# ONE LAST

## ALASKA AIR ONE RESCUE | BOOK TWO

# *CHANCE*

# SUSAN MAY WARREN

## Revell

a division of Baker Publishing Group
Grand Rapids, Michigan

© 2024 by Susan May Warren

Published by Revell
a division of Baker Publishing Group
Grand Rapids, Michigan
RevellBooks.com

Printed in the United States of America

Library of Congress Cataloging-in-Publication Data
Names: Warren, Susan May, 1966- author.
Title: One last chance / Susan May Warren.
Description: Grand Rapids, Michigan : Revell, a division of Baker
  Publishing Group, 2024. | Series: Alaska Air One rescue ; book 2 |
  Summary: "As an Air One rescue swimmer, Axel Mulligan will do anything
  to save lives - including sacrifice his own. When wildlife researcher
  Flynn Turnquist enters his life, he falls hard and fast. But is she
  really who he thinks she is?"-- Provided by publisher.
Identifiers: LCCN 2023050492 | ISBN 9780800745486 (paperback) |
  ISBN  9780800745950
Subjects: LCGFT: Christian fiction. | Romance fiction. | Novels.
Classification: LCC PS3623.A865 O54 2024 | DDC 813/.6--dc23/eng/20231103
LC record available at https://lccn.loc.gov/2023050492

For more information about Susan May Warren, please access the author's website at the following address: www.susanmaywarren.com.

Published in the United States of America.
Cover design by Emilie Haney, www.eahcreative.com

24  25  26  27  28  29  30      7  6  5  4  3  2  1

For Your glory, Lord

# ONE

H E WAS TIRED OF THE RIVER WINNING.

Axel Mulligan crouched on the bank, the cold seeping into his bones despite the dry suit, shivered, and tried to read the foamy, lethal water. His entire body shook, his hands scraped and a little bloody, and he shut out the sound of a man keening behind him.

Grief. Horror. Regret. Guilt, maybe.

Axel got it. His jaw tightened. "Where are you, Cally?"

"She's not . . . it's not worth risking your life, buddy. Don't be stupid."

"Stupid might be my middle name. Just set up the rope."

Axel glanced at his fellow kayaker, Sullivan Bowie, and the man walked away to set up the belay system. But the guy was right.

This could be epically stupid.

Mist rose over the river from the Glacier Veil falls, but she was out there, he could feel it—

Okay, he couldn't feel it. But he wanted it to be true.

*Needed* it to be true.

This river owed him.

The falls dropped thirty feet—not a terrible fall, but with enough force along the forty-foot edge to create a churning hole at the base, a swirling upstream boil, and frothy backwash that could swallow a kayaker, or in this case seventeen-year-old Calista Roberts, whole.

"You about ready on that belay system?" Axel got up and glanced over at Sully, who had unwound the line from one of their rope bags and secured it to a nearby tree. Sully wore his golden brown hair back, square jaw tight as he worked.

Axel glanced at the spray over the falls, toward the fading sunlight. It wouldn't get completely dark, not this far into June in Alaska, but the shadows and the fact that time worked against them put a fist in his gut.

"I'm going to say it one more time. You sure this is a good idea?" Sully walked up and hooked a carabiner to the clip on the back of Axel's life jacket. He'd stopped shivering, despite being soaked. But he'd been busy setting up a tent, then helping Axel rescue fifteen-year-old Adrienne, tucking her into a sleeping bag while Jude Remington tried to keep the girls' father from going into shock. Jude kept talking to him, asking Guy—a lawyer from Georgia—how he'd ended up on this arm of the Copper River, kayaking with—in Axel's opinion—his severely undertrained daughters . . .

This was why Air One Rescue never ran out of callouts.

"Not even a little," Axel said. "According to Guy, Cally passed an advanced kayaking course last year and worked with the Copper River Rafting company last summer. She's a good swimmer."

"Even good swimmers drown," said Sully, his voice lowered. He gave Axel a pointed look.

"I won't drown. Listen, if I go in and don't come up for four minutes, then get me out of there."

"Four minutes?"

"I'd say five, but I'm cold." He pointed to where water splashed against a granite wall near one side of the falls. "The water is pil-

SUSAN MAY WARREN

lowing there, but I think that could be an undercut. When I was a kid, we shot the falls, and the water was really low. I remember it being a cauldron there—it could easily be an undercut in these high waters."

"You think she's trapped in there?"

He lifted a shoulder, glanced at Jude, who was barely holding the girls' father back from diving into the water.

The father looked almost ferocious with grief.

"I don't know. But . . . be ready for anything. Do you think Levi has reached cell signal yet?"

"Probably. It's been forty-five minutes."

"It'll take Air One at least twenty minutes to fly here from Sky King Ranch, so . . ."

"So we need to keep her alive if . . ." Sully looked at him. "Don't die on me, Axe."

"I was born for this."

He stepped out then, life pouch first, and bellied into the water.

He started to swim along the edges of the shore, where the water couldn't jerk him into the boil.

*Please, please, be there.*

Frankly, Axel and the boys might not have seen Guy and his daughters at all if they hadn't stopped under the falls. They'd gotten out of their kayaks to scout the blind spot ahead, where the river simply vanished over a hard horizon line, smoky mist rising to suggest a brutal—albeit possibly fun—drop.

Not so fun once he'd gotten a look at it. Forty feet down to a narrow cauldron of boiling water. Axel hadn't remembered it being this lethal.

Or maybe he'd simply been younger and more stupid back when he'd run this river before.

He'd been looking upriver, his thoughts on, well, mistakes, when he'd seen the paddler drop over the upper falls.

A red kayak nosediving, then pinging up in the foam and mist.

9

"Is he upright?" said Jude, next to him at the time.

"Dunno," Axel said and took off his sunglasses, a little hazy with mist. "There—"He'd pointed to a white helmet and blue jacket that'd surfaced with the red kayak. "It's stuck in the backwash."

Indeed, the cauldron had caught the kayak, swirled it around, pulled it into the froth and back toward the falls. The paddler fought to escape.

"They're going to have to flip, get into current and let it pull them out." Sully had come up to them.

And that's when the second kayaker came over. A bigger paddler, he splashed down hard, and the weight propelled him deeper into the water. He caught the current and jetted out of the cauldron.

"Like that," Sully said.

But then the kayaker turned, paddling back toward the falls even as the rapids grabbed him.

"Look out!" This from Levi Starr, standing upriver. "There's a—"

*Downed tree.* A strainer, it lay in the water like a net, and with the paddler's back to the obstacle, the river ran him right into it, tangling him.

He lost his paddle and grabbed onto the tree as the flow dragged him under.

"For the love—"Axel started up the shoreline even as Levi hustled to the kayaks for rescue rope bags.

And then the third kayak came over. Axel got a better view this time. Orange helmet, orange kayak, long dark braids—

A girl. She splashed down on the far side of the falls, tipped, rolled, and . . . vanished.

Horrified shouts from the trapped man turned the moment from trouble into disaster.

While Levi and Jude pulled out their rope bags and fought to get the man to shore, Axel slid into his kayak and pushed out into the eddy beneath the falls. He paddled close enough so that his voice might lift over the thunder.

No sign of the orange kayak.

The first paddler, red kayak, had big blue eyes, dark hair, and so much fear on her face he nearly got in the water. A girl, midteens, fighting to escape the grip of the falls. "You're too high in the water!" His voice lifted over the thunder of the falls. "You need to paddle upstream, then ball down in the water and catch the suspended load, let the current carry you out. I'll be right here to catch you."

She nodded, and brave kid that she was, paddled out into the boil, rolled to her side, got deep—

The current shot her past the boil line and into the outwash. He grabbed her kayak.

But she was still under, fighting to get upright, and clawed at him. Pulled.

He went over. Under.

The water, even on a hot Saturday in June, sent needles through him and grabbed his breath. For a second, the shock blew out his thoughts.

Then—*stop. Calm down*. He could hold his breath for nearly five minutes. And he'd been kayaking since he was a kid.

He pushed away from the girl, his hand still on his paddle, and righted himself.

Then he reached out and pulled her up.

She came up screaming, shivering, terrified, and grabbed at him again, but he held her away. "You're okay. You did it. Good job."

Her breaths cascaded over each other. "Where's my dad?"

That's when the pieces clicked together. He pointed to shore, where Levi stood with the father.

"And Cally?"

*Cally.* The other kayaker. "You get to shore!"

The orange kayak hadn't popped out of the foamy clutter yet, so maybe . . .

He followed the red kayak to shore, secured her into Sully's grip, and headed back out to the boil under the falls. The water leaned out, a curtain over a granite wall. Maybe she'd been caught behind it.

He paddled along the length and didn't spot the kayak.

But he knew these falls, so that's when he'd had the bright idea of being bait on a string.

Or perhaps a bobber, because now he fought the current, going under, back out, blinking hard to keep his eyes on his target—the overhang of granite where water splashed up, flushing back into the roiling water.

The rock crumbled like eggshells under his gloved grip, but he clawed at it, managed to hang on. He looked back at Sully and flashed a thumbs-up. Then put up four fingers.

Really, he could do five if he had to.

Then he spotted it. The orange of the kayak shoved under the rock, held tight.

Oh no—no—

If she hadn't released from her skirt . . .

He yanked at the kayak, barely moved it, and dug in.

The kayak eased out until the current grabbed it, then popped free, out into the churn.

Empty.

He stared at it as it floated downriver.

Bodies were heavy, especially ones without air. Which meant that she could be at the bottom, where the friction of the rock could hold on, pin her down.

He blew out a breath. What choice did he have, really?

*So that others might live.* The Coast Guard creed to save others, no matter the cost.

Didn't matter if he wasn't with the Guard anymore—the promise still stuck. He drew in five deep breaths, and went under, into the cave.

He kicked hard, the river yanking at him but also pushing, twisting, and just like that, it snarled him up, slammed him against the rock. He grabbed for a hold, but the waves buffeted him, nearly jerking out his breath. He tried to keep his eyes open, but the debris bit at them.

The current turned him and shoved him down. He scrubbed the bottom with his shoulder and searched the floor for a body.

No body, at least not that he could feel or see in the wan light.

His breath burned in his lungs.

He got his feet down, his fingers into the granite, the water still violent around him, and tried to orient himself.

*Get out.*

The thought pulsed at him, and he tried to turn, to catch the outgoing current, but the roil fought him.

His breath started to leak.

And the rope at his life jacket tugged.

He put his arms up so as not to hit the ceiling, and kicked, fighting to escape.

Something grabbed his wrist. Yanked. And just like that, a weight slammed him to the bottom.

His breath burned, bursting against his ribs.

Then hands grabbed his jacket.

He put his hands up, kicked.

Found just a foot or less of water, but air. At least for a second. Then a wave crashed in, buried him, and he clung to the cave wall.

The water receded, and he blinked.

The girl with the orange helmet stared at him.

"You're alive."

"Yeah. Barely. I was pinned, but I got out, and then the current drove me in here. I thought I was going to die." Her voice cracked on the last of her words.

Yeah, him too, but he didn't say that. "They have me on a line. Hold on to me and we'll get out together, okay?"

She nodded.

He tugged on the line and felt it start to grip. *Attaboy, Sully.* He probably had Jude helping.

"Deep breaths now—"

She drank in a couple deep breaths, and he did the same. Then he grabbed her hand, put it on his life-jacket harness, and wrapped his hand around hers, making a fist.

She held on and he ducked under, pushing off the rocks, and swam hard.

With the tug of the rope and the current catching him, they shot out of the cave and surfaced. He rolled over, grabbed her by her life jacket, and backstroked to shore.

Her father fell to his knees, weeping as they crawled over the rocks. She dropped into his arms, and Adrienne crawled out of the tent to join them.

Axel sat on the shore, shivering as Sully unhooked him.

"Thought we lost you there."

"Wouldn't be the first time people thought that," Axel said.

Sully grinned.

And overhead, the air thundered. A big red chopper came into view. Sully stood, waving his arms. "Looks like big brother came looking for you."

"I can see the headlines now," Jude said, packing up the rope. "'Hometown Hero at It Again.' Maybe you can get your own reality show."

Axel got up. Shot him a look.

"What?"

"That's enough, Jude," Sully said, looking back at Axel.

Behind him, the falls fell, the fog rising into the golden shadows. Above them, from the chopper, Shep was coming down on a line. Axel got up to reel his teammate in. "Let's get out of here before the river changes its mind."

Today, they'd been lucky. Real lucky.

But the river kept score.

And Axel was no longer down by one.

He was out there; Flynn knew it in her bones.

*You can run, but you can't hide.*

"Wait until we get there, Flynn." The voice came through her earwig, attached by Bluetooth to her cell phone. Yes, she should probably listen to Chief Burke if she wanted to hold on to her job.

But she also wanted to catch the 1039 Killer, and time gave them no favors. Which was why she stood under the Broadway Avenue Bridge in Minneapolis, down by the water, in the shadows, in the rain, waiting, her breath tight, her eyes peeled at the banks of the river.

He dumped them here. Or around here. Every time.

Girls he'd picked up at the nearby 1039 Bar. It had taken them only six months to figure that out, one strangled, sexually-assaulted victim at a time.

But lately, he'd gotten reckless, maybe frustrated, even thirsty.

"I'm pulling up to Broadway Pizza," Burke said into her ear.

"Don't scare him away," she whispered. Her eyes had adjusted to the wan light of the overhead lights across the bridge. Rain, however, pinged down around her, and mud covered her pants, her boots, her jacket soaked through. She wore a baseball cap, but that didn't help much, not with the downpour earlier.

Felt like heaven might be weeping.

Not tonight. Tonight the carnage *ends*.

"I'm coming to you."

"No. I need you above me, on the bridge, watching in case he drops her on the other side."

"And what if he sees you? He could snatch you too."

"You just keep your eyes peeled for him. This is his night; I can feel it."

Burke made a sound, something deep inside his chest. Probably frustration. She hadn't exactly extended him an invite to this. He'd heard about her stakeout through his ex-cop partner, Rembrandt, who'd probably heard it from his wife, Chief Crime Scene Forensic Examiner, Eve Stone, Flynn's self-appointed mentor after Flynn had interned with her.

Yes, Eve might be a bit of a mother hen, her worry igniting the scrutiny of Flynn's boss, Chief Inspector Andrew Burke. But Flynn wasn't going to go crazy, try to apprehend the guy right here without backup. She just wanted to spot him, confirm, follow, and then, in the light of day, she'd track him down and bring him in. With the appropriate backup.

*Maybe.*

*Aw, probably not.* Because she wasn't going to let him go to kill another day.

Still, she was armed with her camera. And yes, a weapon, albeit holstered. Because she wasn't stupid, thank you. She hadn't become one of the youngest detectives in the Minneapolis Police Department by rushing in without thinking.

No, she'd planned this rainy, midnight stakeout for two weeks, right after the 1039 Killer dropped his last victim into the muddy waters of the Mississippi, under the Broadway Avenue Bridge, and she'd figured out another piece of the puzzle.

Her cell phone vibrated in her pocket, and she reached down to turn it off. Probably her mother, wanting to check in despite the late hour. She owed her parents a call. A visit. Maybe even an apology.

Raising her night-vision monocular, she scanned the shoreline.

His MO meant he'd drop the body on the Minneapolis side, probably parking his car along the river road.

"See anything?" she whispered to Burke.

"No."

"It's the rain. No moonlight, darkness as cover."

"How long have you been out here?"

Given the sogginess of her clothing, the burn in her knees—"An hour, maybe more."

"You sure about this, Flynn?"

Not entirely, but, "As sure as I can be. I've spent the last six months getting inside this guy's head."

"Remind me who I'm looking for."

"The victim is in her twenties, a frequenter of the 1039. I think he knows them, so he probably hangs around the bar, maybe even makes friends. He reminds me of the Charmer Killer in Seattle. My profile puts him in his midthirties, handsome, charming, but also a sociopath. Might have lost his mother, maybe had a young stepmother, felt rejected by her. Takes out his hurt on these women. He has a sibling—a sister, but I haven't been able to track her down. It's possible she was his first victim."

"It scares me a little how much serial killer information you keep in your brain."

"You definitely don't want to see my apartment, then."

"Eve told me about the wall."

Oh, that was for a different case. But she didn't contradict him. "Well, if I were better, I'd have found him before he killed another woman. But I've staked out the 1039 Bar so much I fear he knows me. None of the murders happened on nights I was there."

"Why tonight, here, in the rain?"

"Because this is the night. The scenario fits—a rainy, live-music night, half-price rail drinks for women. The last two victims disappeared during ladies' night. And until I figure out option three—his actual identity—I need to stake out the place he dumps the bodies. Some of the bodies have washed up into the rain culvert just under the bridge, so my guess is that he drops them upstream and they float down. Maybe you should go up to the parking lot near the Park and Rec building. But don't look suspicious."

"What? I've got my best Idris Elba on."

"Yum," she said. "Maybe Rembrandt should make you the hero in his new book."

She heard breathing, and it sounded like Burke could be running. The guy didn't do much in the way of field work anymore. He'd probably made a special provision for her.

But she worked alone, didn't like the complications of a partner. *Don't get hurt, boss.*

Stationed here, under the shadows of the bridge, she had a view of the shoreline and anyone rolling a body into the murky waters—*wait* . . .

"Chief. There's someone onshore, coming down the path right off the River Road split."

"Not. Quite. There—"

"I got him." She raised her camera and took a number of shots, the light terrible, of course.

She needed a better look. Her gut fisted, though. She knew tonight was right—*knew* it. The bouncer at the 1039 should have listened to her, called her. But really, with so many patrons coming and going on a music night like this . . .

The figure was carrying something over his shoulder. He dropped it onto the shoreline.

More camera shots, but even as she peered into her viewfinder, she knew it wouldn't help her case.

"I'm moving in."

Nothing from Burke, but she wasn't helpless. She dropped her camera into the bag at her feet, pulled her Glock, and ventured out of the shadows.

Her eyes had long adjusted to the night, and she waited another half second to blink away the residue of the viewfinder. The rain still pinged down, not as violent, but enough to shatter the silence of the night. Above, traffic whooshed through puddles on the bridge.

The man crouched, then rolled the body into the water.

Washed his hands in the water.

Got up.

And turned.

She stood just twenty feet away now, her gun raised. But the light caught his face, and she froze.

Not a man.

*What?*

The face under the hood of the rain jacket wore no makeup, but her features appeared young, female, and shaken.

Something wasn't right here, but—"Stop!"

The woman's mouth opened, then closed, and she turned, sprinting away.

Flynn started after her, slipped, nearly fell down the muddy bank, then scrambled up. "Burke! It's a woman!"

"On it!"

"She's headed for the road."

Flynn fought for purchase in the slippery soil, reaching the grassy edge, tripping over a downed tree, catching herself. "She's getting away!"

"I see her—"More breaths now, and he grunted over the phone.

She plowed through the bramble, headed for the path—

A blow slammed into her, like a branch across her shoulders, and she fell so hard that the gun bounced away into the night.

Then a knee landed on her spine, the weight of a body pressing her into the loam and grime. She tried to twist, fighting, throwing her elbows back, but the hand grabbed the back of her neck, forced her face into the mud.

"Thought you'd catch me, huh?"

She tried to turn her head, fighting for air, but the voice registered. *Deep.*

*Male.*

*What?*

Then he grabbed her, flipped her, his knees on her arms, his body over hers. In the dim light, she made out a man in a hoodie, his face gaunt, his eyes hard on hers.

"Help—"

His hands viced, his thumbs against the well of her neck.

She kicked at him, her breath fading, dots blackening her vision.

Her right hand found a rock embedded in the soil, and she closed her fist around it. His knees pinned her upper arms, but as her breath burned in her, she flung it at his head.

It hit him—enough that he loosened his hold, jostled his perch—and in that second, she got an arm loose. Brought it in front of her, slamming her hand into his jaw. He fell back.

She hooked her leg around him, brought him down, then twisted, got her other leg free, and slammed her foot into his jaw.

Scrambled away—

He grabbed her ankle and jerked. She went down, but her hand landed on the hard metal of her Glock.

She turned and fired.

The bullet hit him, center mass, tearing him away from her.

He crumpled even as she scooted back, breathing hard.

"Flynn!" The voice echoed through the drizzle, not her earpiece, and she looked up to see a light pinging off the trees, coming near.

"Over here!"

She shook, her entire body on vibrate as she stared at the man. Footsteps squished through the loam and grass, and in a second, the light shone on the wounded body.

Her breaths still came out hard, her heartbeat in her ears.

"You're okay. I got you." Chief Burke, behind her, crouching down and now easing the weapon from her hand. He set a big hand on her shoulder as he pulled out his cell phone. "We're going to need backup. One casualty, one in custody, and we'll need a bus. Officer injured. And the coroner, as well as the crime scene unit, pronto."

"I'm fine."

"Yeah. I know." He shone the light on the man again. "This our guy?"

"I don't know." She looked up at him. "The woman was dumping the body."

"She was pretty freaked out. Not sure if she's a victim or—" Burke cut off.

"It could be his sister." And she didn't know why the thought came to her, just something in her gut, maybe.

Pushing up, she went over to the man. Midthirties, short dark hair, could be handsome in the dim lighting of a bar. She blew out a breath. "She might have even been the mastermind. Or maybe she just got roped into it after his first kill." She took a breath. "Whatever happened, they probably both suffered the same childhood trauma."

"That's a leap, Flynn."

She sighed. "Probably. Just a gut feeling. But it happens. Family bonds—especially sibling bonds are . . . they can be pretty strong. Cause people to do things they would never dream of. Get themselves in over their heads."

"This your professional opinion?"

She glanced at him, nodded.

*But uh, nope. That would be personal experience.*

Sirens moaned in the air. "Where is the woman?" she asked.

"Cuffed to a lamppost."

She grabbed her gun from Burke, sheathed it, then pushed past him out onto the path.

"What are you doing?" Burke followed her out.

"I need to talk to her."

"You need medical attention."

She looked at him, and her hand went to her throat. "I'm fine." Although she could barely make him out in the darkness, she guessed his signature mouth-pursed grim expression. "Fine. But no one interviews her before I do."

"Done." He walked out onto the path ahead of her, waving to a cruiser as it pulled up. But then he turned to her, and this time, the lights revealed his expression. "Good job, Detective. You saved lives tonight."

He turned back, jogging out to meet the officers. She stood in the rain, her gaze on the woman cuffed to the pole.

The woman stared back, unblinking, her jaw tight, fear in her eyes.

*No, not the mastermind.* Maybe even a victim of the killer's psychosis.

Flynn turned, flicked on the flashlight of her cell phone, and followed it down the pathway back to the riverbank.

The victim lay on the shore, her hands and feet bound with duct tape, her mouth also taped, just like the ten plus victims before her.

Flynn knelt next to her, shone her light on her face.

Held her breath. *Please—*

She took in the dark hair, the green eyes, now open, affixed in horror. But it wasn't Kennedy.

Of course it wasn't Kennedy. But sometimes—no, *every* time—she braced herself, just in case.

Flynn got up, stared out at the dark river, the lights of the Minneapolis city skyline rising downstream to glare upon the river.

Then she closed her eyes and let the rain do the weeping for her.

# TWO

"STOP CIRCLING."

Axel looked over at Sully, who sat in the front seat of Levi's truck, his arm hitched over the console, looking back at him.

"You're caught in a rescue loop."

Axel nodded, his mouth pinching along the edges. Except, of course, it wasn't the loop Sully thought—the one with the Roberts family. No, this one went way back, surfaced every time he ran that stupid river.

"Have you heard from Moose?" He leaned up to Levi, in the front seat. It had taken over two hours after he'd dispatched the Roberts family into the Air One chopper for the guys to gather their gear and portage their kayaks up the Bowie Camp road, where they waited for Levi to retrieve his truck with the racks. They strapped on the kayaks, then climbed into the four-door cab and headed toward the town of Copper Mountain.

"He called in just as I was picking up the truck, said they made it back to base. The sheriff met them at the airport. I guess they went to the clinic," Levi said. He looked at Axel. "Maybe you should, too."

"I'm fine."

"You got pretty scraped up in the water."

Axel gave him a look, and Levi lifted a hand in surrender.

"How far did you have to go to get a signal?" Axel asked. "And maybe I'll let you turn up the heat."

Levi grinned and turned it up. "Not even to the highway. I would have gone up to Sully's place, but he still uses smoke signals."

"It's off-grid for a reason, bro," Sully said. He'd dried off too, now wore a baseball cap over his long hair. Levi wore a bandanna over his brown hair, and beside him, Jude Remington had tied his own bandanna around his short dark hair like a redneck. He looked like one too, in his military pants and black pullover. Like he might be a prepper, maybe. Or an outlaw. Or just . . . a maverick, living on his own terms.

But maybe that was the Alaskan life as a whole. Sully lived in the woods for most of the year, a hunting and fishing guide with Bowie Mountain Gear, while Jude helped run his family's gold-mining operation west of town.

Even Levi had vanished off grid for a while, although now he ran a pizza joint in Copper Mountain. Which, apparently, Jude remembered. "How about we swing by the Northstar and grab some overorders?"

Levi glanced over his shoulder. "Anything for the television star."

Axel rolled his eyes.

Sully shook his head.

"I like it. How many episodes are there?" Jude asked. "I've only seen two."

"I think six. Or eight." Axel looked out the window. He really hadn't expected the show to air so quickly. Should have given the whole thing a little more thought, perhaps, because . . . well, he braced himself for a phone call any day from a reporter looking to stir up ghosts.

Regrets.

"I can't believe you spent a whole month with Oaken Fox. Looks like he's an okay guy," Levi said.

The sun had just slipped past the mountains. The entire sky turned to fire, the Denali range dark and forbidding, still white-capped, so deadly even in summer. Maybe more in summer, what with the queue of tourist climbers waiting to summit.

Moose had talked about parking the Air One chopper in the Copper Mountain airbase to help Dodge over at Sky King Ranch, ferry all the wannabes who tapped out down the mountain.

Air One Rescue had also assisted in a few callouts on the mountain. So that probably accounted for Moose's ready appearance in the skies.

"He's a decent guy," Axel said now of Oaken. "He lived with us for a couple weeks. I helped him with some songs."

"Now you're a songwriter," Levi said. "Wow—and you still don't have a girlfriend?"

"Funny. And no. Women are trouble."

"You need a dog," Sully said. "Like Hondo."

Axel grinned. "I do like Hondo. How is he?"

"Scaring the guests, chasing rabbits, and generally ruling over the Bowie Outpost."

"You leave him alone, out there in the woods at the fishing camp?"

"No. He's in town with Mal and Hud. Tangled with a badger and needed some stiches. I'll pick him up in a few days."

They hit the highway and drove north just a few miles to the town of Copper Mountain. A skeleton in the winter, the town came to life in the summer, the resorts, motels, bed and break-fasts, and hostels packed with tourists, hikers, climbers, fishermen, photographers, and all-around lower-forty-eighters who found themselves in over their heads here in the last frontier.

Levi passed the Welcome to Copper Mountain sign, then turned onto Main Street and drove past the Midnight Sun Saloon, the gravel lot packed with cars, grill smoke piping into the sky, seasoning the air with the smell of barbecue. The windows of the Last Frontier Bakery were dark, as was the Good News office and the timber-framed storefront of Bowie Mountain Gear.

Levi pulled up in front of Northstar Pizza, the twinkle lights bright around the outdoor patio, where a few people sat at yellow painted picnic tables.

"It's nearly eleven. How late are you guys open?" Axel said, piling out.

"We changed it to midnight on Saturday nights during the summer. And even that feels early." Levi shut the door. "I'll see if they have any overorders." He headed inside.

Axel lifted out his kayak and carried it over to his Yukon, tied his kayak to the roof with bungee straps, then retrieved his pack and threw it in the back.

He joined the guys at a picnic table. Frankly, he couldn't imagine eating, his gut still roiling. Moose always went out for a shake after a callout. Axel preferred to wait until his gut stopped churning, pacing through all his choices in his mind, trying to throw out the regrets.

Yeah, he should stop circling. Today, no regrets.

A waitress came out, blonde, dressed in a pair of jeans and a black Northstar Pizza T-shirt, and plunked down a pitcher of water and four glasses. "Hey, guys."

"Hey, Parker," said Jude.

"It's getting around that you guys rescued Cally and Adri on the Copper River tonight. At the falls, no less."

Axel put her at about seventeen, so yeah, Cally's age.

"Where'd you hear that?" Jude tore his attention off a table of locals sitting across the patio.

Axel glanced over. *Oh.* Shasta Starr sat among them, her gaze on them. She was pretty for sure—long dark hair, a smile that belonged in a magazine. But she had penchant for trouble, too, and that had semaphores waving him far, far away.

Thanks, but he wanted safe, quiet, and trouble free. Maybe he would get a dog. He looked back at Parker.

"Dad was here listening on the radio when Moose picked you guys up."

Right. Her father was the ranger in charge in the area.

"And he was having dinner with the sheriff and Wilson Bowie—"

"My uncle is in town?" Sully said. "When did he get here?"

She shrugged.

Sully picked up his straw. "Shoot. I wasn't expecting him for at least a week."

Jude raised an eyebrow.

"He's going to want me to take him out fishing. And I'm booked with a group coming in tomorrow for a week."

"So,"—Parker said, "—"anything you guys want to drink?"

"I'm good," Axel said.

The others ordered a couple sodas.

Shasta slid onto the bench beside Jude. "Hey, guys."

Jude glanced over at her, smiled. "Hey, Trouble."

"Stop, Jude. I'm here on official business." She leaned in, her eyes on Axel. "I want an exclusive."

It took Axel a second, and he blamed it on Jude, and maybe the way Sully smirked, but—"A what? You want . . . a what?"

"An exclusive article on you being a hero and rescuing Calista and Adrienne Roberts, thank you." She looked at Jude and punched his shoulder.

"What was that for?" Jude said.

"You called me trouble. I'm not trouble." Her mouth tightened.

"I'm just . . . curious." She turned back to Axel. "Which is why I'm now a reporter with the Copper Mountain Good News."

Silence.

Then, "Um, why do you want . . . I mean—"

"Because of the show. Everybody's watching it. And now you did it again—you rescued somebody. You're a hero, Axel. And everyone loves a hero."

Sully smirked.

Jude quirked an eyebrow.

"C'mon, Axel. You're like . . . I dunno. Jack Powers."

"He's a fictional super spy."

"Yeah, but he always shows up right when you need him."

Jude rolled his eyes.

Axel grinned and folded his arms. "Okay, hit me."

"Great." She pulled out her phone and pressed record. "So, that was pretty brave. I heard the whole thing over the radio, too. That's pretty dangerous—the Copper River. Glacier Veil Falls. Like . . . people have died there."

Axel froze, and Sully glanced over at him.

Jude cringed. "Aw, Shasta, maybe not—"

"Wait." She sat back. "Wasn't that where Aven—"

"And we're done." Axel pushed up from the table. "Actually, Shasta, here's your headline. Nobody died. Not today. That's all that matters." He climbed out.

She stood up. "Axel, c'mon. I didn't mean to—"

"Nope, we're good." He was walking backward and smiled, lifted his hands in surrender, then winked, pointed at her. "Stay out of trouble."

She scowled at him.

He turned and headed to his car. Got in and pulled out.

Yeah, all this television hype was going to his head.

He pulled away from town and headed for his parents' home, the family's hand-built log A-frame overlooking the Copper River just outside town. Passing the airport, he spotted the red Air One chopper tied down, so apparently Moose had stuck around.

North of Copper Mountain, the terrain thickened, the forest closing in. His parents only lived a mile from town, but it might have been in the depths of the bush for all the population this direction. He passed a few timber-framed homes set back from the road, and of course, if he kept driving north another ten miles, he'd end up at the Starr Lodge.

He turned onto a dirt drive and followed it back to the clearing where the A-frame house sat, perched over the river, the apron porch wrapped around the first-story exterior, the lights glowing from the ground-floor media room, the guest room, and his father's beloved sauna.

Moose and the old man were probably hashing out today's adventure.

On the first floor, the light-blocking blinds covered the master bedroom, his mom probably asleep with her earplugs and mask. Even in summer, with the sun at its twenty-three-hours-a-day height, his mother kept her sleeping hours. Had to, really, because the Last Frontier needed its five a.m. cinnamon rolls for the early hiking crews.

He pulled in and parked, left his kayak on the rack but retrieved his pack and climbed the stairs to the entrance. The door whined, but the front room and kitchen were empty, and yep, the master-bedroom door was closed.

From the media room rose the sounds of a hockey game—probably the final games of the Stanley Cup tournament, so likely instead of the sauna, his old man, Ace, would be settled into his recliner, occasionally yelling at the screen.

Axel untied his boots and left them by the door, along with his jacket, then brought his gear up to his room on the upper floor.

A short hallway separated the lofted area into two small rooms, a window at the end of the hall overlooking the river. Moose's door was shut. Coming home always felt like he'd reverted back to his teenage years.

Really, he should get his own place. But he liked staying with Moose down in Anchorage. Had the run of the basement of Moose's luxury, palatial, inherited home.

He dropped his gear on the bed, pulled off his shirt, and headed to the bathroom for a steaming shower.

Twenty minutes later, fatigue hit his bones, and he emerged shirtless, wearing his pajamas. Past midnight, and still it looked like it might be twilight through the hallway window.

Moose opened the door to his bedroom, just across from Axel's room, and leaned against the frame as Axel walked down the hall.

"You're still up?"

"Heard you come in. Waited. You good?" Moose, always the big brother. He wore sweatpants and a cut-off thermal shirt, folded his arms over his chest.

"Yep."

"Guy told me about what you did. Apparently you freaked them all out, going into that cave."

"I knew what I was doing." He reached for his door handle.

"I know. But . . . you know."

Moose's soft tone stiffened Axel. He took a breath, nodded. "I'm good."

Moose's mouth made a tight, grim line. Then he sighed.

*Oh.* "What's going on?" Axel asked.

Moose looked out the window, toward the river. Back to Axel. "He's back."

It took a second, and then—"What? No."

"Yeah. That girl we found in the Copper Mountain ski area— she was shot with a—"

".270 Winchester."

"Yeah. And the bullet matches the others."

Axel looked away, shook his head, his chest tightening. "Does Deke know?"

"Of course. He got the news from the coroner in Anchorage and is the one who told me But more, the news knows, which mean . . . Aven's name is going to come up."

Axel nodded, swallowed. "Yep."

Moose paused. "You saved lives today, Axel. Focus on that."

"Yeah. Whatever." Axel turned and headed into his room.

He lay on the bed, staring out at the bright sky, not bothering to pull his blackout curtain. Circling. Circling. Circling.

Darkness or light, the nightmare simply wouldn't end.

Flynn should have stayed the night at the station. Because three hours of sleep did no one any good.

She stood in front of her refrigerator in her tiny two-bedroom loft apartment overlooking the Mississippi River, just three blocks from the downtown precinct, and wondered what the shelf life was on blueberries.

And spinach.

Maybe if she didn't look closely at them and added enough vanilla almond milk and some peanut butter, she wouldn't notice the taste. No one died from bad blueberries, right?

She pulled out the plastic containers, opened the spinach, and picked out a few non-slimy leaves. After sorting the berries, she added them to her blender along with the milk and peanut butter. Some ice cubes.

Clearly, she should take her mother up on her invitation to tomorrow's Sunday brunch. Her mom had left a voicemail last night, and one this morning, of course. But the invitation probably also meant church, so . . .

Maybe not.

She dumped the containers into the trash, then whirred the blender. Poured the mixture into a tall shaker bottle, capped it, and headed over to her bicycle. Picking up the remote from the table, she powered on her flat screen and opened up a YouTube biking video—this one through Rome.

Then she rolled her exercise bike into the open space beside her sectional.

Light shone through the floor-to-ceiling picture windows that overlooked the river, the rays of sunlight gleaming against the wooden floor all the way to her U-shaped kitchen, the stainless-steel appliances shiny against the white quartz surfaces. The loft at least smelled good, her cleaning lady leaving a lilac scent with her products. When Flynn had arrived home in the wee hours this morning, she'd fallen into the cloud of fresh sheets, her eyes closing hard.

She'd forgotten to turn off her alarm, so it buzzed way too early, and she might have slept in, but her head ached after way too much information from the sister of Magnum O'Conner, the man behind the 1039 murders who now lay on a slab at the coroner's office, along with his victim, Kaitlyn Swenson.

Of course, Flynn had also dreamed, which meant she'd tangled herself in the sheets, a hot, sweaty mess. These cases always dragged up the what-ifs surrounding Kennedy. Longing, maybe, or simply relief that the body found didn't belong to her twin. Still, the one good thing—besides justice—about ending the crime spree was that Kennedy came back to her in her dreams. Still alive. Still whole. Laughing. And with the dream, a revived hope that maybe, somewhere . . .

Flynn hiked up the volume on her TV, pressed play on the bike tour, and hopped onto her NordicTrack, the skinny seat a reminder to stay on her toes, that she wasn't out for a joyride, even if they might be exploring the streets of Rome.

She dug down, pedaling up cobblestone streets, then down

through the hills of the Forum and over to Trevi Fountain. A line of sweat trailed down her back when the doorbell rang.

She slowed the bike even as the bell rang again. Then whoever stood on the other side of the door sat on the buzzer.

"I'm coming!" For Pete's sake.

She got off and grabbed a towel from the back of her Ikea rocker, wiped her forehead, and grabbed her protein shake.

Taking a drink, she walked to the door, then peered through the peephole.

*Seriously?* What was Chief Eve Stone doing in her hallway, especially this early in the morning?

She opened the door. "Eve?"

Her mentor grinned at her, her auburn hair pulled back into a messy bun, still wearing her clothes from last night. "I was on my way home, and then I remembered." She held up a tiny box. "Happy birthday."

*Oh.* But it was a nice gesture, so Flynn found a smile. "Right. Thanks. Come in."

Eve walked inside. "I can't stay long. Rem has an afternoon on the lake planned, and I need a few winks before then, but"——"she set the box on the counter—"you did really well last night. I'm proud of you. Oh, and your security system here needs updating. I walked right in after a jogger left the building."

"I know. I've complained a few times. Want some coffee?"

"Sure." Eve opened the box. "Burke said that you called it—the woman was O'Conner's sister."

"I wasn't sure." Flynn walked to the kitchen, and her hand went to the two jagged half-heart pendants on a chain around her neck. Habit. "But something about the way she looked at me on the beach, part panic, part anger, part fear—just reminded me . . . you know." She filled the coffeepot with water.

"Of Kennedy?"

"Yeah. She wore that same look sometimes." She poured the water into the maker.

Eve had taken out an oversized cupcake and now set it on the counter. "It's not your fault, Flynn. She left—her choice."

"I know. But . . ." She had added coffee to the filter and set the pot to perk. Now she turned and looked at the cupcake. "This looks good."

"Red velvet. Your favorite."

"Kennedy's favorite. But I like it too."

Eve cocked her head. "Okay." She glanced at the television. "Rome?"

"It's a biking video."

"You could go outside, you know. It's a gorgeous day. Rem says it's going to be upper seventies. Ride a real bike; take to the trails around Minneapolis."

"That is a real bike."

Eve arched an eyebrow.

"Listen"——"Flynn opened her silverware drawer—"if I were outside, I'd have to pay attention. Watch out for other riders."

"Stay on the trail."

"There is that." She handed Eve a fork.

"Such a sacrifice." Eve took the fork, then slid onto a high-top chair.

Flynn picked up her remote and exited the app. The TV reverted to live, and she turned it to mute. Closed captioning filled the screen.

Eve glanced up at the show. "That's that new reality show with Oaken Fox—the one where he joins the rescue team."

She set down the remote, her gaze on the screen. The country-music star stood in a hospital somewhere, covered in snow, saying something heated into the camera. She scanned the words, but only caught a few of them. Something about searching for a lost woman.

Probably staged.

She returned to the counter.

"I saw your mom in church last week," Eve said as she peeled the paper from the cupcake.

*Oy.* The perils of having parents that went to the same church as the Stone family, along with Eve's family, the Mulligans, in Minnetonka.

"She said that she and your dad were going on vacation."

*Really?* Okay, so maybe Flynn should catch up.

"What's that face?" Eve set the cupcake on the paper and pushed it between them.

Flynn took the other stool. "I haven't talked to them for a couple weeks."

"Really? Why not?"

"They want to have a memorial service." She took a bite of the cake. "This is good."

Eve nodded with her mouth full. She put the fork down. "That's not a bad idea. Closure."

"Except that Kennedy isn't dead."

Eve drew in a breath.

"Listen—"Flynn said. "I know what you think. But her body has never been found, and—"

"And you're wearing her necklace. Taken off a dead woman who was found in the Copper River, just like thirteen other women."

"A lead that led nowhere. They tested the DNA. It belonged to Kennedy, but they couldn't identify the dead woman, so the Copper Mountain sheriff gave it back to me."

Eve sighed. Nodded. "Okay."

"No, you don't get it." Flynn pressed her hand to her chest. "I feel her. In here. She's my twin. *Identical* twin. And no, I don't buy all the crazy things they say about twins feeling each other's pain, but . . . maybe sometimes I do. Maybe sometimes I wake up suddenly and feel like she's talking to me. Or calling for me. Or . . ."

Her eyes had started to burn. "What if she needs me and ... I can't find her? And I don't show up?" Flynn looked away, closed her eyes. "I'm just tired."

But Eve had slid off the stool and now put her arms around her, pulled her tight. "Yeah, that's it." She held her a long moment, then pushed her away. "But if you believe she's still alive, then you should keep looking."

"I don't know where to start."

"Alaska." Eve slid back onto her stool.

"Yeah, well, I was there three years ago. They had nothing for me. The sheriff in Copper Mountain is this younger guy with zero investigative experience. I tried to interest the Anchorage police in the case—linked it to the Midnight Sun Killer, but they didn't bite." She took another forkful of cake. "Said that people disappear into the bush all the time, and that I'd have to get in line. Last I checked, they'd added her to their missing persons list, but it's listed as a cold case."

"Things can happen. New clues ... I don't remember you taking any PTO for the last three years. Maybe you have some time coming ..."

"I do. Over a month. But ..." She sighed and picked up a napkin to wipe her mouth. "Maybe Mom is right. We do need to move on. But I'd like to move on with the happy idea that Kennedy is out there, somewhere, living her best life."

"Is that why you have a crime-scene board that covers an entire wall of your office?"

A beat.

"So, is this really a birthday call or ..."

"It's a birthday call," Eve said. "But if I could give you one gift ... There are things you can change and things you can't, and knowing the difference is the key to a happy life."

"Thank you, Dr. Stone."

Eve winked and slid off the stool. "Happy birthday, Flynn."

Flynn walked her to the door. "Thanks for the cake. Tell Rem I loved his new book."

"Stop by. He'd love to bore you with some of his old cold-case files. He keeps copies of them in a box in his office—untouched. Maybe someday you can help him solve them."

She laughed. "Maybe."

Eve didn't. She stopped at the door, turned. "Flynn, you're one of the best detectives I've ever met. Even better than Rem. But you spend an awful lot of time in your head, and . . . I just don't want the what-ifs to consume you. Get out of the house. Go live your life. Take a risk."

"Let's not get crazy here. How about if I just finish the cupcake on my own?"

"Start with that." Eve pulled her in close. "You're my favorite student."

Flynn laughed and let her out. She walked back to the counter and folded the cupcake back into the paper, put it in the box, and added it to the refrigerator.

Yeah, Kennedy should be here to celebrate.

She turned back to the television, picking up the remote to continue her workout. But the show's ending caught her eye. A picture of a woman—probably the one they'd been searching for. And a shot of a reporter giving an update. Flynn flicked on the volume.

"According to local police and the sheriff's office in Copper Mountain, this murder might be linked to the notorious Midnight Sun Killer, although officials are quick to point out that the killer might be a copycat of the serial murders over a decade ago. Still, women out hiking or driving along the Copper Highway are urged to take extra care—don't stop for stalled vehicles, and always hike with a PLB and a friend."

The show then switched to a voiceover of where the body was found and then shots of Oaken at a restaurant, eating with a group of men.

*Yeah, see*—a woman was dead, and the world carried on.

Or most of it did.

The rest stayed stuck, circling, wondering.

Hoping.

She turned off the TV and walked into her office, the report sparking inside her. Standing in the middle of the room, she stared at her wall, the one with the blown-up Alaska map, the timeline of the deaths, the reports from the Copper Mountain sheriff's office, pictures of the area, and finally, the news clippings about other women who'd vanished over the years in the same area.

She sipped her protein shake, not sure if she tasted something rotten or not.

*"There are things you can change and things you can't, and knowing the difference is the key to a happy life."*

There would be no happy life until she found the truth.

She brought the shake into the kitchen, poured the rest out, rinsed out her cup, and left it on the counter to dry as she headed upstairs.

To pack for Alaska.

# THREE

"FOR THE LOVE, PLEASE TURN THAT OFF." AXEL closed the basement door, freshly showered, having worked off some of the weekend stress in Moose's home gym this evening after he'd returned from Copper Mountain.

Clearly, Moose had arrived home in the last hour, after flying the chopper down to the Air One base in Anchorage, then driving his truck up to his home on the Knik River. Axel had left after stopping into the Last Frontier and grabbing one of his mother's homemade cinnamon rolls.

The news of the rescue made the local gossip chain, and he'd been stopped by no less than Hank Billings, Charlie Yazzie, and Sully's uncle Wilson, who acted like he might be a hero or something.

He'd pasted on a smile, glad-handed them, and then headed out the door before he ran into Shasta or some other media person. He didn't know what he'd been thinking agreeing to Mike Grizz's reality show. Clearly, he *hadn't* been thinking, really.

*Stupid, stupid—and even more stupid . . .* Especially as he stood in his brother's main room watching the rescue play out on the screen.

Moose sat on his leather sofa, his feet up on his massive oak coffee table, watching the show on the flatscreen that hung from the two-story stone fireplace. He drank a cup of hot cocoa and now glanced over at Axel.

"Why? This is the part where you practically dive in to save that girl—what was her name?"

"I don't remember," Axel said. *Ashley.* Blonde, scared, a possible kidnapping victim. "What I do remember is not being able to rescue the driver."

He walked over to the refrigerator. Moose had inherited the house from a donor of Air One Rescue—one who owed his life to Moose. Then again, a lot of people owed their lives to Moose, including himself, probably. Who knew how many times he'd nearly been swept away in the Copper River, or driven himself into a ditch, only to have Moose come looking for him in the dead of night? Or even track him down during those dark days after he'd left Kodiak. Probably Moose ran a dry house because he didn't want to tempt Axel back into his nightmares.

No need—he wasn't that guy anymore. Even if the nightmares had never left. He just knew how to keep them tucked in better.

Now he retrieved some eggs and put them on the counter. Got a pot of water and filled it, set it on the stove. "There's only six eggs left."

Moose looked at him. "Is that not enough for you?" He shook his head.

"What? Eggs are good for you." He put all six into the pot.

On the screen, he pulled Ashley out of the dark, roiling waters of the Eagle River, helping her and a drenched Oaken Fox, their celebrity trainee, to shore.

The camera caught her being attended to by Boo Kingston, their EMT, and Shep Watson, another rescue tech. Axel noticed how their other rescue tech and copilot, London Brooks, made herself a little scarce—he hadn't exactly spotted that before. In fact, he'd seen only a few of the shows, but he didn't remember her appearing in any of them.

Oaken came on in a cameo to talk about the rescue, and Moose popped the volume down. He got up and walked into the kitchen as Axel watched the water boil. "What's with you and this show? I would have thought you'd be more excited to see yourself on TV."

"I've seen myself on TV before, Moose. I'm not a fan."

Silence.

He looked at his brother, who folded his arms over his heavily muscled chest, all flannel, all north woods—the nickname Moose exactly right. The man always barreled into a person's space without permission.

"What?"

"You're being a little hard on yourself."

"Really? You ever had to make a choice that cost a life? Watch a family be shattered because of you?"

His mouth tightened, and *aw,* maybe Axel was wound a little tight. He blamed his mood on the sleepless night and the nightmares the river always dredged up. On Aven and her haunting laughter, the smile she'd given him a moment before he missed her grip.

Her scream, lifting into the air, shaking him down to his soul.

"I've seen my share of rescues gone south," Moose said quietly.

*Yeah, probably.* Axel glanced at the screen. The footage caught him diving back into the river, tethered to Shep on shore, swimming out to the submerged caravan that had careened off the road into the river, then tumbled into the rapids. It showed him catching up to it, searching it, then canvassing the rocks and shoreline.

A voice came over the screen as the shot faded out. "The driver, still unknown, was never recovered."

*Nice. Perfect.*

His eggs had started to float to the top, so he pulled them out with a ladle and set them in a pan of ice water in the sink.

Outside, the day had turned grim, with the clouds low, a slight drizzle in the air. He poured himself a glass of milk.

Moose picked up the remote to turn the TV off when scenes of the next show began to play.

The snowstorm up at the Copper Mountain Lodge. The missing women from the bachelorette party, and then Oaken's small tirade. They'd even caught footage of the guys eating out at the Skyport Diner, that pretty waitress Moose liked serving them midnight chicken.

Funny, but it occurred to him that Moose hadn't been back to the Skyport in weeks.

Still, the footage stirred up the memories, especially of the woman, one of the lost, who'd been found, murdered.

Shot.

With a .270 Winchester.

Just like Aven.

Now, as he transferred his hard-boiled eggs to a plate to peel them, he looked up at Moose. "What if the guy didn't die? What if he got away . . ."

Moose turned off the television. Turned to Axel, his expression grim. "What do you mean?"

"What if the guy in the caravan was the Midnight Sun Killer and I let him get away?" He couldn't believe he'd voiced it, but that fear had been circling his brain for the better portion of a month. Maybe letting it out would ease the burn inside.

Moose gave a huff that sounded a little like disbelief.

"What was that for?"

"Just . . . no. You didn't let the Midnight Sun Killer get free. If there is such a killer out there—"

"Oh, I think there is—"

"Still at work, after fifteen years? C'mon. I think they've at-tributed a handful of accidents to one sociopath—"

"Accidents? Seriously, Moose, have you listened to any of the news? Done any research? This guy picks up women off the high-way—sometimes lures them to stop, even, then takes them out to the woods, sexually assaults them, then sets them free to hunt them down. He's killed, like, thirteen women, that they know of. And dozens of others are missing."

"And you seriously think your missing driver is this guy?"

"Ashley said he'd followed her, picked her up—"

"She left a bar. He grabbed her in the parking lot, from what I remember. And this was nowhere near where the Midnight Sun Killer left them."

Axel stared at him. "What do you mean this was nowhere near where he left them? What do you know that I don't?"

Moose got very quiet. "You're not the only one who grieves Aven. Who wishes he'd done something different."

Axel let that sit.

"But I don't blame myself. And I don't let it tell me who I am."

Axel brushed off his hands. "I know who I am. I don't need any reminders." He picked up the plate and grabbed the salt and pepper shakers along with the bottle of sriracha. "Next time you decide to rent the Air One team to a reality show, I'm out."

He headed downstairs, back to the basement, which felt a little like a dungeon, maybe, but also contained the media room, with the surround sound and one-hundred-twenty-inch screen, so he'd take it. Moose had let him rent the two bedrooms—one for an office—so it wasn't like he was a freeloader.

Axel just needed to figure out what getting back on his feet looked like. How to swim out of the cauldron.

Sitting on the leather sofa, he set his plate on the ottoman, along with his condiments, and turned on the television.

Weather report, of course—a storm coming in from the Bering

Sea, across the Alaskan peninsula, on the way to Kodiak Island and the Gulf of Alaska. No doubt the Coast Guard in Kodiak was on full alert.

He picked up an egg, slathered it with sriracha, and ate half in one bite.

"That looks wicked."

Moose had followed him downstairs, holding a glass of orange juice. "Thought you might want some. I just squeezed it."

Axel doctored the next bite, then popped it into his mouth and reached for the glass. Nodded.

Moose stood behind the sofa, watching the weather. "Wind gusts of ninety miles per hour? That's nearly a cat-three hurricane."

"Yeah. Hard to get a trail line down in those conditions. Even with a twenty-pound weight on the line, the wind just takes it."

A pause, then, "Personal experience?"

"The Heritage wreck." Axel salted another egg. "It was just off the coast of Kodiak, but it took us two hours to go five miles. I've never seen it so bad before, or since."

"Except now."

"Yeah. Nothing worse than being on scene and hearing those voices on the radio and not being able to save them. Want one?" He lifted the plate to Moose.

"This isn't usually storm season." Moose took an egg, then the proffered sriracha sauce bottle, and doctored it. Took a bite. "This is good."

"Mm-Mmmhmm."

"Hey, I'm sorry about earlier—I just . . . you know . . ."

"Don't like me taking up space in your basement?"

"No. It's a big house. Lots of room. But if being here is somehow keeping you from doing what God wants you to do—"

"Bro. Step back Not everyone has your faith. Or wants it."

Moose frowned.

"Listen. God and I aren't at odds. It's just that . . . I just . . . I feel like—"

"You failed him?"

Axel leaned back into the cushions, picking up the remote. "Maybe. I don't know. Or maybe God failed me. Sometimes it feels like both. But I don't want to know the answer."

"Faith is hard when you don't trust the one you're putting your faith in."

"Leave it, Moose." Axel turned the volume up to hear the reporter.

Upstairs, from Moose's office, his pager rang. *Oh,* that couldn't be good.

Moose headed up the stairs.

The reporter stood in the rain and gusts outside Air Station Kodiak, talking about the deployments of the current teams—four crews, three out on rescues, the other standing by.

Axel headed upstairs and stood outside Moose's office, listening to Moose on his radio.

His chest tightened at the way Moose stared at the map, running his finger down to the Cook Inlet, near Homer. Nothing but rocky shore and underwater scabs there to hang up a boat.

"Roger, Sector Anchorage, we'll deploy to the F/V Lady Luck. Will notify when we're on site."

Moose hung up the radio. "There's a charter fishing vessel that's adrift near the mouth of the Gulf of Alaska, west of Homer. Thirty-foot swells, ninety-knot winds, and they think they're going to roll. The seas are too high to send out a cutter, and all the available Coast Guard teams are currently deployed, so they called us in for backup. You'll probably get wet."

"I'll call Shep," Axel said and headed for the door.

Moose picked up his keys. "Should have slept at the office." He headed out the door. Axel grabbed his jacket and followed him out through the drizzle to Moose's truck.

Overhead, thunder rolled, and as he got into the passenger seat, he was already cold.

But nothing compared to the gusts rolling into the deck of the chopper some ninety minutes later as Moose tried to hover over the pitching fishing boat. The thirty-seven-foot fishing vessel seemed like a bath toy in the dark, foamy water, violent waves crashing over the flybridge, ripping over the boat, and roiling into the deck cabin. The lifeboat swayed from the front, caught up in fishing line and rope, banging on the hull when the boat lifted out of the water.

Axel spotted people in orange life jackets clinging to the cabin inside even as one of them came out to wave at the Air One chopper.

Yeah, he was getting wet.

"Can you hover?" Axel said, attached to the chopper with the safety line, helmet on, garbed in his dry suit, gloves, a life jacket, and harness.

"For now. Let's get you down there. Shep, check swimmer."

Shep, their flight mechanic, checked Axel's equipment, then hooked him into the line and grabbed the pendant. "Checking swimmer. Going out the door for load check."

Axel pushed off and let the line hold him, Moose adjusting for the weight, then Shep gave him the thumbs-up, and he headed down to the dark ocean.

On the line, Axel spun, the wind trying to take him. He heard Shep barking distance and directions to Moose. *Hit the deck, Moose. Hit the deck—*

A wave thundered down over him as his feet touched the boat's deck. He slammed into the rail, caught it, held on as the boat pitched.

Even in June the water ripped out his breath at a bracing fifty degrees. The wave cleared and he turned, searching for the passengers.

*Oh no,* a family. A man, a woman, two kids, and the fishing captain.

Clearly terrified.

The family huddled together, the father, early forties, his arms around a little girl, maybe ten, skinny, her blonde braids sodden. The boy seemed older, maybe twelve, trying to look brave, jaw set. He held his mother's hand.

The father wore a makeshift splint on his leg, a paddle roped to his shin. The woman, too, appeared bloodied, her arm wrapped in a towel, saturated.

"What happened?" He braced himself at the door.

"We were trying to loosen the lifeboat, and it slammed into us!" This from the woman, who looked at the captain with no small amount of anger.

"Okay, everyone calm down. We're going to take you up, one by one—"

"We don't have time for that," shouted the captain. Axel had gotten his name on the ride over—Captain Russell. Midthirties, a Kodiak local. Grew up on the sea.

Axel agreed with him. "Shep, I'm going to unclip—send down a basket. We need to get these kids up, ASAP."

"I'm not going without my mom," shouted the boy, and Axel held up his hand even as he unclipped.

"Don't worry. We'll get you all out." Promises. But he meant to keep them.

The line fell away, Shep hoisting it up even as the boat pitched hard. Axel grabbed the doorframe of the tiny cabin, the water drenching him. His dry suit helped, but the family had to be slowly sinking into hypothermia.

"What's your name, kid?"

"Aiden. And that's Sophie."

"Okay, Aiden. I'm putting you in charge of your sister. You hold on to her when you go up, okay?" Protocol said that he should ride up with them, but Aiden gave him a nod, and the ocean wasn't playing fair.

A basket came down, swinging in the wind, and Axel stayed away until it hit the deck, then grabbed it in. Russell helped, and they dragged it to the door.

"Aiden, you're up."

He stood, looked at his mom, and she nodded. Aiden ran over, ducked into the basket.

Sophie was crying, but her father pushed her away, met eyes with her brother.

The look in his eyes shook through Axel, right down to his bone. He hardened his jaw, then grabbed the girl and helped her inside, strapped them in with a safety line, then radioed for the pull up.

The basket swung as it lifted off the boat, a wave right behind it, as if hoping to steal them back to the sea.

He let out a breath when Shep reeled them in, then sent the basket down again. Axel had gotten the names of the couple—Brian and Danae—and Axel set up Danae.

She disappeared into the chopper.

"How're you doing, Moose?"

"We're nearly at Bingo, Axe. Hurry up. And don't die!"

*Right.* "Shep, send down a sling with the basket."

Water crashed over the boat, slamming Axel into the cabin wall. The boat moaned.

"We're taking on water!" Russell said.

"Yep." He braced himself, then headed out to grab the basket.

"What are you doing?" Russell said as the basket came down, a sling attached.

Another wave hit, skidding the basket to the rail, nearly engulfing the cabin with water. Axel held on and the boat righted itself, but not before it had sucked out the fight from Brian, and maybe even Captain Russell. They shivered openly, both of them wan, fear in their eyes.

"We're running out of time!" He grabbed Russell by the arm. "Help me get Brian in the basket."

The water seemed to have pummeled the man, and he gasped for air, his eyes wide.

"Almost there," Axel said. "This will hurt. But we'll make it fast."

Russell picked up Brian's torso, and Axel moved his legs and ignored his shouts, although maybe the frigid water had helped curtail the pain, and in a moment, they wedged him into the basket. Axel grabbed the sling. "Get in."

Russell climbed in, sitting on the sling.

"Hang on to the basket." He sent a thumbs-up to the bird.

The boat pitched hard into a trough as the basket swung away, and Axel turned.

*Oh. No.* A wall of water curled over the boat, and at the rate of descent, would crash down over the basket—

Maybe even drag the chopper into the depths.

"Moose, pull up. Pull up!"

He scrambled inside the cabin, then shut the door and threw the latch. The boat rode the trough up the front side of the wave—*aw*, they were going to pitchpole. But if the cabin could stay water-tight—

He threw himself down into the lower cabin and pulled the airtight hatch.

Then, as the boat pitched up, nearly vertical, he found the berth strap, slammed himself onto the berth and clasped it.

He grabbed a nearby rail as the boat slammed backward into the trough, the sound deafening as the wave thrashed it under the water. Then, caught in the submerged current and pushed horizontal, the boat rolled.

The strap caught him, but the roll slammed him against the berth, the walls, burning a line into his body.

But it held.

The boat finally stopped rolling, caught in the current under the surface—his best and most pitiful guess, because he hung from the bunk like a fish on a stringer, upside down.

And even as Axel unhooked and let himself down onto the ceiling-slash-floor, as he looked out the windows to the dark-hued shadows of the sea, he knew.

He was going down with the ship.

Flynn had traveled to the end of the world for nothing.

Two flights, including a delay, an overnight layover in a seedy hotel in Seattle, then a flight to Anchorage—and of course, the rental company had given away her car—so another night in an even seedier hotel near the airport, and then, finally, a drive through the drizzly day north to the chilly town of Copper Mountain.

At least the sky had stopped weeping. Three hours north of Anchorage, the spectacular Denali mountain range sat under a vivid blue sky, the clouds high and wispy, and the fresh dump of white on the peaks glistened like diamonds.

Not the place for dreams to die.

Now, Flynn stared at the massive map of Alaska that spanned the sheriff's office, the one with the roads marked, including the dirt forest service paths into the woods. *Where are you, Kennedy?*

County sheriff Deke Starr clearly hadn't been expecting her to show up again, but he'd been willing to listen to her request to dig through the evidence and maybe unearth something new.

She sighed and turned as he arrived back at his office, holding what she considered a terribly thin file.

"Only because you're a fellow detective," he said, handing it to her. "Those are copies. It's considered a cold case because, well..."

"You never found a body."

"We're not sure she's even dead, Ms. Turnquist."

"Flynn. And I'm not either, to be honest. If it weren't for this..."

She touched the jagged half-heart pendant. "Thank you for sending it back to me."

"Seemed like the right thing to do. All the DNA evidence we gathered is in the file. Only two matches—your sister, and the victim, still unknown. And with the wounds consistent with the Midnight Sun Killer's MO, and you coming here to search for her . . .we're sorry we've never had any more leads."

She nodded. "Me too. Is the victim's information in here too?"

He shook his head. "That's an open case, what with the newest victim."

She sighed. "I heard about that. A woman near the Copper Mountain Ski Resort?"

"Yes. She and a group of friends got lost during a snowstorm and all but she were found. A SAR team found her, shot, on the edge of the property, not far from the chalet. We didn't know if she was running from the lodge or toward it. But the bullet matched the rest—a .270 Winchester."

Flynn had turned to the map to find the ski resort. Put a finger on it. "It's next to Remington land, where a couple of the other victims were found."

"Yes. But there were others, located farther downstream. I'm not sure there's a connection to Remington land."

She opened the file and looked at the summary. "There's no mention of an interview with the owner."

"Oh, we talked. I know Ox personally. He runs the gold-mining operation west of here. That land was bought by his father years ago, before he arrived here. Hunting land. He never uses it."

"Someone does." She closed the file. "Maybe a son, or a relative?"

She liked Deke, overall. Good-looking, dark hair, pale blue eyes. He seemed like he cared, like he wasn't putting her off.

"Maybe. He has two sons who work the claim with him—Jude and Nash. I saw Nash in town earlier, talking with Peyton, his fiancée, over at the forest ranger's office."

"Peyton Samson?" She opened the file again. "That's the ranger who runs the wolf-tracking program. She was Kennedy's boss."

"We've already interviewed her—the copy is in the file. She didn't sense that Kennedy was in any distress when she left her at the cabin."

Flynn turned to the map again, checked the black-and-white copy of the map in the file, then found it on the grid. "Here, on the Copper River, just a few miles from the Bowie road."

"That's the one." He stepped up to the map. "You can only get there by four-wheeler—or dogsled in the winter. Or good, old-fashioned hiking. Only trouble out there is black bears and grizzlies."

She gave him a look.

"Sorry. I . . . Listen, Flynn. People go missing in Alaska all the time, whether by choice or by animal accident or, yes, occasionally foul play. I'm sorry to say that there is no reason to believe that Kennedy was murdered."

"Except for her necklace ending up on a murder victim."

He lifted a shoulder. "She could have lost it, maybe in the bathroom at the Midnight Sun, and it got picked up by this girl. Any number of scenarios could explain this."

He spoke quietly, gently, and she recognized the tone. She'd used it herself, especially when talking to relatives of people gone missing, family who were desperate for answers.

And she couldn't argue with him—she might hand out the same explanation. Except, "My parents want to have a memorial service. It's not like Kennedy to just . . . vanish. We were on good terms. I mean, yeah, we had a disagreement the last time I saw her—"

"Where was that?"

"Actually, the Copper Mountain resort. We came out here to go skiing, and she wanted to stay." She palmed the file. "Apparently she did." She looked out the window to the ranger station down the street. "You know that feeling as a detective, when you just feel that you're missing something, but it's out there just beyond your reach, like you're reaching into a fog, and if you just put your hand on it . . ."

"I think that's called faith."

"Or just desperate hope."

"Could be the same thing."

*Right.* "You said Peyton was here, with Nash?"

"Probably stopping in to see her folks before she heads out to the bush again. The Samsons have a summer home in Copper Mountain. Try the ranger station first, though. And, Flynn, I'm not saying that she's dead or alive. I just don't know where to go from here."

"Thanks, Sheriff," she said and shook his hand.

The air smelled of fresh river, summer flowers, a chilly breeze from the north sweeping into the valley, with the slightest scent of smoky barbeque hinting the air. She checked her watch—still early, before six, but it didn't matter really. Not with the sun up almost twenty-four hours a day.

She headed across the street to the ranger station, a few backpackers sitting on the apron deck, probably waiting for permits. One of the women, her auburn hair tied into two braids that fell out of her yellow bandanna, laughed, and the sound and sight of her nearly made Flynn stumble, the sense of Kennedy suddenly deeply, painfully raw.

The girl turned then and looked at Flynn and smiled, and no, she didn't have Kennedy's green eyes, the smattering of freckles across her nose, but still.

Her sister *couldn't* be dead.

Flynn pushed inside the ranger station. A small line in front of a permit window confirmed her guess, but she went to the counter and a teenager with blonde hair, dressed in cutoff shorts and a white shirt asked if she could help her.

"I'm looking for Peyton Samson," she said.

"Parker, you're not supposed to be helping guests," said a woman from a side office. She emerged as the blonde stepped back, hands raised, and Flynn immediately recognized her.

Hard woman to forget, really. Dark-skinned, with hints of Native American in her features, her dark hair pulled back under a yellow bandanna, wearing a ranger uniform, patches on her arm that suggested a long tenure with the park service.

"I'm Peyton," she said. Then frowned. "Wait—it's Flynn, right?"

"Good memory," Flynn said. "I was hoping I could talk to you about my sister."

"Kennedy." She gestured Flynn back to her office, unlatching and holding onto a swinging door. "Still no word from her"

"No."

"I'm so sorry." She gestured to the open door and walked in. A man leaned up from where he'd perched on a credenza.

Peyton gestured to him. "This is my fiancé, Nash."

Good-looking guy, wore a hint of a beard, had a Brad Pitt-goes-to-Montana sort of aura about him in his khaki shirt, jeans, and boots.

Flynn shook his hand.

"Flynn is a detective from Minneapolis. Her sister went missing a few years ago around here. She's still looking for her," Peyton said.

"I'm sorry."

"She was working for me as an intern—staying at one of the cache cabins over by the Copper River, near your land."

"Really." He crossed his arms over his chest. "I've never been there, but that's pretty wild country."

Deke's words pinged inside Flynn. "Yeah. It's possible she was attacked by a bear or—"

"Oh, I don't know. That's right near the Bowie hunting lodge. I think the bears stay away. Was she a kayaker?"

"Yeah. Loved the outdoors."

"Then better bet is that she got tangled in the river somehow."

She frowned. "Really?"

"There's a tributary off the river—a lot of fishermen get salmon there. But I know that Air One Rescue has pulled more than a few kayakers off the river after going over the falls." He stepped forward and leaned over the desk. "I'll see you in a few days. Please stay safe." Then he kissed Peyton.

"Nice to meet you, Flynn," he said, and left.

"Are you going somewhere?" Flynn asked Peyton. "Why do you have to stay safe?"

"Actually, I'm headed out into the bush—in that direction, just a little south. We're studying the migration patterns of a number of wolf packs, and one of them has been spotted way out of their territory. I'm taking a four-wheeler in to see if I can figure out why." Peyton considered Flynn. "You as outdoorsy as your sister?"

"Absolutely. We're twins, after all."

"I can see that. Okay, I'm leaving in an hour. If you want to check out the cabin where she stayed, I'll drop you off on the way. Meet me outside with gear."

"What kind of gear?"

"Do you have a sleeping bag? Food?"

"I will. Thanks, Peyton."

She stepped outside. The sun gleamed on the river down the street, deep blue, fresh, alive. And she felt it in her soul.

Hope.

An hour later, she'd purchased a sleeping bag from Bowie Mountain Gear, along with hiking boots, a rain poncho, a kit of kitchen supplies the good-looking owner had suggested, along with some dehydrated food, and even a pack. Then she joined the other hikers on the deck.

Peyton came out of the office wearing her own pack and waved her over.

They got into a truck, a four-wheeler parked on the bed. Despite the mud-caked wheels, it seemed clean, with a couple jerry cans shoved alongside it on either side. A couple ramps were tied across the back, over the tailgate.

Peyton dropped her pack up front, behind the front tire of the four-wheeler. "There's a space on the other side for yours."

And then they were off.

An hour later, Peyton parked the truck at a private home, waving to the owner, then unloaded the four-wheeler and told Flynn to climb onto the back. They drove another hour into the woods, following what felt like deer trails, hopping off now and again to move downed trees, and even driving down a rugged shoreline to follow the riverbed all the way to . . .oh no. The last place Flynn had imagined she'd sleep tonight was a one-room shack that shared space with a nest of mice.

Flynn had to admit, when she'd heard the words "drop you off," she'd imagined Peyton pulling up to a cabin set in the shadow of some mountainside with a flowing creek and maybe handing her more than a handheld radio and a promise to return in two days.

But Peyton seemed nonplussed by the condition of the cabin, a one-room timber shack that served as a way-side rest for local forest rangers. It contained a wooden bunk bed, a stove, a small rough-hewn table, and a counter and sink.

But the porch did overlook a river, wide and glistening under the afternoon sun.

"A good sweep, some fresh air, and you'll be golden." She checked the potbellied stove. "No nests, and there's some fresh wood in the bin"——"she pointed to a wooden box—"so you should be warm enough. The river is fresh, but you can boil the water if you want."

She pointed to a cupboard where Flynn found a kettle, some dusty metal plates and forks, metal coffee cups.

Then she handed Peyton a handheld radio. "I'm on channel six. And I'm only a couple miles away, downstream. We keep a kayak under the porch if you need it, but if you're not a proficient paddler, I'd stay on the hiking trails. If you need me, call me. I'll be here in a jiff."

*A jiff.* What was that in Alaska time?

"Oh, and I almost forgot. If you get desperate, there's a ham radio." Peyton opened the bottom cupboard. A small radio sat on the shelf, and she pulled it out and turned it on. It powered up. "Oh good, it's working. I replaced the twelve-volt battery last time I was here, so it probably has plenty of juice. We keep it out here for emergencies. Or if you get lonely, you might find someone listening on the other end." She winked.

Flynn didn't have a clue how to use such a thing. She followed Peyton out of the cabin.

Peyton paused before she got onto the four-wheeler. Then her smile fell. "You sure about this?"

Flynn stood in the yard. Actually, despite her first impression, the cabin seemed like a haven in the middle of all this wild. A small front porch held a homemade Adirondack chair, and inside, the bunk bed would at least have her sleeping off the floor. She had food, and the river glistened a deep blue under the sun. *Sheesh,* it could nearly be called paradise.

And then there was the silence. Or maybe just . . . the absence of clutter. Of voices and demands and people calling her and knocking on her door and . . .

Maybe she should have left more than a voicemail on her mother's phone. But she didn't need questions. Or fear.

Or . . . well, reminders that she was the only daughter left.

"I'll be fine."

"You will. Oh, and . . . I brought a bear gun. Just in case Nash is wrong." She pressed a little Glock G20 into Flynn's hand. "I'm assuming since you're a cop—"

"I know how to use it." She checked the safety, found it on.

"It won't kill a grizzly, but it might scare it away. Radio me if you need anything."

Flynn waved as Peyton took off, hating how hard she held onto Peyton's words. But if Kennedy could stay here, so could she.

Except Kennedy had gone missing . . . from . . . here.

But Kennedy wasn't a cop.

And if Flynn wanted to figure out how or why her sister went missing, maybe staying at her last known location could unlock something.

Even if it was only how to say goodbye.

She took a breath. Stared at the river for a long time. Frothy and wild, it mesmerized her, but she couldn't nail why. Or why she'd so easily dismissed Nash's words. No, Kennedy hadn't gone missing in the Copper River. Or maybe Flynn simply didn't want to believe it.

Heading inside, she found the kettle, then a pot and pan along with the silverware and plates, and took them to the river. Washed them out, left them to dry on a towel from her pack, then went inside and swept out the entire cabin, including the rafters, the windows, the bunk beds, the cupboards, and finally the floors.

She put away the clean dishes and was wiping down the wooden table when she spotted the hash marks.

No, not hash marks—a carving. She ran her finger over it. A bird. Probably a sparrow, to be more precise.

Her throat tightened. *Hey, Kennedy.*

She blew out her breath. Closed her eyes. *Okay.* Maybe this crazy feeling could be attributed to faith. Oh, she wanted to believe that.

She walked outside and stood on the porch. "Kennedy, if you're out here, send me a sign. Something—"

The crackle emanating from behind her nearly shot her out of her skin.

"CQ, CQ, CQ, this is . . . um, KL7SEA . . . CQ, CQ, CQ, this is KL7SEA . . ."

She turned. The voice came from the ham radio, still on, sitting on the table. A small box with a handheld mic. She picked it up. "Hello? Um . . . hello?"

"Hello! Hello—um, QRZ?"

"I'm sorry—I don't know ham-radio-speak."

"Who is this?"

It needled through her that whoever was on the other end just might be . . . well, maybe not Kennedy's killer, but the last thing she needed was to tell him she was here alone, right?

"Just a researcher. You can call me . . . um . . ." Wait. "Sparrow."

"Sparrow, I need your help. My name is Axel Mulligan. I'm on a capsized boat in the middle of Cook Inlet. And I think my team believes I'm dead."

She had nothing.

"Hello?"

"I heard you. What . . . can I do?"

"Get ahold of Air One Rescue in Anchorage and tell them to come back for me."

And how—Peyton could probably figure that out.

"Roger. Okay. Um, I'm sort of . . . out in the boonies?" Oh, please let him not be a serial killer. "But hang on. I'll try. Stay there."

"Yeah, no problem."

He sounded a little sardonic, maybe.

She picked up the radio Peyton had left her. "Peyton. Calling Peyton. Come in, Peyton."

Static.

She tried again.

Nothing. *C'mon, Peyton.*

Just static.

She closed her eyes. *Breathe.* Then she picked up the mic. "You still there?"

# FOUR

THIS WAS NOT HOW HE WANTED TO DIE, THANK you. Buried alive at the bottom of the ocean, the air slowly turning to poison in the tomb-slash-cabin of the fishing boat Lady Luck.

Maybe not so much on the luck, although if Axel was honest, the fact that he'd gotten inside the lower compartment and latched the waterproof seal in time to create an air pocket did seem on the lucky—or even the divine providence—side of the equation.

He now sat on the ceiling, the contents of the entire cabin scattered around him—pots and pans, dishware, books, pillows, life jackets, blankets—anything that wasn't latched down, and even then, cushions had broken loose, along with the contents of the freezer. Frozen fish, some coffee beans, and a bag of raspberries—that seemed like an interesting combination.

A few canned goods rolled across the ceiling with the below-surface current.

He couldn't tell if he might be sinking—or maybe the air pocket of the cabin was keeping the boat afloat. And it might not be the only air pocket. It was possible that the captain's cabin and even the flybridge contained air.

He didn't want to chance it.

The windows peered out to murky water, but the barest of light suggested he might not be too far below the surface. Hopefully the keel still stuck out of the sea, something to catch the sunlight, tell the world he wasn't on the bottom.

Yet.

The static of the mic buzzed through him, and he tried again. "Hello?" Axel held the mic to his forehead, breathed out.

*Nothing. Okay. Think.*

It had been a long shot anyway, hoping the ham radio he'd found tucked in the cabinet might work. Radio frequencies struggled underwater, but the ham operated at a 136 kHz band, so—

"Axel?"

Her voice crackled through the line, igniting inside of him.

"Hello! I'm here! I'm here!"

A pretty voice, although he might be biased. He'd take *any* voice on the other end. Still, he wanted to imagine her as pretty, maybe a brunette, someone who wouldn't give up on him.

Mostly that last part.

"I thought I lost you," she said. "I'm trying to get ahold of someone over the radio, but she's not answering. I'll keep trying."

"I'm still here."

He wanted to suggest she turn the dial, find another channel—in fact, Moose possessed a ham radio, but the chances that his brother had parked the chopper and returned home to his warm bed came in at negative zero.

If his brother could get a bird in the air, he would search the ocean blue for him; Axel knew it in his bones. But the chopper's fuel had been almost spent right before the boat went over, so chances were Moose had headed to Homer to drop off his crew.

And by the time he returned, Axel might be at the bottom of the sea.

Not to get too dark and gloomy, but the hope of his brother finding him in the swells . . .

The woman on the ham might be the last person on earth he spoke to.

"Are you okay? Are you hurt?" she said now.

"Maybe some bruised ribs, and my shoulder took a hit, but I'm fine." For now. Gurgling from somewhere above suggested the boat gulped water somewhere. But so far his ears hadn't popped, so no depth pressure yet.

Oh, so much to look forward to as he slowly asphyxiated. Or drowned.

"What happened?"

Maybe she was trying to keep him talking—probably not a terrible idea, given the fact that at least he'd know how far he'd sunk. When he lost transmission, well, he'd lose any chance of contacting Moose too.

"There's a storm coming through the area, and my team went out to rescue some fishermen. The boat got swamped."

"Are you alone?"

"Just me and Davy Jones."

"Who?"

He laughed. "You know—the pirate? Dead pirate? Captain of the Flying Dutchman?"

"Oh." Silence. "That's . . . not very funny."

"That's all I've got."

"That's pitiful. Okay, listen. Can you swim out?"

He frowned. "Not in seas with thirty-foot waves, and fifty degrees. You saw *Titanic*, right?"

"Jack could have totally fit on that door."

"Right?"

"But then Rose would have had to marry him, and maybe he was just the holiday-romance guy and not the real guy."

"The holiday-romance guy?" He found a jug of water and uncapped it.

"You know, the guy who's lots of fun but deep down can't make a commitment."

"Maybe she was the holiday-romance girl." He took a drink, wiped his mouth.

"Rose was still trying to figure out who she was. At least Jack knew—he was a guy just trying to figure out how to survive."

"So which one are you? Jack or Rose?" He put the cap back on.

"I don't know. Rose, maybe."

A sigh on the other end. *Interesting.* "So, who are you, Sparrow?"

"I'm a . . . researcher."

"What are you researching?"

A pause. Outside the window, bubbles rose, which meant that air below him was escaping.

He pressed his ear to the ceiling boards. Sloshing. The more water that spilled in, the heavier the boat would get.

"Um, the migratory patterns of wolves?"

He leaned against a pole that connected to the bench seating above. "I have a friend who does that—her name is Peyton. She's from my hometown."

Another pause, this time so long that his voice held the smallest edge of panic when he keyed the mic. "Sparrow? Are you there?"

Another beat. Was the ocean getting darker outside his window?

"Sorry. I tried the radio again. No answer. How are you doing?"

"I've been better." He grimaced, hating the desperation in his voice. Blew out a breath. He wasn't dead yet. "So, Sparrow, are you from Alaska?"

"No. I . . . I came out here because of a friend."

"Where're you from?" The boat was turning, starting to roll to its side. He braced himself on the cabinet.

"Minnesota."

"I have family there. My great-uncle and some second cousins. They live on a lake."

"Everybody lives on a lake. There's ten thousand to pick from."

He liked her. She was no-nonsense, had a bit of wit to her. "Have you always been a wolf researcher?"

Silence. Another beat. For a second he feared—

"No. I was . . . a detective."

"Like Sherlock Holmes?"

"Maybe. I hunted serial killers."

"Sort of a dark hobby."

"It paid the bills."

"So does river-monster hunting, but nobody is signing up for that."

"What is river-monster hunting?"

"You know, that show where some guy shoves his arm in an underwater cave or log and pulls out a catfish with teeth the size of my hand clamped on to his bloody arm."

"And now that's an image I'll have to sleep with."

"Not if you never go river-monster hunting." The boat continued to turn in the water.

"I'll cross that off my bucket list."

"What else is on your bucket list?"

Another pause, and he found himself smiling.

"Okay, in truth I don't have a bucket list."

"Yes you do. Everybody has a bucket list." Canned goods rolled across the ceiling, fell onto the bench.

"Fine, what's on yours?"

He blew out a breath. "Besides living through this?" He caught a can of peaches before it beaned him. Set it on the bench.

"That's a given."

"Fine. Bungee jumping."

"You aren't serious."

"I think I am. I'd like to just . . . fall. And know that I'm going to be caught."

"And if you're not?"

"Maybe I won't know?"

A laugh on the other side as she toggled her mic, and something warmed him to his bones. "Okay, fine. If you started a bucket list right now, what would be on yours?"

She sighed. "I think I might be willing to skydive."

"So very Rose of you."

"What?"

"Standing on the bow of the ship, believing she could fly?"

"Only because Jack was holding on to her," she said.

"And we're back to Jack."

The boat had righted itself. At least he wasn't upside down. But he might be going straight to the bottom.

"We're always back to Jack. He believed in . . . everything. Hope. Tomorrow. That he could be anything, do anything."

Something about her voice . . .

"You don't believe that?"

Quietly, "I think I used to. Or maybe a missing part of me does."

He hated how much he could agree with her. "Once upon a time, I think I used to believe that too."

Oh, he wasn't sure why that came out.

"So, who are you, Axel? Jack or Rose?"

"Neither. I'm the captain—going down with the ship."

"More dark humor?"

Maybe just truth. He shook his head. "I should have dove into the sea when we were hit by the wave. Then my brother could have picked me up."

He knew that made no sense to her, but he just had to voice it to someone.

"We all have would've and should've, but this is what is. So, how are you going to stay alive?"

*Huh.* "You sound like my Coast Guard instructor."

"You're with the Coast Guard?"

"I was. Rescue swimmer. Top of the class—"He wasn't sure why he'd added that. "Got my pick of stations and came up to Kodiak. I could swim farther, last longer than anyone . . . Thought I was really something."

Silence. Finally, "And then? Because it sounds like there's an 'and then' at the end of that."

She was dangerously easy to talk to. "And then I went out on a rescue. It was in October and the seas were high—like today. A fishing boat was taking on water, seven souls on board, all a family. By the time we got there, four were in a lifeboat, three in the water—a mom, dad, and one of their sons. Twenty-five-foot swells, water breaking over their heads. Thirty-two-degree water. I went into the water and got the mom—direct deployment with a sling. I put it around her and took her up, and by the time she was onboard, I couldn't feel my hands, and ice blinded my face mask. But I went back into the water after the next two. I got my hands on the dad, but the waves kept washing over us and my hands wouldn't work. He got away from me."

Pressure started to build in his ears. *Aw, yeah,* he was going down, albeit slowly. The air pockets probably acting like buoys. Still, he was definitely sinking. He held his nose and blew out, popped them.

"Then what happened?"

"The son grabbed me and climbed into the sling. Put his legs around me, and the chopper lifted us out. By the time I got on deck, my hands were frozen, the radio on my helmet frozen. Another rescue boat radioed in that they were picking up the guys in the lifeboat. But there was still that guy in the water, right?"

*Wait*—was that water near the edges of the ceiling board, coming out of the toilet?

*Shoot. Not watertight.*

"So what happened?"

"My crew chief wasn't going to let me go out again, but I pushed out and refused to come back in, so they lowered me down. I searched the sea for twenty minutes until they reached bingo and had to haul me up. By then I had hypothermia and was nearly a casualty."

*Yep, water.* It ran across the boards of his cabin. *Shoot.*

"The Coast Guard censured me and put me on leave. But I was a little messed up in the head, all that time in the water, the frustration sort of . . . I don't know. Sometimes I still hear the mom screaming, the kid crying. It got inside me and . . . anyway, the Coast Guard decided I should take more time off. Like, permanently."

He was going to have to ditch. He'd already stood up and now searched for a flare or a buoy.

"I'm sorry."

"Yeah. Well, I'd wanted to be a rescue swimmer all my life, since I was a kid and I saved another kid from drowning—at the time, I thought I was some kind of hero or something." He found a flare. Blew out a breath. "Maybe I am Jack after all."

"Desperately trying to survive?"

"Something like that. Listen. Um. So, I'm taking on water here. And . . . I think I'm going to have to swim out. Any luck on the radio?"

"I'll try again, but . . . are you sure? It sounds like you'd have a better shot inside the boat."

He stood in water to his ankles. "Pretty sure." Although he thought he would have sunk faster. "Maybe there's more air in the captain's cabin."

"The longer you can wait to get in the water, the better, probably, right?"

She had a point.

Silence hung on the other end while he ripped one of the cushions from the bench. Supposedly flotation devices, but he wasn't holding out hope.

"Axel?"

"I'm here."

"I tried again. Sorry—still no signal."

"What time is it?"

"Nearly midnight."

He found a waterproof bag amidst the pillows and picked up the ham. Shoved it into the bag. Maybe if the next compartment wasn't flooded . . .

"Axel?"

"Yeah?"

"Just checking. You were quiet there."

"I'm trying to figure out how soon I abandon ship."

"Oh. Okay, listen. Look around you. There's got to be something you can use to self-rescue."

"I have a flotation cushion and a flare."

"How about a life raft?"

"It's hung up on the bow of the ship."

"What?"

"The lifeboat. It's hung up—"

"But isn't there a redundancy on the ship? A lot of boats have lifeboats and a life-raft suitcase. It's usually at the back, near the rail."

"Who are you, Captain Ron?"

"Ten thousand lakes. Go check."

"I can't, not without leaving the boat." But maybe it was time. The water had risen to his knees, his feet turning frigid. "I think it's time to ditch." Especially since the pressure had hit his ears again.

Every ten feet, which meant he might be under by twenty feet. Any deeper and he wouldn't have enough breath to reach the surface.

"Sparrow?"

"I'm here."

"Thanks."

"I'm not going anywhere—I'll keep trying. Stay alive."

No promises, but he didn't say that. "Yep." Then he shoved the mic into the bag and zipped it, securing the bag across his body.

The water had sloshed up to his thighs, and he popped his ears, then stood at the hatch to the captain's cabin. Five deep, fast breaths, then another, to fill his body. He shoved on his helmet and reached for the door.

It swung up more easily than he'd expected, and while water gushed in, it didn't fill the cabin. He scrambled out, up the stairs, into the cabin.

Not filled full, but water seeped in.

Through the windows, the sea gulped the last rays of light. The air had buoyed him, but the ocean would win. And given the froth and current above him, the sea still raged.

*Life-raft suitcase. Near the back rail.*

He slogged through the water toward the door. Still had breath left, but let it out and took five more quick breaths, then another, deep, then more.

Then he fought open the door.

The ocean blasted into the room, and he held on to the frame as the pressure equalized.

The boat would sink fast now, so he pushed out and grabbed the rail.

Yes—there, the orange life raft, in a suitcase.

Pressure built behind his ears—*C'mon*—

He reached for the latch. No frozen hands today, but it slid under his grip. He held the rail, the pressure burning through his brain—and hit the latch again.

The suitcase popped open, and like a balloon, the raft deployed. He grabbed it as it inflated and rode it to the surface as the boat dropped away into the depths.

Then held on with everything inside him as he surfaced into the raging sea.

She couldn't just stand here and let him drown.

But thirty minutes since his last transmission said . . .

No, Flynn wasn't going to jump to conclusions. Except jumping to conclusions was sort of her job—jumping, then sorting through, then jumping again, rinse and repeat until finally she landed on the *right* conclusion.

Please let it not be that Axel had drowned.

She picked up her radio again. "Axel, are you there? Axel?"

Nothing, and she set the mic down and got up, running her hands behind her shoulders, kneading them, then moving to her neck.

She stepped outside for a breath of air despite the nip, knowing she should go to bed. But how, exactly, was she supposed to sleep with him out there, maybe—hopefully—fighting for his life?

But in all likelihood, the ham radio had gone down with the ship. So even if he was alive . . .

He was alone.

She picked up the radio again. "Peyton, come in." Nothing. "This is Flynn. For the love, come. In!"

Nothing. *Shoot.*

The sun had set—or the closest it came to that in Alaska at the height of June. Really, it simply hung just below the horizon, turning the sky to blood red, dotted with deep magenta clouds, scarred by the jagged thrust of the faraway Alaska Range. The rays glistened on the river, turning the water into a molten lava flow.

In the east, the moon also hung, pale and ghostly, muted by the light of the sun.

It felt like twilight, shadows climbing out of the forest. The makings of a horror movie. How had she ever thought this might be a good idea?

Except, if she *hadn't* been here, then Axel would have been completely lost. Now . . .

*Now what?*

If he'd made it into the sea, and if it hadn't already gobbled him, maybe . . . Well, he had said he was the top of his class.

*C'mon, Axel. Don't die on me.*

She went inside. Picked up the mic, tried to call him again.

Nothing.

Then she picked up the bear gun and went outside. Peyton had said she would only be a couple miles away. Maybe . . .

She pointed at the sky and pulled the trigger. *Aw,* the stupid gun made a silly pop. And with the river . . . but she shot again. And a third time, just in case someone thought it might have been a mistake.

Then she stood in the yard, listening to their conversation about hope.

*"You don't believe that?"*

*"I think I used to. Or maybe a missing part of me does."*

Maybe she needed to channel the part of her that was Kennedy. Or, rather, Sparrow.

She went back inside, paced. Okay, maybe she could walk out. Or . . . follow the trail of the four-wheeler to Peyton's camp—

"Hello? CQ, CQ—"

*What*— She swept up the mic. "Axel! Is that you?"

"Just hanging out in the tub."

She closed her eyes, holding the mic to her chest. Breathed. Then, "Where have you been?"

Crackling, then, "Fighting the high seas, Sparrow. Good call on the life raft."

She sank into the chair, fighting the crazy urge to weep. She barely knew this guy, and yet . . .

Maybe it was the desperation of his situation. Or maybe . . .

Maybe she just longed for someone to have a happy ending. To be found and not lost. She found her voice. "You escaped the ship."

"It went down like a rock. I rode the raft up and it inflated right there in the ocean. Managed to get inside it and zip the covering shut. I might hurl, though. I strapped myself in, but . . . oh, yep, I'm going to . . . Hold please."

She scowled. Waited. Her own appetite had vanished over the past few hours.

He came back. "That's better. But gross. The ocean is wicked out there. Please tell me you got ahold of someone."

"No. Sorry. I . . . maybe I should try to scan the channels?"

"Yeah. Maybe. But I don't know if anyone is up—what time is it?"

She checked her watch. "Two a.m."

"It'll get light soon. Maybe . . ."

"I'll keep trying, Axel."

"Good, because I can't feel my legs. There's water on the bottom of the life raft, and I think I have a hole in my dry suit."

Which meant he was slowly freezing to death.

"Don't go to sleep."

"Yeah. I get that."

"No, seriously—you have to stay awake."

"I'm throwing up. I don't think I'm going to sleep."

She ran her hand across her face. "Okay, tell me—tell me about your brother. What's his name?"

"Moose. Except that's not his real name. His real name is Arlo, and he hates it. For a while, people called him Arlie, but he's always been a big guy, so around fifth grade someone dubbed him Moose and he grabbed hold of that."

"No nickname for you?"

"Oh, I had a few, but . . ."

"C'mon."

"Moose used to call me Lugnut."

She laughed. "Really?"

"He thought it was funny. I didn't. I tried to get people to call me Phoenix."

"Really? Like, you rise from the ashes?"

"Naw. There's a guy named Phoenix from Alaska who plays in the NHL. I wanted to be him for a while. Actually, I just wanted to be like Moose."

"And then he called you Lugnut."

"The jerk."

"So, have you risen from the dead?"

"Huh?"

"Like a phoenix."

"Absolutely. I have at least five lives left."

"That's a cat, not a phoenix."

"Still. At least five."

She imagined him as handsome, to go along with the smile she could feel through the ham.

"Do you have any siblings?" he asked.

The question caught her like a hit to the boards. "Um. Yeah. Yes."

"You sound unsure."

"No, I'm sure. A sister. She's a lot like me."

"Smart, brave, and faithful?"

*Oh. Wow.*

"Too much?"

"I—"

"I'm freezing to death here. It might have shut down my brain a little, but . . . I'd like to meet you, Sparrow."

*Um.* "Let's just keep you alive there, Phoenix. Then we'll talk."

Laughter. It swept into her, through her, and found her bones. Heated them.

"So how'd you get into the serial killer hunting business?"

"I failed out of river-monster school."

"Aw, I like you, Sparrow."

She smiled, but his voice had softened. Fatigue, or possibly the cold, creeping over him. *Stay awake, Axel.* "I like you too. So I'm going to be really peeved with you if you die."

"Roger," he said softly.

*Oh boy.* "Okay, so when I was ten, we lived a neighborhood near uptown, in Minneapolis, with alleyways and detached garages, and one day I was walking home from school, and I found a dead body in an abandoned garage a block from my house. My sister was with me, and she completely freaked out, but I . . . I was curious. We ran home and my mom called the cops, but I sneaked back and watched them bag her up and take evidence, and I thought . . . someday, I want to do that."

"Bag up dead people?"

"No—search for evidence. Find the killer. I actually met a cop on the scene—his name was Rembrandt Stone, and he was nice. He liked that I was curious. He explained what the crime-scene techs were doing—one of them was actually his wife, Eve. And then, later, he came by the house and gave me a detective book. Turned out he lived in the neighborhood. He quit being a cop after that, started to write novels. But after I graduated from high school, I tracked him down, and he introduced me to his wife. They became my mentors as I went to college. Then the police academy. And then into the forensics department. But I really wanted to be an investigator, so I became a beat cop and finally made detective."

"And started specializing in serial killers."

"Actually, that was . . . that's a more recent focus. But I did recently catch one."

Silence.

"Phoenix?"

"Mm-Mmmhmm."

"Stay with me."

Silence.

"Axel?"

Nothing.

"Lugnut!"

Crackling, then. "I heard that."

"Do not sleep."

"Not. Sleeping."

"Listen. You can do this. You managed to escape a sinking ship! You're tougher than you think—I know it. So, *stay awake*. Your turn to talk."

"Fine. We have a serial killer in Alaska. The Midnight Sun Killer." His voice was fading.

"I know," she said. And oh, in that moment she wanted to tell him. Why not? Clearly it wasn't him. What would it hurt? "Actually, I came to Alaska in search of—"

Outside, the sound of a motor hummed in the air. "Stay there. Don't move. I'll be right back."

"Where am I going to go?"

She didn't answer—just set down the mic and headed outside. And wanted to weep when, through the dusty shadows of the forest, Peyton emerged, riding hard on her four-wheeler. Head down, helmet on, thundering over the field, throttle open.

Flynn waved, stepped off the porch, and Peyton almost skidded to a stop. Threw up her visor. "Why didn't you answer me?"

Flynn jerked, stared. "What? I've been calling you for hours! Over and over!"

Peyton just looked at her. Then she grabbed the radio. Closed her eyes with a face. "Channel sixteen."

"You said six!"

She drew in a breath. "Okay. Yeah. That's the channel I use when I'm out with Echo—sorry. I got worried when you didn't answer. Did you shoot off a gun?"

"Yeah, I did—"

"Are you okay? Are you in danger?" Peyton pulled off her helmet.

"No—but I have a guy on the ham radio who is."

"What?" Peyton got off the bike and headed into the house.

"He's a rescue swimmer, and he got caught in a storm. I've been talking to him for the better part of the night. He was on a ship but it went down, and now he's in a life raft, but I think he's hypothermic and he's barely talking—"

Flynn charged in behind her, but Peyton had already picked up the mic. "CQ, CQ, this is AL7RAC—"

"I don't remember my numbers," said Axel, barely mumbling. *Oh no.*

Peyton's eyes widened. "Axel? Is that you?"

"Mm-Mmmhmm."

"This is Peyton. Where are you?"

"I'm . . . in a life . . . raft."

"He's in the Cook Inlet somewhere," Flynn said. "He keeps asking me to call his brother, Moose, and some rescue team."

"Air One. Okay." Peyton toggled the mic again. "Axel, you stay alive. I'll get Moose to you. Hang in there."

She turned the dial to another frequency. "This is AL7RAC, Alpha Lima 7 Romeo Alpha Charlie calling AL7SKY, Alpha Lima 7 Sierra Kilo Yankee on the Copper Mountain repeater. This is AL7RAC calling AL7SKY. Mayday, Mayday, Mayday."

Her gaze fell on Flynn. "Breathe. We'll get him."

*Yeah. Breathing.*

Flynn stood at the door, her arms around herself as Peyton repeated the call signs.

Then a female voice came on the line. "AL7RAC, this is AL-7SKY 5-9. What's your Mayday?"

"Echo, we got a call from Axel. He's alive but in a life raft in the Cook Inlet. He lost communication with Moose. Can you ping Moose?"

"Roger. Dodge will call Moose."

Peyton blew out a breath. Looked at Flynn. "You scared the pine out of me. I've been trying to call you for hours. And then, halfway here, I heard that gunshot."

"Sorry. That was me panicking."

Peyton raised an eyebrow.

Flynn stood up. "Who's Dodge?"

"He's an Air One rescue pilot, stationed up here in Copper Mountain."

The female voice came over the line again. "AL7RAC, this is AL7SKY, I got ahold of Shep. The team is in Homer. Moose is receiving the message."

Flynn leaned over to Peyton. "Tell them he's in a life raft. The ship went down. And he's really cold because he thinks it has a leak and—"

Peyton held up her hand. "Okay." She relayed that information to the other operator.

"I need to talk to him. Let me talk to him."

Peyton turned the channel to Axel's frequency. "CQ, CQ, this is AL7RAC."

No answer.

Peyton tried again. "CQ, CQ, this is AL7RAC—"

Flynn leaned over. "Axel, wake up! Wake. Up!"

No answer.

"Listen, Axel," Peyton said. "Moose is on the way. Just hang on. Hang on."

Still no answer.

Flynn looked at her, eyes wide. "We should go find him."

"What are we supposed to do? They are hundreds of miles away in the middle of the ocean. The best we can do is stay right here in case he comes back on the line."

*Right.*

Peyton gave her a sad look. "I've had my history with wandering off. We're staying right here where people can find us." She got up then and went outside. Returned with a sleeping bag and her pack. She shoved the bag on the top bunk. Then she pulled out coffee. "Coffee?"

"Absolutely." Flynn sat down at the table. Picked up the mic. "Axel. Come in. Come in."

Nothing. Her finger caught on the scratching of the bird.

Maybe it wasn't a sparrow. Maybe it was a phoenix.

Maybe it was her one last chance to save a life out here in the bush.

"Moose, you okay in there?"

The voice came through the bathroom door from where Moose stood over the toilet, pretty sure that, nope, he wasn't okay.

Might never be okay.

But maybe his stomach had called it quits for now.

He ran water, washed his face, rinsed out his mouth, and stared at himself for a long moment. His eyes bore the agony of the past five hours, reddened, raw, furious—and not just at Axel but at himself for not sticking around.

He'd left his brother to die in the frothing, roiling ocean.

Axel *couldn't* be gone.

He opened the door to see the team EMT, Boo Kingston, standing there. Petite but fierce, her dark hair pulled back in a severe bun, she wore the red jumpsuit of the Air One Rescue team and held a Sprite and a stack of saltines. "You need to eat something or you won't make it back out. And you need sleep."

"Don't talk to me about sleep with my brother out there." But he did take the can of soda and walk to the massive hangar windows that overlooked Coal Bay. Outside, wind and rain lashed the Bell 429 chopper, sitting under the bloom of tall tarmac lights. The runway lit up the night, a trail of white into blackness. Voices and the bitter scent of burnt coffee languishing in the pot filtered into the room. Cessnas undergoing their 100-hour inspections filled the massive hangar, the mechanic boxes lined up against the walls.

Boo came up beside him. Said nothing, just stood, silent.

No amount of hopeful talk could deny the truth.

"How is the family?" he finally said.

"Alive. The father has a broken leg, and the mother is getting stitches and is being treated for a concussion. But the kids are alive and so is the captain." She took a cracker from the sheath and took a bite. The crumbs spilled onto the floor.

He held out his hand, and she put a cracker in it.

If his brother, by some miracle, managed to stay alive, he wanted to be on his feet. Which meant that yes, he needed shut-eye or the FAA would shut him down and he'd have to rely on the Coast Guard, or maybe even Dodge from Copper Mountain to fly down and take the chopper out.

"Where's the bunk room?"

She motioned toward the office area in back. "They don't have a proper SAR bunk room, but they set up cots in the waiting room."

"Thanks."

He felt her gaze on him when he walked away. It wasn't every day that their fearless leader lost it as completely as he had after they touched down and after the winds hit ninety knots.

He'd barely made it to the head.

But he'd never been as sick as he'd been watching from a safe three hundred feet above as the Lady Luck pitchpoled, bow to stern, then rolled over, exposing her keel before plunging under the waves.

Axel trapped inside.

*Oh God, please save him.*

He'd said the prayer then and again a thousand times as they tried to reach Axel via radio, and as he'd flown the crew back to the Homer Airport, where they'd tried to locate the boat on radar.

His brother had simply vanished.

Moose came into the waiting room and spotted London lying on a cot, her eyes closed, curled under a blanket. The other cots remained empty. He found one in the corner and lay down.

Behind his closed eyes, he watched the horror replay, over and over. *"Moose, pull up. Pull up!"*

He'd have to try harder. He dug out his phone, opened a sleep app, and set it to waves. No, not waves. An airplane. No, not that . . . A train.

A nice constant, loud locomotive.

Then he lay on his side, the sound pressed to his ear. Closed his eyes.

And all he saw was waves, thundering down over the boat.

He sighed, his gut churning again.

*Please, God. Save Axel. Please, save Axel. Please . . .*

He must have dozed off, because a hand on his shoulder jerked him awake. He stirred, turned over, and stared up.

"You were making sounds." London stood over him, her blonde hair tied back, concern in her blue eyes.

"That was the locomotive."

"Sounded more like—"She frowned. "You okay?"

He sighed. "No." He sat up. "What time is it?"

"About three a.m."

"I didn't mean to wake you."

"I wasn't sleeping." She sank down on the nearest empty cot. "I'm worried too."

He scrubbed his hands down his face. "I should have never asked him to jump aboard this . . . team. I knew he was reckless—"

"Moose. He's the best rescue tech I've ever seen. No one dies on his watch—not if he can help it."

Moose sighed. "That's because he has history."

"The Coast Guard rescue gone bad. I know about it—Shep told me."

How Shep knew, he didn't know, but Moose nodded. "But not just that. Years ago, when Axel was about fifteen, our cousin went missing. She got lost on a camping trip and was never found. A month or so later she showed up, dead—shot."

London's eyes widened. "That's terrible."

"What's more terrible is that she was with Axel when she went missing. They were swimming in the Copper River. She got swept downstream and . . . he couldn't get to her."

"That explains a lot."

"Yeah." He shook his head. "I was trying to give him . . . I don't know . . . purpose, maybe. A way to sort out all that grief inside. Maybe get free of it after he saved enough lives. But it's always with him. Always telling him he's not quite enough, that he needs to be better."

She touched his arm. "If anyone can survive out there, if it's even possible, it's Axel."

He nodded. And for a second wished he was back in Anchorage, waiting it out at the Skyport Diner, his favorite waitress—no, friend, at least for a while—Tillie sitting across from him, listening to him with that way she had, her face in her hands. Wow, he missed her. She seemed to know how to soothe the prowling frustration inside him. And it had less to do with the diner's pie or chocolate shakes and more to do with the fact that she asked. Listened. Cared.

And she wasn't a teammate that he had to protect, emotionally, physically, or financially.

London got up. "I'm going to check the weather—you try and sl—"

The door banged open. "Moose. Get up." Shep came into the room. "Axel is alive."

Moose hit his feet. "What?"

Shep always seemed so reserved, the kind of guy who thought first, left his emotions at the door. But now he slammed on the lights. "We got a call from Echo—Axel used the boat's ham radio and got ahold of someone. He's on a life raft—at least, he was a few minutes ago."

Moose headed out the door to the office just down the hall. Boo stood in the doorway and stepped away as he barreled inside.

A big room with radios and weather monitors, and the female director standing behind the radio operator seated with earphones, listening.

"Angie, what do you know?"

The director looked up at Moose's question and stepped away from the radio operator.

"We got a call from a ham-radio operator out of Copper Mountain," Angie said. She nursed a cup of coffee in a well-seasoned cup. "They gave us the frequency of the boat's ham radio, but so far no answer."

He looked at Boo, then Shep and London. "We gotta go back."

"The storm's still pretty rough," said Angie. "Wind's at forty knots, easy. And who knows what it'll be out at sea?"

He turned to her. "The sun is on the upside—it'll be full daylight soon. The ocean always dies a little in the morning—we'll use that window." He looked at his team. "Wheels up in five."

They took off and he grabbed a cup of coffee, emptying the pot. Then he turned to Angie. "Keep trying. And alert any ships in the area."

"It's a pretty big area, Moose. You keep track of that bingo."

"Roger. But I'm not coming back without my brother."

She raised her cup and he left, finishing his coffee on his way out of the hangar.

The rain spat down on the chopper, but London had already climbed into the copilot's seat. Boo was sliding the door of the belly shut, and he got into the pilot's seat.

He commenced the check with London, then, "To be clear, I won't risk your lives. But I do want to bring Axel home."

London looked at him. "Let's get him."

He radioed the tower, they cleared him, and he eased the bird into the air. The rain had died, but the wind fought him as he rose. Still, he'd flown in worse conditions in Florida, and even the Gulf of Alaska.

Okay, none of those included rescuing his brother. But he'd searched the sea many times for lost sailors.

*Please, God, help me find him.*

The sea still churned, and he rode high, the winds less brutal as he headed to Axel's last known position. Below, the vastness of the foamy gray sea seemed an endless lethal cauldron.

"Get out your glasses! Boo, portside, Shep, starboard. London, log our coordinates. We'll search in a box pattern . . ."

The sun had risen, brilliant gold over the horizon, the mountains white-capped and glistening. Below, the sea also gleamed under the light, creating impossible shadows, the glare blinding.

The sea had simply gobbled him.

A dispatch came through the radio from Homer. "Air One Rescue, advise that we have picked up an EPIRB. Sending coordinates. Hold."

Moose looked at London and she nodded. The lats and longs came in and she adjusted their course.

Five miles to the southwest.

"Keep your eyes peeled!" He angled the chopper toward the

coordinates, the wind still fighting him, but over the last hour, it had died nearly to thirty knots. He spotted Augustine Island to the west, the volcano rising from the ocean, less than a mile away, maybe. Beyond it, from the mainland, the McNeil range rose, a rocky, forbidding game land.

No boats to be seen amidst the vastness of the water, and in the sunlight, the water turned a ghastly green.

He could almost see the shoreline of the island now, the waves breaking at ten or twenty feet over the shallower shelf. "Where are we on those coordinates?"

"Right above them, sir," London said.

"Anything?"

Silence. "Not from starboard—"

"Wait! I see something—over by the island!" Boo kept her eyes trained to her glasses. "It's orange—a life raft."

He angled the chopper west and spotted it too. A crumpled hull of rubber beached on the shore, half-deflated.

Abandoned.

It couldn't be from the Lady Luck. He'd plainly seen her life boat caught on the cables at the bow.

"It's not from the Lady Luck," he said quietly. "And no signs of—wait."

As they drew closer, the raft started to sway—although it might be the rotor wash. But then—

A body rolled out of the raft.

Red suit, helmet, boots . . . He crawled onto the rocky shore, then fell onto his back.

Lifted his arm.

"It's him!" London shouted. "It's him!"

"Not sure I can land on this shoreline," Moose said. "It's pretty narrow—"

"I'll grab him," Boo said. "Shep, you work the winch." She was already climbing into a harness, attaching a sling to the winch hook.

He held the bird steady, fifty feet over the shoreline, as Boo went down the line. Shep gave him a play-by-play. "She's on the beach. He looks pretty whipped—she's attaching the sling around his back and shoulders. Okay, coming up."

He managed to hold it in as Boo and Shep pushed Axel into the deck.

His brother sprawled there, barely moving. "Is he alive?"

"He's alive," said Axel, pulling off his helmet. "But he's cold. Really cold."

Shep shut the door. Boo wrapped a blanket around him, and London took the controls as Moose turned. Found his brother's eyes, his smile. And had nothing.

But Axel just grinned at him, his body now shaking so hard his teeth chattered. "I hope someone brought sandwiches, because I'm starved."

Moose turned back, took the helm. *Yeah, me too.* "Let's go home."

# FIVE

F LYNN, WAKE UP. WAKE UP."

A nudge to her shoulder and Flynn jerked, the words piercing the dark veil of her dreams—the ones where she and Kennedy stood together on a mountaintop, surveying the world. Funny, a flying dream too, because she'd definitely wanted to lift off, to soar into the clouds.

She hadn't had a flying dream in years.

Now she blinked it away and tried to orient herself as she lifted her head from the cradle of her arms.

Light streamed into the cabin through the windows onto the rough-hewn table, and her body ached, the few hours of sleep still sitting in her bones. Peyton Samson stood over her, her dark hair back in a yellow bandanna, wearing her light brown ranger shirt and pants, concern in her eyes. "Wow, you were sleeping hard."

"Yeah. When I sleep, I drop like a rock." She ran her hand behind her neck, then, "Wait—"

"They found him." Peyton moved over to the counter where a small camp stove heated a kettle. "I got the call early this morning, but you were dead to the world, so . . . But I need to get going, so I thought I'd wake you."

Flynn stared at her. "Please tell me he's alive."

"Oh. Yeah. Sorry. They found him alive." She turned off the burner and lifted the kettle. "Eggs? They're dehydrated but are pretty good heated and scrambled. And I made some hot cocoa too." She pointed to a thermos.

"Thanks." Flynn got up, blew out a breath, and went to the door.

Opened it and stepped outside, her hand grabbing the post on the porch. Her legs trembled, and she simply covered her face, holding on to the words, letting them crest over her.

*Found alive.*

She didn't know why the urge to weep overtook her.

The door opened behind her. Peyton handed her a metal Sierra cup with eggs rehydrating and a metal spoon. "You'll want to stir that."

She took the cup and sat on the porch, her feet on the steps, and began to stir, the focus helping to tuck everything back in. Maybe she was just tired.

"Do you know any details?"

Peyton sat beside her. "Only that they found his life raft half-deflated on a volcanic island in the southwest of Cook Inlet. He's in the hospital—hypothermia and dehydration."

She nodded.

"If you hadn't been here to get the call—"Peyton looked at her. "You saved his life."

Flynn drew in a breath. "Fate."

"Yeah. Sure." Peyton blew on her eggs. Took a bite. "Listen, I need to head back up to my research marker and finish my observations. Do you want to come with me?"

Flynn shook her head. "I think I want to nose around, see what Kennedy saw. Maybe try to figure out where she might have gone."

Peyton nodded. "I should have kept better track of her. She

seemed so eager to stay out here alone, and she checked in every day on the ham. I never thought—"She looked at Flynn. "I'm so sorry."

"That was Kennedy. A free spirit ever since we were kids. We may be identical twins, but we're very different on the inside."

Peyton cocked her head at her.

"What?"

"You seem every bit as free-spirited and curious as she was—just focused on a different subject."

"I don't know that I'd call myself free-spirited. Driven, maybe. And . . . until I figure out what happened to Kennedy, maybe trapped."

"You're out here in the middle of the Alaskan wilderness, tracking down someone who went missing three years ago. That feels big and bold and very much like your sister." Peyton touched her hand, squeezed. "I do hope you find her." She released her hand. "I'll never forget coming back to the cabin and finding it empty, all her stuff cleared out."

Flynn looked at her. "Wait—her sleeping bag, her pack, everything? But—we got that back."

"Yeah. We found the pack, or at least a lot of it, in the area of a research marker. Animals had gotten into the contents, we think, although nothing was torn or eaten, so we weren't sure what happened. And we didn't find any blood . . . or a body."

And then there was the case of the traveling necklace. Flynn's hand went to the jagged hearts. "How do you think her necklace ended up on a victim of the Midnight Sun Killer?"

"Yeah, that. I don't know. I'm sorry." Peyton got up and headed to the river. It sparkled, rushing, alive, foamy and bright, the waters inviting despite their lethal secrets. Peyton crouched and rinsed off her Sierra cup in the water.

Flynn finished off her eggs, her stomach suddenly awake and

ravenous, then got up and followed Peyton. She too rinsed her cup in the water.

Peyton stayed crouched, shaking off the water but also picking through the rocks on the shore. She emerged with a shiny green rock, about the size of her palm. Handed it to Flynn.

"What's this?"

"Nephrite, otherwise known as jade. Alaska has a number of deposits—most of them in the Seward Peninsula, but one of them is connected to this river. Sometimes we get lucky."

Flynn held the rock in her palm. Black with greenish veins, it almost seemed polished, the surface smooth. "I thought jade was green."

"It comes in all colors, but this black is really green." She took the stone out of Flynn's hand and dipped it in the river, then held it up to the light. "See how the light turns it dark green?"

"And it's spotted green."

"That's the jade inside the rock—it's translucent. This could be worth cash." She handed the rock back to Flynn. "You never know its value until you hold it to the light."

"Kennedy would have loved this. She was into rocks—had a collection back in Minnesota when we were young. Used to love to go to the north shore of Lake Superior and go agate hunting."

Peyton stood up. "She did that here too. Had a collection of rocks along the windowsill." She drew in a breath. "I'll never tire of the fragrance of the woods."

Flynn gave a smile. "You remind me of Kennedy. She was always the stop-and-smell-the-pine type."

Peyton laughed. "Yeah. She struck me as a live-off-the-land girl—subsistence gardening, fishing, maybe even jewelry-making." She reached into the neck of her shirt and pulled out a necklace on a lanyard, a shiny green pendant on the end.

Flynn took the pendant in her hand. "An infinity symbol. Is this jade?" She let it go.

"Yeah. They're made by a local community. Jade is supposed to mean the protector of generations. My father gave this to me a few years ago, and I showed it to Kennedy. I think it sparked an idea." She tucked it back into her shirt. "The jade stones were still on the windowsill after she left, so I think she meant to return."

They walked back to the cabin. "So you think she went on a day trip to observe the wolves, and never came back."

"Or an overnight trip. She took her pack and her sleeping bag. And food, but—oh wait, I found something in the debris of her pack. Maybe—"Peyton hustled up the stairs, inside the cabin.

Flynn followed her in.

Peyton had opened a cupboard—the same one where she'd tucked away the ham radio. Flynn's gaze went to the lifeline.

Home safe. She didn't know why, but the sense of it had stirred more hope inside her.

Or maybe it was Peyton's memories. In her mind's eye, she easily saw Kennedy hunting for jade by the river . . .

"Was the river near where the wolves were?"

Peyton emerged with a weathered journal that had a folded map tucked inside. "Yes." She set the book on the table. "Are you thinking she went to find more jade?"

"I don't know. But you said her belongings were scattered but not torn or eaten, right? Maybe she took them out to make room for the rocks."

Peyton considered her a moment. Then she set the journal on the table and opened it to the map. "This journal belongs to the cache. We use it to record wildlife sightings, anything unusual that might happen, or just our general thoughts. Think of it as a traveler's journal. Sometimes campers stay here and they add their thoughts. Kennedy added a number of entries."

Flynn sat on the chair and pulled the journal over, recognizing Kennedy's handwriting. Her throat thickened, seeing her sister sitting on the bunk, maybe writing in the journal by fading sunlight.

*"Spent most of the day watching Koda and Luna and their pups, along with the few beta males and females adopted into the pack—Storm, Aurora, and Fang. Koda and his betas took down a moose a few days ago, and they're still feasting on the kill—the adults going out to gather food and bring it back to the pups as a regurgitated meal.*

*"One of Luna's pups is wounded—I don't know how. It won't eat and I fear it won't survive."*

She turned the page and found another entry, a few days later.

*"Returned from watching Koda and Luna. They lost their pup and have moved dens, this one closer to the river. Storm seems to be missing also. Not sure if Koda put him out or if he's hunting.*

*"I found a piece of jade in the river, downstream from the wolves."*

"You might be right about the jade theory," Peyton said, obviously reading over Flynn's shoulder. She stepped away from the table. "I'm going to pack up. Last chance—"

"I'll stay. Read the journal." Flynn opened the map. "Maybe do some hiking. Where are we?"

Peyton came over as Flynn unfolded the entire map. It covered the table.

Flynn stood up as Peyton pointed to their location. "We're here, on one of the Copper River tributaries. The CR, as you can see, runs all the way from the Denali basin, down to the Cook Inlet. This tributary—Jubilee Creek—leads to a number of falls and runs into the Jubilee Lake south of here before emptying out into the lower Copper River."

She pointed to a road southwest of the cabin. "This is Bowie Road. It leads to the Bowie Outpost, for fly fishermen and hunters.

If you get into trouble, you head to that road and follow it out to the highway. There's the Copper Mountain Ski Resort." She pointed to the lodge, maybe twenty miles overland. "And between Bowie land and the resort is Remington land." She put her hand on the map, spread out her fingers. "It's huge and wraps around the resort area and bumps up to Bowie land. Nash's family never uses it, but since it's between two key resources, they sometimes rent it out to hunters, and of course, the Copper River runs through both Bowie land and Remington land, so it's popular with kayakers."

She then pointed to one of a number of circles on the map, located inland, about a mile or less from the cabin. "This was Luna and Koda's main den, where the pups were born, usually every year. Except this year—they're over here." She pointed to a place downriver on the creek. "This isn't normal, so I'm trying to figure out why they moved."

"Maybe something happened to their den."

"I don't know. But the den by the river, where they moved the pups, is here." Another circle closer to the river marked the spot. "They usually move them here when they're about two months old. I think the place inland is more secure—it's near a small lake and located in the cliffs. I think Kennedy used to watch them from this point here." She indicated a nearby mountain. "This was where we found her pack, by the way. I'm not sure why she was there."

"Have you checked the den?"

"Not yet."

"I'll do it."

"You know how to read a map and compass?"

"I went to the same wilderness camp that Kennedy did."

"Okay. Follow the river until you come to this ravine." She used her thumbnail to trace the route. "Then cut north and you'll find the overlook. And remember, channel sixteen. *Sixteen.*"

Flynn smiled. "I'll be fine."

"I'll be back tomorrow night. Don't be missing." Peyton lifted her pack, slung it over her shoulder. Paused by the door. "And if you can't get ahold of me, I wrote down the channel for Echo's ham receiver in the back of the journal."

"Thanks." She didn't ask about Axel's channel. Probably she should put him out of her head, keep her focus on Kennedy.

She stood on the porch, watching as Peyton motored off, drinking her cup of hot cocoa. The air did smell amazing, and an eagle lifted from a nearby tree, soaring into the blue.

Maybe this was her day to fly too.

Packing up a day bag, she filled her bottle in the river, added some iodine tablets, took a couple power bars, the notebook, flashlight, binoculars, a compass, and the bear gun—freshly loaded—and headed out along the river.

The air gathered the sun's heat, and a bell on her pack jingled as she picked her way along the rocky shoreline, away from the river.

She expected Kennedy to slide into her brain, but Axel sat down instead, his tenor warm and sweet.

"What is river-monster hunting?"

"You know, that show where some guy shoves his arm in an underwater cave or log and pulls out a catfish with teeth the size of my hand clamped on to his bloody arm."

"And now that's an image I'll have to sleep with."

She laughed at the memory.

Okay, she clearly liked his voice too much for a guy she'd never met.

The ravine cut north a half mile up the shoreline, and she took it, climbing away from the river, up a rocky mountainside. It rose maybe two thousand feet, and her breaths came out hard when she finally reached the peak.

But the view. Oh, the view.

The mountainscape fell to the east and north into a valley of lush greenery, dissected by blue rivers and a handful of lakes, puddling like the footsteps of giants. To the northwest, the Alaska Range rose jagged and white against a pale blue sky, scattered cirrus casting blue-gray shadows into the wells and granite runs that creased the peaks.

The air here smelled of wildflowers, a little brisk, but for a moment, she spread her arms and wondered what might happen if she simply ran off the edge.

Instead, she walked to the summit, stood looking down into the ravine. And spotted the trouble, maybe the answer to why the pack had moved wintering locations.

A rockslide on the other side had dammed up the better part of the river, scree and boulders probably blocking the entrance to the wolves' den. She'd have to make a note of it in the journal.

But why would Kennedy come here if the pack had moved closer to the river?

She stood, hands on her hips, staring into the horizon. North, then west, then south, toward the cache cabin, then—

*Oh no.* Smoke lifted from somewhere between the lower foothills to the east. Except it didn't seem the deep black of a forest fire but gray, as if coming from a factory.

So, that was weird.

A shot cracked deep in the valley, echoing. She jerked.

And then another shot split the air.

This time, rock chipped off below her.

*What—*

She stepped back as another shot blew up rock behind her.

Was someone—*shooting*—at her?

The next shot was so close it nicked her pack. She spun, fell.

Another shot hit the rocks behind her.

She scrambled down the side of the mountain, jumping from rock to rock, her heart slamming into her throat.

Then a shot pinged off a rock right where she put her hand, and she screamed.

Tripped.

Just like that, she was falling, slamming against rocks, launching into the air, and careening for the valley, some two thousand feet below.

"For the record, this is a bad idea."

*Yeah, whatever, whatever.* Axel ignored his brother, who stood like a sentry at the end of the bed, arms folded, legs apart, as Axel pulled out his IV. Gently, but enough that some blood formed on his forearm. He grabbed a nearby cloth and held it as he swung his bare legs out of the hospital bed.

"Six hours ago, you were dangerously close to dying."

"And now I'm not. I'm fine and I want to go home." He stood up on the linoleum. Okay, yes, a chill still ran through his body, but other than hunger—he still wanted that sandwich—and some dehydration, maybe some fatigue, he felt fine.

Aces, actually. Because who lived through both a sinking boat and a deflated life raft to land on the only island in the Cook Inlet?

He didn't want to suggest some sort of divine favor—didn't want to get used to the idea, really—but this time, he'd let God have the credit, no argument.

"No, you don't," Moose said. "You want to go find that woman on the other end of the ham radio."

Axel didn't look at him as he waited for Boo to return from her mission to score him some clothes. "Listen. I need her to know I'm safe."

"I'm sure Echo radioed her."

"I want to tell her personally."

Moose gave him a look, rolled his eyes.

"Yeah, well, you weren't there. She ... Not to be too dramatic, but she kept me alive. It was her idea to find the life-raft suitcase— if not for that, I would be swimming with the fishes."

"Agreed. Great idea. But it doesn't mean you should get out of bed while you teeter on the edge of death and trek into the bush to find her."

Boo came into the room smiling like a thief, holding clothing wrapped in plastic under her jacket. She tossed it to him. "Hope you're a large, because that's all I could find."

"It'll work," Axel said as he caught the open back of his breezy hospital jammies and headed to the bathroom. His red jumpsuit, thermal shirt, long johns, and underclothes lay soggy and wadded into a plastic bag hanging in a closet, his boots, now mostly dried, on a shelf at the bottom. He untied the gown and climbed into the surgical pants, pulled on the shirt, and even found socks at the bottom of the package. *Sweet.*

He emerged, the bag of soggy clothing over his shoulder, his boots untied, the laces trailing. "Let's blow."

They were down the hall before he heard a nurse calling his name, but he ignored her and hit the stairwell, taking the steps two at a time, Boo keeping up.

Moose hit the door as it was closing, taking his time. "Sheesh, you're not escaping prison. Simply ask to be discharged—"

His voice cut out on the ground-level door closing behind Axel.

And then he was free. The sky had cleared, the debris from the storm littering the parking lot, turning the air soggy, but overhead, simply bright blue, the scent of pine and ocean in the air.

"Still hungry?" Boo said. "I saw Jell-O on your tray."

"Find me a burger, and fast."

Moose came out, holding the keys to the truck he'd borrowed from someone over at the airport. "I'll call the others, get Shep to fuel up the chopper."

Axel slowed, fell into step with Moose and Boo. "So, do we get food here, or wait until we get to Anchorage—maybe stop by the Skyport Diner?"

Moose glanced at him. "There's a burger place on the way to the airport."

*Oh. Huh. Interesting.*

"Besides, my guess is that you'll want me to fly you up to Copper Mountain."

Axel grinned at him. "I like how you think."

"What I think is that you've created the woman of your dreams in your head. You do know that whoever was on the other end of the radio was probably a fifty-year-old woman with bad teeth who has lived in the bush for thirty years, bathes once a year whether she needs it or not, and spends more time talking to her sled dogs than humans, right?"

"She sounded younger." Axel grinned at him. "Calm down, bro. I just want to thank her, not ask her out on a date."

"Sure you do." Moose unlocked the doors to the truck with a beep. "Boo, you sit in the middle so I don't have to smell him."

"What?"

"You do smell like the ocean," Boo said.

Axel gave himself a sniff before he got in. Okay, so maybe he'd stop for a shower at the Air One base first.

Moose was grinning, however, as they drove through a fast-food joint and grabbed a stack of burgers, enough for the entire crew.

Okay, so maybe Axel did harbor a smidgen of wishful thinking. Because she didn't sound like a fifty-year-old toothless woman with a shotgun, dressed in pelts. She'd mentioned being a wolf researcher, yes, but so was Peyton Samson, and every guy in town had mourned the loss of her on the list of single women when Nash proposed.

Sparrow could be just as hot as Peyton. And better—her laughter sat inside him, even after the wave had filled the life raft and shorted out his radio.

He'd survived the next three hours shivering and replaying their conversation about river monsters and bungee jumping and the stories about her life as a serial-killer hunter . . . He'd even told her about the Coast Guard.

Really, she'd kept him alive.

*"I like you too. So I'm going to be really peeved with you if you die."*

Yes, he was most definitely tracking her down.

Three hours later, showered, full, and awake, he disembarked from Air One's Cessna 206 onto the tarmac in Copper Mountain. His father waited beyond the gate, his hands shoved into his jacket, the wind blowing his thin brown hair as Moose tied down the plane.

Axel secured the tail and waved to Ace. Moose joined him. "Any idea where this woman is?"

"Not a clue. In the bush somewhere. I thought I'd start with Peyton. Hey, Dad."

Ace glanced at Moose, then put his hand around the back of Axel's neck, squeezed. Gave him a nod. Then he let go and headed for the truck.

Axel glanced at Moose. "You told him."

"All of Copper Mountain knows, bro. Peyton called in the rescue to Echo who called it in to Air One, but we couldn't get ahold of Echo when we brought you in, so we called Hank, and I'm sure word got around." He reached the front passenger door, his father climbing in on the other side. "You scared a lot of people."

He didn't know what to do with that and simply climbed into the back seat.

Despite his bracing shower, fatigue had caught up with him on the flight north and now sat in his bones as they drove into town. "Can we stop by the ranger office?"

"After you see your mother. She's minding the store."

*Right.*

They pulled up to the family store, Ace's Hardware, and he got out. His mother wore the last twenty-four hours in her expression as she came out from behind the counter and simply pulled him into a hug.

He put his arms around her. She was a sturdy woman, physically and emotionally, she wasn't usually given to holding on quite so long.

Then again, he'd seen what losing a child had done to her sister, so—

"I'm okay, Ma."

"Yep." She patted his back, his shoulders, and leaned away. "Yep. Yep." Her eyes glistened, however, and she ran a quick hand across her cheeks. "I'll make you some pasties for dinner."

"I'll never leave."

"I won't argue."

He kissed her cheek. "I gotta find someone. I'll be back to pick you up."

Moose stood at the door and lifted his hand to their mom, followed Axel out to the ranger's office.

For a moment, Axel thought the offices might be closed and checked his watch. Only four in the afternoon, but the place seemed quiet.

He went inside and spotted Parker reading a magazine behind the reception desk. She dropped it and stood up, smiling at Axel. "Hey. You okay?" Her eyes glowed and she seemed just a little too smiley. Weird.

"Yeah. Hey. So, is Peyton around?"

Parker wore a black T-shirt with the words *Be a Wolf in a World Full of Sheep*. Another wolf fanatic. Peyton had her own little club.

"She's out in the bush checking on a pack."

"Do you know where?"

She made a face. "Not exactly."

"Is your dad here?"

"No. He's dealing with a hiker gone missing up in the park."

"Shoot. I was really hoping to track down Peyton."

"I do know that he called in an update on a cache cabin on the river this morning. I heard him in his home office . . ." She came around the desk, through the swinging gate, and out to the massive topographical and elevation map tacked to the wall. Along with all the hiking trails in the area, the service had designated all the fire towers and cache cabins in their district. Most of the cache cabins were marked by a number.

Parker ran her finger down the highway, then over, along the river, up a tributary, and then stopped at a cabin located on the Jubilee Creek. "Number forty-seven. I think that's right." She looked at Axel. "But I'm not sure."

"Axel, you can't go all the way—"Moose started.

Axel shot him a look, then pulled out his phone and took a shot. But really, he knew the area.

Probably too well.

"Thanks, Parker."

She grinned at him. "I loved the last episode of your show."

"Oh?"

"The one with you rescuing Oaken Fox out of the river?"

"It's not my show."

She shrugged.

*Oh brother.*

"Tell your dad thanks for his help today," Moose said, and held the door open for Axel.

He stepped outside.

"She has a crush on you," Moose said.

"She's seventeen."

Moose grinned. "If this bird lady doesn't work out, you wait a few years and—"

"Get away from me, you creep." Axel walked down to the truck.

Moose caught up. "Now what?"

"Now I go home and get my bike."

"Here we go—"

Axel rounded on him. Held up his hand. "Moose. You did enough. I've got this."

His brother had been joking—Axel knew that—but as he took a breath, his expression grew solemn. A moment passed between them.

"Sorry," Axel said quietly.

"For what?"

"For . . . nearly dying."

Moose's shoulders rose and fell, and he nodded, looked away.

Another beat. Then, "If you do that ever again, I'm going to have to kill you." He smiled, mouth closed, a little danger in his eyes, and headed toward the truck, parked in front of the store.

Well, that was settled, then.

But wow, Axel hadn't realized his brother cared so much. *Huh.*

He got into the back, and Moose got into the driver's side. His mother slid into the front passenger seat, glanced back at Axel. "I'll bet you're tired."

"I have a little errand to run. I'll be home by dinner."

She eyed him but nodded.

His dual sport dirt bike sat under a tarp in the big garage his dad had built for their motor home and other northern equipment, including the plow, a tractor, four-wheelers, and snowmobiles. He pulled off the tarp and ran a hand over the bike, made for both off-road and highway.

He'd given it a bath after taking it out a month ago, but it still bore scrapes and a couple dents from the off-roading.

So many memories.

So many near tragedies.

"You sure you don't want me to go with you?" Moose stood at the door of the garage. "We can take dad's truck, put the four-wheeler in the back."

"I feel the need for speed."

"Oh brother."

He grinned. "Listen. I'm just going to take a run out there. Four hours, tops."

Moose made a noise deep inside his chest but nodded and headed to the house.

Axel grabbed his helmet, strapped it on, then eased the bike off its kickstand.

The machine roared to life as if angry, and he sat back on it, feeling it rumble under him.

Yeah, this was right.

He pulled out of the garage, got out and shut the door, then tucked his earbuds in under his helmet, turned his phone to a local channel, and motored out of the dirt driveway and down the highway.

The local radio station, WBEX, played country, and wouldn't you know it, Oaken Fox crooned out one of his recent hits. Of course.

Axel thought he might have written it for Boo.

*"Out on the open road, I've been searching high and low,*
*For a love that's true, a heart that knows,*
*Through dusty towns and city lights, I roamed,*
*Seeking a love that felt like coming home."*

Yeah, that sounded like Oaken. Axel liked the guy, and the country singer had done a great job of putting Air One Rescue on the map, but frankly, some people were cut out for the limelight. Like Oaken.

And some people weren't.

Like him.

Axel hunkered down, leaning into the song as he motored past the turnoff to Copper Mountain and headed south, ten miles until he turned off onto Bowie Road.

*"But then you walked into my life, like a sunrise over fields,*
*I saw forever in your eyes, and all the past wounds healed,*
*Now I know, deep in my soul, I'm the luckiest guy alive,*

*For in your love, darlin', I've found my guiding light."*
Oh brother, he'd started to hum. *Whatever.*

Really, he just wanted to thank her. Even if she was a fifty-year-old woman dressed in furs and wielding a shotgun. He owed her that much.

He shut off the music when he turned off onto the Bowie camp road. He followed the dirt along the river until it veered south, then turned off-road, north toward Jubilee Creek. The terrain was built for four-wheelers, the path narrow as he drove across meadow and tundra, and he slowed, bumping along, easing the bike over boulders and gravel along the shoreline. But it was faster than walking. Even when he slowed to cross the creek at the shallows, the water washing up to his feet. But he gunned the bike through the river, spitting up mud and gravel as he hit the other side.

The terrain fought him as he traveled along the gravelly, rocky shoreline. Around him, the mountains rose, and as he gained elevation, the terrain turned bumpier.

But he knew he'd made the right choice when a path cut through the forest.

He slowed, coming out the other side, and spotted the cabin seated on a rise above the river. Small but cozy, with a front porch and a scenic view.

He understood the allure.

Parking away from the cabin, he took off his helmet and looked around. "Hello?"

Peyton's four-wheeler didn't appear to be parked anywhere, but maybe she was out stalking some wolves or something.

He went up to the cabin, knocked on the door, and when no one answered, pushed it open.

A sleeping bag lay on the wooden bunk, rolled out. Camp gear—a stove, dehydrated food, a watertight bag for clothes—so Peyton was around.

He'd just have to wait for her to return, see if she knew where to find Sparrow.

He stepped outside, stood on the porch, his hands to his back, stretching, watching the river—

"Good try, but I'm not in there."

He paused at the voice. "What—"

"Keep your hands where I can see them."

Gravel crunched to his left, and he looked over to see a woman—a hurt and bleeding woman—with a bear gun trained on him. Blood ran from a wound on her head, or at least had run—now it stuck her hair to her face, the blood dried and dark on her cheek and neck. And she limped, dragging her foot. And a sling around her neck with a binoculars cord held her arm close to her body, her left hand gripping her pistol. She wore canvas hiking pants, boots, a blue thermal shirt, and he put her in her late twenties, maybe early thirties.

He cocked an eyebrow. "You do know that you probably can't kill me with that."

"I can hurt you. And then I can take your bike and leave you here."

*Oh.* "Okay. Listen, I don't know who you are, but you're clearly hurt. Let me help you."

Her eyes narrowed. She blinked at him.

He started to turn, to lower his hands—

She shot at him. Maybe missed purposely, but the bullet chipped off wood from the pillar beside him.

"Sheesh! Are you crazy?"

"Who are you and what are you doing here?"

"I'm . . . Listen, I'm nobody. I came out here to find Peyton Samson." He took a breath. "Do you . . . um . . ." He took his eyes off her to scan the area. "Peyton! It's Axel! Shout if you're here!"

"Axel?"

He looked back at the woman. She'd swallowed, her gun hand shaking.

And then, right then, he got it.

Or at least, he *thought* so . . . because she wasn't a fifty-year-old woman dressed in a bear skin.

In fact, she looked more like she'd been *mauled* by said bear.

*"Sparrow?"*

And right then, even as she nodded, her legs gave out, and she collapsed onto the dirt.

# SIX

PLEASE LET HER BE RIGHT. TO HAVE HEARD the truth and not just what she hoped.

Please let her not have been followed as she struggled off the mountain, only to collapse here in the dirt for the shooter to finish her off.

She couldn't die here—

"Sparrow, just calm down—calm down!"

Flynn hadn't even realized she'd been thrashing, pushing Axel's hands away from her as she came back to herself.

One second she'd nearly shot the man standing on her porch, the next she'd been trying to grapple with his voice—so wonderfully familiar—while the world spun.

"What happened?"

She opened her eyes to find herself tucked into her sleeping bag on the porch, Axel bent over her with a wet cloth, dabbing it to her head with one hand while the other held her wrist.

Her hand was balled into a fist.

"Did I punch you?"

He bore the faintest hint of red on his cheek. "It's nothing. You were a little confused. I think you might have had a seizure."

She remembered nothing except—"Axel."

"That's right." He met her eyes. Blue eyes, just like she'd imagined. Almost brown hair, except for highlights that turned to deep bronze in the sun, and a smattering of golden-brown whiskers across his face, as if he hadn't shaved in his hurry to get to her.

Oh yeah, she'd hit her head, and hard, careening down that mountain.

"What happened to you?" He leaned away, his eyes on the wound on her head. "That needs a stitch or two."

"I fell down a mountain."

"You did what?"

"After someone shot at me."

His frown deepened.

"I thought . . . I thought maybe he'd followed me back to the cabin. Then I heard your bike and I hid and . . ." She winced, her head really starting to bang now. "Sorry I shot at you."

"Please tell me you were trying to miss."

She closed her eyes, but her mouth tweaked up one side. "Yep."

"Okay. Listen, I need to take a look at your wrist, and did you hurt your leg too?"

"Yeah, I sprained my knee. Landed pretty hard on it. And it's not my wrist—it's my shoulder."

"Hence the sling. How far did you fall?"

"All the way?" She opened her eyes.

Now he narrowed his eyes at her. "Smarty pants, huh?"

"Listen, Mr. I-Scare-People-To-Death-And-Don't-Answer-My-Ham-Radio, I think you had it coming—oh, ah. Okay, no more talking."

"Agreed. And I only went dark because a wave took out the ham. Yeah, your knee is really swollen." He'd zipped open her sleeping bag and now put his hand on her leg gently, moving it around the joint. "As for your shoulder, lemme see how bad it is. I don't want to try to put it back into place if your shoulder is broken."

He put his hand on her shoulder, kneading gently.

"I don't think—oh, oh, that hurts. Okay, that's good—that—oh." She grabbed his wrist. "Thank you so much, doc, but I think let's leave it to the professionals."

"I am a professional."

"If I remember correctly, you're a professional *swimmer*. Not shoulder-setter."

He leaned back. "Okay, from what I can tell, it's an anterior dislocation. It can be reset. And the longer we wait, the more damage you'll do to it. How long has it been—"

"About three, maybe four hours. I don't know. I fell about twenty feet, onto a ledge, and then sort of worked my way down the mountain. There might have been more falling. I was pretty . . . well, I did mention the shooting, right?" She tried to sit up and he caught her, one strong arm behind her back as she eased up.

The world started to spin again. She grimaced.

"I think I need to get a chopper in here."

"No . . . no, I just need to rest."

"Have you lost your ever-lovin' mind? You need a hospital!"

She looked at him. Smiled.

He frowned at her. "What?"

"What are you doing here? You're supposed to be in a hospital, recovering from hypothermia."

"You can't figure that out?" He leaned close to her, those blue eyes on hers. Then he smiled.

Oh wow. And just like that, she felt like she could fly.

*Sheesh.* She'd been knocked harder in the head that she thought. For Pete's sake—

"Now, let's set that shoulder."

*Oh.*

"Listen, there's an old cowboy trick I know—a guy I used to

swim with taught me. He was from Oklahoma—had an itch to live by the ocean. But he rode bulls for a while too and showed me how to self-set a dislocation." He hopped off the porch, eased her legs out of the bag, grabbed her by the hips and turned her. "I'm going to help you stand up. Don't fall."

She nodded, wincing as her knee bent. But she let him pull her forward so her feet touched the ground.

"Okay, I got you." He tucked an arm around her waist. "Now, lean forward and let your dislocated arm dangle down."

"That's going to hurt."

"Yes, yes it is." He leaned down. "But you're tougher than you think."

"Oh, I see where we're going with this."

"Lean over. I won't let you fall."

She grunted, grabbing her arm to ease it down until it dangled.

"Okay, bend your knees and tuck your fingers beneath your foot."

"My knee is swollen. I can't bend it."

"Right. Okay, um . . ." He knelt in front of her, his face near hers. "I'm going to slowly pull down on your hand. Don't stand up. Brace your other hand on me."

She put her hand on his back—he had wide, firm shoulders—and closed her eyes as he started to apply pressure. Gritting her teeth, she bit back a moan.

"Almost there."

Her muscles stretched and then—*pop*. Her shoulder moved back into place. She let out a gasp, then a whimper, and opened her eyes.

His gaze fixed on hers, so close, too close maybe, and truthfully, all these feelings probably had way too much to do with the last twenty-four hours of panic, then relief, and now rescue than actual attraction, so *hello. Wake up and calm down.*

But oh, Axel Mulligan was a handsome man.

"It's back in the socket?"

"Yeah." She straightened, then swayed, and he grabbed her waist.

"Hokay, I think it's time to close up that cut on your forehead and head back to Copper Mountain."

He picked her up and set her back on the porch, just like that. He moved her onto the sleeping bag. "Lie back. Let me see what you've got around here for first aid."

"I bought a kit in town, at the outfitter's," she said. Probably. At least she said it in her mind.

He emerged holding the bag and now crouched beside her and opened it. "Yep. Butterfly bandages. Perfect. That'll get us started."

She let him doctor her cut, adding ointment, then taping it shut. Then he wrapped her knee with an instant ice pack and an ACE bandage.

"You're a regular Doctor Quinn, Medicine Woman."

He looked at her.

"Except you're a guy."

"Thanks for noticing." He tucked the kit away. "Do you think you can ride on my bike?"

"I can try." She pushed herself up. "I did manage to walk down the mountain by myself."

He considered her a moment. "Okay. Let me pack up your gear. Or is it Peyton's?"

"Peyton! Oh, we need to call her—"

He held up his hand. "Where's the radio?"

"I . . . think it might be in my pack?"

He found the pack and pulled out the radio. "You didn't think to use this?"

"You remember the shooting part, right? The last thing I wanted was to bring Peyton into that."

He considered her for a long moment, then nodded.

"Channel sixteen," she said.

He stood up and went into the cabin, and she heard him call up Peyton. Tell her that he was bringing Flynn into Copper Mountain.

He also mentioned the shooter, then someone named Hank—oh, right, she knew Hank—and as she closed her eyes, she heard him say he'd called Nash.

How could she have thought he might be a killer . . .

"Don't sleep!"

His voice jerked her back, her eyes open. He stood over her, the pack over his shoulders. "Don't sleep, Sparrow."

Sparrow. She should tell him her . . . name . . .

"Okay, that's enough. We're going. But I don't trust you to hang on." He whipped off the pack, stepped into the cabin, and in a moment he'd returned with the empty pack, her supplies gone.

"Let's go."

*What—*

And then he simply bent and swept her up into his arms.

He smelled good. Like the woods, and maybe soap, and something tough and durable and determined.

"Sparrow!" He jostled her hard.

Her eyes opened. He'd reached the bike.

"Okay, I'm hoping this works—I need you to sit behind me, and then I'm going to put the pack around both of us."

*Huh?*

He settled her on the bike, put a helmet on her, then pulled off the pack and loosened the straps. "Put this on."

"Sure."

But he helped because her arm still hurt, and frankly, the world wasn't quite right either.

He got on in front of her, reached down, gripped her thighs, and pulled her up against him. Then he reached back and put his arms through the straps, pulling her tight against him. She put her arms around his waist, tucked in tight, the helmet thumping against his shoulder blades.

Yeah. She wasn't going anywhere.

He reached down and put her right foot on a peg that he flipped out.

Then he took hold of her leg with the damaged knee and carefully lifted it, holding her knee against his thigh. "I know this isn't ideal. But we need to get you to help, and soon, and this will be faster than bringing in the Air One team. I promise to go easy."

She probably made a sound of agreement, because he started off. Easy, navigating with one hand while working the throttle.

Her arms tightened around him, and despite her helmet, and against her will, her cries of pain leaked out, even over the sound of the engine. They motored down the shoreline, then through a river, and she closed her eyes again as they hit the other side and he drove a little faster.

Breathe. She gritted her teeth, stealing herself, but the pain cascaded through her, took hold. She bent her head, closed her eyes.

He reached the dirt road and opened up the bike a little, kicking up dust.

And then, suddenly, they were sliding, the bike almost spilling out beneath him.

She gasped, gripped his waist.

He braked and righted it. "You okay?" She breathed out. Not even a little. But as she lifted her head, put her hands to his back, she discovered he was sweating. "Axel?"

"Yeah. Just . . . give me a second."

She lifted the visor and spotted a rabbit on the side of the road. "Did we almost hit a rabbit?"

"The rabbit almost hit us, but—yeah. I think . . . this might have been a bad idea. Once we get on the highway, I'm going to need both hands. Unless . . ." He breathed out. "Okay, I got this."

He reached into his jacket and pulled out his cell. "Good. We finally have service."

She closed her eyes, but in a moment she heard—

"Hey, Moose, I found her."

His voice, his words just . . . well, she was definitely concussed, because they simply settled inside her, bathing her insides with a sort of warm goo. *I found her.*

"Okay. Meet me at the highway."

He hung up. Looked over his shoulder. "Put the visor down. It's going to get dusty."

She did, and he motored up the bike, still holding her leg, and pushed off.

They crawled along, stones and rock pinging off the tires, his body taut, clearly trying to keep them from sliding.

And all the while he kept a firm grip on her leg.

She closed her eyes again, surrendered to the buzz of the motor, the sense of him, stalwart, in front of her.

She didn't know how long they'd traveled before she heard the engine cut down. He stopped, his legs bracing them.

She lifted her head and spotted a pickup on the side of the road. A man, dark hair, a canvas jacket, and jeans walked over to Axel. "This is your fifty-year-old bush woman?"

*Huh?*

"She did show up with a gun, so you weren't wrong there. Help me get her off the bike. Easy. She fell down a mountain."

"You two are a pair."

He eased out of the pack and leaned up, still holding her leg. "Sparrow, I'm going to put your leg down and lift you off the bike."

He looked at Moose. "Take her helmet off. Then catch her because she's in and out of consciousness."

Yeah, well, if she'd been sleeping before, she woke when Axel got up, trying not to jostle her leg. Her knee must have swelled six sizes since getting on the bike, and a noise that she'd never heard before came out of her body.

"Okay, okay—"Even he sounded panicked. He came around and scooped her up again into his arms. "Listen, I'm going to put you in the back seat of the truck, and Moose is taking you to the Copper Mountain hospital. They'll assess you, and if you need it, we'll fly you down to Anchorage."

She looked at him, dust on his skin and his clothing, his eyes holding a fair amount of worry, and she couldn't stop herself. "You'll be there, right?"

He smiled. "Yeah, Sparrow. I'll be there as soon as I can."

Then he stepped up to the back seat and placed her inside. She slid back onto it and let her leg lie straight.

The big guy got into the driver's seat. "I'm Moose, Axel's brother."

"The one who called him Lugnut."

He considered her for a moment. Then chuckled. "Don't you worry, Sparrow. I'll take good care of you."

"Stay alive," said Axel as he stood at the door. Then he winked and shut it.

Fear not. Because her sister's murderer was in those mountains; she just knew it.

And she wasn't going anywhere.

"You did hear the part about someone trying to shoot her, right, Deke?"

Axel didn't mean to raise his voice, and despite the lingering late-evening sun, a nurse had walked by twice with a finger to her mouth to shush them.

He didn't care when visiting hours ended, he wasn't budging. Not until Sparrow came out of a CT scan for her head, her MRI for her knee, and X-rays for her shoulder.

And not until he got some answers about who might have been shooting at her on a mountaintop in the middle of a national forest.

So there was that.

The moment Axel had arrived at the Copper Mountain hospital—a five-bed hospital attached to the clinic and the new maternity ward—and discovered Sparrow getting a head and knee CT, he'd left to track down the sheriff.

"I did hear you, Axel," Deke said. He was out of uniform, Axel having dragged him out of the Midnight Sun Saloon. He'd gotten a takeout box from Vic, the owner, for the man's hot wings, so what was he complaining about?

Now Axel, Deke, and Moose stood in the waiting room of the ER, and Axel wanted answers. Or at least . . . some action from the sheriff's office. A BOLO maybe or . . .

"What exactly do you want me to do, Axel?" Deke said. "You know that area is near Bowie land. Could have been a stray bullet—"

"It's *fishing* season, Deke. No one should be shooting anything, let alone a person."

"People have a right to bring a gun into the bush any time of year. You know that. And they can shoot an animal in self-defense."

"You really think that woman in there could be confused with a *grizzly bear*?"

"Take a breath, Axel," Moose said, stepping between him and Deke. "No one is saying that this is okay. And yes, Deke—and Hank, really—will get to the bottom of this. But let the man finish his wings."

They did smell good. Maybe he should have picked up an order too. "Does that have Vic's special bacon sauce?"

"Yeah. Ribs, too. And I'll bet they're cold."

"Sorry."

Deke nodded. "Listen. I'll talk to Hank, see who's picked up any permits for fishing in the area. Sully should know too—he's out on a fishing trip with his uncle right now. He'll be back any day."

Axel nodded. "Okay. Can you stay and get a statement from her?"

Deke had picked up the container. "Of course." He went over to the sofa and opened the container.

"You want me to go over to the Midnight Sun, get you some ribs?" Moose asked.

Axel pressed his empty stomach, churning. "No. Did Mom make pasties?"

"She was midroll when I left, so probably."

He walked to the window. A haze, what might be considered night this time of year, had started to settle over the valley. The hospital sat away from Main Street, overlooking it at a distance. From here, he spotted the airport, the train station, and the Bowie lodge along the river.

And the RV parking lot, jammed with tourists, hikers, and fishermen here for the summer of the eternal sun.

Yeah, Deke was right. Could have been anyone. And . . . maybe Sparrow wasn't even the target.

"By the way, I know your girl."

He looked over at Deke, who was finishing off a rib. Deke took out a wet wipe that came with the dinner and cleaned his hands, then his face. "Her name is Flynn. Flynn Turnquist. She's a cop from Minneapolis."

*Huh.* He sort of liked Sparrow better. But why hadn't she told him her name?

And he knew about her being a cop. Still, "How do you know that?"

"She has a sister who went missing here three years ago. Kennedy Turnquist. She worked with Peyton, studying wolf patterns. Went out on a hike one day and never returned." He picked up another rib. "They found her belongings—her pack and other items—scattered near one of the research sites. Peyton reported her gone, and we issued a search warrant, but nothing ever came of it, and she just disappeared into the system. Hank thought she might have been attacked by a rogue grizzly we had roaming around at the time, but—"He bit into the rib.

"But what?" Moose said, sitting on the opposite sofa.

"We found a victim in the Copper River—maybe one of the Midnight Sun victims—about a year or more after she went missing. The girl was wearing a necklace that supposedly belonged to Kennedy. Flynn flew out here, and we went through the evidence. I was a deputy at the time, and I remember her being like a dog with a bone. But we just . . . came up empty. Couldn't even connect it to the Midnight Sun Killer. So we released the necklace to Flynn, and she left." He took another bite of the rib.

"Why's she back?" Moose said.

"I know," Axel said, looking up as the elevator opened. "It's because of me."

A nurse wheeled Sparrow—*er, Flynn*—out of the elevator and down the hall to her room. He headed to follow.

Moose blocked his way. "What do you mean it's because of you?"

He held up his hand. "Because I let the Midnight Sun Killer get away in the river two months ago."

"Please. That is not true."

"You don't know that." Axel stepped past Moose. "And then he struck again. And now Flynn is here, hurt and . . ." He lifted his hands. "Just sayin'."

"That's a pretty big blame leap there, bro."

"I'm a pretty athletic guy. Not hard to make." He turned and headed down the hallway, then followed the nurse into the room.

Flynn was awake, her head wound stitched and bandaged, her arm in a real sling, and her knee on ice and elevated. An IV ran into her vein, probably painkiller along with fluids, and she gave him a wan smile. "Hey. You're here."

The nurse rounded on him. "No, he's not."

He didn't recognize her. "Aw, c'mon. I'm the one who rescued her."

"It's past visiting hours—"

"Please." He gave her his best local-hero smile.

It worked. The woman—he put her in her early forties, short brown hair—shook her head. "Celebrities," she said, but smiled. "Five minutes."

"She can't sleep anyway, right?"

The nurse sighed, stuck her hands into her pockets. "Fine. But no trouble from you." She pointed at him.

"Me?"

She rolled her eyes and left the room.

"Really, she means me?" He looked back at Flynn.

Oh, shoot, she was lovely, even with all the wounds. And sure, maybe she'd left an imprint on his heart over the radio, and only in his wildest dreams would it belong to someone who wasn't fifty and in bearskins. But nope, she had pretty copper hair, burnished by the fading sunlight, and now that he could see them clearly, beautiful green eyes, a petite nose, pert lips, and a crooked smile that now creeped up one side.

"I don't think she means me," she said.

"What—I'm not the one sitting in a hospital bed, having taken a flying leap off a tall mountain." He came over and sat in the bedside chair. "What, did you think you could fly?"

She leaned her head back in her pillow. "I wish I could. I just . . . ran. Down the mountain, at break-my-neck speed." She sighed, her gaze on him.

Silence.

"So, I need to tell you something," she said quietly.

"Shoot." He leaned back, propping his ankle on his knee, folding his arms.

"Now you're being weird."

"Go on."

"Fine—I was going to tell you before you almost drowned the second—or wait, was that the third—time."

"Only the one time there, skipper. What were you going to tell me?"

And he didn't know why, but he held his breath, hoping—

"My name is Flynn."

And there it went, his last reason for not really liking her full out. He sighed and leaned forward. "So, Flynn . . . Sparrow is, what, your call sign?"

"My sister's nickname."

*Oh.*

"She went missing three years ago, and I . . . I'm here to find her." He pressed his hands together, then touched them to his lips. "I know."

Her eyes widened.

"Deke told me."

She leaned back. "Right. Deke. You two know each other."

"Pretty well, yeah. He told me about the case. And how it went nowhere."

"Yeah. Until a few days ago when I saw a newscast about a woman who was shot in the woods near Copper Mountain Ski Resort. I don't know . . . I just . . ." She looked out the window. "I've never been able to get it out of my head that Kennedy's still alive. But my parents want to declare her dead and have a memorial service. And I . . . I can't. Not until I know."

"You think she was killed by the Midnight Sun Killer."

"I think she could have been. She matches the profile of his victims. Young—between the ages of seventeen and thirty. Independent. The kind of woman not afraid to hike alone, drive alone, or even stop to help someone on the side of the road. And she was camping near the Copper River where—"

"All the bodies were found. Or most of them. The girl at the ski resort was found away from the river, up the hill, frozen."

Her eyes widened. "Really?"

"Mm-Mmmhmm. I was there for that."

"Oh."

Maybe, since she'd come clean, he should too. But . . . somehow, looking at the price she'd paid to discover the fate of her sister, he just couldn't tell her that he'd been the guy who had . . . possibly . . . let . . . Okay, yeah, maybe Moose was right—it was a gulf of a blame jump there.

Still. "Not long ago, Air One rescued a woman who we think might have been picked up by the guy."

"What?"

"Yeah. They were in an accident in a river. We rescued the woman. The man . . . got away."

She nodded, swallowed. "He's still out there."

He lifted a shoulder.

"Twenty years is a long time to be killing women." She looked at her hands, closed them. "So many victims. So many untold stories. So many people waiting for answers."

Aw, she had no idea that his family might be some of those people waiting.

She looked up. "I need to find the guy who was shooting at me."

"You . . . *what*?"

"I need to find the shooter. I don't know why he was shooting, but . . . what if he knows something about Kennedy?"

A beat.

"Okay, I know that sounds crazy, but listen, here's my working theory. What if he lives around there, or maybe hunts in that area every year, and he saw me? And . . . you know, I am Kennedy. We're identical twins. And maybe he thought . . . I was a . . ."

"Ghost?"

That seemed to take the wind out of her. She frowned. "Okay, you're right. That's nuts. I just . . . I got nothing here." She leaned away and closed her eyes. "Maybe this is a crazy wild-goose chase. Maybe I should just take my hits, learn my lesson, and go home." She opened her eyes, met his, relaying so much grief that the pain reached in, twisted everything inside him. "Tell my parents to have that service, bury my sister, so to speak, and move on with my life."

She looked away, her eyes filling, and *man,* he couldn't stop himself—

"I'll help you."

She turned back.

"You'll . . . help me?"

And maybe yes, it had to do with a little blame leaping, and maybe a dose of seeing that frustration and grief on her face, but really . . . he didn't want her to leave.

Not yet.

Because somehow Sparrow, the girl on the other end of the radio, still had ahold of him, was still keeping him from drowning.

And he wasn't ready to let go.

"Yeah, I'll help you find Kennedy, or the serial killer. Both. Whatever. Maybe we start with talking to Ashley, the girl who got away."

She smiled, wide and bright and full, her eyes shining. "Thanks, Phoenix."

He'd forgotten he'd told her that nickname.

But maybe he didn't mind.

Maybe, in fact, it was time for him to rise from the ashes.

The nurse poked her head in. "Okay, superstar, it's time to go home."

"I thought—"

"Listen, we'll take care of the mountain climber. I'll be in every hour to annoy her. Go home."

He got up. "What's your name?"

"Aw, Axel, c'mon, don't you remember me?"

He shook his head.

"Right. Okay, it's probably better that way." She smiled at Flynn. "Say goodbye to Mr. Rescue, and I'll be in to check on you soon."

She left and he stood there, looking at Flynn.

And she looked at him.

"Right, then. See you in the morning."

"I'll be here."

Another beat. Then he took a breath, nodded, and fled the room before he did something really stupid.

Then again, stupid seemed to be his MO.

He met Moose in the hallway. Deke was there, waiting.

"She'll give you a statement in the morning," he said. "It's late and she's not going anywhere." At least, he hoped not.

"Seriously?" Deke shook his head. "I ate cold wings and ribs for nothing?"

Axel grinned and followed Moose out to the truck.

And was asleep before Moose pulled out of the parking lot.

# SEVEN

FLYNN COULD ADMIT TO LIKING HAVING A partner. At least for a few days.

She wasn't bringing him back to Minneapolis or anything, but right now, she didn't hate having him around to the address of the survivor of the recent river rescue, Axel at the helm of his Yukon.

Especially since he fed her. She took another bite of the crispy pastry, still warm from the tinfoil he'd wrapped it in. Talked with her mouth full. "What are these called again?"

"Pasties. They're a Minnesota dish—although I think they're originally from England. My mom has relatives in Cornwall."

"It's delicious. What's this—steak and carrots—"

"And potatoes and even rutabagas. Garlic and onions. But you can put almost anything in it. My mom makes them for the Midnight Sun Saloon sometimes. It's her secret recipe."

He'd warmed the pasty in the microwave after they'd arrived at the Air One headquarters in Anchorage late this morning.

She'd needed something to combat all the coffee swimming around in her gut after her two-hour interview with Deke earlier this morning, right before her discharge. She'd given him everything she remembered . . . Probably lost a few things. Frankly, she didn't see her statement as much help—she hadn't gotten even a glimpse of who might have shot her.

Axel had picked her up and driven her right to the airport, where Moose's Cessna waited. She'd never been up in a small plane before and clutched her third cup of coffee while staring out the window at the lush, breathtaking beauty of Alaska.

The sun turned the peaks of the Denali massif white and glistening, a ridgeback that stretched as far as she could see. It shadowed the valley below a deep emerald green, and running through it all was the deep indigo of the Copper River and the Knik Arm.

The majestic view scattered the lingering fatigue of her sleepless night and even distracted her from her throbbing knee, now in a brace. At least the swelling had subsided. And, she had hobbled out of the hospital this morning on her own power.

Although, honestly, as she limped beside Axel, dressed in jeans and a dark blue button-down shirt, smelling freshly showered, his hair burnished under the sunlight, looking every inch the hero who'd practically carried her out of the woods, she wouldn't have minded leaning on—

*Stop.*

The light of day had scattered the shadows of yesterday, given her a clear view of reality.

*Sheesh,* she'd practically *swooned* into the man's arms.

Yeah, it would help to keep the reason she was here—finding Kennedy—in the forefront of her brain.

She had a life in Minnesota, *hello,* and Axel had a full and necessary life here and . . .

And until she returned home, she wouldn't push him out of her life, because, well, again . . . maybe having a temporary partner wouldn't be terrible.

As long as he didn't get in her way.

"Your mom is amazing. My mom makes some killer cookies. Sadly, I can barely boil eggs."

He looked over at her. "I love boiled eggs. I can teach you my trick."

She looked away from his impossibly blue eyes with the feeling his tricks could get her in trouble.

He turned off the highway onto a rough paved road. They passed a sign for the Glacier View mobile home park, then turned onto a dirt road where twenty or so single-wide homes sat maybe ten feet apart along each side of the road. Most had two or even three cars parked in the front grass, some of them newer model SUVs and trucks. Decks jutted out from a few, covered with flowers, manicured front patches of grass. Others overflowed with debris—old furniture, rusty appliances, and weeds growing up around propane tanks.

She supposed it looked like any other neighborhood in any other city. Axel read the numbers on the homes and finally slowed, a boxer running out, barking and growling, pawing at the chain-link fence in front of a green single-wide.

"You can stay in the truck if you'd like." He put the SUV into park.

"No, I'm good." She had finished the pasty and now folded the tinfoil into a square, tucked it inside a napkin, which she used to clean her fingers. "Let's do this."

Okay, she might have more desire than actual ability as she eased herself out of the car. He came around and offered her a hand. She took it, let herself cling to his grip for a moment.

Then she turned and closed the door, sizing up the place.

Curtains hung closed at the window. A blue tarp slung over the top of the home suggested a roof leak.

Axel held out a hand to the dog, shushing it.

The boxer ran to the end of the yard, leaped up, still snarling.

"He's clearly immune to your charm."

"I should have saved him a pasty."

"I'd fight him for it."

He laughed.

It threaded inside her. Oh, how she liked that laugh.

"Ashley knows me, so—"he headed up the stairs—"maybe she'll be willing to talk."

Flynn could have called the Anchorage Police Department and asked for a favor, but this felt simpler. Besides, it was a personal investigation. For now.

He knocked, and in a moment, the inner door opened.

A woman, young twenties, gaunt, wearing a pair of sweatpants and a T-shirt, stood holding a cat. She didn't open the screen door. "Yeah?"

"Hey," Axel said. "Ashley? Remember me, from the river—"

"I remember you." She gave him a wan smile, swallowed. Then glanced at Flynn.

Maybe it helped that Flynn still looked pretty banged up, with a leg brace and head bandage. A fellow victim.

"Can we talk to you about that night—the guy that picked you up?"

Ashley looked again at Axel, drew in a breath. Swallowed. "I don't want to talk about it." She stepped back, reached for the door—

"I'm looking for my sister. I think that might be the guy who took her," Flynn said. Sometimes putting the victim in a place of power helped. "You could help us find him . . ."

Ashley's mouth tightened around the edges, and only then did Flynn see the tiniest bruise on her face. Maybe Axel saw it too because—

"Are you . . . safe?"

She glanced down the hall, back to Axel. "Yeah."

But then she stepped out onto the deck. She wore threadbare slippers, and her hair hung in greasy tangles. The sweet odor of something other than cigarette smoke emanated from her clothing.

*Oh boy.* Flynn tried to assess whether she was high but couldn't tell.

Ashley let the cat go, and it ran to the fence and hissed at the still-growling boxer. She pulled out a vape pen and inhaled. Blew out smoke. "What do you want to know? I already talked to the police."

"I know," Axel said.

She looked at him. "Did you get any money for the show?"

He glanced at Flynn, back. "Um, I think Air One got a production fee, but not me—"

"They made me sign a waiver that night. Didn't pay me anything."

"Sorry."

"They made me look . . ." She shook her head. "He followed me out of the bar, pulled me into the car. I didn't ask for it . . ." Her gaze met Flynn's. "Did you ask for it?"

Flynn drew in a breath. "No. He shot at me."

Ashley's eyebrows rose. "Oh." She took another hit off her vape. "He had a gun too. Shoved me into the back of the van and tied me up. But I got free." She raised her chin. "I caused the accident."

"You saved your life," Flynn said. "That was brave. And smart."

That earned her a half smile.

"Do you remember what he looked like?"

"It was dark. He wasn't big—maybe"——"she glanced at Axel—"shorter than you. But he took me by surprise. And he smelled bad, like he'd been living out of his car. Or an old motel. Anyway, I didn't get a good look at him. Dark hair, maybe. Or not. Sorry."

"You said he followed you out of a bar? What bar?"

"The Tenderfoot. Off Highway 3. But now that I think about it, maybe he wasn't in the bar,, because he got out of his van as I

walked by. Maybe he was just waiting for someone to come out..."
Her hand shook a little, and she inhaled again on the vape.

Flynn took a step toward her, paused, then touched her arm.
"You're safe now. He's not here. You lived."

Ashley looked up at her, nodded.

"You want to talk to us about that bruise?"

Ashley's mouth pinched and she shook her head. "I need to get back inside."

Flynn glanced at Axel. He had taken a deep breath, glanced into the house, what looked like worry on his face.

She slid her hand into his, tightened her grip, but spoke to Ashley. "Listen. You ever need help of any kind, you call Air One Rescue, okay?"

Ashley wrapped an arm around herself, swallowed. Nodded.

Then she turned and went into the house. Shut the door.

Axel just stood there. "I really want to go in there."

"I know. You can't. C'mon."

He stayed a moment longer, however, then surrendered to the tug on his hand and followed her down the stairs.

The cat jumped onto a nearby lawn chair and hissed at him.

He held the car door open for Flynn as she climbed in. "That was unhelpful."

"Actually, it was super helpful."

He gave her a look, then closed the door and came around to the driver's side. Got in. "How so?"

She glanced over to the mobile home and saw the curtain fall as they pulled away.

A lump formed in her chest.

"You all right?"

She sighed. "Yeah. She just reminded me a little of ... well, Kennedy."

"Your sister? How? I thought she was your twin—"

"She is. But . . ." She looked at him. "I mentioned that I found a dead body near my alleyway as a kid, right?"

"Yeah. It led you into being a cop."

"It led my sister into darkness. She kept having nightmares. She started drinking and then got into drugs and . . . I spent a lot of time in high school and even college tracking her down in the middle of the night, holding back her hair as she detoxed in my dorm room. We finally got her into a drug rehab place, and she turned it around. Mostly."

They'd pulled out onto the road. "Mostly?"

"She came out to Alaska because she was running from an old drug dealer named Slade. She'd been clean for a few years, and we thought he was out of her life. But he tracked her down at this convenience store where she was working and . . . anyway, she owed him money. He followed her a couple times, and it was my bright idea to leave town. We actually came out here in March, went skiing at the Copper Mountain resort, and she fell in love with Alaska and stayed. I thought . . . well, I thought it was the start of a new life for her." She looked out the window at the deep blue of the Knik Arm as they drove back toward Anchorage. "She got the job working for Peyton a month later, and by June she went missing. I never dreamed . . ."

And just like that, his hand covered hers. Squeezed. "It's not your fault. Stop jumping."

She glanced at him. "Jumping?"

"It's a thing my brother said. Jumping to blame yourself."

"It's not a big jump."

"Pretty big there, Sparrow. You couldn't know that she'd go missing."

She didn't hate that he called her Sparrow.

"Did you ever consider, however, that this drug dealer followed her to Anchorage?"

She shook her head. Almost didn't tell him why but, "Slade

showed up on a slab in the morgue a couple weeks after I got back from Alaska. Months before she went missing."

"Oh."

"I didn't . . . I didn't kill him, in case you're wondering."

He looked at her, eyes wide. "I wasn't. Wow."

"It's just that, you know . . . I shot you."

"At me. I hope."

"Yes. I wouldn't have missed if I'd wanted to hit you."

"That's ever so comforting." He let go of her hand but gave her a grin. Then he signaled and turned at a light and pulled up at a diner.

"You're hungry?"

"I'm always hungry. But my brother Moose hangs out here—or did—and the shakes are amazing."

She opened the door, and he was right there with a hand out to help.

They walked into the Skyport Diner. Something out of the fifties, maybe, with a long counter bar with round stationary stools. A few patrons sat at red vinyl booths along the window wall. An order wheel held paper orders, and a bell dinged with an "order up!" from the cook in the back kitchen.

The place smelled deliciously of fried food, and pies spun slowly in a refrigerated case behind the counter.

Axel slid into a booth, and a woman came over. Long dark hair, a sort of exotic beauty, she wore a blue uniform and plunked down a couple waters.

"Hey, Tillie," Axel said. "How about some fries, chicken, and a shake."

"Not until you tell me where Moose has been for the past month." She smiled at Flynn. "He's a regular who vanished on me."

Axel lifted a shoulder. "He hasn't been around?"

Tillie sighed. "He might have asked me out."

Clearly Axel hadn't known, because his eyes widened. "And—"

"I can't date a customer . . ."

"Please—"

"Okay . . . I have my reasons. But they have nothing to do with Moose. Please tell him to come back. We're overflowing with pie and . . . I miss him."

Sweet. "If Axel doesn't, I will," said Flynn.

"Fries are on me," said Tillie, and winked. "What flavor shakes?"

"Surprise us," Axel said.

"Living on the wild side?" Tillie said.

"I need some adventure in my life."

"Oh yeah. You lack adventure." Tillie laughed and headed toward another table.

He laughed too, and for a moment, Flynn simply . . . couldn't. How did this happen that she was sitting across from this painfully handsome, sweet man who'd not only saved her life, maybe, but had shouldered her desperate investigation?

More, she liked it, this temporary partnership.

Yeah, Burke might not recognize her. She barely recognized herself.

And oddly, something Axel had said days ago over the radio filtered into her head. *"Maybe he was just the holiday-romance guy and not the real guy . . ."*

Jack, the handsome rogue who made Rose feel alive. Yeah, she could embrace that.

Axel put down his water. "Okay, so how was our conversation with Ashley helpful, except to make me want to go back there and figure out that haunted look in her eyes?"

"And on her face."

"That too." He folded his arms. "I can't figure it out—why people let themselves be treated that way."

"Because they don't believe they deserve better. A happy ending. A life of joy."

He looked at her then, something enigmatic in his eyes. "Yeah. So . . . what did you learn?"

"The Midnight Sun Killer isn't the kind of guy who has to kidnap women to get them into his car. From all accounts, he lures them to him. I recently worked on a case where the guy picked up women from a bar, luring them home to—"

"I don't need to know."

"Right. Well, there's a type. Not all killers are creepers who live in the basement and come out at night. There are plenty who live among society, have families, work in normal jobs, and might even be religious. We call them charmers. Like Gacy, the Killer Clown."

"Okay, that's the definition of creepy."

"For sure. And then there's Ted Bundy? He killed over thirty women by pretending to have a broken arm and need help. Or the Casanova Killer . . ."

He shook his head. "So you think this guy isn't the same as the Midnight Sun Killer."

"I don't know. It also doesn't fit the timing of the deaths. Most of the victims were killed in late June, early July. The more I look at it, I think the MSK could be a tourist. That's why he's never been caught. He's only here for hunting season."

"Except hunting season in Alaska starts in the fall."

"Right. But . . . people still carry guns."

"In the bush, yeah. For protection."

"Could be a hiker. I think we need to be looking at people who are seasonal, every year, in the area around Copper Mountain."

"That's a lot of people. There's an entire RV park of seasonal regulars."

"He's probably single. Or at least here, he's single. Maybe he leaves family behind to get it out of his system in Alaska. Something about the frontier stirs a feral need in him."

Axel's mouth tightened.

"I don't see him committing the same murders where he's from. Unless he gets sloppy, and desperate."

"Wow," he said, shaking his head.

"What?"

"You are a river-monster hunter."

Her mouth opened.

"Reaching into the darkness, pulling out the scary fish."

She gave a small laugh. "I guess."

Tillie returned with a plate of fries and another of fried chicken. "Shakes on the way."

"I might have lost my appetite," Axel said after she left. He took a fry. "Or not." He reached for the ketchup. "Ever thought about doing something different?"

She took a fry. Salty. Crispy. *Yum.* "Like what—move to Alaska, live in the bush, and track wolves? Been there, done that."

He lifted a shoulder. "Or just not get shot at?" He blobbed ketchup onto his plate.

Sweet. "Sorry to drag you into this. I know it's gruesome."

He looked up at her then. Put down the ketchup. Then he sat back and sighed. "What I haven't told you, Flynn, is that ... I really don't have a choice."

She stilled. "What?"

"I know more about the Midnight Sun Killer than I've told you."

He hadn't meant to trek into the past, to the worst day of his life, but it'd just sort of spilled out, and now Axel's words lay on the table between them.

"What do you mean you know more about the Midnight Sun Killer?" She'd put down the piece of chicken she'd reached for.

Stared at him, her expression unreadable. *Angry? Curious? Worried?*

"My fifteen-year-old cousin, Aven, was one of the early victims of the Midnight Sun Killer."

He blew out a breath, watching how the words landed. She blinked, then nodded and leaned back. "I see."

"And it was my fault."

She gave him a dubious look.

"Okay, before you say anything, just . . . listen." He pushed his plate away. Sighed. Looked out the window. The sun hung over the backside of the day, still high but casting rays across the mountains, the shadows almost blue.

A gorgeous Alaskan day. The kind of day where people died.

"We were out camping, just the kids—Moose and me and Aven and some of my cousins from Minnesota who were visiting, along with the Bowie brothers and Nash Remington and the Kingston triplets—a whole bunch of us. My parents knew where we were— we'd camped on the river for years. And actually, they were camping with their friends—the Bowies and my aunt and uncle and a few others—just down the road so . . . Anyway, we were below the lower falls, toward Jubilee Lake. Usually a really safe area."

She hadn't moved, just listening. The sun swept into the window, turning her hair that copper red, and he suddenly wanted to ditch the story, grab her, and drive.

"Go on."

"Right. So we were all pretty accomplished kayakers and swimmers, and we'd taken the run down the river, over the falls—the river wasn't high or anything. Moose and a few of the others decided to haul in, set up camp, make dinner. But not me. And not Aven. She was . . . well, maybe a little crazier than I was. She had this wild side—not rebellious, just . . . she liked to do all the things—cliff jump and kayak and ride dirt bikes and . . . we were close." He lifted a shoulder. "She was like a sister, maybe. Anyway, we decided to take another run, and I went first over the falls, then waited for her at the edge of the churn pool." He ran a hand over his mouth. "She hit it all wrong. I don't know why or how, but she came over backwards, hit the pool already coming out of her kayak, and by the time the boat surfaced, she was out of the seat."

He swallowed, his voice turning hoarse. "I spotted her in the churn and dove out of the boat for her—our fingertips met, but then she went under."

He looked away, blowing out a breath. "She never surfaced." He met her eyes again. She wore a haunted look in her expression. He did too, probably.

"I was screaming for help, and Dodge and Moose showed up, and by that time I was in real trouble. I'd hit my shoulder on one of the rocks searching for her and then went down again and managed to get a foot jammed. I would have drowned if Moose hadn't dragged me out. As it was, they had to carry me out. I broke my tibia in two places, dislocated my shoulder, and sort of lost it in the hospital when I found out the sheriff's office couldn't recover her."

She nodded. Didn't speak. But her eyes glistened.

He looked away. "But that wasn't the worst of it." He met her eyes. "A month later, a hunter found her body. It was washed up onshore, down the river. But the thing was, she had been shot."

"With a .270 Winchester."

"Yeah. Of course, I didn't know that detail until years later—I just knew that she'd survived going over the falls, and if I'd kept looking . . ."

"Axel."

He held up a hand. "No. See, that's not a huge blame jump, is it?"

Her mouth made a thin line. "My mentor, Eve, says that you can't blame yourself for the actions of others. You tried. And yeah, you couldn't find her. But her getting murdered is not your fault. That is the fault of the killer. She was in the wrong place at the wrong time."

He shrugged.

"But you still feel like you have a chain around your neck, pulling you down."

"Like I'm drowning and can never get enough air." And he'd never told anyone that before. "How did you—"

"Me too. Regret. The sense of frustration. The helplessness. Right?"

He nodded. "Every time I rescue someone, it feels like I can breathe. Only for a moment. It doesn't last, but . . . it helps."

"Yeah. I get that too. My chief thinks I'm obsessed. I'm not. I'm just trying to . . . well, as you put it, stay above water."

She leaned forward. Reached out and touched his hand. "So maybe we just need to figure out how to both get on the door."

It took a moment. *Oh, right.* Rose and Jack. He turned, wove her fingers between his. Met her eyes.

What was happening here? He'd known her for all of twenty-four hours, —maybe forty-eight if he included the radio chat. And yet . . .

And yet she'd found her way past all his barriers as if they weren't even there. As if she'd always belonged inside his heart.

"I hope you like salted caramel. This is one of my favorites."

He let go of Flynn's hand. Tillie set a creamy milkshake in front of him, another in front of Flynn.

"I put toffee pieces on the top. It's amazing."

Flynn reached for the cherry on top of the whipped cream. "It looks amazing."

He unsheathed his straw. "Thanks, Tillie."

"Okay, then. Eat your fries; they're getting cold." She tucked the tray under her arm and headed away.

"She's a little bossy," Flynn said.

"I think that's why Moose likes her. He doesn't have to be in charge for once."

She stuck her straw in, took a sip. He did the same.

"Delicious," she said.

He reached for a fry, suddenly ravenous. Maybe they'd get a box for the chicken.

"Thanks for telling me the story, Axel."

He dipped a fry into the whipped cream.

"What you don't know is that I have an entire wall of information on the Midnight Sun Killer and his history in my extra bedroom."

He stared at her. "What?"

"Yeah. And I know all about your cousin Aven's case."

"What?"

"I mean, I didn't know about the first part, but I know that she was found near the Bowie camp road. What you don't know is that she'd been killed a month earlier, even before the first victim, although the first one—Jennifer Greene—was found first. Which makes Aven our first victim, although she's listed as the second."

She stirred her shake. "The Bowie camp road follows the river for quite a ways before the river turns south into Remington land, where she was found."

"It's a huge swath of land," he said. "Lots of unknown hunting happening around there. Especially after the Bowie parents were killed."

"Killed? How?"

"Mac Bowie was a state senator as well as a private pilot, and he was coming back from Juneau when his small plane crashed. He and his wife were killed, along with another couple. Donors, I think. Anyway, the oldest son, Jericho, was already in his twenties, as was Sully, and Hudson was already over eighteen, so they inherited the estate, and Hudson took over the resort as well as custody of his little brother, Malachi. They grew the family's ventures—Sully works as a trail guide."

"And Jericho?"

"He hasn't been around for a while. He was in the military when his folks died, but that's all I know."

"Was he around when your cousin went missing?"

"No. He was gone by then."

She helped him with the fries.

"What about the Remingtons?"

"Ox? He and his wife are separated, although not at the time. I remember them camping with my parents that weekend—they're still pretty close with Ox. I think his wife lives in Montana along with his daughter and oldest son. It's just Nash and Jude running the gold mine. I don't think Ox hunts, but I don't know."

"Right. Okay." She took another sip of shake. "We could really use a fresh lead."

"Sorry that Ashley didn't pan out."

"I'm not."

He frowned.

"You were worried that you let this guy get away." She leaned forward. "You didn't. Like I said—I don't think it's him. Our guy finds his victims around the Copper River area for some reason. I'd like to know that reason."

She leaned back. "The killing at the ski resort was an anomaly. He doesn't kill in winter—maybe because he's not usually here. We need a list of guests at the resort . . . See if it lines up with anyone who regularly visits the area in the summer."

"How would we know that?"

"Copper Mountain is a small town. Maybe Deke or Hank has a list of regulars. Hank has to issue fishing permits, right?"

"And hiking permits." He signaled Tillie and she came over. "Can we get a box for the chicken?"

She took the plate. "I'll box it up."

He turned back to Flynn. "I'll bet Hank has a database of all the regulars. We can ask him to run it and see if any permits match the dates the women went missing."

"I like how you think. I might just give you a junior investigator's badge."

He laughed as Tillie came back with their chicken. She'd written "To Moose" with a giant red heart and her name scrawled on the top. Axel looked at her.

"I added a few of his favorite pieces in there." She shrugged. Then she tore off the bill and put it on the table. "Stay safe."

He picked it up and slid out to pay. When he returned, Flynn had finished her shake, gobbled down the rest of the fries. "I was hungrier than I thought."

"I like a woman who eats."

His cell phone buzzed and he pulled it out. "Moose needs us back at the Tooth."

"The what?"

"Air One HQ. We call it the Tooth. Like, you know, the Moose's Tooth."

She lifted a shoulder. "Is that something?"

"It's a cliff around here. It . . . never mind." He scooped up the warm container and followed Flynn out to the parking lot. Handed her the box as he got in.

The smell of hot chicken filled the Yukon as they drove the mile over to Merrill Field and the Air One office, located in a building at the edge of the tarmac.

"This is quite the office," Flynn said as she stepped inside. "That's a huge map." She pointed to the topographical map on the wall.

"And it's only the middle of Alaska, where we operate. Doesn't even include anything north of Fairbanks or the Juneau area."

"Seems like a pretty big area for one team."

"Oh no. We're the second team. The Coast Guard, the state patrol, and the military have massive operations. But every year, tourists and hikers find themselves in over their heads, and sometimes the wait for help can be hours, or days." He set the container on the stone island. "We're privately funded, out of an endowment from a man who helped Moose get started. But we do fundraising every year—hence the TV show. Moose needed to fill the coffers, so he hired us all on as guinea pigs."

"Celebrity guinea pigs," Moose said, coming down the hallway. He wore a red jumpsuit, carried a file folder wrapped with a rubber band, and a held a radio. "I think I saw T-shirts with Axel's face on them."

"They'll make a killing," Flynn said.

Axel glanced at her, a little heat in his face. She winked.

*Oh wow.* Yeah, he was in way over his head here.

Moose raised an eyebrow but nodded and set the folder down on the table. "We got a call from Hank. They need help. There's been a run of climbers trying for the summit, trying to outrun an oncoming storm. At the same time, Dodge and other local pilots are busy hauling people off the mountain. They're short on resources. Apparently, Sully called in and needs help with a hiker who fell. Said it's not urgent, but they can't get to him, so they need the chopper. I need to head back to Copper Mountain, and I was hoping you'd come with me, Axel. We'll leave Boo and Shep here to assist locally, if they need it."

"Yeah, sure. Flynn? Ready to head back to Copper Mountain?"

"Axel, we're heading right to the rescue site. I don't think—"

"She needs a ride back to Copper Mountain."

Moose considered Flynn for a moment. Glanced at her leg.

"I promise not to get in the way."

Oh, she was already way in the way. But Axel let out his held breath when Moose nodded.

Two hours later, however, his only thought was on the fourteen-year-old kid who'd gone on a walkabout from the guys' fishing trip, slipped, and found himself thirty feet down, on the edge of a cliff, unable to climb up, with a hundred-yard drop to the river shore below.

Axel had donned a harness while London, who'd ridden as copilot, clipped on the rescue harness. Flynn wore a helmet, clearly listening to the conversation as London communicated with Moose, positioning the chopper above the kid, who appeared panicked and a little bloodied, but standing as he gripped the rock some thirty feet below.

"Rescue out the door," said London as Axel maneuvered out of the chopper.

From inside, where she sat against the wall, Flynn gave him a thumbs-up.

"Descending," London said and lowered him down on the hoist. Not a windy day so he caught the rock easily, waved to London to stop, and braced himself in front of the kid.

"Hey! My name is Axel. I'm with the rescue team. What's your name?"

"Laramie."

"Nice to meet you, Laramie. How's the view?"

The kid smiled a little. "Big."

"Yep. Okay, let's get you off this rock." Axel put the sling over Laramie's shoulders, then under his arms, and stretched it out so it also encompassed his backside. "I got you, so just sit back and hold on to me." He patted his harness and the kid grabbed the straps. He motioned to London and pushed away from the rock.

Laramie grunted and Axel put his arm around him, mostly to protect him from the rotor wash, but it never felt great to dangle in midair. At least, not the first time.

Now, Axel drank it in, despite the tremor that scurried through him every time he stepped away from terra firma. He put his hand over Laramie's head as they came to the chopper bed. London raised them up and pulled them in and onto a stretcher.

Axel climbed right in over the kid, then reached up to hook them into the safety line before London unhooked them from the winch and closed the door.

"You okay?" Axel asked, his voice raised as he climbed away and sat on the deck.

Laramie lay there, looking at the ceiling, breathing out.

Axel patted his chest. Leaned over to talk to him. "You'll be fine. It's just the adrenaline drop."

He took a deep breath. Looked at Flynn. She was grinning.

"Breathing?" she said into the mouthpiece.

Yes. A full breath.

She wore something bright and sweet in her eyes.

Okay, yeah, he didn't hate that she was here to see that.

They touched down on the riverbed, Moose finding a clear area. Sully, Bowie, and a number of other men stayed back until the rotors stopped spinning.

Then London opened the door.

Laramie's father, a muscled guy, lean and built, was the first in, grabbing up his son. He looked strangely familiar, but Axel couldn't place him. Maybe he'd seen him in town.

Axel glanced over at Moose, who was grinning, watching the father and son embrace. He'd endure some crazy celebrity to be able to have this moment.

London got out as Axel worked off his helmet and followed.

Sully came up. "Love watching you guys in action." He met Axel's hand. Then he looked past Axel and jerked.

Flynn had gotten out of the chopper, also taken off her helmet, shaking down her copper hair, then looking up at him and grinning.

Until, that is, Sully said, "Kennedy? What the heck? What are you doing here?"

Then he stepped up to her, put his hand around her neck, and kissed her.

# EIGHT

FLYNN DIDN'T MIND A GOOD KISS FROM A
handsome guy, but *hello*—wrong guy, wrong girl. And sure,
she felt the desperation behind it, but—"Hey!" She slammed
her hand into his chest, pushed hard.

She'd count him as handsome, with long golden-brown hair, a
bit of scruff on his tanned face, pale blue eyes, and built like any
of the Alaskan men that suddenly crowded her life.

But yeah, this might be too crowded. "What do you think you're
doing?"

Even as she stared at him, however—at the confusion on his
face, the hurt that swept into his eyes, the way he startled at Axel,
who'd taken a step toward her—it clicked.

*Kennedy.*

He knew her sister.

She just blinked at him, breathing hard, and thankfully Axel
came to the rescue.

"Sully! What are you *doing*? This is Flynn Turnquist." He now
had himself planted in front of her, a wall of red, literally, and well,
it was sort of . . . sweet.

Even if unnecessary. She could usually—minus the knee brace—take care of herself.

"No, it's not. That's Kennedy. Wait. What?" Sully took another breath, wrapped both hands behind his neck, turned as if trying to walk off whatever stirred inside him.

"This is Flynn, Kennedy's sister," Axel said. "But more important, how do you know Kennedy?"

Sully rounded, clearly undone. Stared at Flynn. Shook his head. "She . . . she looks exactly like Kennedy. Except for the—"He pointed at his head, the location of the wound on her forehead. "Although, yeah, even that. That's—you're definitely Kennedy. What's going on, babe?"

He took a step toward her.

Axel held up his hand. "We're not prankin' you here, Sul. Seriously. This is Kennedy's twin sister. Identical twin sister."

Sully stopped. Swallowed. "She did mention a sister." He blew out a breath. "But she didn't say twin."

"Sorry," Flynn said, and added a softness to her voice. Clearly this man was distraught.

And a witness. Possibly the last person to see her sister alive. Clearly very much alive because something, *ahem*, had gone down between Mr. Outdoors and Kennedy, the free spirit.

They were probably perfect for each other.

"Listen." She stepped, or rather limped, past Axel. "Can we talk?"

Because at the moment, they had the arrested attention of the entire party, including Moose and London as well as Laramie and his dad, plus a handful of other fishermen.

"In private?"

Sully nodded, but she turned to Axel. "Except for you."

"I wasn't leaving even if you asked nicely." He glanced at Moose. "Give us a few minutes."

"I want to check out Laramie anyway," London said and went back to the chopper to retrieve a med kit.

Flynn still couldn't believe what she'd witnessed up there. Axel, dangling from a line no bigger than her pinkie finger, a hook on a line. And he'd brought up a scared kid like he might be Superman.

Okay, that felt dramatic, but still, seeing him at work, she got it. A full breath.

Sort of like how she'd felt when she put the 1039 Killer and so many others under arrest.

A small piece of justice won, another light against the darkness.

And for him, maybe another soul brought back from the brink.

She slid her hand into Axel's, feigning a need for help as they walked away from the group to the other side of the chopper, then down the riverbank.

Sully stopped, his gaze falling, then bouncing off their hooked hands.

She let Axel go and found her way to a boulder. "Did I hurt you?"

Sully frowned. "No. Uh . . . did I hurt you?"

She smiled. "No. I can see why my sister liked you."

He smiled.

Axel didn't. He looked at her with wide eyes. "Seriously?"

"But Kennedy isn't me, okay? Are we clear?"

Sully nodded. Glanced at Axel. "Sorry, man."

Axel held up a hand, shook his head. "Listen . . . uh . . ."

She didn't need any crazy, mispurposed showdown here. "Sully. How do you know my sister?"

He drew in a breath. "Okay, for the record, I don't know where she is."

"That was pretty clear," Axel growled.

"Right. Okay, so . . . uh, she showed up at the Bowie cabin about . . . three years ago, I guess. In May, right after fishing season started. She was wounded . . . shot, actually, across the shoulder.

I think she must have gotten lost—I don't know where she came from. But she wouldn't let me take her into Copper Mountain. She said someone was stalking her and had found her. She was really scared, and—"

He looked at Axel. "Believe me, I wanted to take her in, but I didn't want to leave her either. She was . . . she had a mind of her own, and her wound wasn't deep. Only needed some stitches. I did it myself."

"Oh, that makes us all feel better," Axel said.

"Hey. I'm really good with knots, thank you."

"Did she say who was stalking her?" Flynn asked. *Down, Axel.*

"No."

"But it's the same person who shot her?"

"Maybe. Probably. She didn't say."

"What happened then?" Flynn folded her arms, gave him a hard look.

Sully looked away, down to the ground, back to her, and met her eyes. "She stayed."

Silence.

"She *stayed*?" Axel said.

*Thank you.* She actually appreciated his tone this time.

"Listen. We . . . the fishing camp has many rooms. And she was a guest of the Bowie Outpost. It was . . . Okay, so yes, we might have had a spark. But . . . it wasn't . . . Okay, listen. She wanted to stay. And—"He swallowed, and to Flynn's eye, it looked like his eyes glistened. "Fine. I asked her to marry me."

*Oh.*

"That's why you stayed at the lodge that winter," Axel said quietly. "I remember Hudson and Mal talking about it. You didn't come in for an entire year."

"They brought supplies out to me."

"So, let me get this straight," Flynn said. "While I was home, crushed at the disappearance of my sister, she was holed up with you? Playing house?"

"I didn't know she was officially missing. She said she came out to Alaska on purpose, and yeah, she mentioned family, but people come out here all the time to leave their past behind. It didn't occur to me to ask Deke if she was on the missing persons list."

Flynn folded her arms. Looked away.

"We did a lot of fishing. And hunting, and I taught her how to make beef jerky and dried fish, and we had a garden, and . . . we played a lot of Scrabble. And Aggravation on my grandfather's old wooden marble board."

He crossed his arms over his chest. "I loved Kennedy. Still do."

"What happened, Sully?" Axel said, glancing over at Flynn.

She saw it but turned her gaze back to Sully, trying to decide if he was the kind of guy to keep a woman captive for a month, or even a year.

Probably not.

And by the kiss, yeah, he'd loved her.

"I don't know. It was fishing season again, and I started getting groups in. I'd have to go to Copper Mountain to get them, and she'd stay behind and make dinner or, you know, work on her jewelry, and then one day, I showed up with a crew and . . . she wasn't there. There was food on the stove, and her jewelry stuff was on the table in her room, and most of her stuff was there too . . . but she wasn't. She just . . . vanished. And never returned."

He ran a hand across his cheek. Shook his head, looked out at the river. "I looked for her. Everywhere. Even sent Uncle Wilson and Hud and Mal out—it was a big Bowie family trip. But nothing. We searched the river, and all the trails . . ."

"And you never thought to tell the sheriff?"

"Uncle Wilson went back into town with my statement . . . I never heard anything from Deke about it. And in the back of my mind, I thought . . . well, maybe she wanted to stay lost, you know? Like, if I tried to find her, maybe it would only cause trouble."

His mouth tightened. "I . . . well, the fact is, I thought maybe she was angry with me about something. She'd been acting restless." He shook his head and looked back at Flynn. "But yeah. It haunts me. I can't go out into the woods without the fear that I'll find her body. Or return without the hope that she'll just . . . be there at the lodge."

She knew exactly how that felt.

Behind him, the wind ripped through the evergreens, the river rushing, the sun glistening on it, shadows casting from the massive cliff behind them.

"What about the missing girl who had her necklace?"

Sully shook his head. "I don't know anything about—wait, are you talking about the Midnight Sun victim? You think maybe she was killed by the Midnight Sun Killer?" His eyes widened.

"It's a theory."

Sully stared at the river, a hand to his mouth. "I should have—"

"Yes, you should have." She met his gaze, accusations roiling inside her. But his story sounded exactly like Kennedy—selfishly independent. And she'd done the same thing to Sully that she'd done to Flynn.

"If Kennedy is still alive, she clearly doesn't want to be found," Flynn said quietly.

He swallowed. "I'd like to hope that she is, but . . ."

"But if she loved you, she would have come back to you?"

"That makes me sound like a Hallmark movie."

"You sound like a guy who loved my sister." She gave him a tight smile, reaching inside for compassion.

He answered with the same.

"Okay," she said finally. "Can I get her stuff? I'd like to look at it, see if I can find anything."

"Absolutely. I'll get it and bring it into Copper Mountain when the fishing trip is over tomorrow."

"Okay." She stood up. "For the record, I think that Kennedy and you would have been perfect for each other. I'm sorry I'm not her."

"I'm not," Axel growled, low and under his breath.

She looked at him, but he just shook his head and held out his hand.

Sully followed them back to the chopper.

London had bandaged up a cut on Laramie's hand and packed up the medical kit. "Laramie and his dad are going to finish the trip with Sully," she said. "So I think we're done here." She stowed her med kit and climbed into the copilot seat.

Flynn climbed into the chopper, strapped in, and pulled on her helmet.

Axel closed the door and settled beside her, also buckling in. "You sorted?"

She nodded but folded her arms around herself as Moose started up the rotors and finally took off.

She couldn't speak over the sound of the rotor wash as they headed toward Copper Mountain, so she let herself sink into her thoughts.

If Kennedy was in love with Sully—and if she knew her sister like she knew herself, Kennedy had fallen hard and fast for the handsome fishing guide—nothing would keep her from returning to him.

Except if she thought she—or he—wasn't safe. If she thought by staying away she'd keep them out of trouble.

And then there was the trouble, the stalker.

Kennedy couldn't know that Slade was dead. But surely she didn't think he'd followed her out into the wilds of Alaska?

No, she was afraid of someone else.

They touched down on the tarmac at the Copper Mountain airport, and Axel helped her out, then London and he unloaded the gear into a storage unit in the offices while Moose tied down the chopper.

Moose and London headed inside the office, maybe to make transportation arrangements.

Axel held out his hand. "C'mon. I'll introduce you to the pasty maker."

"What I really need is clean clothes. I can't keep wearing what you brought me to the hospital in. And you dumped all my clothes out at the cabin, thank you." Her eyes widened. "And the journal."

"What journal?" He held open the gate to the parking lot.

"It's a journal Kennedy kept at the cabin. It was in my pack. I completely forgot about it—can we go back?"

He stopped, looked at her. "To the cache cabin? Seriously?"

"I . . ." She sighed. "Okay. I just . . . I just thought there might be something in the journal about who she might have been afraid of."

He turned to her, put his hands on her forearms. "I'll call Hank and see if he can get ahold of Peyton and . . . I'll do my best."

And suddenly her eyes started to fill. Maybe the rush of adrenaline from the rescue or the surprise of being kissed or even the fact that her sister had been found and loved . . . but, aw, she started to cry.

"What . . . Hey—"

He pulled her against himself, his strong arms around her, and simply stayed right there in the parking lot, holding her while she quietly fell apart.

"It's okay. I'll get the journal—"

"No, it's not the journal. It's . . ." She leaned back. "I don't know. It's being here, so close and yet so far, and then . . . you. You just keep . . ."

"What?"

"Being nice! And getting me out of trouble and . . . and . . ." She stared at him, not even sure—

He cupped his hands under her face, met her eyes. And then he slowly bent down and kissed her.

Oh, it was sweet, his touch, like he didn't want to break her or hurt her, his lips soft, perfect—

But she wanted—something else. More of him. All of him, maybe, and she reached up with her good hand and grabbed his shirt.

Lifted herself on her toes and kissed him back. Hard. All in. Practically inhaling the man because this, right here, was air. Breath.

It took him a second, but he caught up fast, his arms going around her, his mouth opening to deepen the kiss, to add urgency and desire and probably everything he'd been thinking—she hoped he'd been thinking—since that moment when he'd reached out for help.

She just hadn't realized that she'd been reaching out too.

His arms tightened around her, holding her as she softened her mouth, slowed them down a little. He still tasted a little of salted caramel, and in his arms she felt at once rescued and needed.

The wind picked up the fragrance of Alaska, the piney forest, the expansive breath of the mountains, the wildness of an untamed frontier and, yeah, maybe . . .

Maybe she did have an answer to his question.

*"Ever thought about doing something different?"*

Yes, yes, right now, she did.

"Okay, listen, I can leave you here and come back later or . . ."

Axel raised his head, looked toward the voice.

Moose stood in the parking lot, grinning.

"Thoughts on that?" He looked down at Flynn.

"I think I need a pasty."

He laughed.

"But for the record, you're a better kisser than Sully."

He held out his fist as he took her hand.

She bumped it.

He didn't have to be in the ocean to know that he was in over his head.

Axel lay on his wretchedly small single bed, staring at the slanted ceiling of his bedroom, the sunlight leaking between the gaps in the room-darkening shades because of course the sun just couldn't leave him alone, even at midnight.

It kept him awake, his mind replaying the kiss.

The. Kiss.

How-*dy*. He couldn't remember being kissed like that—or kissing someone else quite so . . . well, like he meant it, all the way down to his soul, if that were possible. Somehow, over the past three days, Flynn had awakened something inside him that he'd thought long dead.

He felt like a freaking hero.

And the way she looked at him didn't help. First in the chopper, then at the airport—and what was a guy to do when she dissolved into tears? Having her in his arms, holding her—

He didn't even have to think about it when he kissed her, the urge just crashing over him, drawn in by those beautiful green eyes, her parted lips.

And okay, the memory of Sully kissing her first—yeah, even now, as he stared at the ceiling, he drew in a breath. Sat up.

He'd been one step from pulling the guy off her.

*Okay, breathe.* He had felt for Sully when he'd realized the truth. And Sully's story about Kennedy . . . yeah, that made sense. Even the part about why he hadn't talked to Deke.

Flynn had been quiet at dinner. Maybe too quiet, although she'd gotten on with his parents all right, helping his dad with the dishes while Axel and Moose secured the trash from the animals and put away the vehicles and Moose checked in with the Air One base in Anchorage.

No callouts, for now.

London had stayed in town, bunking at a local Airbnb she frequented.

*"But for the record, you're a better kisser than Sully."*

Great. Now he was back to thinking about Flynn, and the taste of her, the way she fit into his arms, the beautiful intensity of how she'd kissed him. She was . . . well, maybe a whirlwind, or an avalanche, or a force of nature.

Or maybe just a hand in the storm, something he could hang on to. But he'd never felt so much like someone had given him back pieces of himself.

He might even be falling in love with her.

*Might be?*

His stomach growled.

*Fine.* He got up, opened the door and, dressed in just a pair of pajama bottoms, headed downstairs.

Paused on the bottom steps at the sight of Flynn sitting on the sofa watching television, the volume on subtitles, remote in her hand.

*Oh no.*

He saw himself onscreen pretending to be a rescue dummy, Oaken Fox dangling from a fake helicopter in the Shed, their training facility—one of the early episodes of *The Sizeup,* the rescue reality show.

Even as he watched, he came alive on the rock, startling Oaken. Poor guy nearly fell, but Axel caught him. Pulled him in.

"Yeah, that was a stupid move." He walked into the room, and she looked up, paused the show. She wore a pair of leggings that she'd picked up in town on the way home. Leggings and T-shirts and underclothes and a thermal shirt and even socks.

She'd forgotten a sweatshirt, however, and he'd given her one of his old Copper Mountain sweatshirts. Which hung on her, of course.

Now she wore a blanket over her shoulders and stood up. "Sorry. I just...I can't sleep. It's too light out. And...your dad mentioned that he's taped all the shows so far. I thought I'd get caught up." She waggled her eyebrows. "You're quite the dish, Axel."

"Well, keep watching. You'll see how dishy I am." He took the remote. "Or—"He tossed it onto the sofa and reached for her, pulling her close.

Lowering his face.

She spun away, leaving him holding the blanket. Backing up.

He eyed her. "What's...happening...uh..." Because her eyes had widened, and suddenly she turned—

And walked out the door.

*What. The—*

He took off after her—probably not his smartest move, but something...

Something wasn't right, because she'd taken the deck steps down to the yard and was limping out to the river, gesturing into the air as if talking to herself.

*Ho-kay.*

He didn't even realize he still held the blanket until halfway across the yard. Then he slung it over his shoulder and kept going.

"Are you serious? Just...c'mon, Flynn!"

He came up behind her as she stalked the shoreline, and she glanced over at him. "Sorry. I'm having a little shout-out with Kennedy."

He cocked his head. "What?"

"Just...stand back and let us duke this out, okay?"

He looked around, back to her. "What?"

She sighed, turned to him. "I know she's not here, okay? I'm not actually losing my mind or anything. Sometimes I pretend she is here, okay? Because, you know, I see her every time I look in the mirror. So it's not super hard to have an actual conversation with her, because I know how she thinks."

*Right.* He hadn't thought about the fact that she actually looked at the likeness of her lost sister every day. *Wow.*

"Okay. I'll just . . . go sit over here, and you can tell me when you . . . two are done fighting."

His parents had set up Adirondack chairs overlooking the river, and he settled into one. "Carry on."

She stared at him. "Now it's weird."

"I have news for you—it was always weird."

Her lips pursed.

He leaned forward. "Okay, fight with me. I'll be Kennedy."

"You can't be Kennedy."

"Why?"

"Because, tough guy, we're arguing about you."

"Perfect. Because I'll be on my side."

She stared at him. "Okay, here's the thing. You might be Jack and everything, but I'm Rose."

"And we're back to *Titanic*."

"It's always about *Titanic*. Jack and Rose. And how they couldn't possibly have lived happily ever after."

"Why?"

"Because it wasn't real. They lived in different worlds . . . Their romance was just . . . for the moment."

"Looked real. Felt real." And maybe he wasn't actually talking about the movie, because he'd seen it when he was about twelve, on DVD, and thought it was overdone and way too dramatic, but then again—he'd been twelve.

And then, as she went quiet, real frustration in her eyes, he realized . . . no, she wasn't talking about the movie.

"What's going on here, Sparrow?"

"Don't call me that."

He had cocked his head at her.

"Because it just . . . makes me . . . like you. Too much. And I lose my brains, and I can't do that, Jack. *Axel*."

"Lugnut, if that works better."

She raised both her fists, shook them. "Stop being . . . charming."

"You saw the reality show. I can't help it." He smiled.

"This . . . thing. This attraction . . . this—"

"Undeniable passion? Unbreakable connection? Unrelenting desire?"

She rolled her eyes. "Whatever. It . . . can't work."

*Oh.* From her tone, she wasn't kidding. And that took the wind out of his smile.

"Don't look at me like that. We've known each other for three days. Three. And I kissed you like you'd just come back from war or something."

"Looked at me that way too."

"You're not helping!"

"Yeah, I am." He stood up. "I'm helping you see that maybe there is something else—for both of us—if you have a little faith." He took a step toward her. "Listen, Sparrow, three days is forever in the rescue world. Every minute is life and death. Three days is an eternity." He took another step.

She swallowed but didn't move.

"There's a reason that you were on the other end of that radio," he said, his voice lowering. "And if you believe in God, like I do, then you have to believe it there was a purpose."

"Maybe to save your life."

"And yours."

She nodded. He took another step, close enough to put a hand under her chin, to lift it.

"And I think you keep saving it, Flynn."

She wet her lips, and his gaze caught on it, stirring the flame inside that didn't need any more fanning.

She stepped back. Put her hand on his chest. "I have a life in

Minneapolis. A job. A family. I'm the only child left, and my parents need me and . . ."

"Hey, hey—"He took a step toward her, but she matched it and stepped back.

"Okay. I won't chase you down." He stood there, his hands at his sides. "But, Flynn, I—"

"What did you mean, I keep saving your life?"

He drew in a breath. Looked out at the river shaded in the dusky after-midnight light. Back to her. "When I was a kid, about ten years old, I was in town. It was summer, and I was throwing sticks into the river, down at the park. There were some families there, and suddenly I looked up and there was this kid playing in the water. Maybe six years old. He fell and the current grabbed him, and there was no one else around—or I didn't see anyone—so I went in after him. He was already struggling, but I grew up on the river. I started kayaking when I was about his age, so I knew how to read it, what to do. I caught up to him at an eddy, and then a few grownups were there and they got us out. And then, suddenly, I was the town hero, and . . . I got it in my head that I could save people."

He looked back at her, and she hadn't moved, listening again, like she did.

"And then . . . I lost that feeling."

"When Aven died."

"Yes."

"And you tried to get it back in the Coast Guard."

He lifted a shoulder.

"Then you lost yourself."

*Huh.* "Maybe, whatever. But when I'm with you . . . I guess . . . I feel like I've found me again. Or at least pieces of me. And not because I saved you or you saved me—"

"Let's be honest. You saved yourself, Axel."

He cocked his head. "If we're really honest, God saved me. But maybe that's it. You make me feel like that guy—the guy I thought I was—is back. Like Rose did for Jack. You make me feel like I can be more."

His voice softened. "Maybe you are Rose. You make it worth it to stay in the water. And wow, that sounded stupid."

"Yeah, that's a real mess." Then she shook her head, took two steps toward him, and put her arms around his neck. Pulled him down to her. "I'm in such big trouble."

And then she kissed him.

Oh wow, did she kiss him. She was a wave, crashing over him, sweeping through him, taking him with her into the kiss. She smelled amazing—she'd taken a shower in the basement guest bathroom and her hair was still a little wet—and he wove his hands into all those copper tangles before wrapping his arms around her waist, pulling her closer. Fitting her perfectly against him.

The flame lit to inferno and he deepened the kiss.

He didn't have a hope of sleeping after this.

She tasted of toothpaste, fresh and inviting, and he wanted more of her. So much more. So he scooped her up, then walked back and sat on the nearest Adirondack chair, her arms still around his neck.

She made a tiny sound and leaned back, met his eyes. "I'm not sure what you're thinking there, Jack, but this is not the backseat scene in the movie, so don't think of getting handsy."

"I'm going to be honest and say that was the only scene I liked."

"I'll bet."

He lifted both hands. "But I'll keep them where you can see them, to quote my favorite ornery detective."

"I still have the bear gun."

"No, actually you don't."

She wrinkled her nose, then slid her hands into his, wove her fingers between his. "Please don't make me fall in love with you."

"Then you should stop kissing me. Because you've seen my press. People all over the world love me."

She narrowed her eyes. "Fine. I'll chance it."

"Attagirl." Then he pulled her close and kissed her again, the midnight sun shining over him, the rush of the Copper River cheering in the distance.

He didn't know why he'd brought the dumb chicken box along.

Moose stood in the light of the refrigerator, staring at the cardboard container.

No, staring at the stupid red heart. The one between his name and hers. Like they might be in middle school and she'd scrawled it in her notebook and he'd gotten a peek.

It made the small part of his heart that was indeed still in middle school thump, hard, against his ribs.

Almost painfully.

But the rest of him, the all-grown-up-and-learned-lessons-in-love-the-hard-way part of his heart, shut the door of the refrigerator.

The chicken had probably gone bad anyway, sitting in his duffle bag all day. He'd grabbed it from the counter as Axel kitted up, as Flynn read the map on the wall, and suffered an insane swell of jealousy.

He missed the Skyport.

No, he missed Tillie. And her beautiful brown eyes, and that teasing smile, and that mane of dark hair.

He should never have asked her out and screwed up the entire thing.

Movement out in the yard made him glance over, through the kitchen window.

He stilled.

They were at it again. For the love . . . And now Axel picked Flynn up and sat down with her on the chair overlooking the river.

Parking them there.

He turned away, refusing to be a voyeur.

Axel deserved a little happiness, but Flynn had come out of nowhere. Still, according to Axel, she'd been a lifeline to him.

And she'd kept her word today and kept out of the way. Mostly.

Until Sully *kissed* her.

He should have known by the look on Axel's face that little bro had feelings for her. But Sully had lived to see another day, and apparently, given the moonlight tango out there, they'd sorted it out.

He had a mind to wander down to the river, though, just to make sure that Axel behaved himself . . .

*Have a little faith.*

He didn't know if it was his voice or God's, but yeah, his big little brother was probably old enough to figure out what kind of man he wanted to be.

Moose headed over to the television. It was paused on—*oh boy. The Sizeup.* That stupid reality show he'd agreed to.

He sat down and pushed play. Laughed a little at the scene of Axel playing the dummy, although at the time he'd wanted to strangle him.

But it played well on the show. Oaken came on, talking about his experience, and then the show cut away to them debriefing at the Tooth. Axel sitting at the table and Boo with him, Shep, standing, his back to the counter. They were talking about training and how Oaken was doing, right before he came in from the locker room. Axel tossed him a rope bag he'd been stuffing, one they'd use for the upcoming river rescue training.

And then someone asked where Moose went.

He froze when Axel grinned and said, "He went to see his girl."

*His girl.*

Yeah, not even a little. He turned off the television.

He walked to the refrigerator and opened it. Took out the container, looked at the heart. "Sorry, Till." Then he opened the trash and dumped it in.

Some mistakes couldn't be fixed.

He glanced out the window. Axel had gotten up, taken Flynn's hand, and they walked back to the house.

He watched as Flynn headed into the downstairs entrance. Axel came up the stairs to the main floor.

Good boy.

He headed upstairs to his room and finally closed his eyes when he heard Axel's door close.

Maybe it was enough to see Axel happy. Healing. Heading toward wholeness.

And maybe he should stop babysitting his brother.

He just didn't know how.

# NINE

FLYNN NEEDED TO GO HOME BEFORE SHE DID real damage to her heart.

Starting with her love for Axel's mom and her baking skills. *What. Ever.*

Flynn walked out of the Last Frontier Bakery, peeling a layer off a hot and gooey cinnamon roll, Axel beside her holding a couple coffees and a grease-stained bag with a cake donut. Overhead, the sky arched a deep blue, although heavy clouds obscured the mountains, a slight chill in the air.

She popped the bread into her mouth. Cinnamony, caramelly . . . "I've died and gone to heaven. How are you not three hundred pounds?"

"Lots of hockey as a child," Axel said.

She could see that. He had a competitor's aura about him. He wore a pair of black cargo pants, hiking boots, and a white long-sleeved shirt, had shaved, and looked like he might have walked off some celebrity movie shoot with the confident stride in his aviator sunglasses.

His words last night—this morning?—hard to keep track with

all this sunlight—returned to her as they sat at an outside picnic table, him setting the coffee cup in front of her. *"You make me feel like that guy—the guy I thought I was—is back. Like Rose did for Jack. You make me feel like I can be more."*

Yeah, any more and she might lose her brains altogether.

Except, she got that. He made *her* feel as if . . . well, as if she might be discovering a part of herself that she'd forgotten.

The Kennedy part of her, maybe.

But not today. Today she was Flynn with a purpose. And on this morning's agenda was a stopover at the ranger's station because Axel had gotten a text this morning from Peyton saying that she'd brought in the journal. But first, a chat with the sheriff and maybe the regional forester, Hank Billings, with the hope of getting a list of recurring seasonal tourists.

She had the victims list plastered in her brain but also on her phone, which Peyton had grabbed also.

"We're getting somewhere; I just feel it," Flynn said, setting the cinnamon roll on a napkin, wiping her hands on a wet wipe from the bag, and reaching for her coffee.

"I'll say," Axel said and winked.

"Stop."

"Just saying that we were getting somewhere last night pretty well."

"Seriously?" But she grinned. Frankly, the fact that he'd called a halt to their campout by the river had her trusting him more than he could know.

Jack was the real deal. And his words to her kept whispering around her brain, even in her dreams. *"I'm helping you see that maybe there is something else—for both of us—if you have a little faith."*

Last night, she'd stood on a cliff facing the valley below, spread her wings, and taken off.

*Wait.* She put down her coffee. "Right before I was shot at, I was standing on a mountaintop, and I saw some smoke in the distance. Like from a campfire or a cabin . . ."

"Could be." He took a sip of coffee, then reached into the bag.

"But didn't you say that was all national forest? Can people camp in a national forest?"

"If they have a permit, sure. And there are a few off-grid cabins that are grandfathered in, so yeah, smoke from a campfire or a chimney isn't unusual."

*Oh.*

"You thought it was a clue?"

"Hoped so."

Around them, tourists wandered the streets, some of them entering the Last Frontier, others walking along the wooden boardwalk between stores—gift shops, Bowie Mountain Gear, a bookstore with a sandwich board advertising a BOGO sale. The outfitters had set a teepee of kayaks out with a rental sign.

And down the street, workers strung lights across the road with American flag banners hanging down.

"Is there a festival this weekend?"

Axel set down his donut, leaned in, his voice low. "Fourth of July? It's sort of a once-a-year thing. Involves hot dogs and fireworks. Don't tell anyone."

"Oh, you're hilarious." She finished off her roll. "No wonder the town is so full."

"Actually, Copper Mountain does it up right—street vendors, the Midnight Sun Saloon sells barbecue sliders that are so good they will melt your face off. And the VFW pays for the fireworks. We even have a street dance."

"I love street dances. They have one in a small town on the north shore of Minnesota every year. My family usually goes up to visit my cousins there. It's a blast."

"Clearly you'll have to show off your street-dance moves," he said, finishing his donut.

"Really."

"Probably with me."

She smiled. "We'll see. I might go with Sully."

"That's not funny."

"It's a little funny."

"You said I was a better kisser."

"Yeah, I dunno."

He leaned forward. "Need more proof?"

"Keep your proof away from me. I have work to do." She wadded up her napkins, got up, and dropped them into the trash, along with the wet wipe and empty coffee cup. "I'm going to talk to the sheriff. You coming with me?"

"Sure. Then I need to duck into Bowie Mountain Gear and pick up radios for Moose. He ordered some after I dunked ours in the Cook Inlet." He shot his wadded bag into a nearby basket, then followed her across the street to the sheriff's office.

It hadn't changed since she'd last visited. A long, ranch-style building with a front porch that creaked as she walked inside, the sheriff's office might have been a house in ages past, although the inside had been gutted for a reception area and chairs. A dividing counter separated the waiting room from a small administrative area. Behind it, windows protected the back offices. The place smelled of age, old coffee, and overwork, indicated by the worn vinyl chairs and the cluttered Wanted board.

No wonder Deke hadn't gotten anywhere with the investigation. They needed help.

So different from the high-tech offices back home. She worked downtown in the Minneapolis city hall building, built in the 1800s with the green copper roof, rose stone, and the breath of generations of investigators, including her mentors, Eve and Rembrandt Stone, and the old chief of investigations, John Booker. But the place had undergone an overhaul over the past few years, with smartboards in every conference room, electronic whiteboards to cast investigations onto a big screen, and two screens at every desk, connected to high-speed internet. She barely left her cubicle when caught in an investigation, knitting together leads, creating profiles, and rewatching surveillance videos and interviews.

So maybe her hands-on sleuthing needed some resharpening.

She waved a hand to Deke as she came in. He had looked up from his computer and now came out of his office. "Flynn. How are you?"

"Better."

"Still limping."

"Swelling's down. Nothing broken."

He pointed to her bruised head, the healing cut. "How's the noggin?"

"Still working. Enough to wonder if the Midnight Sun Killer might be a seasonal tourist. All the murders happened in the spring—late June, early July. Right during tourist season."

He motioned her back to his office, met Axel's hand. "Saw the latest episode last night. The blizzard on the mountain. Rough. The father took it badly."

"Anyone would. Her fiancé had to be sedated," Axel said.

She got that too. Maybe it was easier to live with the hope that Kennedy was still alive. Although, since yesterday, the feeling had started to loosen its hold.

How could Kennedy walk away from a man who loved her?

Flynn glanced at Axel, leaning against the wall of Deke's office with his arms folded, and shook the thought away. *Reasons. Good reasons.*

And she wanted to find them.

Deke sat down at his desk. "Seasonal visitors. Yeah, that makes sense."

"I'm wondering how we'd get a list of the yearly campers at the RV park. I have no jurisdiction here, but you could ask for it, as a matter of your investigation. You might not even need a subpoena—it's not private information."

"I could do that. And we have a good relationship with the park owners. We run a patrol through the park once a day, just to keep trouble down."

"Lots of seventy-year-old rabble-rousers?" Axel smiled.

"You'd be surprised. Most are great folks, but people get up here, out of the lower forty-eight, and the midnight sun does something to them. Turns on the serotonin, revives their youth. We have more accidents from the over-sixty crowd than the risk-loving youth. Usually in over their heads with a four-wheeler or a river raft or even a hike that they can't get back from and, most often, a barbeque pit out of control."

"Thanks, Deke. How soon can you get the list?"

"I'll call over in a bit."

She stood up. "Great. I'll round back after I talk to Peyton."

Axel held open the door, and she walked through, noticing a couple guys at the counter.

"Hey, Mal, what's going on?" Axel said. He shook hands with a younger man, good-looking, with long blond hair, wearing a T-shirt with Bowie Mountain Gear on the chest.

He stood next to an older man, maybe early sixties, dark hair cut short, looking fit in a denim shirt and jeans. He wore a cap with Bowie Fishing Tours on the front.

"Wilson," Axel said. "Didn't know you were still in town. How's the fishing?"

"Good. Got a freezer full to take home." He turned to Deke. "I wanted to report that my truck is missing."

Deke had followed them out. "Oh?"

"I left it on the camp road, near the trail to the Bowie fishing lodge, and it went missing." He looked at Mal. "Of course, I left the keys in it so . . . I don't mind anyone using it—but it hasn't turned up. Can you keep an eye out for it?"

"That old '84 Ford? Blue with the white stripe? You still have that thing?"

"That's the one. It's not worth much, and I just use it when I'm here, but . . . you know. Hate for it to get into the wrong hands." He looked at Axel. "Keep an eye out?"

"Yes, sir. You heading back to Montana?"

"Yep. Stay safe out there." He shook Axel's hand as Flynn exited into the sunshine.

Axel came out after her.

"Who was that?"

"Wilson Bowie. Mal's uncle. He was the executor of their estate for a while. Now he just checks in on them a couple times a year."

"Every May and June?"

He gave her a look. "Wilson is a great guy. He has his own family down in Montana, a ranch, and is real close with the guys. I promise, he's not a"——"he pitched his voice low—"river monster."

She glanced at him. "You'd be surprised."

"I hope not. I'm heading over to Bowie Mountain Gear for the radios. I'll meet you at Northstar Pizza." He pointed to a place with hanging lights and a deck, the smell of pizza stirring in the piney breeze.

"All you do is eat."

He laughed. "A guy can't live on donuts alone."

He walked away, and she watched him even as he looked both ways and jogged across the street, toward the outfitters.

Maybe that was her problem—she had too many river monsters hiding in the shadows to have faith in anything but disappointment.

Still, faith—or hope—had brought her out here. Maybe she should start leaning into it . . .

A truck filled with dogsled boxes passed, and she crossed the street after it, walking up the stairs to the ranger's office.

Hank was at the desk, talking with a couple of hikers. He pointed to a side office as she came in.

Peyton sat at her desk in front of her computer, wearing her uniform, her dark hair washed and fluffy around her head. She looked up with a smile. "You. Sheesh. Seriously, how much trouble can you get into in seventy-two hours?" She got up and gave Flynn a hug. Leaned back and pointed to her head. "Ow."

"Yeah."

"So, what exactly happened?"

"I got shot at."

Peyton's smile dimmed, her eyes narrowing. "Are you sure? Because that's a national forest area. Could it have been a shot that carried? The Bowie land is nearby—maybe some fishermen, firing at bears?"

"Yes, I'm sure. It pinged off rock at my feet." She sank into a chair. "I can admit to some panic."

Peyton folded her arms. "I'd be panicked. I'm glad Axel showed up." She gave her a smile, something of tease in it. "So . . . there are rumors . . . I saw London today at the Last Frontier."

"Wow, can this town get any smaller?"

"Probably not. The ham-radio date worked out, then?"

"I don't know." Flynn looked out the window to the river in the distance. Back to Peyton. "I have a life in Minneapolis."

"Yeah, you do." Peyton smiled. "That's what my dad said. But he and my mom are back here every summer because this is her hometown. They make it work. You want something enough, you make it work." She reached down beside her desk and hauled up Flynn's backpack. "The journal is in there, and I put your phone in the side pocket."

"Wow, thanks." Flynn stood up. "Hey, do you think I could get a list of recurring hikers in the area who've gotten permits for the national forest where we were?"

Peyton frowned at her. "Why?"

"I can't help but think that the Midnight Sun Killer might be a tourist."

Her friend went quiet.

"What?"

"I don't know. Most of the hikers I meet are crunchy granola types. And I don't know much about the case except for the rumors, but the Midnight Sun Killer seems more ex-military. Like a tracker or a sniper or . . . a big-game hunter. I think you'd have more luck asking some of the guides around here for their client lists. You could start with Sully. He brings a lot of groups in all year round."

"We've met."

Peyton smiled. "Okay, I'll ask Hank. You going to be in town for the festival?"

"Not sure. Thanks, Peyton." Flynn grabbed her pack.

"Glad you're okay." Peyton gave Flynn a hug on the way out.

Flynn stopped in at Bowie Mountain Gear and searched for Axel but didn't spot him, so she headed over to the pizza place and took a seat at one of the yellow tables.

Opened up her backpack. The journal sat at the top and she pulled it out, along with the map.

Spread it out.

"Can I get you something to drink?"

The question came from a teenager, clearly a waitress, her long blonde hair pulled back. Pretty. She wore a nametag—*Parker*. "Water is good."

"Menu is on the board in the middle of the table." She pointed to a blackboard, chalked and shellacked. "But we have a lunch appetizer special on breadsticks."

"Sure." Why not eat all the bread in town?

She dug the phone out of her backpack's side pocket. Dead, but she'd powered it down when they left civilization, so she pressed the power button.

It came to life, vibrating, and suddenly a slew of messages came in. She thumbed open her app.

All from Eve. She opened the text loop.

Eve

How's Alaska?

Have you found anything?

Hello?

I'm getting worried.

Call me before I send out a search party.

Flyyyyynn!

She sent a reply.

Flynn

I'm fine. Safe. Still searching. XO.

She set down the phone, opened the journal, and found the last page she'd read. She hadn't noticed it before, but a tiny sparrow was drawn at the bottom of the page. Her thumb ran over it.

Reading through the entries, she saw that most of them were about the wolf pack, Koda and Luna and the pups. And then—

> *Met a trail guide today near the river. He carried a bear gun and had another man with him. The other man called him a name—something like Indiana, or Iowa. The first guy reminded me of Slade. Handsome, but dangerous. I think they're poaching.*

Poachers. She hadn't thought about that, but it made sense.

Her sister had drawn something on the page again. Not a sparrow—it looked like a wolf with a tribal tattoo woven into the hair at its neck. She ran her thumb over it.

Her phone rang. *Eve*. Wow, talk about hovering. She picked it up.

"What? I said I was okay."

"Five words—that's all I get? It's been five days, Flynn. And radio silence?"

"Sorry. I was in the bush." Seemed like the simplest explanation.

A pause. "I don't know what that means, but I'm going to assume you were searching for Kennedy. Anything?"

*Where to start?* "Maybe. I'm checking into seasonal tourists. And maybe . . . poachers."

"Listen. Don't do anything . . . well, don't be you."

Funny, in a way she felt more *her* than she ever had. Or maybe a part of her she'd always known existed and had never let free.

"When are you coming home?"

"Why?"

"It's just that . . . I think we have a copycat on our hands. 1039-style kills. Young women taken from a local bar after hours, found days later in the river—it's eerie. I could use your brain."

She drew in a breath.

"Flynn?"

"You're the one who said I had months of leave."

"Right. Yes, you do . . . Is there something . . . happening out there I need to know?"

"No!"

"That was too quick."

"Okay, I might have met someone." She looked out into the street, and there he was, that someone, heading out of the gift shop.

"An Alaskan woodsman?"

"Sort of. But it . . . I have a life in Minneapolis."

"Yeah, you do. But what if—"

"No. No what-ifs."

"I'm just saying that everything happens for a reason. A purpose. And I know you have to figure out everything, but what if you didn't? What if you just had a little faith it would work out?"

"I don't know, Eve. Maybe this whole thing is . . . just . . . Maybe I should come home."

"Or maybe you should trust that God has a plan."

Axel came over and sat down opposite her. Smiled.

"See if there's a pattern to the nights the victims were killed. I gotta go."

She hung up.

"More river monsters?"

"Something like that. Hey, have you ever heard of a hunting guide called Iowa or Indiana?"

"Idaho?"

"Maybe."

"He was a poacher—got arrested last year."

*Oh.*

"Why?"

"Nothing. It's in the journal." She closed the book. "What did you get?"

He pulled out something wrapped in tissue. "The gift shop is having a sidewalk sale. I saw this and thought of you." He drew a necklace out of the tissue and held it up. A small black bird with veins of green, tiny wings spread. "It's a sparrow."

She took it in her hand, stared at it. Ran her thumb over the smooth surface. "Where . . . Is this locally made?"

"I don't know. Probably. But . . . it's a sparrow."

And with his words, something simply took hold inside her.

She might even call it faith.

Axel didn't want to pay attention to the storm on the mountain. The one obscuring the peak of Denali and drifting southeast. But a breeze worried the trees, and it picked up their paper plates and tried to toss them from the table.

"Whoa—"He grabbed Flynn's cup before it went over.

She was too late to stop her plate from frisbeeing away.

He got up and chased it across the deck, out to the street.

"That's not a good sign."

A foot stepped on the plate, and he looked up. Shasta Starr stood on the sidewalk, dressed in a pair of jeans, a sweatshirt, her dark hair loose in the wind. "Hey, Axe."

"Shasta." He leaned down and picked up the plate. "What do you mean, not a good sign?" But he already knew.

"Storm on the mountain." She shaded her eyes, gave Denali a grim look. "It moved in fast. Hopefully there are no climbers on the summit."

He'd bet against it—Denali, from June to July, had turned into Everest, a virtual highway of climbers trying to conquer the tallest peak in North America.

"I saw Moose in town and heard about the rescue yesterday. You're at it again."

"I'm at nothing again." He glanced at Flynn, but she had her head buried in the journal.

"Oh please. You saved a kid off a cliff—"

"That's my job."

"Because you're a *hero*."

He held up his hand. "Shasta, I'm just an ordinary guy."

She gave a laugh. "Why can't you get it through your head that ordinary people don't do the things that you do?"

"It's not extraordinary if you were made to do it."

"It is to the people you save."

He stared at her.

"Why don't you want to do an interview?"

"Because . . . it's . . . Listen. Things go south in a rescue. A lot.

174

And I don't want to be some kind of hero and then have everything implode, okay? Just . . . leave it, Shas."

He walked back to Flynn, who set the book down.

She considered him as he sat down.

"What?"

"What was that about?"

"Oh, that's just Shasta. She works for the newspaper."

Flynn's attention went to Shasta. "What did she mean, hoping there are no climbers on the summit? Is she talking about Denali? Isn't this the climbing season?"

"Oh. Yes. And it's crazy busy on the mountain. The park service has a permanent base camp set up at 7200 feet, on the Kahiltna Glacier. People flying in and out every day—they even call the runway there the KIA—Kahiltna International Airport. But there's a storm coming in, so people want to get off the mountain."

"In July?"

"Yeah. The mountain is constantly between storms, and it can get to twenty below up there. Or colder. It's one of the most dangerous mountains to scale because of the weather."

"Have you climbed it?"

"No." He leaned back. Every year we pull people off the mountain who have their fingers or noses or toes frozen off. And then there's the ones who just freeze to death. I happen to like my fingers and toes."

She reached out, touched his hand on the table, wove her fingers into his. "Me too."

Aw, really, he shouldn't get used to this. Because, well, because of the very reason he didn't want to give an interview to Shasta.

The minute he started to believe in something . . . that was the minute he had something to lose.

And that thought shook through him and loosened his grip on her.

She didn't seem to notice. "So no climbing for you."

*Calm down.* He wasn't going to lose her just because he'd started to care . . .

"My worst nightmare is being stranded on the mountain in a snowstorm, watching my fingers turn gray." He opened the pizza box. "One piece left."

"Knock yourself out."

"You ever want to climb a mountain?" he asked.

"Not even a little. It's too . . . unpredictable."

"And yet you want to go skydiving."

"Skydiving is vastly different than climbing a mountain. Besides, I only *talk* about skydiving. Never going to happen."

"Why not?" He took a bite.

"I just like to keep my feet on solid ground."

"You might like scuba diving. It's like flying."

"Except for the no-air part."

He laughed. "Seriously—you're weightless and underwater with all the fish—it's breathtaking."

"Literally."

"Right."

"So." She took a sip of her soda, put it down. "She's right, you know. To the people you save, you're not ordinary. Speaking from experience."

He looked at her. "You heard that."

"So you do the interview, and people think you're awesome. What, you think you might get a big head?"

"Wow. I haven't heard that phrase for years."

"My mom is Lutheran. It's a thing—no big heads."

"Right. Well, no. I mean, most of the time I'm just waiting for the other shoe to drop—if we're speaking in idioms."

She leaned forward. "Why?"

He frowned.

"Why are you holding your breath, waiting for disaster?"

He drew in a breath. Swallowed. "Maybe it's just better to expect disappointment."

He didn't know where that'd come from, because yesterday he'd been telling her to have a little faith.

Except yesterday it hadn't felt like this might be real. He'd hoped it, and now suddenly they were holding hands and sharing a pizza, and he'd purchased her jewelry and . . .

*Oh.*

His chest tightened.

"Axel? You okay?"

He nodded. *No.* "I'm fine." *Not in the least.*

Because howdy, he had something to lose. Something big and painful and . . .

And no, he didn't have an ounce of faith that it wasn't going to crash and burn. Because fate didn't play fair.

Parker came to the table. "You done?" She gathered up the plates, the pizza box. "You guys going to the festival this weekend?"

He pulled out his wallet and handed her a card.

"Axel!"

He turned and spotted Moose headed across the street. His brother stepped up on the deck of the pizza place, walked over.

"I picked up the radios, if you're wondering. They're in the truck," Axel said.

"Good. We have a callout. Dodge called, and he's been ferrying climbers off the mountain all day in his Otter, but there's been a fall. The wind took a couple of climbers off Squirrel Hill, and they're on a slab overlooking Peters Basin."

"That's pretty high elevation."

"We can be up for thirty minutes without supplemental oxygen. C'mon—we need to go before the winds get worse. We're meeting Dodge at Sky King Ranch—he'll be my copilot. I need you on the line—London will run the hoist."

Axel was already swinging his leg over the bench. "What about Flynn?"

"She can take your Yukon back to the house—"

"Or I can go with you," Flynn said.

Moose looked at her. "Not to Denali. Not this time."

Flynn's mouth tightened.

And Axel didn't know why he said it. "She could wait at Sky King Ranch. Maybe man the radio. She's good on the radio." He looked over at her, winked.

"I think Echo can handle it," Moose said. "But that's okay with me. Let's go."

Axel drove the Yukon to the airport, then left it there and retrieved his gear from the storage unit. Moose arrived with London, and ten minutes later, they were airborne, Flynn strapped into the seat, her helmet on.

He didn't know why he'd lobbied for her to come with them—it would probably have been better for her to wait at home.

Except . . . weirdly . . . Okay, yeah. He couldn't get past the idea that he didn't want her out of his sight. Or at least, not roaming Copper Mountain alone.

Because . . . shooting. And her bum knee. And maybe because he didn't want it to end.

*Sheesh,* yeah—what she said. He was in big trouble.

Flynn stared out the window as the Air One chopper flew over the roaring Copper River and to the western hills and valleys that made up the Denali basin. Mostly homesteaders out this way, but Sky King Ranch owned a decent swath of land, a lodge, some cabins around their own lake, and had for years run a bush pilot service. Dodge still managed that, in between rescue flights.

Axel spotted the ranch from a distance—the Quonset hangar for Dodge's Otter and the Air One chopper, the red barn for their cars and gear, the lodge, with the front porch and stone chimney jutting from the roof. A runway ran along the back of the yard.

The storm hadn't yet reached the valley, clogged on the jagged mountaintops. Echo stood outside, a sweater wrapped around her body, not quite able to fit over her nearly-to-term belly. She wore a pair of oversized sweatpants, a stretchy shirt, her dark hair back in a messy bun, and now stepped back, away from the rotor wash.

Axel opened the side door, and he and Flynn got out. He walked her over to Echo and introduced them.

"Flynn can help with the radio, if you need."

"Good, because my back is killing me." She stretched, her stomach larger than her body, it seemed. "Dodge flew up to the base camp. He'll meet you there."

Axel turned to Flynn. "We'll be back as soon as we can."

"Stay safe," she said, and stood there. And he wanted to lean over, give her a kiss goodbye, but suddenly that felt too . . . domestic. Real. Like they somehow belonged to each other.

He nodded instead and ran back to the chopper.

Moose lifted them off, and Axel glanced down to see Flynn bracing a hand over her eyes, watching them go.

He should have kissed her. *Stop panicking.* Everything was going to be fine.

The storm hit them twenty miles away from the mountain, catching the chopper in its flurries, but Moose kept it steady, and they landed neatly at KIA. Dodge's DHC-3 Otter sat on the snowy tarmac, and he helped load the plane with packs and other gear.

He wore a parka and a wool hat and looked up as they landed. His aviator glasses reflected the activity at the base—orange tents flapping in the wind, climbers sitting on their expedition sleds, packs, and other gear, a few climbers digging tent platforms in the snow.

Axel counted maybe fifty climbers, all hanging out, waiting for the weather window to pass. Around them, the north face of Mount Hunter rose, a forbidding jut of sheer ice and granite. Fresh snow lay like a creamy layer on Mount Foraker to the southwest, the mountain only slightly dwarfed by Denali. The afternoon sun turned the eastern slopes to a deep blue-gray.

Dodge lifted a hand to the chopper and trudged over, wearing snowshoes. Moose opened the door.

"Hey. So, the update is that they're on a serac outcropping on Peters Basin. They fell about two hundred feet and lost their packs, and the wind is gusting off Motorcycle Hill, so rescue teams can't get down to them."

"What's the wind at up there?"

"About thirty knots. There's been at least one avalanche sighted, and that serac could let loose at any time. Still need me on copilot? We're still waiting on some climbers to finish packing up."

Moose nodded and turned to London, who was already un-buckling.

She worked her way to the back, and Dodge climbed in at co-pilot, pulling on a thermal rescue jumpsuit and donning a helmet.

He and Moose huddled in the cockpit, working out how to reach the climbers, Moose with his tablet out, tracing a route down.

London wore a tight-lipped look.

"What?"

"I was on a rescue like this in the Alps. Nearly went down with the gusts." She drew in a breath, forced a smile. "I'm not a fan of mountain rescues."

Moose turned and held up the screen. "This sounds crazy, but with the angle of the mountain and the size of the serac, I think we can get a skid on it and, Axel, you can just climb out and haul them in. We'll put you on a safety line, and London will lower down a double sling. I think we only have one shot at this, so work fast."

Axel gave him a thumbs-up, and Moose lifted them off the snow and into the air. Axel had never had a desire to climb the Tall One, as it was called by the locals, and as they rose now, past the dark granite walls, deep glacial runnels, and thick snow-capped ridges, that resolve settled into his bones. He wasn't fueled by adrenaline and risk—he just wasn't afraid of it.

Although, as he spotted the two climbers clinging to the massive serac the size of an oil platform jutting out from the white face, a tremor strummed through him.

He'd be glad to get off this mountain.

Moose had judged correctly—they could set a skid down on the serac and load up the climbers in one fell swoop. But Axel would have to get out and assist them into the sling because the way they both clung to the ice, their axes dug in, they weren't moving. Ice crusted their face masks, and one might be hurt, because his arm hung loosely, his grip unused.

London checked Axel's secure line as Moose lowered them to the lip of the icy protrusion; then, when he'd settled the skid, she opened the door.

The frigid wind swept Axel's breath away.

"Make it quick!" Moose yelled.

Absolutely. Axel ducked his head, glad for his helmet and visor, his thermal suit, and stepped out onto the skid, still attached to the safety line in the chopper. London had released the hoist with the two slings attached. He grabbed it, then stepped off into the snow.

He landed thigh deep in the fresh layer and fell, still holding the slings. He moved to lie on top of the snow and army-crawled over it, distributing his weight.

The guys were shouting at him, but he couldn't make out their words over the rotor wash. He reached them, and they grabbed on to him, pulling him close.

"Get in!" He held out the hoist, and one of them pulled it over himself, under his arms, then let go of his ice axe and wrapped his arms around the sling.

The other shook his head.

"C'mon, man! It's cold out here!"

He reached out for the sling, grabbed it—

A gust of wind sailed over the top and sent snow funneling down over them like a waterfall. Axel tried to brace himself, but the snow whipped him back, turning him, tangling him in his line.

The chopper ripped away from its perch, jerked him, and in his peripheral vision, he saw the line rip away from the mountain. One man hung on, inside the yoke, safe.

The other hung onto the yoke with both arms, dangling.

"Get them in, London!"

The chopper dragged him, snow crammed into his visor, blinding him.

And then he was hanging. Simply twisting in midair, eleven thousand feet in the air, nothing but a carabiner saving him from a plummet to the earth below.

He shoved up his visor, tried to clear his eyes even as the wind whipped through his ears, freezing his body. Shouts came from the duo on the line as London tried to reel them in.

Moose, in his ear, talked over London, fighting for control of the chopper.

Then, "The hoist is breaking free!" London shouted.

*No, no—*

And Axel's safety line might be next—

Moose's voice came through, even, calm. "We're going to put down on the pass above Motorcycle Hill. Hang on, Axel."

What—he was going to do *what*?

But the chopper suddenly lifted into the air, some one thousand feet, and he swung like a trout on a line, deaf from the wind, his eyes burning, nearly frozen shut as Moose angled them toward the pass.

Snow swirled up under him as he skimmed over the plateau, Squirrel Hill rising in front of him. "Put me down!"

As if he heard him, Moose descended, the snow a tempest, churned up by the blades.

Then the chopper started to spin. Axel looked up, saw it fighting the wind that churned over Squirrel Hill, spinning and bobbing. The bird dragged him through the snow as it descended.

He lost sight of the climbers as he tunneled into the drifts, his body tugged along by the failing chopper. Please, let him not crash into a granite outcropping. He rolled, trying to get his hands on the carabiner, but snow crusted his gloves and—

And then, suddenly, he stopped.

He rolled over.

Then everything inside him died as he watched the chopper disappear into the mountain in an explosion of snow and ice.

# TEN

**W**HAT JUST HAPPENED?"

Flynn stood behind a man named Barry Kingston, Dodge's father, who manned the radio in the office at the ranch. Not a big office, but the window overlooked the runway as well as the cloud-shrouded Denali range.

Now, Flynn stared out of it as if she might see the red chopper caught somewhere on the mountain.

"Did they go down?"

Barry wore glasses, but she sensed that his eyesight might not be clear, given the way he ran his fingers along the walls when he walked and feathered a touch over the dials and radio equipment on the desk. An icon spun on the computer, and a map of the area, including the individual peaks of the Alaska Range, hung on one wall, a collage of pictures on the other, most of them of his three sons in various outdoor settings, one of his daughter standing in front of a small airplane.

He reminded her of the older version of Indiana Jones, worn wisdom in his leathery face, salt-and-pepper hair, heavier on the salt. He wore a denim shirt and a pair of jeans, leather loafers, and he sat in an office chair listening to the chatter, a microphone in his hand.

Barry held up a hand to her question.

She said nothing, just listened to the static. Finally, he lifted the mic. "Air One, this is Sky King Base, come in."

Nothing.

He repeated the call.

She stalked away, her hands on her stomach.

Moose had radioed in trouble with the chopper, something about air gusts, and then one Mayday had issued through the line.

Then it had gone dead.

Barry put the mic down. Folded his hands, leaned his forehead down to them.

"What are you doing?'

"The only thing I can." He'd closed his eyes.

"Wait, are you *praying*?"

Now she might really be ill. She held on to the door frame. "Is it that bad?

"It doesn't need to be bad to pray, but it might be, so . . . yeah." He had lifted his head, and he now resumed the position as she stepped back into the hallway, bent and grabbed her knees.

Okay, so praying might help, but really, someone needed to *do* something.

"Flynn, are you okay?"

Echo stood in the hallway, her hands on the small of her back. She had abdicated the radio control for a recliner in the great room of this beautiful home about an hour ago, after Moose reached the base camp.

"They went down." Oh, she probably shouldn't have said it like that, but why mince words?

"What?" Echo braced her hand on the wall.

"The chopper. We lost contact. I think—" he glanced back into the office. Barry sat, still praying. "They went down."

Echo stood there, swallowed, nodded. "Okay, then." She turned and headed back to the great room.

What was with this family?

Flynn followed her out to where Echo sat in the recliner, her head down, her hands on her lap, breathing. "Are you praying too?"

Echo looked up. Blew out a breath. "Not really. But sort of."

"Then . . . wait. Are you in *labor*?"

Echo leaned back, her eyes closing. "I think so. I don't know. Could be Braxton-Hicks."

"How close are the contractions?" Not that the answer would mean anything to Flynn—she knew nothing about labor and delivery. Still, maybe some knowledge of the situation would help her should she need to call 911.

"I don't . . . Oh . . ." Echo pressed her hands to her belly, then looked up, her eyes wide. "Can you get a towel?"

"What?"

Liquid saturated the chair as Echo leaned forward, pushed herself up. Her leggings dripped. "My water broke."

"I see that—"Flynn fled to the main-floor guest bathroom. Grabbed the towels on the rack. But then stopped and looked in the mirror. "Everything's fine. You can figure this out. Just breathe."

Her reflection nodded, as if in agreement, and then she headed back out and handed Echo a towel, put the other on a chair. "I'll get Barry."

"No." Echo reached out. "I'll call my mother. She's an ob-gyn."

*Right.*

"Check on Barry." Echo waddled to the island and slid onto a stool, picking up her phone from a bowl in the middle of the island.

Flynn hustled back down the hallway and found him standing at the window, staring out as if he could see through the veil of clouds, talking to someone. "They had already picked up the climbers, according to Moose. I think they must have gone down just above Motorcycle Hill, but who knows?"

"I'll alert the rangers at Camp Three," said the voice. "See if they can get down to them."

"Keep me posted. Thanks, Hank."

He clicked off.

She walked into the office. "I know Hank. Over at the ranger station in Copper Mountain."

Barry looked at her, seemed to focus on her. "He got the call from one of the guides going up Squirrel Hill. Said the chopper was intact, just sitting in deep snow."

"And . . . Axel?"

"They didn't say."

She nodded. "Okay, well, we have other problems—Echo is in labor."

"Oh no. Did she call her mom?"

"She's doing that now."

"Okay. You help Echo; I'll stay here," Barry said.

"And do what? We need to send help or . . . maybe send up another chopper or—"

He held up a hand. "There's nothing we can do. There are planes on the ground at base camp. They can fly over if they need to, and the rangers at Base Camp Three can climb down to them. We haven't even heard from Moose yet—it could be that the chopper just needs to be dug out."

"Or it could have dragged Axel off the mountain—he wasn't even in the bird yet!"

Barry had taken a step toward her and now put his hands on her shoulders. She was shaking her head. "What am I even doing here. This is . . . I should be . . . doing . . . finding . . ." She looked at Barry, found his blue-eyed gaze on her. "I'm a detective from Minnesota. I came here to find my sister—or at least what happened to her. And maybe hunt down a serial killer. I . . ." She put her hands to her face. Shook her head. Lowered them. "What am

I doing here? I . . ." She sighed. "I don't do helpless. This . . . this waiting thing . . . This is not me."

"Have a little faith, Flynn. I know we can't see what's going on, but it wouldn't matter—we have no control over what's happening on that mountain right now. None. We just have to trust that God is with them."

"And that he'll rescue them?"

"Yes. If that's his plan."

She stared at him. "Okay, see that's why I don't . . . I'm not . . . Faith is not something I'm signing up for. I need—"

"Assurances?"

"Maybe, yeah. I need to know that who I'm putting my faith in is going to—"

"Do what you want?"

"Yes!" She shook out of his grip, not trying to be a jerk, but— "Why should I have faith in God if he's not going to help me out?"

Barry just nodded.

"Listen. I know that God exists, okay? There's no dispute there. But . . . the world is a dark place, and I've seen too much to put my life into the hands of a God who seems largely absent."

"Really." Barry folded his arms. "Seems to me that according to Dodge, you've been intricately involved with a God who hasn't been absent."

And suddenly, Axel's words filled her head. *Fine.* "Axel said that God has a reason for why it was me on the other end of the radio. But I've never . . . I mean, after my sister went missing, I prayed a lot, you know? And nothing." She swallowed. "I'm not sure God cares."

Barry nodded. "Faith is believing even when you don't feel like it. You really think that God doesn't care even after he sent Axel to save you? Or sent you to save Axel?"

*"If we're really honest, God saved me."*

"I guess I don't know what I think."

"God still holds us accountable for what we refuse to see."

Her mouth opened. Closed. "Okay, sure. He shows up when he wants . . . how he wants. But that's certainly not someone you can *trust*."

"So you only want to trust someone who does what you want."

She sighed. "Listen. It's not that I need God to do what I want—"

"Because you're in charge."

Her mouth tightened. "I don't need to be in charge, but . . . I just want to know that . . . everything is going to . . . Fine, yes, I'd like to be in charge, thank you. If I was, people wouldn't go missing or get shot at or crash on a mountain—"

"And they'd never see the salvation of the Lord."

"They wouldn't need it."

"I don't think a world where we don't need God is possible." He had taken a step back and leaned against the table. "Because if you're in charge, then what if . . . I want to be in charge, or Dodge, or Moose—who wins?'

"It was metaphorical."

"No, it's not. That war is going on all the time. In politics, in governments, in the lives of communities and families, and even in your own heart. Who is worthy to be in charge of our lives—your life? That's a lot of responsibility."

She looked past him, out to the storm moving over the mountains, the jagged peaks splicing through the clouds. "At least I know what's best for myself."

"Do you?" He reached over and picked up his glasses. Put them on. "I was a bush pilot for the better part of forty years. And then my eyesight went south and I crashed my plane." His eyes focused on her. "And because of it, my sons had to come home, one by one, reckon with this place and, as a result, their past. See, a terrible fight in our family ripped it apart, and I'd prayed for years for God to put us back together. If I was in charge, I would never have crashed my plane. But God, in his wisdom, used the crash to heal our family."

"Are you saying he caused the crash?"

"As much as you can blame the maker of the wind. But I also live in a body that is decaying—it's destined to decay. We're not meant to live forever. So, could God have healed my eyesight? Absolutely. Did he use the natural order to breathe new life into our family? Yes. When God is in control, even death and decay can turn into good."

His voice softened. "You said you came here to find your sister. Why?"

"Because I . . . I . . . Fine, I feel like she's alive."

"So, you have faith?"

"I have hope."

"The devil wants to keep our eyes on the finite, the problems, the pain, the feeling that if we let go of control, everything will spiral out and become chaos. But God says, 'Trust me.' He is not a God of chaos but peace. And when we trust him, we can know he will be with us, here in the valley or up on the mountain or even in the depths of the sea. And it will be good, even if it doesn't feel that way."

The radio behind him crackled.

He picked up the mic but glanced at her. "Faith isn't weakness. Faith is aligning yourself with true power. True control."

"Sky King Base, this is Air One Rescue chopper, come in."

Moose. Her eyes burned.

"Go ahead, Air One Rescue, this is Sky King Base."

"We made an emergency landing on the mountain. All souls accounted for. No casualties. We're sitting in a drift, however, so it might be a bit before we can get out."

"Confirmed. Hank wants to know if he should send rangers to your position."

"Negative. It's an eight-hour climb from here. We'll assess and call for help if we need it."

"Roger. Standing by."

She'd stepped up to Barry. "Tell him about Echo."

Barry shook his head. "No need for them to take undue risks. This is her first baby—she has time—"

"No . . . no, I don't." Echo appeared at the door, her breaths hard, her face white. "I think the baby is coming. Now."

Flynn turned back to Barry. "Tell Dodge to get down that mountain as soon as possible. We'll meet him at the Copper Mountain hospital."

Axel could admit that being dragged through the snow like a buoy felt a little like drowning in the Cook Inlet.

He might be just as cold. The snow and ice had burrowed into his thermal suit and down his neck and into his bones, and Axel shoved his hands between his knees to stop shivering.

He ground his jaw shut as London closed the door. She turned and wrapped him in a space blanket, having already secured and wrapped the climbers, who were dazed, terrified, and probably traumatized into deep shock.

Outside, Moose and Dodge had assessed the structure of the chopper, tromping around the bird in their snowshoes.

The fact that his brother had brought the aircraft down to the pillow landing despite the wind sheer and the pull of the human anchors was a testament to his Navy piloting skills.

Still, Axel probably had snow burn on his face, the way it felt on fire.

He closed his eyes, trying to shake away the churning inside him, the sense of terror that sat in his bones.

Always sat in his bones, if he was honest. He just never let it out to fill his lungs, his throat.

"You all right?" London said, sitting beside him. "You sound funny."

"I'm fine. I just . . . I, uh . . . um."

"I'm taking your blood pressure." She reached for her medical bag under the seat, but he grabbed her arm.

"I'm too cold for that. I'll be fine. I just need to get off this mountain."

"Roger that." She looked at the climbers, also shivering. "Probably a sentiment shared by everyone."

Moose climbed into the cockpit. "I think we have the skids cleared. We need to get out of the snow before they ice over."

Dodge came in the other side. "Let's get going."

They ran a systems check, then Moose fired up the bird. It shook to life, having been manually shut down right before they'd put down onto the shelf of snow. The loosened snow kicked up and stirred into the blades.

"Hang on." Moose's voice came through the headphones. Axel had taken off his helmet, now wet with ice and snow, but put his headset back on.

The chopper eased forward, broke free, shuddered, then lifted into the air.

Axel's hand tightened around a bar on the edge of his bench seat. *Breathe. Sheesh,* maybe he did need his blood pressure checked, because he might be in a full-out panic attack.

Shoot—this was supposed to be in his past . . .

He focused on his breathing.

"You good back there, Axel?" Moose, in his headphones.

"Mm-Mmmhmm." Sounded more like a grunt.

"You sound like you're hyperventilating."

Uh, thank you, big brother, for alerting the entire chopper.

"I'm fine." He didn't open his eyes in case anyone might be looking at him. He just needed a full minute. Or two.

The chopper beat the air down the mountain, the wind less turbulent as they fell in elevation. He opened his eyes and spotted the Kahiltna base coming into view as Moose angled the chopper down and landed sweetly on the snow.

Like they hadn't nearly careened down a mountain, dragging Axel and two others like a tail off the mountain and into . . .

He couldn't bear the rest.

Moose powered off the rotors, and Dodge got out, opened the door. "We have a plane waiting to bring you guys into Copper Mountain hospital." He helped the two climbers out, still unsteady on their feet.

He got that. So Axel stayed put in the chopper, even after London exited. Moose had taken off his headphones, and now Axel watched him greet someone—looked familiar. *Oh, wait*—Orion Starr, Shasta's cousin. He'd heard he'd returned to Copper Mountain with his wife, Jenny. Must be working as a guide, maybe.

Axel shivered, the wind tugging at him. Maybe someone should have shut the door.

Moose came over. "You good?"

Axel looked away, nodded.

"I don't think so, bro." Moose got in and shut the door. "Maybe you should take a ride down to the clinic with the climbers."

Axel looked at him. "Don't."

Moose held up his hands. "I'm just saying that . . . you know. It's a thing—panic attacks—and—"

"Listen. I'm fine. Just . . . trying to get out of my head the feeling of being a drogue anchor."

"Sorry."

Axel closed his eyes. "I knew it would happen. I don't know why I'm so . . . whatever."

"Freaked out? And what did you mean by you knew it would happen?"

He opened his eyes. Took a breath. "I was happy for a full moment and then . . . you know . . . just a good reminder that I need to dial it down."

"Dial it down?"

"Expectations. I try, you know, to keep it light and happy and not let it in, but . . ."

"Wait, are you talking about the past and—oh, right. You think God is out to get you."

"No, I just think . . . Listen. We both know I've made some pretty big mistakes, and, well—karma."

"That's a bunch of crazy talk. First, there's no such thing, and second, God doesn't get even by messing up your life, Axel. He very much wants you to be whole and free—"

"And happy?"

Moose shook his head. "He's not interested in your happiness."

Axel frowned.

"He's interested in your joy. Happiness is circumstantial. It's fleeting and momentary. Joy is . . . it's a state of being. It's living in the place where you know that you're loved by God, that he is at work in you, and that you can trust his control. And that beats any kind of happiness, all day long."

Moose scrubbed his hands down his face. Leaned back. Fatigue lined his face.

Reminded Axel of how Moose had looked when he'd plucked him off the shore. "Sorry I keep nearly dying."

"I'd appreciate it if you'd stop that." Moose opened his eyes. Smiled. "I know you were built to be a hero. But one of these days . . ." He sighed. "Ever since you grabbed that kid out of the river, you wanted to be the guy who saves the day. First in the water, last off the boat. You thought if you were just strong enough, could endure enough, be the best, then you could save anyone."

"And?"

"And then you didn't."

Axel stared at him.

"Aven. The guy on the fishing boat . . ."

"What, are you keeping score?"

"Not even a little. But you are."

Axel swallowed.

"You've disappointed yourself, and that infuriates you."

"Of course it does."

"Because you can do better."

"Maybe, yeah."

"Save everyone."

Axel opened his mouth. Closed it. "What are you getting at?"

"Just pointing out the arrogance of that statement, Captain America. Without you, the world would . . . we'd all end in disaster."

"I thought you came in here to make me feel better."

"What makes you think that? I'm your brother. But listen. If you feel shame that you couldn't rescue someone who was beyond rescue, then you're saying that you're better than God."

Axel narrowed his eyes at his brother. "I'm not saying that I'm better than God."

"You are. Deep down inside you're angry because you thought you were enough. That you should have been able to save them."

Axel blinked at him. "I guess so. I'd call it regret, not anger."

"And I'd call it pride. You know what happens with pride . . ."

"Oh, this is fun. Can I call a friend?"

"A fall. A big fall. Because to even the score with the disastrous you, you've told yourself that God doesn't love you. Isn't for you. And that he's actually working against you." Moose leaned forward. "But what if God is right here, saving you, over and over, because he is actually for you? What if he doesn't think you're a disappointment? Even if you are a little bit arrogant."

"I don't think that word means what you think it means."

Moose had pulled out the medical kit and opened it. Now he grabbed a bottle of water. Handed it to Axel. "Drink. It will slow down your heart rate."

"Maybe you should stop talking—that'll slow my heart rate."

"Drink."

Axel put the bottle to his lips while Moose talked.

"Regret is one part shame and one part lesson. But if the only lesson you've learned is that you are on your own, then that is the wrong lesson."

He wiped his mouth. Okay, the drink helped. "What is the right lesson?"

"Forgiveness. Focus. Faith. Focusing on regret keeps you entangled in sin and darkness and futile thinking. But God says, 'Let me forgive you of your pride. Put your eyes on me and my love, and trust that I have good waiting for you.' That's joy. And that's how your regrets lose their grip."

Axel finished off the water. Looked at Moose. "Is that how you live with Aven's death?"

Moose drew in a breath. Smiled. "Trying."

"Mm-Mmmhmm."

"Listen. I like Flynn, and I'm happy to see you happy. But don't for a second think that your happiness is going to last without getting free."

"Wow, thanks. I'll be sure to send you a wedding invite."

Moose smiled. "What are you talking about? I'll be your best man." He got up and opened the door.

Dodge had come over. Stood on the tarmac. "I'm heading back to Sky King Ranch. My dad called, said there's another storm coming. I didn't see it on the radar, but he's watching the weather so . . ."

"I'm right behind you," Moose said and climbed out to get into the front.

London joined him, pulling on her earphones. She handed back a chocolate bar. "Get your sugar up."

Axel took it and let the chocolate dissolve as they took off. Moments later, Dodge's plane passed them.

Axel closed his eyes, Moose's words rattling around inside.

Maybe, if he was honest, he'd been angry for a long time. At himself, at God. And yeah, maybe it was arrogant to think God should have done something different. Or that Axel could have stopped Aven's murder. Or, well, saved any of the other rescues that had gone south.

Which did sound a lot like pride, too.

Out the window, the sky had turned a deep blue, the clouds fewer here, the sun shining into the valley, turning it a deep, rich green.

*"Joy is . . . it's a state of being. It's living in the place where you know that you're loved by God, that he is at work in you, and that you can trust his control."*

*Sheesh,* he'd said almost the same thing to Flynn.

*"If we're really honest, God saved me."*

He drew the blanket around himself. That wasn't the only confession . . .

Because at the end of the day, his greatest fear was anyone finding out that he *wasn't* enough . . . and he was going to let them all down.

They landed, the plane already parked on the tarmac. Moose shut down the rotors, and Axel opened the door.

He caught Moose. "Maybe let's not tell Flynn . . . just . . . let's . . ."

"I got it." Moose held up a fist. "What happens on Denali stays on Denali."

Axel bumped it and dropped the blanket into the chopper. He'd give his life savings for a hot shower.

But as he came to the house, Flynn appeared at the back door, her face so stricken he slowed.

Moose, behind him, did the same.

Flynn launched herself at Axel, her arms around his neck, holding on so tight they cut off his breath.

"What—what is it?"

She leaned back even as Moose walked past them, shot him a grin.

"Don't do that again," she said to Axel.

"What?"

"Crash."

"Oh, I didn't crash. That was Moose. I was . . . not in the chopper."

She narrowed her eyes at him. "That's at least two lives you've used up there, Phoenix. You're down to three."

Wow, she had a way of bringing him back from the edge. He might indeed be a phoenix with her around.

And then, from the house, a scream lifted, high pitched and agonized. He froze. "What—"

"That's Echo. She's in labor."

"Here? Now?"

"Her mom is in there. We were going to go to the hospital in Copper Mountain, but her mom is an OB-Gyn, so . . . she wanted to wait for Dodge."

"Oh, right." Axel slipped his hand into hers. Held it, maybe tighter than he meant to. But he didn't care what Moose said. Happiness was having someone that cared waiting to throw herself into his arms, and that was enough.

They walked into the house, into the main room, and the sight stopped him cold.

Echo sat on the recliner, her knees up, breathing hard, her body draped in a sheet.

She was having the baby right here, in the living room.

He knew Dr. Effie Yazzie by reputation—she'd been gone most of Echo's life but had returned a couple years ago. Dark hair pulled back, dressed in jeans and a T-shirt. Now she pulled off gloves and dropped them into a bag. Looked at Dodge, who knelt beside Echo. "We need to go. Now."

A moment of silence and then, "Go where?" This from Dodge, but it could have been anyone.

"The baby is breech. And I can't turn it. And unless we get to a hospital, they're both going to die."

*What?*

Axel glanced at Dodge, who had gotten up.

"Okay, okay—I have fuel in my chopper—"

"No. We need to take your Otter, Dodge," Moose said from where he stood at the counter. "It's faster. And you're in no condition to fly. London, you come with me." He turned to Axel. "Help me get the seats out of the plane."

*Right.*

He followed Moose out onto the tarmac. Moose grabbed the preflight checklist and started a quick walkabout while Axel and London and Flynn removed the seats.

Dodge appeared with Echo in his arms, wrapped in a blanket, her mother behind him, carrying a medical kit. They got in.

London grabbed the med kit from the chopper and shoved that in also, then climbed into the copilot's seat, starting the interior preflight routine.

*Huh.* He didn't know she could fly a plane too.

"You need me, Moose?" he asked as Moose came around and closed the door.

"No. But you could pray."

He could pray.

He looked at Flynn and she nodded. *Right. Okay.*

"I'll call you from Anchorage," Moose said, then went around and got in.

Axel stepped back, holding Flynn's hand as Moose turned the

plane for takeoff. In moments, it arched around the lake and headed south.

And suddenly, he prayed with everything inside him that Moose was right . . . and that God was on their side.

And this was why he should never get married. Never have kids.

Moose stood in the parking lot outside the Tooth, watching as the rescue truck pulled away, Boo and Dr. Effie in the back with Echo and Dodge, Shep at the helm.

He wrapped his hand behind his neck, blew out a breath.

"You good, boss?" London glanced at him, her medical bag over her shoulder. She so often stayed in the shadows that sometimes he forgot she was around. She preferred it that way, and he knew why, but sometimes he looked up to see her standing there, watching, thinking, listening, and she seemed more like a covert agent than a woman trying to shake off her broken past.

But she'd come highly recommended last year—pilot, rescue tech, with medical skills, and Shep had vouched for her too—so he'd taken her on.

Hadn't regretted it. And she'd joined the team without hesitation, even if she kept pretty close-lipped about her past.

Maybe they all did. He didn't exactly open up about—

*"Is that how you live with Aven's death?"*

Axel's words in his mind added to the silence between himself and London, and he finally just nodded.

"I'm exhausted," London said. She keyed in the code to the door of the Tooth and headed inside, down to the supply room. "I'm headed home, unless you want to grab a pizza or something."

He followed her in, turned on the light "No. Not hungry."

Actually, starved, but maybe not the kind of hungry that meant sharing a pizza with London. Maybe he could wait for Shep and Boo to return, but . . .

Nope, only one place he wanted to be.

Should be, really.

He pulled out his phone and called Axel.

His brother picked up on the first ring. "How's Echo?"

"Not sure. She's headed to the hospital. Her pressure dropped in the air, but the baby's heartbeat is still beating strong. Where are you guys?"

"Back at the house. Mom's making dinner. Flynn got a couple of reports from Hank and Deke and is doing some internet sleuthing. Dad is catching up on *The Sizeup*. Did you know that Oaken used that song he was working on at your house in the show?"

"No." He paused. "You okay?"

"Fine."

"You're not . . . everything's—"

"I'm fine, Moose. If you hear anything about Echo, call."

"Axel—"

"We all made it off the mountain. And thanks for the pep talk. You headed back to Copper Mountain?"

"Not tonight."

Another pause. "I'm not the only one who needs to consider his regrets. G'night, bro." Axel hung up. Moose watched London lift her hand in a wave as she headed outside.

So maybe pride sat behind his regrets too. The regrets that kept him from returning to the Skyport.

And he needed a shake in the worst way after today. A shake and some midnight chicken and . . . Tillie. Even if they'd only be just friends.

If he believed God was in control, then clearly she'd turned him down for a reason. And who was he to tell God that reason wasn't good enough?

*Right*. He flicked off the lights, then headed outside to his truck, sitting in the parking lot. Climbing in, he glanced in the rearview mirror, then decided he'd have to live with the two days of beard growth.

She'd seen him in worse shape, maybe. Probably. *Whatever.*

He pulled out and headed over to the diner. The sun glinted off the green roof of the fifties-style diner, the name painted onto the windows, along with pictures of pie.

He parked in his spot in the corner, backing in. Then sat for a moment, replaying the memory of helping Tillie get her decrepit car started one cold night.

And the way she'd sat down with him once, to share onion rings.

She had drawn a heart on the top of the takeout box. Maybe it was a just-friends heart. But it was a heart all the same.

*Regret keeps you entangled in sin and darkness and futile thinking.*

He'd done quite a bit of futile thinking...

Time to trust that God had something good waiting.

He got out, swinging his keys around his finger, and entered the diner.

It smelled of coffee, buttermilk-battered chicken, frying burgers, and fresh milkshakes.

*Home.*

Not busy—one other man sat at a booth. It was after nine p.m., so he didn't expect it. But Tillie worked the late shift, and he preferred it quiet.

Maybe she'd have time to sit with him, just for five minutes.

He spotted a waitress in the Skyport's blue uniform grabbing a couple plates from under the heat lamps behind the counter.

Not Tillie. He didn't see her around, but she could be in the back.

He walked down the row of red-vinyl booths and slid into his regular spot, three booths down, facing the door.

Folded his hands.

Tried to sort out what to say.

*Hey, Tillie, sorry it's been so long*—no, that just made it sound like he'd stayed away on purpose. Except, yeah, but . . .

Okay, maybe, *Hey, Tillie, how about the usual?*

That felt too . . . well, like he was just a customer and she was just a waitress.

And she had drawn the heart on the container . . .

*Tillie, I'm sorry I screwed things up between us.*

Maybe closer.

*Hi, Tillie, thank you for the chicken. I . . . missed you.*

Could work, maybe over the top, but—

"Can I help you?"

He looked up. Stilled. The other waitress. He put her in her midtwenties, brown hair pulled back, a little hanging down and tucked behind her ears as if she'd had a trying shift. Her name badge read Sami.

"Hey, Sami. Um . . . is Tillie here?" He didn't want to be obvious, but this was her section . . .

"Oh." And the way she said it, the tiny sound of surprise, maybe awkwardness, had him sitting up. "Um . . . she's not here."

He leaned forward, raised an eyebrow. "Where is she?"

"Actually—" She glanced toward the kitchen, then back. "She . . . hasn't been in for three days."

Silence.

"Is she sick?"

"I don't know. I . . . they called me to work her shifts. I don't know if she's fired or what, but nobody knows where she is."

Moose just sat there. Swallowed. "Is your manager here?"

"No. She works days. But Lyle is here. He's our night cook."

Moose slid out of the booth and headed back to the kitchen.

"Sir—"

Moose turned, held up his hand, then pushed through to the kitchen. The place swam with grease, the griddle sizzling with a couple burgers, fries bubbling in the deep fryer. A stainless steel countertop ran the length of the wall opposite the griddle, and farther down, a scrawny teenage boy loaded dishes into the industrial dishwasher. An office with a closed door sat at one end of the kitchen, a deep freezer at the other, a back door led to the parking lot. And Lyle, the king of the kitchen, glared at Moose, his spatula raised, wearing a stained apron, his shirtsleeves rolled up, a hairnet over his prison-short hair. The guy looked fresh out of Spring Creek Correctional Center.

"No customers back here," said Lyle.

"I'm just looking for Tillie. Do you know where she is?"

He flipped the burgers, pressed the grease out of them. "No. She took off a few days ago, right in the middle of her shift. Told our manager that she needed to take some time off."

"No idea where she is?"

"You could try her house."

"Where's that?"

"Dunno." He scooped up the hamburgers and stacked them into a bun, open on a plate. Added some lettuce, onions, and tomato, then closed it up and went over to the fries. Dumped them into a bin and salted them. Looked over at Moose. "You still here?"

"Listen . . . we're . . . friends. And it's weird, right? She never misses work."

"She missed it once, last year."

"Okay, she rarely misses work."

The cook scooped up fries and dumped them onto the plate. Grabbed a couple pickles from a stainless steel bin and plopped them on the plate too. Set it under the lights. "Order!"

Then he grabbed a towel and wiped his hands. "Listen. I don't know where she is. Tillie's a tough broad—she can take care of herself, trust me. But if you're asking me, I think she's in some kind of trouble and doesn't want to be found. You pickin' up what I'm layin' down here?"

He took a step toward Moose.

Moose held up a hand and tried very hard to breathe, keep his heart rate down. And nod. "I just want to know she's okay."

"Get out of my kitchen."

Okay, he didn't need an altercation.

"If she comes back—"

"She ain't comin' back, man. Now, unless you want something to eat, you need to do the same."

Something . . . it just didn't . . . "Fine." He backed out of the kitchen, spotted Sami standing near the cash register, her eyes wide. The burger still sat under the lights.

"Do you want a shake or something?" Sami said as he passed her.

He shook his head as he headed toward the door.

He'd lost his appetite. At least for food. But he'd figured out what he wanted to say. *Tillie, where are you?*

He took out his wallet and pulled out a business card. Then he grabbed a pen and wrote her a message. Handed it to the waitress. "Give this to her if she ever comes back."

The woman nodded and tucked it beside the cash register.

Then he headed out into the night, wishing he hadn't waited so long for pie.

# ELEVEN

FLYNN WASN'T SURE WHERE SHE'D GONE OFF the tracks and lost control of her heart, but she was in big trouble. Axel stood in the moose-burger line, his dark-blond hair curling out of a baseball hat set backwards on his head, his hands in his faded jeans pockets, wearing a blue flannel shirt with sleeves rolled up over his powerful forearms, smiling in greeting at locals, just a casual hero hanging out . . . Yeah, she needed to run, run away, as soon as she could if she ever had a hope of returning to her life in Minnesota.

Except, what life? Tracking the river monsters, residing in the darkness? She'd sort of gotten used to all this light, the sun pouring over the mountains, glistening on the river, the fresh piney air . . . All of Alaska felt awake and alive and . . .

Maybe Kennedy had brought her here, but staying had suddenly become about . . . living. In fact, it felt sort of like she'd forgotten how to be a detective.

But maybe there wasn't a trail. Maybe Kennedy was gone.

And maybe it was time to let her go.

"Hey, Flynn." Peyton walked up holding a piece of beef jerky. "I didn't know you were still here." She wore a fleece, a pair of jeans, her dark hair pulled back. Her fiancé, Nash, walked behind her, holding a couple of frothy beers. He also wore the uniform of Alaska—a gimme hat, flannel shirt, jeans, boots. Dark hair, a hint of whiskers.

Alaskan men. No wonder they landed on calendars.

"Yeah. I—" She glanced at Axel, now standing by the cashier. "I like it here."

"I'll bet." Peyton winked. "You look like you're getting around better."

"Knee's back to normal, almost."

"Good. Any luck with that report Hank gave you?"

"It's not very long—I thought there'd be more repeat hikers."

"Our repeaters are locals, usually."

That didn't fit with her profile, but she just nodded. "I compared the list to Deke's list of RV regulars. Just a couple crossed over, but most of them have social media posts that put them in the lower forty-eight at the time of the most recent, um, incident."

"Sorry."

"There's got to be another clue to Kennedy's disappearance out there . . ."

Axel had paid and, carrying two burgers wrapped in paper, headed over to her.

"So, you're going to stick around until you find it?" Peyton glanced again at Axel, grinning.

Or maybe she'd stick around for other reasons.

*What—no. Oh—*

"Hey, Peyton," Axel said as he came up. "Nash."

"Lug."

Axel grinned and handed the burger to Flynn. "How's gold mining?"

"Busy. We found a new lode and are opening operations, but Dad's trying to get some financing for it, so he's meeting with investors today." He took a drink of the beer. "Going to throw today?"

She looked at Axel. "Throw?"

"Axel here is a champion axe thrower. At least in Copper Mountain."

Axel held up his hand. "I won a couple years in a row."

"Four. Four years. He was only unseated because he went away to be a Coast Guard hero." Nash singsonged the last word.

Axel rolled his eyes.

"The Remington brothers are in it, so . . . you know. You might have a rep to defend."

"I don't need to defend my rep. I'll always own those four plaques in the VFW."

"I knew you still cared." Nash grinned. "See you at the pit." He put his arm around Peyton's shoulder and steered her away.

"Axe throwing?" Flynn said.

"Hey, it's a thing," he said as he unwrapped his burger. He smiled at her, but it seemed reserved. Something had shifted between them over the past two days since he'd come off the mountain.

Maybe she could blame the hug she'd given him—clearly a little desperate—and maybe that's when her heart had left the station, because all she could think was she'd nearly lost him on the mountain and . . .

And wow, she'd only known him for three, now five, days and she'd practically unraveled. So, yeah, maybe they should both just cool off these flames.

She unwrapped her burger and bit into it. Tangy, with sauce and pickles and lettuce—"This is delicious."

"It's actually part moose, part hamburger—the tourists wouldn't love full-on moose. Too gamey. But this sells."

Booths lined either side of Main Street, most of them local artists hawking their wares, everything from knitted goods, dream catchers, polished rocks, oil paintings, and wood carvings to canned jams, wild honey, relishes, fresh-baked nut breads, and monster cookies. A country band played an Oaken Fox cover from a stage set up beside Northstar Pizza, the music drifting into the street. Tourists walked with their leashed dogs, children eating cotton candy and standing in line for pony rides around the block.

Sale signs hung from Denali Sports and Bowie Mountain Gear, as well as the Last Frontier, and even Gigi's, a cabin turned grocery store, had a sale on their homemade granola bars.

A crowd in front of Bowie Mountain Gear watched a demonstration of a beautiful Bernadoodle as he hunted for the KONG that his handler hid. The handler, a man in his early thirties, maybe, dressed in a pair of green canvas pants and a black T-shirt emblazoned with a logo of some sort, handed the black KONG to a girl, maybe ten, and asked her to hide it.

She found a place behind a flowerpot of geraniums.

The handler let the dog loose—he found it in less than a minute.

"And imagine now that the KONG is a person buried under two feet of snow. Orlando is trained to find you."

Clapping. Next to her Axel stilled. "You've got to be kidding me."

As the crowd dispersed, he finished off his burger and walked over to the man, crumpling his wrapper and throwing it in the trash. "Jericho Bowie. I can't believe it." He held out his hand.

Jericho wore his brown hair clipped close to his head, had a military build, a sort of self-possessed aura about him.

Flynn followed Axel, also finishing her burger, trying to remember why that name sounded familiar. Clearly a Bowie... Wait. The other brother, gone for years.

And now back...

But that didn't fit the profile either.

Jericho met Axel's hand but clearly struggled to place the name. "Moose?"

"Close. Axel."

"Right. Lugnut?"

Axel laughed. "What are you doing here?"

"Back to see the bros. Hud roped me into doing a demonstration." His shirt emblem read Highland K-9.

Axel noticed it. "What's Highland K-9?"

"It's a K-9 SAR school in Montana. We're located right outside Glacier National Park, and we train dogs to track the lost and missing. Orlando here is a former avalanche SAR dog. I'm going to take him into the park for a few days and do some training."

"You should talk to Moose. He started an SAR team—Air One Rescue."

"Right. I heard about that from Hud. Dodge runs a chopper for Air One?"

"Yeah."

Jericho had dropped his hand to Orlando's head, glanced at Flynn. "You have the look."

"What look?"

"You can pet him." He looked at Orlando. "Down."

Orlando lay down and Flynn crouched in front of him. "Hey there, Orlando." She put her hand on his paw, and he raised his eyebrows but didn't move.

"I heard about the accident on the mountain a couple days ago. You okay?"

She looked up to watch Axel's response. He'd said little about the accident even when she'd asked, although he'd slept in yesterday and had spent the day at home, icing his shoulder. He still moved as if he ached. Maybe she just didn't want to know.

Except, the three hours from radio silence to the chopper's touchdown at Sky King Ranch had taken everything out of her.

She could hardly breathe with his answer.

"I'm great. You know—living the dream."

Jericho laughed. "Right. I remember you. Weren't you the one who went cliff-jumping into the Jubilee River?"

Axel gave him a thin-lipped smile. "Yep. Great to see you, man."

Flynn stood up, eyed Axel. There went that hooded look again.

He glanced at her as they walked away. "Really, I'm fine."

"You don't seem fine. I . . . You want to tell me what happened up there?"

"Not really."

*Oh.*

He slid his hand into hers, however, held it, and the strength of it seemed to fill her veins. Yes, something had definitely shifted between them.

They stopped at booths, looking at paintings and photographs, and he pointed out a couple landmarks. "That's the real Moose Tooth," he said of a picture of a jutting granite peak. They sampled honey and some homemade granola from Gigi's, and never once did he release her hand.

They stopped by the booth outside the gift shop, and she found more jade necklaces like the one she wore, the one Axel had given her—the sparrow. And other shapes—turtles and hearts and teardrops and an eternity symbol. She picked up the artist's card. "It's from a local art colony," said the vendor when she inquired.

She stopped at a place that made soaps and got a lotion sample. "What is this smell?" A woman in tie-dye and dreadlocks handed her an ingredients card. "Cedar and pine, with a little lavender. All natural."

She rubbed her hands with it, then put it on her neck. Axel leaned in. "I like it."

It felt so much like a date, so much like she'd shed a part of herself. The day soaked into her, turning her warm and sunbaked.

They ended up at the end of the street, in the gravel lot of the Midnight Sun Saloon, where the smell of barbecue could make her barter her future for a basket of tangy ribs or salty fries.

"You'll love the fries. They're battered." He ordered a basket from a hearty blonde woman.

"Thanks, Vic," he said and took a number for the fries. He pulled

Flynn away, toward a picnic bench. He sat, straddling the bench, one arm on the table.

She sat next to him, facing the lot, her gaze on the crowd. Habit, really.

"Vic used to be a cop somewhere in the lower forty-eight. Found her way here and never went back."

"Sounds mysterious."

"Maybe she was just looking for a new life."

She looked over at him, and his blue eyes landed on hers.

*Oh.*

"I—"She turned to face him, putting her leg over the bench. Took his hand. "Listen, I might have gotten a little worried, and I know that I sort of—"

"Threw yourself into my arms?" He quirked an eyebrow, added a hint of a smile.

"I panicked."

His smile fell as he looked away toward the mountain. "Me too."

*Huh?*

He grimaced. "After I got in the chopper, I had . . . maybe a little smidgen of a panic attack. Or started to. Whatever."

*Oh.* "You okay?"

"Yeah, but . . . aw, shoot. Okay, it wasn't the first time. In fact, I had to leave the Coast Guard because of them." He made to let go of her hand, but she tightened her grip.

"It's okay, Axel. I get it—"

"No, actually, you don't. See, it was really bad after the . . . incident in the Gulf of Alaska. And I couldn't get it out of my head, and I couldn't sleep. It's mandatory to have a psych eval after rescues that go south like that, but I . . . I didn't pass. What kind of born hero doesn't pass a psych eval?"

*Oh, Axel.*

"Anyway, they recommended time off and . . . I got angry. So I quit."

"I see."

"Not my best move, but Moose gave me a chance, and I have it under control."

"Mostly."

"Mostly." He sighed. "But it's always there, the sense that it could happen again and I'd be in over my head and . . . let's just say out at sea, without a way home."

"You could call for help." She meant it as sweet, but he frowned. Swallowed.

"I could. I . . . keep thinking about that, actually."

"Our ham-radio conversation?"

"Yes—sort of." He met her eyes and took her other hand. "I want more than just right now, Flynn. Something Moose said to me won't leave me. He says that I keep reaching for happy moments when instead I need joy." His thumb ran over her hand, and he looked at it. "I guess I don't know what joy feels like. But I'd like to." He glanced around, nodded at a local.

Turned back to her. "Everyone calls me a hero. But really, inside I'm just that guy in the river, frantic to find my cousin. Searching, I guess."

She didn't know why his words sat in her chest, filled her throat, burned her eyes. *Shoot.* What was her problem that this guy could so easily unravel her?

"Maybe I shouldn't have told you all that. I think our fries are up." He made to stand up, but she tugged him back.

"I get that. I came out here searching for . . . well, my sister was the reason, but maybe I was looking for something more. Maybe to let go. To find peace." She offered a smile but looked away, blinking hard.

He reached out, touched her wet cheek, brushed the moisture away. "Sorry."

"For what?"

"For scaring you."

She looked at him. "Shoot."

"What?"

"I told you not to make me fall for you. Now . . . I'm a mess. How do you expect me to go back to Minnesota—"

"Maybe you should stay."

The words fell between them.

He wasn't kidding.

Oh. *Oh.*

His gaze landed on hers, and a smile slid up his face, sweet like honey, and it warmed her to her bones, her cells, her very core. She leaned forward, the man nearly hypnotic with his power to—

"Axel. Seriously, your name isn't on the list. What's going on?"

She jerked away and looked up to the voice. The man had dark hair, no baseball cap, a chamois shirt, the sleeves rolled up, and jeans. Axel stood up, reached out his hand. "Mr. Remington."

"It's Ox, Axel. Every time we play this game." He clamped a hand on his shoulder.

Flynn stood up.

Ox Remington. Handsome man. She tried to remember what Axel had said about him—miner, although he seemed pretty slicked up to be a gold miner.

He turned to her then and seemed to frown. "Have we met?"

"No, I don't think so. Flynn Turnquist."

"Flynn. Nice to meet you." He held out his hand.

Her gaze fell on a tattoo on his arm, and her heart hiccupped, even as she shook his hand.

A wolf's head.

"Flynn is from Minnesota," Axel said.

"Just visiting?" Ox said and she tore her gaze away, met his eyes. She nodded.

"Right in time for the fireworks." He winked at Axel.

Axel laughed.

"Listen. I remember you throwing as a kid. Jude's competing. I thought you'd want to get your name back up on the wall in the VFW."

"Not today, Ox. But thanks."

The man made to walk away, but she couldn't stop herself. "That's an . . . unusual tattoo."

Ox lifted his arm. "Stupid impulse as an eighteen-year-old. You'd think I would have thought ahead fifty years to sixty-eight-year-old me. But no. Used to play for the Silver City Wolverines. We won the state championship, and we all got tats. Or some of us. Not my smartest move." He looked at Axel before walking away.

"What's going on?"

"That tat," she said quietly. "That was in my sister's journal."

Axel stared at her.

"C'mon," she said. "Let's get our fries and follow him."

"Follow . . . What?"

She looked at him and grinned. "Ever been on a stakeout?"

Maybe he should have done a little axe throwing. It might have helped Axel feel less like he was walking around naked, his heart on the outside of his body.

What had he been thinking? *Inside, I'm just that guy in the river, frantic to find my cousin. Searching, I guess.*

Could he be any more of a pansy?

No wonder Flynn hadn't answered him when he'd suggested—he could hardly believe the words had come out of his mouth. But she had just sat there listening, those beautiful green eyes fixed on his, holding his hand and . . .

Aw, what an idiot. She'd been here less than a full week, five days since he'd met her, and already he'd thrown out his heart to her, asked her to stay . . .

Even he'd be running.

Except she hadn't run, just ... not answered. But she had gripped his hand and dragged him along with her as she followed Ox Remington around the festival.

They'd started at the axe-throwing contest, and Axel had watched Jude win, glad-handed him afterward, then caught up to Flynn, who'd stood looking at some mittens while she watched Ox stop at the real estate office in town and stare at a few postings in the window.

"What's he doing?" he'd said into her ear, and she'd nearly jumped through her skin.

"I don't know. Looking at land?"

Then he'd left and they'd looked at land too while Ox went into Ace's Hardware.

He'd come out with Ace, and they'd headed down the street, toward the music.

"You do know that my dad will recognize me and wonder what I'm doing skulking around town," he'd said as they'd wandered toward the tent. Flynn had stopped at a pottery vendor and picked up a bowl. Brown with swirls of turquoise and gold. A Bible verse was printed on the rim—Proverbs 3:5 and 6, about trusting God.

The woman in the tent had stood up. "There's a fish symbol on the bottom. It's my signature." She had dark hair, and a baby lay in a sling fitted to her.

"You're the potter?" asked Axel.

"Yes. We're traveling the country this summer, attending festivals," she said. She wore a printed skirt, a turquoise necklace. Had a bit of a free spirit about her. "Also held a workshop at a nearby art colony."

A man in the booth had packaged up an order and handed it to a customer, along with a card.

"Do you attend every year?" Flynn had asked as she put down the bowl.

"This is our first year," the man had said. He'd handed her a card, and she'd tucked it into her pocket.

His dad and Ox had taken seats at a picnic table in the beer garden, so Flynn had edged over to the music festival, buying popcorn from a popcorn cart.

"Hungry?"

"It's a prop. Stand right there."

So now he stood, eating popcorn, his back to the beer tent, watching the band, acting like nope, nothing to see here.

"This is a stakeout? It feels like stalking. Except with a lot of food."

"Mm-Mmmhmm," she said as she held a piece of popcorn, her body angled toward the band, her gaze on Ox in the nearby beer tent. "Who's he sitting with?"

He looked over his shoulder.

"Don't turn around!"

"You asked me who he was with. What—I can't see behind me."

"Fine." She tossed the popcorn into the trash, then grabbed his hand and pulled him over to a cleared area where a few people were dancing. Put her arms around his neck. "Now you can look."

He wanted to look nowhere but at her, the feel of her body warm against him stirring up everything he'd been trying to tamp down over the past two days.

Frankly, her hug—the desperate nature of it—had shaken him to his core. Mostly because he'd needed it. More than he wanted to admit, even hours later.

He was falling for this girl, and ... despite his teasing about her staying, having a little faith, suddenly it felt way too ... well, maybe the thought of her walking away had him by the throat, just a little.

So maybe he wasn't exactly teasing.

In fact, he wanted nothing more than to put his arms around her, pull her tight, twirl her right off this swath of dirt, maybe over to the wan shadows between the beer tent and the ranger's office, and resume their conversation.

*Searching, I guess. Searching for you, Flynn.*

*Oh boy.* Instead, he unlatched her arms, moved her hand onto his shoulder, his around her waist, so he could move her around.

"You know how to two-step?"

"Not even a little."

"Okay." He swayed with her, then turned her and peered into the tent. "Okay, sitting with my dad are Ox Remington, Barry Kingston—you know him—"

"The other guy?"

"That's Wilson Bowie."

"That's right. I knew I'd see him before." She sighed.

He looked down at her. "What?"

"Maybe this all just . . . maybe I need to accept the fact that Kennedy is gone and stop seeing clues where there aren't any."

"What clue did you see?"

"None, just that wolf tattoo on Ox's arm. And Wilson Bowie, a seasonal fisherman, and then there's Peyton's dad, who shows up every summer but isn't a hunter. And if you want to go wild, Sully, who tromps around in the woods and knew my sister and maybe isn't telling us the truth. And . . . I don't know, Axel. I'm so far out of my element here . . ."

She looked up at him. "And there's you."

"I'm a suspect?"

She smiled. "No. But you are . . . I . . ." She pushed away from him and walked away from the dance floor, down the street, and—*w— here was she going?*

He caught up to her, grabbed her hand, then tugged her over to exactly where he'd been eyeing and dodging—the space between the tent and the ranger's station, a nice, secluded space that meant trouble, probably.

But, "What was that about?"

"That's about the fact that, yes, I want to stay here. That being here is . . . magical. And perfect, and I can see why Kennedy stayed and . . ." She shook her head. "But this isn't real life. This isn't my life. Even if . . ." She closed her eyes.

He had leaned against the building and now pulled her closer, his hands on her waist. "Even if—"

She opened her eyes, and they looked almost tortured. "I'd like to stay."

A beat. And he saw the word in her expression. "But."

"But I . . . I am too curious for my own good. And your own good. Because that usually gets people I love hurt."

He frowned. She put her hands on his chest. "My sister had a reason to run from . . . well, me, and Minnesota and . . ." She swallowed. "I caused her trauma. I caused her drug abuse. And maybe I even caused her death."

He had nothing.

"That woman I discovered in the alley when I was a kid—she wasn't the first victim. There'd been rumors of another girl who went missing in our neighborhood, and I got it in my head that maybe I could find the killer. So I started to sit in my dad's car at night and watch the neighborhood. I'd pack sandwiches and pretend I was, you know, some cool female detective, like Veronica Mars."

"Did you find the killer?"

"He found me. Sort of. He found my sister. Maybe he knew I was there—I don't know. But she knew what I was doing, and it drove her crazy with worry, so she'd come out and sit in the car with me and . . . one night she left to go to the bathroom and didn't come back. So I got worried. And then I heard screaming, and then . . . He'd grabbed her, dragged her back into the alleyway behind our house."

"Oh my—"

"I called 911 and then picked up a tire iron and tried to stop him, and I was thirteen and he was in his thirties, and both Kennedy and I were hurt. But we weren't taken or raped or killed, and when the cops showed up, they caught him."

He wanted to shake away the images flashing through his head.

"So you see, her trauma, her drug use, her . . . everything. That's on me. And you'd think I'd learn, but I . . . I can't stop. I was made to hunt . . . river monsters, I guess. And in the end, the people with me get hurt. That's why I don't have a partner."

He touched her face. "You do now."

"You said that in the hospital."

"I meant it in the hospital. And I mean it now."

"Yeah, but . . . Axel . . ."

And shoot, here he was, at it again, but, "I said I was searching. But maybe you are too."

"Searching for what?" she said softly.

His gaze roamed her face, landed on her beautiful green eyes, widened. "For something that makes it all worth it." Then he lowered his mouth to hers.

She slid her arms up around his neck, her mouth opening, sweetly surrendering to his, and it only stoked a sudden and urgent fire inside him.

The kind of fire that woke from a place deeper than his body, from his heart.

Even, his soul.

Searching, yes, for happiness. For a partner. For someone he could rescue, over and over, and who might let him.

So she got into trouble. He'd be okay getting her out of it, no matter what it cost him, as long as it meant holding on to her.

He tucked her in close to him, angled his head, and heard her emit a tiny sigh. *Oh, wow.* A rumble shuddered through him, and he caught his fingers in her silky auburn hair, wanted to wrap himself around her as the twilight settled over them. With the music serenading them, the scents of the festival, and then—

Fireworks. A thousand sprinkles of exploding light arching above them.

She leaned away and looked up. Gave a laugh.

"Right?"

"Oh wow, Axel." She turned back to him, her eyes on his mouth. "I've never . . . I don't normally . . . You are a good kisser."

He laughed. "I haven't had a ton of practice. You just bring out the best in me."

She met his gaze then. "Really?"

*Oh.* But, "I think so. You see me, and it's okay." He swallowed, because it was more of a question, too.

"It is, Phoenix. It is." She leaned close, brushed her lips against his, and his arms tightened around her as the fireworks burst overhead.

Barking jerked him back. He hit his head on the building.

"Sorry! Sorry!" Jericho came tromping into the space, scooping up Orlando's lead. The dog sat, barking, then panting, as if smiling. "C'mon, buddy. This is not your show."

Jericho held up a hand again. "Don't know what his problem is—just took off on me, running after you."

"Did you get him?"

The voice came from behind him, and Axel rolled his eyes as Sully appeared. "Oh. Hey. Oh. Wow." Sully pointed at Axel. "I get it now." He nodded, then followed Jericho away.

But Flynn pushed away and followed Jericho and Sully out onto the street. "Jericho."

He turned, Orlando in hand. The dog sat and whined.

"Why did your dog run after me?"

"I don't know. I was talking with Sully and he was petting him, and suddenly, he just acted like he scented something. I don't know . . ."

Sully was frowning too. Then, "Oh, wait." He knelt and held out a bandanna tied around his wrist. "This was Kennedy's. She wore it in her hair and sometimes around her neck. Maybe he picked up your smell."

"That's a Hail Mary there," Jericho said.

Sully brought the bandanna to his nose. "Nope, it's hers. Seeing Flynn sort of . . . I don't know, made me miss her. So I got out her box of stuff and found this. Been wearing it ever since. Cedar and pine. She got the soap from town, I think. But it was homemade."

"There's a booth in town selling soap," Flynn said. She knelt in front of Orlando. "Good dog." She looked at Jericho.

"Go ahead."

She petted Orlando, rubbing him behind his ears. He groaned with it. Yeah, Axel knew how he felt. *Jerk.*

"We're getting pizza—wanna join us?" Sully said. He was looking at Flynn, a sadness in his gaze.

"Yeah." Flynn stood up.

"You're hungry?" Axel asked.

She smiled and took his hand. "You can eat. Admit it."

*Fine.* He followed Sully and Jericho to the pizza place and sat down, Orlando lying at Jericho's feet.

Sully played with the bandanna around his wrist, looking at Flynn, something in his eyes. Any thought that maybe he might be a suspect seemed crazy, given the expression he wore. Sorrow, grief. Helplessness.

Axel got that. Because as Flynn sat there, smiling, her russet hair tossed by the wind, her hand trailing down to Orlando's fur, he knew . . .

If Flynn went missing, he'd follow her. And he'd find her, no matter what it took.

Levi came out to their table. "Can I get you guys something?" He wore a Northstar Pizza shirt, a pair of jeans.

"You waiting tables today?" Sully asked.

"Yeah. We're busy, and we're short. Parker didn't show up for work."

*Huh.* "A small pepperoni for us." He looked at Flynn to confirm. She nodded.

*Us.* He reached across the table and took her hand and didn't care what anyone thought.

Sully and Jericho ordered, and Levi promised drinks and left them.

Axel turned to Sully. "So, I saw your uncle in town. I thought your fishing trip was over."

"It was—he left but came back with Jer, here."

"Uncle Wilson is a big contributor to the K-9 school. We use his ranchland for some of our training activities."

"He lives in Montana?" Flynn asked.

Jericho nodded as Levi showed up with the drinks, put them on the table. Levi's phone rang, and he pulled it out as he walked away. Axel unsheathed his straw as Flynn turned to Jericho.

"Where in Montana?"

"Near Silver City, north of Helena. It's where my dad grew up."

She looked at Axel, back to Jericho. "The Silver City Wolverines?"

Axel stared at her, and heaven help him, he was even starting to think like her. "Did he play football?"

"Absolutely. His team won the state championship when he was a senior. Dad was a sophomore. We heard the story so many times—they had three overtimes, and the entire town came to watch them play in Bozeman. They all got tattoos afterward—except Dad. He wasn't old enough. But Uncle Wilson has one."

"A wolf," said Flynn.

"He's not the only one," Jericho said. "Remember Idaho? He had one too."

"You do know he was arrested, right? He's in jail."

Jericho frowned. "No, he's not. I saw him maybe a month ago. At Uncle Wilson's place."

Sully's eyebrows rose. "He's free?"

"Not allowed back in Alaska, but you know Idaho."

Sully shook his head. "I never liked him. He hunted on Remington land illegally. And took others there too. Came by the house once when I wasn't there. Kennedy said that he and one of his hunters came in and took food. She was shaken up." He took a sip of his soda. "I ever see him again, I'll run him out of Alaska myself."

Flynn took all of that in without a word. Now stared past him, toward the tent.

Axel leaned forward. "Are we going on stakeout again?"

She gave a half smile and pulled out her phone. "Stand by for further instructions."

He laughed. But his smile dimmed as Levi came up to the table. He held a pizza and set it on the table but something . . . he almost looked stricken. "You okay, Levi?"

Levi stared at Axel for a beat, then drew in a breath. Shook his head. "Not sure. I just got word from Deke that Parker's car was found on the highway, near the Bowie road."

Axel looked at Flynn and saw the horror written on her face even as she said it, soft, a realization that struck him cold. "He's back. The Midnight Sun Killer . . . he's back."

"He's a fighter; that's for sure." Moose stood next to the plastic bassinet, cradling little Chase Kingston, with his brown eyes and dark tufts of hair, cooing up at him, and wow, he might even tear up. "Sheesh, he's cute."

"Just like his dad," Dodge said, standing near Echo, but close enough to catch his son if Moose should drop the ball there.

*Not likely.*

Moose had enough regrets.

"You doin' okay, Echo?" He glanced up at her. She looked whipped, pale and fading into the pillows and blankets, her eyes bloodshot. An IV of morphine and fluids ran into her veins, and an oxygen cannula boosted her stats.

Moose had heard the story from Dodge—the emergency C-section that'd nearly happened in the hallway, and how Dodge might have lost both of them if Effie hadn't once been chief of OB here at Alaska Regional.

As it was, Echo had had a brutal C-section, barely going under before they cut Chase out, and even then, the kid had been in pediatric ICU for the last twelve hours.

But he seemed fine now, robust and crying. "Is he . . ."

"Probably. Echo fed him about twenty minutes ago."

"Back to Dad you go, big guy," Moose said and handed him into Dodge's arms.

Moose walked over to the window, staring out. The night had started to flood into the valley, shadows hovering like a haze over the city. He sighed.

"You all right, Moose? I sort of thought you'd be heading back to Copper Mountain by now."

"I had some things to take care of."

Things like trying—vainly—to wheedle Tillie's address out of the diner's day manager, who'd been less menacing than the night cook but just as unhelpful. He'd left feeling like some kind of stalker.

He'd even called Dawson, asking the Anchorage police detective for help. But what was family for? He pulled out his phone. *Shoot. Still nothing.*

Pocketing it, he turned to Dodge, who was just finishing changing Chase. The little guy's arms and legs sprang out, and he wiggled, squeaking, then mewing in protest.

"I don't blame you, kiddo. It's cold without pants."

Dodge finished reswaddling him, then tucked him against himself, rocking his son.

Okay, maybe Moose should loosen his hold on bachelorhood.

He wouldn't mind having a kid. Although babies seemed like a lot of work.

"Family heading this way?" he asked Dodge.

"I think Colt and Tae might be coming up from Florida. Ranger and Noemi are in Minneapolis, so I don't know. Oh, when you get back, can you check in on my dad? He's pretty capable, but his eyesight isn't super."

"Absolutely. Do you want me to fly the Otter up or take my truck?"

Dodge glanced at Echo.

"We'll drive, thank you," she said. "I'm done with airplanes for a while."

"What? I'm a fabulous pilot."

"I think it was more about the entire experience," Dodge said, glancing down at Echo. "Something about trying not to give birth in a plane."

"I hear that's overrated."

"And messy—trust me on that," Dodge said.

Moose held up a hand. "I believe you. All right. I'll leave the keys at the Tooth. You can drive my truck up when you get discharged . . ."

"In about a week, if I have my way," said a voice behind him. He turned and Dr. Effie Yazzie came in, wearing a white lab coat, her hair back, looking every inch the awarded doctor. "Thanks, Moose," she said, her hand on his arm. "You kept it cool and you got us here safely. And by the way,"—she looked at Dodge—"Charlie went over yesterday and brought your dad to the festival last night. I think he's staying over at the ranch to keep him company."

"I'll handle the hauls off Denali until you get back," Moose said. "My plane is parked at the Copper Mountain airport."

"The Sky King Ranch chopper is at your disposal," Dodge said.

"Thanks." Moose's phone buzzed and he pulled it out. *Finally.* "I gotta get this. I'll see you guys."

He stepped out into the hall. "Daws? Please tell me there are no bodies in the morgue that look like Tillie."

"Rose tattoo on her neck, right?"

He was standing in the hallway, and Daws's question made him put a hand on the wall. "What? Yeah—"

"No bodies."

"What is wrong with you?" He bent over, his stomach nearly heaving. "Sheesh—"

"Sorry. I just needed to confirm. We have a body—about that age, height, weight, but no rose tattoo."

He sank down into the seats. "Okay. Okay. So, is she in the database?"

"You didn't give me a lot to go on. Good thing Tillie isn't a common name. We have a couple Tillies in the system—both of them in their fifties. A Mattie, which is another form of Mathilda, but she's in her early twenties. And of course, these are women with criminal records, so . . . Too bad you didn't get a plate on that car. I checked, but there are so many listings for a Ford Focus, especially older than ten years. So, sorry, cous.'"

"That's okay. Keep an eye out, okay?"

"For . . . dead bodies with a rose tattoo?"

He sighed. "You need to work on your delivery."

"I'm a cop, not a nurse. Invite me to dinner sometime—I'll beat you in pool." He hung up.

Moose blew out a breath. Wanted to hit something.

*Where are you, Tillie?*

He'd spent most of last night trying not to let what-ifs tear through his brain, but hello, there was a serial killer out there.

Maybe.

Probably.

Which meant Aven had also stepped into his head and walked around, and he'd finally gotten up early this morning for a workout at the Tooth. And then a fruitless visit to the Skyport.

She hadn't picked up his note, still sitting by the cash register. The whole story, especially the part where she left in the middle of her shift, still sat in his gut, churned.

His phone buzzed in his hand. *Axel.* He swiped open the call. "Hey. How are you?"

"Where are you?"

"Anchorage." Something about his tone . . .

"How soon can you get here?"

"Uh, in the Otter, maybe thirty minutes?"

"Bring the new drone. And hurry."

Now Axel's tone had him by the throat. "Why?"

"Parker Billings is missing. Has been for twelve hours. And we think she's been taken by the serial killer. Which means our window is closing."

"On my way." He hung up, turned, paused, then headed into the hospital room. Because if he were Dodge, he'd want to know that a local girl, and daughter of a friend, was missing.

He was right. Dodge stared at him, at Echo, then, "I'm going with you."

"Yes, you are," Echo said and took baby Chase.

"I'll be in touch." He kissed Echo and headed out down the hallway.

"You taking the chopper?"

"Yep." Moose handed Dodge his keys. "Meet you there."

Because he was going to find Tillie. But first, he was going to find Parker Billings.

Alive.

# TWELVE

**W**HERE ARE YOU, PARKER?

Flynn stood in the tiny conference room of the Copper Mountain sheriff's office, staring at the crime board that she'd constructed in the wee hours as the sun cast a shadow over Copper Mountain, then rose again, despite clouds tumbling over the jagged purple mountains.

Now, the sunlight was a blade through the one window in the room, a slice of light across the board, dissecting the map as if God might be trying to tell her something.

Thirteen pins on the board. Thirteen faces down the side, with details of most of them. A handful remained unnamed. All of them with dates of when they'd gone missing, when they were found, and their presumed death, along with orange yarn trailing from their faces to the locations where they were found. And on the other side, a profile of the target. Male, possibly married. She'd put him forties or older. He kidnapped them as if the victims knew him, or at least weren't threatened by him. A hunter, or maybe just an outdoorsman.

And he'd been hurt by a woman, or women, enough to want to hurt one back.

*Please, God, save Parker.* Maybe Flynn didn't have faith, but she needed *someone* to turn to.

"Moose is flying up from Anchorage," said Shasta Starr, who'd come in to man the radio. She stood at the doorway of the room, and her eyes widened at Flynn's board. "What is this?"

"These are all the victims of the Midnight Sun Killer. Where they went missing"—she indicated a point on the road connected by yarn to another push pin—"and this is where they were found."

Shasta came in and stared at the board, her arms folded. "They were all taken by the Bowie camp road, where it connects to the highway."

"Some of them. We don't know where a few of these Jane Does were taken." Flynn pointed to the yellow push pins.

"They're unidentified?"

"So far. This one was found wearing my sister's necklace." She pointed to a picture of a girl, early twenties, with long dark hair.

Shasta stared at her. "Wait—your sister is an MS Killer vic?"

She didn't love how Shasta said that, but maybe that had more to do with the way she'd flirted with Axel before. Aw, she should let that thought go.

*Wait.* Shasta was a reporter, right? "What do you know about the victims?"

"Not much, just the local rumors." Shasta stepped up to the board. "They were all found on the Copper River. Although this one"—she pointed to the most recent victim, found near the resort—"was quite a ways from the others."

"It's a panic kill, which can happen if killers get desperate." Flynn pointed to a list. "Those are the dates of the finds and their supposed dates of death."

"There's a five-year gap between the first two and the others."

"Yes. Or maybe we're just missing victims."

Shasta nodded. "All in June or July."

"Tourist season."

"*Fishing* season. Tourists aren't here until mid-June. Climbers earlier, but they're here with the purpose of Denali, so . . ."

"Right." Flynn stepped back from the board. "And given the river location, the killer might know the Copper River."

"This is Bowie land here." Shasta palmed the northern section. "But most of the victims were found in Remington land."

"They could have been dumped in the river and swept downstream."

"I guess." Shasta stepped back, scanning the list of faces. "Wait, that's Aven Mulligan."

"The second official victim. She was fifteen and also an anomaly. She was swept downriver and found a month after she disappeared, dead by gunshot. .270 Winchester."

"A deer gun."

"That's why we were looking at hunters."

"It's an open-range gun," Shasta said. "It uses a scope and a bolt action, single-shot big-game rifle. For people who sit in a deer stand and wait. My dad has one that belonged to my grandfather. They're a terrible gun to ward off a bear, so any hunter using that gun out of season is poaching."

She turned her attention to a picture of Idaho that Flynn had downloaded from the arrest files in the department. "You should be looking at his clients."

"You'd make a decent detective."

She glanced at Flynn, grinned. "Investigative reporter."

"Right."

"Besides, my family has been in the area since the dawn of time. My brother Deke is the sheriff. And my brother Levi runs the pizza joint."

"How many of you are there?"

"Five. Goodwin runs Denali Sports, and Winter is a pilot. And there's me . . . Local investigative reporter, waitress, and front desk for the local sheriff department. And I know things."

"Like what?"

"Like the fact that Starr Air ran a lot of flights for Idaho into the bush, and Winter might have a list of his clients."

"Can you get it?"

"It's on the family cloud. Which I have the password to."

"You're my new favorite person."

Shasta looked at her, winked. "You're not bad either, even if you are taking Axel off the market."

Flynn shrugged. "We'll see."

"Really? I saw you guys snoggin' behind the ranger building. That didn't look like 'we'll see' to me."

Flynn's eyes widened.

"Just saying, everyone in the beer tent was watching."

*Oh.* Her face heated. Shasta grinned, then turned back to the map. "By the way, this whole area used to be Bowie land." She put her hand over the Remington property. "Senator Bowie sold it to Ox when he first came here. I think he needed money for a campaign or something. Ox thought he might mine jade, I think, but then his gold claim hit big, so he focused on those operations."

"Ox bought it from a Bowie?"

"Their families are connected. Ox's wife and Wilson's first wife were sisters.

She used to come up here with him in the spring, when Wilson came for his annual fishing trip."

"With Sully."

"Wilson still comes up. Brings his son Dillon with him. And sometimes his grandson, Laramie."

*Laramie.* She knew that name. She took a sip of coffee, made a face, then set it down. Cold. *Wait.* "Laramie was the kid Axel rescued last week. He was on a fishing trip with his father."

"I've seen them in town."

232

In the next room, a voice came over the radio. Axel, out with Levi Starr, checking in.

Flynn walked over to the door and listened.

"We've checked the river all along the Bowie camp road. Nothing so far. We're going back to the road. Moose is on his way to Copper Mountain and he's bringing a drone."

"Roger," Shasta said.

"Any word from the other team?"

Sully had left with his brother Jericho, and Orlando to see if the K-9 could pick up the scent. His uncle Wilson had gone with them.

Another search party—Ox along with Peyton and Hank, had taken four-wheelers out into the deer paths and woods.

"No joy," Shasta said.

"Let me know when Moose arrives."

"Roger." She looked at Flynn. "Should I order food from the Midnight Sun?"

"I can't eat." She went back to the board. Then she pulled out a topographical and elevation map of the area and spread it over the conference table.

Grabbed a yellow highlighter.

She traced all the roads in from the Bowie camp road, including old fire roads and ranger trails. Then she put the map up over the grid of yarn and ran an orange highlighter over the yarn.

If she had her smart board, she'd be throwing this up on a screen, seeing it all overlaid, but Copper Mountain was old-school.

Still, when she put the map on the wall, over the area, a few of the lines intersected. More than a few.

And most of them on Remington property.

"Shasta?"

The woman came in carrying a hot cup of coffee and set it on the table.

"For me?"

"You're doing all the big thinking."

"Yeah, well, I need help. There are ranger trails in Remington land. Why?"

"Those aren't ranger trails. Those are hunting trails. Senator Bowie used the land for hunting trips for his big donors." She looked down at the spots. "I've been out there—just flown over it—but I think this is an old hunting cabin. It's on the river. And this . . . this is a hunting bunker." She pointed to a spot near the Copper River. "I don't know what this is . . . Oh, wait, this is an old homestead. O'Kelly's cabin. It was on Axel's show—the first episode. Where Oaken met Mike."

She'd seen it. "That's on Jubilee Lake. The Copper River runs into it."

"Abandoned, though. That's probably why they used it for the show."

Flynn stared at it. She hadn't thought about a guy like Mike Grizz as a suspect. But he was seasonal and knew how to hunt.

Flynn stood up. "Okay, so the killer snatches a girl off the road. Parker's car was here. She was on her way to a friend's house down in Willow. Why would she stop?"

"She wouldn't. She's smart—she knows about the MS Killer. Everybody does. It's a thing . . . Women know not to stop."

"But she did. So why?" Flynn turned and looked at the board. "She has to know him. Not fear him. Not remotely think that he's the killer." She looked at her list. "Who would she know?"

Shasta stood next to her. "Who *wouldn't* she know on this list? She practically grew up here. She works at the ranger's office with her dad, so she knows Sully because he picked up permits. She works at the pizza place, so she knows Levi and sometimes helps out Anuk Swenson at the vet clinic. I mean . . . it's a really small town."

"Does she know Ox?"

Shasta frowned. "Ox Remington? Of course. Everybody knows Ox, and he attends their church—"

"Where is that? I haven't seen one in town."

"Most people go to Church on the Rock, just out of town."

"So, Ox goes to her church."

"And so do the Bowies. Which means Wilson and his family, when they're in town, probably. And . . . yeah. She knows everyone."

"That's a big help."

"Sorry. But—"She stepped up to the board and pointed to the picture of the Jane Doe with Kennedy's necklace. "I *can* help you with this Jane Doe. I knew her. I think that's Dori Cooper. But I didn't even know she was missing."

"How do you know her?"

"My sister brings supplies to their commune. It's . . . here." She tracked a finger north of Bowie land, east of the national forest and cache cabin.

"Wait. There's a commune here?"

"The art colony. Or maybe a commune. It's called Woodcrest. It used to be this place for hippies, and then Jesus people, and then, I don't know. They grow their own food and send crafts out to sell, and homeschool their kids. Nice people, keep to themselves. Don't like outsiders much—I mean, they're not going to shoot anyone, but generally, they like to stay off the grid."

"And Dori was from there?"

"Yeah. Sometimes I'd go along with my dad, and we'd hang out while he delivered supplies or chatted up the elders. I liked her."

"What was she doing on the highway? That's, like, thirty miles. More."

"Maybe she wasn't on the highway. You don't have an origin pin for her. But she was found here . . . near O'Kelly's cabin. If you follow this trail, it leads into the national forest."

She picked up a blue highlighter and ran it into the forest.

Flynn stood there, mentally placing herself on a mountain. Oh, she was an idiot. From there, it was a short hike to the cabin. "What's this?" She traced a faint line along the bottom of the property.

"That's Silver Salmon Drive. It's a high-end, seasonal residential area. Gated properties. It's near Willow."

"Seasonal?"

"Yes."

"I need a list of every single owner."

Shasta nodded.

"Why was this not on any map?"

"It's new . . . like, in the last ten years."

"Who is the developer?"

"I don't know."

"Let's find out." Flynn pulled out her phone and started a search. "Says . . . Oh my gosh. Wolverine Construction." She put down her phone. "Out of Montana."

Shasta shrugged. "I don't understand."

Flynn walked back to the map. "Who was Parker visiting?"

"Um, I don't know. Maybe someone from the youth group in Willow? She's pretty active there."

*Right.* "Call Hank, find out."

The door opened in the front area, and Flynn looked up to see Moose and Dodge walk in. She walked to the door of the office as Shasta went back to her reception desk.

"How are Echo and the baby?" Flynn asked.

"All good now," Dodge said. "I have a son."

"Congratulations," Shasta said.

"What do you need from us?" Moose set his sunglasses on top of his head, backwards.

Flynn motioned them into the office and walked over to the map. "Axel said you have a drone?"

Moose and Dodge followed her in. "I do. And I brought London and Shep and Boo with me. Shep can run the drone, Boo watching the screen, while London and I search by chopper. Dodge will take his plane, do a big sweep of the river."

"Okay. I really need you guys to focus here, down by Jubilee Lake. The rest of the teams are on the Bowie camp road and searching the Remington property, but I have this feeling . . ."

Shasta came back in. Shook her head. "I talked to Parker's mom. Sarah said she was visiting Laramie Bowie. She was meeting Calista and Adrienne Roberts, along with a few other kids in the youth group. Apparently, they were going to go swimming. Except she never showed up, so Calista called her folks, and they found her car."

Flynn stilled. "Right. Laramie Bowie is the grandson of Wilson Bowie."

"Yes. His father is Dillon," Moose said. "You met him last week—we rescued his kid."

She hadn't exactly met him. She'd been busy untangling herself from Sully. But now she repeated the information Shasta had given her. "So they were here on a fishing trip."

"They come up every year, even after Wilson's first wife died."

"When was that?"

Moose paused, then, "I think she died about twenty years ago. Dillon was about nineteen or twenty at the time. Really sad. Dillon is about ten years older than me, so I never really knew him. I barely recognized him at the rescue. He had to remind me."

He took the cup of coffee that Shasta offered.

"He was a little lost after his mother died. And then when Wilson got remarried. I think he didn't get along with his stepmom. I don't blame him—she cheated on Wilson, and they divorced a couple years later. I remember my folks telling me about it."

"Wilson got remarried? When was that?"

"Maybe fifteen or sixteen years ago? Dillon was already married.

I remember Wilson and Dillon on the camping trip the weekend Aven went missing."

"How old was Dillon?"

"I don't know. Midtwenties?"

"And how old was Wilson?"

"I don't know. He's early sixties now, so, maybe midforties."

"Still in the range for a serial killer."

Shasta made an *O* with her mouth.

Flynn grimaced, shook her head. "It's just a hypothesis. But the first death happened fifteen years ago, right after Wilson's second wife cheated on him, so . . . could be a trigger."

Silence as they gaped at her. She decided not to mention the wolf tattoo. "Listen, it's how we sort it out—follow one lead to the next."

"Wilson is a fixture in this community. He's been coming up for years, helping his nephews . . ." Dodge said quietly. But his voice trailed off and he looked at Moose. Shook his head.

Moose lifted a shoulder.

"I'm going with you," she said to Moose. "I need you to take me right to O'Kelly's cabin on Jubilee Lake. And call Axel—we'll meet him at the cabin."

She turned to Shasta. "I think you're in the wrong profession. They could use your detective skills around here."

"Or yours." She smiled.

*Huh.* Flynn headed outside and got into a truck Moose had borrowed from the airport.

"What are you thinking?" Moose asked.

"First, that Ox Remington is not our killer."

"I didn't know he was a person of interest."

"He's just lower on the list, but now I'm thinking Wilson Bowie fits our profile. He's here every year, and he has a home near the Remington land. Women in town know him, and he's flying under the radar, undetected. It feels close. And he could have intercepted

Parker on her way to the party. Jericho and his dog are searching, but I fear that he put her in his car and drove away. And then stashed her in the cabin and drove to the festival."

Moose looked over at her. "That's dark."

"That's a river monster for you."

He started up the truck. "I just . . . Wilson?"

"You'd be surprised—serial killers can be very Jekyll and Hyde."

They pulled into the airport, and she spotted Shep working the controls of a drone. Lifting it, maneuvering it in the air, landing it.

Moose walked over. "You all set?"

"It's a video game. I got this." He picked up the drone, about twelve by twelve, maybe a couple pounds by the way he handled it. Four arms came off at angles from the body, on which was attached a camera. "This is a thermal imager," Shep said, probably picking up Flynn's silent curiosity. "And Boo will have the iPad with the map. I also have a display on the controller, but she'll get a better lay of the land. And she can send you coordinates."

He got into the chopper and held out a hand for Flynn. She sat beside Boo. London and Moose took the front seats.

"I was at O'Kelly's cabin a couple months ago when I dropped off Oaken," Moose said. He indicated headphones which hung from a hook near Flynn's seat. She put them on.

Shep closed the door and strapped in.

The chopper shuddered, then wrenched itself into the air. The headphones blunted the whir of the chopper blades, and maybe Flynn shouldn't have drunk so much coffee, because her stomach swayed with the movements of the bird.

But then again, she always felt a little woozy before venturing into the darkness. And it made her think of Axel.

*"You see me, and it's okay."*

Yes, and he saw her. And it was okay.

And maybe that's how love was supposed to be. Reaching into darkness, trusting that he'd hold her hand on the other side.

Maybe, in fact, that was faith.

Oh, she was going to be sick. She opened her eyes. "I need a bag."

Shep's eyes widened.

"We're nearly there," Moose said.

She swallowed. *Oh boy.*

"I see the cabin," said Moose. "I'm setting down in the yard."

He used some superior pilot skills and set them down softly.

Shep opened the door, and Flynn nearly rolled out. Ran toward the woods.

By the time she'd emptied her stomach, Shep and Moose were inside the cabin and back out.

She turned, walked toward them, and if she'd had any more, she would've lost it again. They held the cut remains of zip-cuffs.

Cut, not ripped.

She took the ends and swallowed. Looked into the tangled dark woods behind the cabin and turned to Shep.

"Get that drone in the air, Shep. Boo, you stay here. Moose, I'm going to need a radio. And please tell me you have a gun."

"No, you're not going after—"

"Yes, I am. And I need you in the air, watching my back and searching."

He didn't move. "Axel won't like this."

"It's my job."

London had walked to the chopper, taken out a gun from under her seat. "It's just a bear gun."

"Okay. It'll do. Shep, find me our girl. Moose, get in the air."

Moose took a breath, his mouth pinched. Then he took the radio from his belt, handed it to her. "Channel twenty-seven. Two. Seven."

"Got it." She stuck it on her belt. Then she turned. "Tell Axel and his team to follow the river. And to pay attention."

"I don't understand—what's going on?" Boo said. "Didn't she get free?"

"Yes and no. He freed her. Maybe even gave her a head start. But the hunt has begun."

"Flynn did *what*?"

Axel stood on the shore of the Copper River where it tipped into Remington property, the river's roar rushing into his ears, Moose's words on the radio trying to find purchase. "What do you mean, she's *going after Parker*. Alone?"

"Shep has her on the drone, and I'm in the chopper. London is watching for her, but Parker is in the wind. Flynn thinks she's being hunted."

*Hunted.*

Axel ran his hand over his mouth, staring at the river.

From here, the river dumped into Jubilee Lake. "What side of the river?"

"North."

He and Levi had trekked along the Copper River, his gut tight as he searched for a body. They'd stopped above the high falls, a half mile from where the Jubilee Creek tributary peeled off toward the lake.

The cache cabin where he'd found Flynn was just a ways farther.

And if he remembered correctly—it had a kayak. He'd seen it under the porch when he found Flynn.

"Levi!"

The guy stood upstream, staring at the long swatch of rapids that led to the falls. He turned and lifted his radio. "'Sup?"

The river thundered, deafening, so Axel stepped away from shore. "Parker is on the move. She got away, and they're searching for her. They don't know how far she got, but my guess is that she'll stay by the river. She's smart, and she knows that the river crosses roads and trails. I'm going to get farther downstream—I'll get the kayak at the cache cabin. You keep searching the river." He didn't add a "just in case," but it lingered in the crackle of the radio.

"Roger."

He lifted a hand, then turned and picked up his pace. Deeper into the woods, a thin deer path cut along the river, and he found it, started to run, his breaths sawing through him.

*Hunted.*

*Oh, God, please don't let Flynn get between Parker and a bullet.*

But he knew her—and, shoot, maybe he was exactly the guy for her, because apparently, she was right . . .

She got into trouble. Purposely.

But he was made for this.

He picked up his pace, found the ranger trail, and took off in a full-out sprint.

The cache cabin sat quiet and lonely in the sunshine. He found the kayak, pulled it out, and checked it over.

Battered and scraped, but seaworthy. And it came with a life jacket.

He grabbed the paddle, then carried it to the river. Strapped on the jacket.

Then he got in. No skirt, but he didn't care about getting wet.

He pushed out into the river, found the current, read the Vs and eddies, the color of the river, the edge drops, rode the outside edges of bends. Spray soaked his shirt, his face, and he kept his body loose, sitting back, letting the waves take him, a bobber in the water, flying downstream.

The first falls roared ahead, a drop that gathered spray, and steam roiling off the boil at the bottom. The waves turned into mini cauldrons, so he moved his body over the bow, digging across the waves with his paddle, pulling harder.

He shot over the turbulence into a breaking wave, the foamy edge trying to upset his upstream edge. He lifted his upstream knee, arced his paddle over the froth on the downstream side, and kept his seat.

He spotted a diagonal wave and turned to hit it perpendicular, his speed high to carry him through.

And then he hit the lip of the falls. He rode the green water over, into the curtain.

He loved falls diving in a kayak, the sense of time slowing as he fell with the droplets—

Today he dropped hard into the plunge pool, punched back up to the boil, and kept moving.

Water had flooded into his kayak, but he let the river take him, and he moved over the bow, paddling hard over the edges, through the Vs. He spotted the channel to the next falls ahead, where the river narrowed, and forced himself to relax.

He rode the current down, the splash soaking him, sliding into two short drops before hitting the ten-foot falls.

The landing took him down, filled his boat, and he surfaced, sodden. But he worked his way to the shore and climbed out.

He rolled the kayak over, let the water dump out, and pulled his radio from the waterproof pouch in his life jacket. "Air One, this is Axel. Do you copy?"

"Copy, Axel."

"Any update?"

"Negative. We lost her in the woods. But Shep has located two heat sources. What's your twenty?"

"I'm on Jubilee Creek, just below Treble Chute, I'd say three miles from Jubilee Lake."

"According to Shep, she's on the north side of the river, about a half mile south of your position—"

A gunshot punched the air.

Axel froze, watched birds scatter downstream. Glanced at his kayak.

Without a skirt, he'd never make the next falls—not without swamping the boat.

"I heard a gunshot—I'm headed toward it."

He tucked the radio into his vest, picked up the paddle, and took off running. Found the trail along the river.

A scream sounded, but it might be a hawk or an eagle—

Another scream, and it sounded close, rising above his breaths and his heavy, water-soaked footfalls.

"Axel, do you copy?"

He slowed, pulled out the radio, still running. "Copy."

"Shep found a heat source—just above Glacier Veil—she's not moving."

*No.* "Is it Flynn?"

"He doesn't think so—Flynn is south, maybe a quarter mile or less. Be careful—"

"Copy." He held the radio in his grip, the paddle in the other, running hard.

The falls ahead roared, growing louder, and he cut toward the shoreline, standing on a rocky outcropping, peering downriver.

Nothing.

*Parker, where—*

Then he spotted her, climbing out onto the rocks, her blonde hair in tangles, wearing a T-shirt and jeans. He didn't see any blood, but—"Parker!"

The turbulence caught his voice, swallowed it. She collapsed onto a boulder, and he took off, skipping across boulders, praying he didn't slip.

Shots sounded in the woods, and Parker screamed, ducking, pulling herself toward the edge—

"Parker!"

She looked up, around . . .

Blood had pooled under her, but from where, he couldn't know.

If she'd been hit by a .270 cartridge, the internal bleeding would be lethal.

The fact that she had made it this far said maybe the killer had missed, mostly.

Except, maybe the hunt was still on.

He scrambled over the wet rocks, hunkering down, then crawling over to her. She lay on the rock, halfway in the river, her arms wrapped around herself, eyes closed, whimpering. "Parker—it's me. Axel Mulligan—I got you."

She opened her eyes. Drew back, her breaths fast and hard. "What—what?"

"It's me. Remember me?"

"Axel . . ." Her face crumpled and she started to cry.

"It's okay. Let me see—are you shot?"

She shook her head. "I fell. I hit a branch—I think it stabbed me."

He wanted to weep with the relief of that, especially when he saw the wound. A glancing swipe against her abdomen, it hadn't even broken the hypodermis, but a long, terrible tunnel gouged across her side. "Okay, it's just a lot of blood, but I don't think you pierced your body cavity. Let's get you wrapped up here." He pulled off his life jacket, then his thermal shirt, wound it into a length, then tied it around her waist, tight against the wound. She cried out, then bit her lip to keep it in.

"What happened—do you remember?"

"Yeah. I was going to Laramie's place—we were having a youth group event—and I saw a guy standing on the side of the road. He was holding a dog—it looked hurt, so I stopped."

A dog. A *dog.* He hadn't even thought about a dog.

"Did you know him?"

"Of course I knew him—it was Hondo—"

Another shot boomed through the forest, shuddering the trees

245

with the lift of birds. Parker screamed and clutched her hands over her head.

"It's okay, it's okay."

Return shots, like pops, short bursts.

Sounded like a pistol.

"Okay, I'm going to get you into some cover and call Moose. He's in the area with the chopper. We'll get you out of here." He strapped his life jacket back on over his bare chest, then he scooped her up.

She clung to him, her fists in the straps of his vest as he picked his way back to the thick of the forest. Found a tall pine, the arms bushy, and tucked her under it. "I'll be right back."

He scrambled back to the shoreline, picked up his paddle, and tugged out his radio, heading back to cover.

"Air One, this is Axel. Do you copy?"

"Copy, Axel. What's your twenty?"

"I'm right above Glacier Veil—north bank. I've got Parker. She's injured, not shot. I repeat, *not shot*. But we need evac."

"I'm five minutes away. Hang tight."

"Roger."

More shots, pops, closer now, and he scrambled under the canopy of the tree, bent over Parker. She trembled, her hands over her mouth, maybe to keep from screaming. "It's okay. Help is on the way."

Then he heard crunching, breaking of branches, cracking of needles on the forest floor.

Parker met his eyes, her eyes wide.

He put a finger to his mouth, took a breath, grabbed up the paddle, then scurried out from their hiding spot.

Scrambling over to a trio of birch, he crouched into the mass, searching. Spotted movement—a body—rolled, his back to the tree, caught his breath, counted—

The loam snapped near him and he sprang out, paddle out, ready to swing.

Flynn jumped back, hands up, bear gun in one grip. "It's me! It's me!"

*Oh . . . wow.* His breaths came out hard, and he dropped the paddle, took a step, and grabbed her against him.

His heart hammered against his chest, his hold probably too tight, but he couldn't help it. "I . . . I thought—I don't know what I thought, just . . ."

"I'm okay."

But she held him back just as hard, her arms viced around his neck, shuddering a little.

She finally pushed away, met his eyes. "You got Parker?"

"Yeah. She's not shot, but she's wounded."

"I saw him—he's out here, wearing camo. But I might have shot him, so—"

"What were you *thinking*?" He didn't mean for it to just erupt out of him, but maybe the adrenaline and the panic and—"You could have gotten killed!"

She just stared at him, blinking.

"You don't just go running after a serial killer, alone, in the woods—that's crazy. That's—"

"My job." She pierced him with a look. "This is what I do, Axel. This is my life. This is who I am."

And he knew that. Really. Except—"What am I supposed to do with that?" And although she took a breath to respond, he couldn't stop. "I can't . . . I can't . . . I've been crazy for the past two hours, trying to get to you, and I can't . . ."

"What? You can't *what*?"

A shot sounded. It ricocheted through the woods, and he grabbed Flynn and shoved her to the ground, his body over hers. The chill of the river had turned to sweat, his heart lodged in his throat.

Silence resounded in the wake of the shot, and he just stayed there, down, holding on to her, hating his answer. Instead, "You okay?"

She pushed away from him. "Yeah—"

A scream came from Parker's nest.

He scrambled to his feet, turned. Parker was out of the nest and running hard for the river.

"Parker!"

Another shot, and this one exploded a tree limb over her head. She tripped, fell—

He took off after her, hitting away the branches, crunching through the loam, breaking out of the forest.

But Parker had scrambled back up, fleeing to the water.

"Parker! No!" He glanced back—*aw,* Flynn wasn't on his six.

Parker hit the rocky shoreline.

Another shot broke the air. Return gunfire, little pops—"Flynn!"

Parker stood at the edge of the river, teetering.

"Parker! Stop!"

He caught up and grabbed Parker a second before she leaped. "You can't go in—you're not strong enough!"

"Run, Axel!"

*Flynn.* Heading toward him in a sprint.

"I'm out of pellets!"

Another shot, and Flynn ducked. But the motion tripped her up.

He caught her a second before she careened into the river. But the movement jerked him off-balance.

He scrambled for purchase, fell back, his grip still on Flynn, and knocked into Parker—

All three splashed into the rapids.

The water grabbed him, spun him, a thousand icy shards into his bones. But he surfaced fast, shook away the haze, and spotted

Parker's head five feet away. She fought the swirl of foam, trying to swim.

"Parker!" He reached for her, but the current ripped her away.

Where was Flynn?

He circled and spotted Flynn downstream, clinging to a rock. She clutched it, fighting the spray.

"Stay put!"

He turned, read the river, and swam hard for Parker. She thrashed in the water but caught the spur of a downed tree, and it slowed her down.

"Hang on!"

She clung to the spur and screamed as he fought the current toward her. Just as her grip broke free, he grabbed her arm. Then he pulled her up to himself, rolled, and shoved his feet against a nearby boulder.

But the rapids jerked at him, the current wanting to send him over. The falls dumped twenty feet ahead, the current inescapable, but maybe—"Hold on to my jacket. Don't let go!"

Parker, *good girl,* grabbed his life jacket. Treading hard to stay afloat, he gripped the rock, got his legs under him, aiming for the edge, out of the flow. The river narrowed at the falls, and if he could get close enough—

Overhead, the air thundered, and he looked up to see—

Air One. Wow, he loved his brother.

London had let down a line with two slings. They rode the current, got caught up on a rock just beyond his reach, downriver.

He glanced at the shoreline, then the slings and—

"Get ready to grab the sling!"

Parker nodded, and he turned, took a couple hard breaths, then pushed off.

The river snatched them up, flung them into the froth and wash, the current merciless. He fought to keep them above water, riding it, stretching out his hand—

Missed!

He rolled, kicked, and his hand caught on a boulder. He gripped it, fighting, the water filling his mouth, his eyes.

The slings broke free, sliding down the river, and he flung himself at them again.

Caught one. He threw his arm into it, then grabbed Parker to himself and shoved her inside the sling. She wrapped her arms around it. "I'm in!"

He reached for the other, got his hand on it, his arm through it, hauling himself—

A scream lifted and he turned just in time to spot Flynn flying into the green, over the lip and into the falls.

The chopper began to lift. He dove into the sling headfirst, barely in before the world dropped out from under him.

The chopper arched them away from the falls, and he searched the plunge pool for Flynn.

Nothing.

*No*—

He looked up. London held the hoist, not reeling them up until they stabilized. "I'm dropping!"

"No—Axel!" London leaned out over the river. "There's another falls—it's too high!"

He knew that. But he also knew this river. And even if Flynn made it out of the plunge pool, she couldn't survive the next drop.

And if he didn't let go now, he'd be too high.

"You got this?" he said to Parker.

"Yeah. Yeah." She seemed to come back to herself, despite her wide eyes.

"London will get you into the chopper."

She nodded, wore an expression of survival.

*Attagirl.*

Then pushed himself out of the sling and dropped into the frothy, unforgiving churn of the Copper River.

# THIRTEEN

THIS WAS NOT HOW SHE WANTED TO DIE.
Flynn gripped the rock behind the falls, her breath exploding inside her lungs, and pulled with everything she had inside her. Up, against the current, plastered against the rock—
*Air.*

She clung to the rock, gulping it in, blinded by the water, the terrible thunder of the falls around her, engulfing her.

*Breathe. Just breathe.*

She opened her eyes, blinked away the water.

Somehow, she'd come up behind the falls, the water a curtain between her and freedom.

But she'd *survived,* and right now, despite the frigid water and the hammering of her heart, that mattered.

Pulling herself up, she found a small ledge. Scooted herself onto it, skinning her knees, bloodying her hands. Then she drew her knees to herself, clasped her arms around them, and shivered.

Last she'd seen of Axel and Parker, they'd been scrambling toward rescue from the sky. But her grip had given way, and she hadn't had a hope of latching on. *Please be alive.*

She closed her eyes, the terror of careening over the falls still razoring through her, catching on her breaths, filling her throat, working out now into stuttered breaths.

*Get ahold of yourself.*

She opened her eyes, blew out a breath. She'd been forced to the bottom, hit the rocks, fought the pummel of the water until it pushed her free, curling into itself and bringing her with it. Blood trickled down her legs—whether from her hands or knees, she couldn't know. But that rock had saved her life.

*Now what?*

Somewhere out there, people—Axel—were looking for her, she knew it in her bones.

Funny, Kennedy slipped into her head. Did she know the same? That Flynn would come looking for her?

Or had she just kept running, afraid, alone . . . into the darkness?

Flynn drew herself tighter, the thought tunneling through her. Clearly she and Kennedy were exactly alike, because she'd done that very thing. Run, alone, into darkness.

And yes, God had saved her. That truth exploded through her, and she gasped.

Maybe that's what she'd been meant to find—not Kennedy in person, but maybe . . . peace.

The kind of peace that Barry Kingston had been talking about. *"God says, 'Trust me.' He is not a God of chaos but peace. And when we trust him, we can know he will be with us, here in the valley or up on the mountain or even in the depths of the sea."*

Or behind a wall of water? Because the falls pinned her in on every side, crashing down three feet ahead of her, the power of it—and the thought of swimming through it—turning her weak.

*Oh God, I really want to trust you—please—*

"Flynn!"

The voice sounded, faintly, on the other side of the veil.

*Axel?* "Here! I'm here!"

"Where?"

"Behind the waterfall!"

Nothing. "Axel!"

Another moment, and then his voice came from a different direction, closer to shore. "Okay, I can see you—are you okay?"

"Where's Parker?"

"She's safe. Are you hurt?"

She looked at her hands, then the shelf, and finally got a glimpse of Axel. He clung to the rock just outside the veil, near the shore, a red life jacket, like a beacon, strapped to his bare chest. "No. I'm fine—but I don't think I can swim through the waterfall!"

"Listen, work your way over and then—just dive in. I'll grab you."

She sat in a pocket, and to move his direction, she'd have to cling to the gritty rock, hope the rush of water didn't rip her away. But maybe—"I'll try!"

Climbing back into the water—it stole her breath—she worked her fingers into the granite, kicking against the pull of the current. Started to edge her way over.

The water pelleted down, hitting her shoulder, her head. She went under, clawed her way back up, and scrambled back. "I can't do it! It's too strong!"

"You're stronger than you think. Duck in and push yourself off the wall. The momentum will carry you out and I'll grab you!"

She spotted him in the water, out of the churn pool.

Yeah, and then her momentum would take him down the river and over the next falls.

"No!"

He slapped the water. "C'mon, Sparrow! Do this!"

Her eyes filled. *Shoot!*

"Wait—stay there."

Where did he think she might go?

He scrambled up onto the shoreline and disappeared.

Please don't let him do anything stupid.

He returned in a moment, holding a stick. No, a paddle. "Listen. I'm going to push this through the curtain—I can't hold it long, so I need you to grab it. I'll pull you out."

Right. This might work. "Okay!"

She scooted over, right next to the wall of water.

He braced himself, then reached the paddle into the falls, breaking into the curtain.

She flung out her hand for it. Missed. The action dislodged her from the rock, and suddenly the pool grabbed her, tugging her down.

*No!*

Her hands scraped the rock, and she kicked hard, slammed her head but scrambled up and came out inside her pocket. Free.

Her name rose above the thunder, Axel completely freaking out. "Flynn! *Flynn!*"

"I'm fine! I—think . . . I don't think—"

"We have to get you out of there! The lower your body temperature drops, the weaker you'll get. I'm coming in after you—"

"No!" The last thing, very last thing, she wanted was for him to die with her. But—"Let's try the paddle again!"

He hesitated.

"I can do it!" Her voice tremored, but she blew out a breath. Another. Then worked her way back to the edge, the water fighting her. "Now!"

He had already rebraced himself against the rock and now stretched out the paddle.

She reached for it, but her fingers only skimmed it. Her end started to float away, caught in the current—

She flung herself at it, blind—

The water took her, forcing her under. But she got her hand on the paddle and held on with everything inside her.

Axel dragged her up, like a fish on a hook, pulled from the

depths. She hit the surface, sputtered, but lifted her chin against the froth and got both hands on the paddle.

He towed her in with a jerk, grabbed her by the wrist, then dropped the paddle and hauled her body to his. "I got you. I *got* you."

She wrapped her arms around his neck, her legs around him, clinging to him as he pinned her to his body.

His breaths came hard against her, but so did hers, and she simply closed her eyes, buried her face in his amazing shoulder.

A full minute, maybe more, went by, and finally she lifted her head. "That was so stupid."

"Yeah, well, stupid is my middle name."

"No wonder your brother called you Lugnut."

He grinned.

And she kissed him. Oh, how she kissed him, practically inhaling him, her entire body, her entire focus, on possessing this man who had become light and courage and the partner she'd always wanted.

Wow, she loved him. And that feeling simply exploded through her.

And then, like the drop over the falls, his words from the forest came back to her.

*"I can't . . ."*

*Oh.*

*Oh.* She lifted her head, breathing hard, the truth breaking over her.

He was Jack. The guy for now, the adventure.

He didn't want her real life. And as if fate read her mind, his next words only confirmed it.

"So, no more of these near-death experiences, okay?" he said, and touched her forehead with his.

She forced a smile. Now wasn't the time. "Agreed."

But a chill had taken her heart even as he helped her to the rock, then pushed her up, out of the water.

He climbed out beside her. Shivered.

"Me too," she said, trembling, her throat thick.

"I think my radio is toast." He pulled it out of his life jacket, dripping. "Hopefully Moose is still circling."

But she didn't see the chopper.

Maybe because a shot cracked the air.

Flynn froze. *No. What?* "He's still out there."

"Is he shooting at Moose?"

*Maybe.* She got up. "Let's get off this shore before he sees us. We make easy targets."

He trekked after her into the woods, and she didn't look behind her, not sure what to do with the slurry of emotions.

*"I can't..."*

Really, she knew that. Knew it. And frankly, she got it.

Had been dealing with the same question ever since he crashed on Denali.

No, they were exactly Jack and Rose—a relationship both explosive and combustible.

She hadn't realized how she was plowing through the forest, going deeper off the deer path, until he grabbed her hand. "Where are you going?"

She turned. "The same place my sister went when Wilson Bowie tried to kill her."

He stared at her. "Wilson Bowie?"

"Yeah. Well known in the community, a fisherman, lost his wife, his second wife cheated on him ... right about the time of the first murder."

"But Parker?"

"She's a little young. I don't know how he got her to stop for him, though."

"I do." He stopped. "Hondo."

"Who?"

"Sully's dog. He was in town with the Bowies after a visit to the vet."

She stopped. "Parker works there sometimes."

"Wow. Call me impressed."

"It's my job to listen." She'd started walking through the woods, her hand in his. "So, Wilson knew she was going to see Laramie. Maybe he saw her in town, picked up Hondo, and waited for her?"

"I can't believe it's him—"

"I can't believe I missed it. He was right there—on Sully's fishing trips, he has the tattoo . . ." She looked at him. "I got distracted. Which you can't do when you're hunting a killer. And Parker nearly died."

He stopped her, pulled her to face him. "This is not on you, Flynn. We found her because of you. And she's safe."

Oh, how was she supposed to walk away from this man? Her eyes burned. "Yeah."

His hand touched her cheek. "Okay?"

"Okay."

A crack split through the forest. Flynn grabbed him, pulled him down nearly on top of herself. "Seriously?"

He rolled over onto his knees. Met her eyes. "I'm going to find him."

"No, you're not. We're going to run. He has a bolt action .270 rifle—it takes time to load, and he needs to be set and tracking us to get a good shot. Running is our best option."

"What about your knee? Can you run?"

She grabbed his hand. "Keep up."

Then she took off, jagging around trees, over downed logs, ducking under branches.

"Do you know where you're going?"

"I hope so!"

They came out of the forest into a grassy field, and she scooted around it, keeping near the trees, glanced at the sky, then plunged back in.

"Who are you? Katniss Everdeen?"

"My sister and I spent every summer at wilderness camp in northern Minnesota. They taught us things. Like in the northern hemisphere, moss grows on the north side of a tree. And of course, the sun goes from east to west in the sky. We're heading northeast. Didn't you go to Boy Scout camp?"

He had kept up with her. Now he stepped ahead of her. "No. I did things like hunt deer and fish for salmon and swim in rivers—and that, girlfriend, is a deer stand." He pointed to a wooden ladder that led up to a platform built against a tree. "Which means there's a deer trail around here. *There.*"

She followed his point and spotted the thin trail not far from the stand. "Now who's Daniel Boone? Good job."

They jogged down the trail, and yeah, her knee had really started to burn, but she gritted her teeth against it because, according to her calculations . . .

They came into another field. Except—"Those are berry bushes with bear cages," Axel said.

Indeed, thick berry bushes sat inside massive enclosures, reinforced with rebar and wire and wood, cloth over the top to protect them from birds.

And beyond that, as they walked over the hill, a garden, almost an acre of fenced area, with more rebar and wood enclosures.

Chickens roamed another enclosure, a dog lifting his head and rising to bark. Big and white, he resembled a sheepdog, enough to spook or even attack a predator.

Like them. "Good dog," she said.

Weirdly, the dog seemed to settle, sat and looked at her.

"He likes you," Axel said.

Something sort of shifted inside her. The action reminded her of Jericho.

The path had widened, and she spotted a barn, along with a number of smaller timber-framed houses. A path ran down to a large lodge, and gray smoke spiraled out of the tall stone chimney.

"Where is this?"

"I think it's called Woodcrest," Flynn said. "According to Shasta, it's an art community."

"Looks like a faith community too," Axel said and pointed to a building with a cross rising from the roof.

They passed what looked like a school, with wooden play structures—a house, a climbing wall, a swing set.

They walked down the path, and beyond the barn, she spotted a corral with horses, and beyond that, another fenced yard with cattle.

"It's like its own world, tucked away in a forest," Axel said.

"That's exactly what it is," said a voice behind them.

She turned, and Axel's hand tightened in hers.

A man stood on one of the porches. He wore a pair of jeans, a jacket, a wool hat, his hair shaggy out of it, a hint of a beard, and Wellingtons. His arm hung in a sling. "Can I help you?"

It didn't sound like he wanted to help.

A couple children, maybe five or six years old, ran around the side of the house into the yard, chasing a cat, who jumped on the deck and into the house. They stopped by the man—probably their father—and took his hand, turned and stared at Flynn and Axel.

"Um, I'm looking for someone," Flynn said, and despite Axel's hold on her, stepped forward. "Her name is Kennedy, and she's my sister."

A beat passed, during which her heart decided to step up and enlarge, cutting off her air, and then—

"Yep, I can see that." He sighed, looked at the kids, back to her. "Sorry, but she's not here."

Flynn blinked, trying to take apart that sentence. "She's not . . . *Was* she here?"

He looked away, back to her. "Why are you asking?"

"Because it's her sister," Axel said. He also stepped forward.

The man held up his hand. Then turned to the kids. "Go inside. Papa will be in in a minute."

Flynn imagined they looked a little suspect—blood had roughed up her hands, and she had wiped them on her pants, and Axel was also still soggy and beat up from the rocks. Had a bit of a scrape on his jaw.

"We don't mean any harm," she said. "I'm just . . . I'm just trying to find my sister. I lost her three years ago, and I thought she was dead. And if she's not, then . . . I'd really like to find her."

The man stood, stoic.

"And I think she's here. And I think . . . I think she makes these—"She pulled out the black sparrow. "And maybe she's not going by Kennedy. Her name could be Sparrow, or maybe . . . I don't know . . . anything. But she's beautiful and smart and creative and brave and loves animals and people and—"Her throat filled. "And if she's not here, then I need to know so we can say goodbye. But—and I don't know why—but everything inside me says that she is here . . . so . . ."

He made a face, then came down the steps. "I'm so sorry . . ."

*Oh.*

She closed her eyes. Nodded.

"I'm not allowed to—"

"Flynn."

Her breath caught. She turned.

And good thing Axel had hold of her, because her knees felt like they could buckle.

Kennedy stood on the porch of the lodge, the door open, a few other people coming out around her. Long red hair tied back with a handkerchief, in a tie-dyed dress, wearing moccasins, her face tanned, freckled. Skinny but fit and . . .

*Oh.*

*Oh.*

And then Flynn's knees did buckle.

"Flynn!"

Kennedy was off the porch, running down the path, even as Axel caught her.

"She's okay. Just shocked," he said.

*Yeah, what he said.* But she found herself just as Kennedy reached her. Pulled Flynn into her arms.

Oh, she even smelled the same—piney, with lavender and a little cedar and lots of crazy sunshine that seemed to emanate out of her. Flynn closed her eyes, felt her heart sink into rhythm with her sister's, and tears ran down her face. Flynn put her hand over her eyes, trying to hold herself together.

Kennedy, *alive.*

No, she didn't have a hope of tucking herself back in. She held on to Kennedy and full-out sobbed.

Axel came around her then, his arm warm on her back. Kennedy must have looked up, because she heard, "It's been a long week."

And then she started to laugh. It came out unhinged, a little crazy, but it made Kennedy laugh, and then Axel and not a few of the people who had come out to see the spectacle in the street.

She finally let her sister go and wiped her face. Axel put his hands on her shoulders as she met Kennedy's smile. "So, that guy there told us that you weren't here."

"That's Donald. He's a little protective." She winked at him.

Donald winked back.

"There's a story—"

Kennedy's smile fell then, and her breath jerked as she looked past Donald, past Flynn, and then opened her mouth and screamed.

"Stay behind me."

It was all Axel could think as he turned.

Because the truth simply blindsided him.

It seemed incredible that the Midnight Sun Killer might be someone he knew. Someone he'd not necessarily grown up with but who had known his family and maybe some of the others that he had killed.

"Dillon. What . . . what are you doing here?"

Dillon Bowie—how had he missed him during the rescue? But it all snapped into place now as the man walked down the street, holding a .270 Winchester, dressed in forest camo, a hunting pack over his shoulders, his face grimy, his hair under a wool cap, a smidgen of blood on his face.

"I think I nicked him," Flynn said behind him.

Or the forest had slowed him down. Whatever—it hadn't been enough to stop him.

And now he stood in the middle of the path into Woodcrest, his gun aimed at, well, Axel. Because he had stepped in front of Kennedy and Flynn.

And wasn't moving.

Axel raised his hands. "I don't know what you're thinking here, Dillon, but this isn't going to go down well."

"Get out of my way, Axel. I've been hunting this girl for three years—"

"It's not going to work!" This from Kennedy, and Flynn was right—they *were* a pair of troublemakers. "I'm not going with you."

"You are. You both are." Dillon fanned the gun around the crowd, and a few of them gasped and stepped back.

"You can't actually be serious!" Flynn said. "Every one of us sees you. Knows who you are!"

Axel stiffened as the man pointed the gun at him again.

"Really?" Dillon said, his voice low. "Maybe you don't know where you are, honey, but no one here is going to say a word. Not when they know what I can do to them."

Axel saw Donald draw in a breath, and his jaw tightened.

"Dori," said Flynn quietly.

"He killed Dori?" Kennedy said.

"I'll bet you wondered why that little girl never came back. She was tougher than she looked. Took me two days to track her down. Even injured as she was."

More gasps, and a couple women started to cry.

"So, here is how this is going to work. I know this is a peace-loving community, and I am gonna leave it at that. All I want is these outsiders. The twins. And I leave, just like that. No harm. And I don't come back. Unless I have to."

He turned to Axel. "Oh, except for you. You're a problem, with your new television show. People might miss you. So I'll give you a head start. You'll have to choose—stay together and die, split up and maybe one of you gets away. But not all three."

"I'm going to have to decline," Axel said.

"Not an option. Move."

Axel stayed.

"Okay." Dillon pulled out a bear gun—

"That's mine!" Flynn said—

And he shot Donald.

The man jerked, fell, rolled in the dirt, moaning.

"Not dead yet, but I can fix that—"

"Seriously! What is wrong with you!" This from Kennedy, who'd come out from behind Axel. She stalked toward Dillon. "Fine. Take me and be done. But leave these people alone—"

And he could have guessed that Flynn would walk out from behind him too, grabbing hands with her sister.

*Sheesh.*

Axel gave Donald a once-over. The pellet had hit him in the shoulder—the one with the sling—but it looked like it had gone through the fleshy part, taking out a chunk of skin.

"Sorry, man," he said and stepped up behind Flynn. "Where do you think you're going?"

Flynn looked at him. "Stay here."

"I'm going to pretend you didn't say that." He scooted in front of them again, his hands up. "Dillon, let's just . . . take a breath here. No one needs to get hunted—"

"I'm going to let you walk past me and start running. I'll give you two minutes."

Axel had entered a *Walking Dead* horror show. "Dillon—"

"Or I could just leave you here with Donald." Dillon raised the bear gun.

Axel reached for Flynn's hand, then Kennedy's. "You said two minutes. Make it five—two is hardly a challenge for a real hunter." He looked at Dillon, his heart a fist, pounding through his chest.

"Axel," Flynn hissed. "What are you—"

"Five. Go."

Axel took off, pulling Flynn behind him. Kennedy picked up her skirt, raced ahead, past the barking dog and the chickens, past the garden and the berry cages, and then she veered away from the path, across the field.

*Where on earth—*

Flynn followed her, limping a little, and he had a strong feeling who might be the pair left behind.

He got Flynn to the edge of the forest. "Kennedy!"

She was twenty feet into the woods and now turned. "Hurry up!"

"Where are we going?"

"C'mon!" She turned back, and Flynn grunted. This wasn't going to end well.

In every single scenario of how his life might end, being shot in the back by the Midnight Sun Killer hadn't even remotely entered his brain. So, yeah, he had nothing.

Except, well, he wasn't done yet.

Kennedy stood at a small clearing, breathing hard. Looked at him. "Help me."

*With what?* And then he saw it—a trapping pit. Layered with loam and leaves and left to rot in the woods.

Kennedy found the handle, tugged, but it barely moved.

He got on the other edge and gave it some oomph. The trap opened, and she let it drop.

A hole, maybe fifteen feet down. The bottom glistened.

Water. Clearly, the top was porous. And the bottom made of rock and clay, poor drainage.

A net was rolled up at the edge. Kennedy went to pull it across.

"The fall kills them or wounds them, and then . . . We need some way to get meat, and we don't have guns."

"You should get some."

Kennedy gave him a look. "Help me get some leaves over this."

"He's not going to walk into this. He's smarter than that."

She looked at him, and *shoot*, she possessed the same green-eyed fierceness as her sister. "Do you have a better idea? Because thank you for bringing my past into my world."

*Oh.*

But maybe that was directed at Flynn. *Ouch.*

Of course Flynn responded. "Hey. You're the one who took off into the wilds of Alaska without telling anyone."

"What do you mean without telling anyone? I sent my necklace out with Dori. With a note. How was I to know that Mr. Crazy Stalker would find her and . . . and . . ." Kennedy's voice crumbled. "I can't believe he killed her."

"Kennedy—"Flynn started.

"Why did you bring him here?"

She blinked at her. "Seriously? Because I was looking for you! Because I love you! Because deep down inside I knew you weren't dead—"

"Of course I'm not dead."

"You acted dead—"

"No, I acted *disappeared*. I didn't want him to find me—and hurt someone I love." Her eyes glazed. "That's why I ran away when he showed up with Sully. Do you seriously think I would leave Sully? I *loved* Sully. But I also saw this man shoot a wolf mother feeding her babies. And he shot at me, and I knew he wasn't going to stop. Just like all those monsters you hunt."

She wiped her hand across her cheek. "So yeah, I left, and I hoped to stay gone, and I'm sorry you thought I was dead. I did try to get a message to you. But I've been safe for two years. Safe from this monster until *you* showed up. Why couldn't you leave well enough alone?"

She let the silence sting. And Axel wanted to move toward Flynn, but honestly, they had no time. "Our five minutes are ticking away. I need you two to put this away so we can stay alive."

"How?" Kennedy said.

He came over to Flynn. "Kennedy, your sister got hurt looking for you. She has a bad knee. And I need you to come over here and help her." He turned to Flynn. "I need you to run."

"No—Axel—"Flynn shook her head, eyes wide.

"Yes."

"And what are you going to do?"

"I'm going to finish this."

She stared at him, her breaths thick. "He'll kill you."

He narrowed his eyes at her. "Have you met me? I have nine lives."

"I think you're down to, like, two remaining."

"That's all I need." He kissed her, hard, a hand around her neck. Then, "Go."

"Wow, I hate you."

"No, you don't."

Her eyes filled. Kennedy had come over, put her arm around her waist.

"Run, ladies. *Run*."

Flynn nodded, then took off with her sister at a half run, half limp.

He watched them go.

*Think.*

But he'd already come up with a plan. Desperate and stupid, but maybe it could work. He threw leaves and moss over the netting, a couple sticks, more leaves, and then covered the open door with loam.

Sheesh, it was a neon welcome sign. *Don't step here. It's a trap.*

Still, he found a spot behind a downed tree and hunkered down. Stopped breathing, only his heartbeat in his ears, swishing.

In the distance, he could hear the women thrashing through the woods, a collective moose, although moose were large, *silent* animals.

These two sounded like buffalo.

They didn't stand a chance.

Probably he didn't either. He wasn't ex-military like Moose or Dodge Kingston. He was a swimmer, not a fighter.

And that's when he got it.

Plan B.

Or maybe the only plan. He scooped up a rock, held it in his fist.

Just in time, because Dillon the Serial Killer edged into the forest, holding his father's old rifle like he might be hunting bear.

The man crouched, staring at the leaves and the trail, a regular tracker, then stood up and listened.

Axel hid maybe fifteen feet away, hunkered under brush, his breath tight as Dillon scanned the forest.

Dillon advanced, one step, then two, and then kept going.

*Please, God, let me be fast.*

Axel flung the rock through the forest, away from him, across the path. Birds scattered and Dillon turned, searching—

Axel lunged toward him.

He might be his own brand of buffalo, but he was also a panther, and he cleared the forest and tackled Dillon just as the man turned.

Shot.

Missed as Axel wrapped his arms around Dillon, scrambled forward—

They hit the net and fell.

It was deeper than he'd thought, maybe from years of accumulation, because the water seemed to suck him down—or maybe that was Dillon's hold on his life vest. But still, they landed in the muck and mud and liquid, and despite the semi-cushioned landing, it blew out Axel's breath.

He shoved Dillon away, fought for footing, and pushed himself up.

It was ten feet deep, easy, and he was treading slime.

Dillon popped up next to him and Axel turned just as a fist slammed into his head. Ringing, but he shook it away, rounded, and dove for Dillon.

The man was thrashing, trying to get to the sides, but Axel grabbed him back and threw his own punch.

Dillon howled as blood exploded from his nose. He reared back and pushed Axel away.

Axel treaded water, also kicking away. It wasn't completely viscous. He could tread and kick, although he didn't want to know what might be decaying in here, the smell rank.

He might not have thought this completely through because, yeah—no exit. At least, not one he could spot. He made the mistake of turning to search, and Dillon grabbed him from behind, an arm around his throat, and pushed him under.

He let himself go, dropping hard, bringing Dillon with him.

Holding onto him at the bottom.

He could hang here all day. Or five minutes—whatever came first.

Dillon punched him, fought to wrench free, and a minute in, Axel let him go.

Surfaced behind him.

Dillon was coughing, hanging on to the side. He stiff-armed Axel. "You're going to die in here."

"But the women aren't, so . . . there's that."

Dillon stared at him.

"You should know that I've won records for my ability to tread water."

Dillon swore at him and lunged.

*Shoot,* he'd hoped Dillon would play the long game.

Dillon took him down, on top of him as he thrashed and punched. Axel touched bottom, and his feet kicked bones—he thought they might be bones. Probably sticks—*please, sticks*. But he grabbed Dillon's grip, shook free, pushed him down, then kicked him away.

Surfaced.

Dillon came up spluttering, swearing.

"All day, man. All day long."

"You're a cocky—"And Dillon finished with a long string of interesting nouns.

"Maybe. But I'm not a murderer. So I'm going to out-survive you and watch you slowly drown, and I'm going to tame my inner hero and let you die, because you or me, pal, and I can't save us both. Your only hope is that my team shows up to rescue me before your boots and silly hunting gear weigh you down to join the other bones at the bottom."

Dillon's eyes widened. He turned and clawed at the edges of the pit. Dirt and rock. And every time he found purchase, he fell back.

Axel treaded.

Dillon shouted, then lunged again at Axel.

Axel kicked him away, bloodied his mouth, kept treading.

"Does your son know you're a killer?"

"Leave him out of it."

"How'd this happen? How'd you start killing women?"

Dillon was breathing hard, his grip sliding off a tree root.

"No. What I want to know is why you killed Aven." He hadn't quite expected the question to rise inside him, take root, to stir a feeling that scared him a little.

He could be a murderer too, if he let himself get too near this guy.

Maybe he needed rescue more than he thought.

"Aven. I don't—"

"She was my cousin. Fifteen. You shot her in the back—"

"The camping trip. I remember—"Dillon smiled now from the corner, an animal. He stopped fighting the water then, treading, staring at Axel. "The girl just floated by. No one saw her but me, so I ran down the shoreline, and she just kept going. And she was tough. Good swimmer. She finally got to shore and just sort of collapsed there. So I went down and picked her up. And then I realized we were near my dad's old fishing cabin on Jubilee lake, and I thought we could have some fun."

"Stop."

"You're trapped. You're going to listen." Something dark flashed in his eyes.

A chill threaded through Axel. He'd stuck his hand into the darkness and was trapped with a river monster.

"She fought me—"

Axel threw a piece of floating debris at him, but Dillon batted it away.

"And she was loud—"

He pushed off, launched at Dillon, grabbed him by the throat. Slammed his fist into his face.

Dillon jerked, looked back at him, his mouth bloody. "But she—"

Axel pushed him under the water. Wrapped his arms and legs around him, holding on to him as they went down.

Dillon punched him in the throat, and some of Axel's breath leaked out. But he had plenty—enough to get ahold of his brain, to slow it down.

He wasn't a murderer.

But Dillon had stopped fighting him. In fact, he went heavy and just let himself sink, all the way to the bottom. With the bones and sticks and mud.

Axel let him go, tried to push him away, to surface.

And that's when he realized—the man had hooked him with the carabiner on his hunting pack—right through Axel's life vest.

Dillon rolled on top of Axel, pinning him in the gore as he let his breath leak out, drowning them together.

# FOURTEEN

F HE WAS GOING TO CATCH US, HE'D HAVE DONE
it by now."

Flynn leaned against a tree, breathing hard.

Kennedy stood a few feet away, also breathing hard. "No—he's out there."

Flynn stood up. "I think Axel did something—I don't know what, but you don't know him. He's not going to let Dillon get us. Or he'll die trying."

Her words froze her. *Oh no . . .*

She looked back along their path. They'd broken branches, trampled leaves, plowed through thickets . . . Anyone hunting them would need to be blind not to find them.

And they weren't moving fast—not with her knee thickening with each step.

"He's back there, with Dillon. And—"She shook her head. Looked at Kennedy. "You're right. I led him right to you. Because I just couldn't let it go. Let *you* go. I should have let it be—"

"Hey." Kennedy took a breath. "Listen. I never meant to just . . . play dead. I was scared, and maybe I found something, too, in that community. But mostly, I just thought—hoped—that he might forget about me. Let me go . . ." She stepped closer. "This is not your fault."

"Oh, yeah it is. I completely roped this poor man into helping me—or at least, didn't say no when he offered. And this is why I don't do partners. But at the very least, Axel is in big trouble, and I'm not going to let him die on my watch." She picked up a stick. "You keep going. Find help—the Air One team is hopefully looking for us—no, *probably* looking for us. Get to the river. Follow it out to the road."

"I know how to get out of here, Flynn. But if you think for one lousy minute I'm leaving you, then you don't know me." She smiled. "I'm you, remember?" She stepped up to Flynn and put her arm around her waist. "I'm tired of hiding."

"I'm tired of letting this guy win."

Flynn didn't think they'd run far, but the trek back seemed an eternity—mostly because they ducked behind trees and treaded in new places, her eye out for Dillon.

In truth, he could probably spot them a half mile away through his scope, and why he hadn't shot one or both of them had her more and more wound up as they fumbled their way through the forest.

They came to the clearing where they'd left Axel.

Nothing.

She looked at Kennedy. Then, "Axel?"

Nothing.

"Flynn—"Kennedy pointed to the pit.

The net had been torn away, and Flynn spotted muddy scuff marks of boots digging into the loam.

*Oh no—no—*

She let go of Kennedy, made to the edge of the pit. Stared down.

An odor of death emanated from the mire, the water murky and dark. She couldn't see to the bottom, but it had recently been stirred up, debris floating on the surface, moving as if the water might have a current.

Or as if bodies were fighting beneath the surface.

"Axel!"

"There!" Kennedy motioned to something surfacing at the far end of the pit. Hunchback—no, a backpack.

Floating free.

"Axel!"

Then another form surfaced. Bobbing up, rolling over, his face pale.

Axel.

He looked dead.

"Is he breathing?" Kennedy said.

"I don't know—Axel!"

He didn't move, and no, it didn't look like he was breathing.

"We have to get him out of there!"

"I'm going in." Flynn dropped the stick and, just like that, jumped in.

Not as cold as the river, but dank and thick, like swimming in oil. She swam over to Axel, put her hand to his neck.

A heartbeat. But . . . no breath. "Get help!"

Kennedy took off running.

Flynn tucked her hand under his neck, moved his face to hers, and breathed for him.

The air spat out of him, water spewing from his lungs.

*That's right, get it out.* She blew again, and his body shuddered. More water.

She blew again, and another jerk.

"Stay with me!"

She kept breathing for him, checking his pulse. Still the heartbeat—

She didn't know how long she'd gone before a body landed in the water next to her.

Shep. "Let's get him out of here!" He grabbed Axel by the arm-
pits and swam him against the wall. Barking sounded above, and
a ladder came down into the hole.

She looked up to see Jericho and Moose above, Wilson beside
them. Moose scrambled down the ladder, grabbed Axel's vest, and
he and Shep pulled him up.

Flynn climbed up after them, stood watching as Boo started
breaths.

Axel's body shuddered again.

"He's getting air, but there's a blockage." She rolled him over
and pressed on his diaphragm, and water spewed out of his lungs.

Then she rolled him back and started again.

His chest rose and fell. Flynn wrapped her arms around herself.
*C'mon.*

Again.

She closed her eyes. *"Trust me."*

Not her voice. Oh, she wanted to—and really, what else did
she have?

*Please, God, save him. Because you can, and you're good, and I
know this with everything inside me. Even when it doesn't feel that
way.*

"He has too much water in his lungs," Boo said between breaths.

Flynn knelt next to him. "Listen here, Phoenix. You have at
least one more life left. So use it!"

Another breath, then his body spasmed and he began to cough.
Boo rolled him, and his entire body turned into a knot as he
retched and spewed water from his lungs.

Then he lay back, spent, breathing hard, his eyes closed.

Flynn took his hand.

He squeezed it.

And then she bent her head to his and started to weep.

Everyone went quiet, just her sobs wracking through her.

Oh, it wasn't worth it, for him, for her. And for a moment, his words hours ago on the river came to her again.

*"I can't."*

He was right. Because she couldn't either.

Finally, softly, she felt a hand on her head. "It's okay, Sparrow."

*No, not even a little.*

But she couldn't tell him that now. She leaned up, wiped her face. "Do not do that to me again."

He looked wrung out, his eyes reddened, his face grimy, but he managed a stupid, beautiful, heartbreaking smile. "Drown with a serial killer? Okay, deal."

She sank into the grass, not sure. *Wait.* "What do you mean 'drown with a serial killer'? Where's Dillon?"

Behind her, Wilson was speaking, or at least making sounds, gasps, and tiny hiccups of horror. "Is that . . . Oh my—no, what—"His knees buckled and he landed in the dirt. "No . . . Dillon. Not like this."

She looked over, and Shep and Wilson stood on the side of the pit.

"He floated to the surface, didn't he?" Axel said, his voice raspy.

She looked away, not sure how to reckon her feelings.

Kennedy came running up, breathing hard. "I went to the village, and then I saw the guys show up with the dog—they found you—I don't know how."

"That would be Orlando," Jericho said. "I don't know how he found your scent. We met Moose and London at the cache cabin, where they put down to give Parker to her dad—she's on her way to the hospital. But Orlando took one whiff of Parker, and the minute we landed, took off this way."

She looked at him, back to Axel. "Parker had his shirt."

Jericho dropped a hand on Orlando's head. "Good dog."

Kennedy dropped next to her sister and put her arm around her. "You okay?"

"Nope." Flynn looked at her sister, then leaned into her embrace. "But I will be."

"Kennedy?"

The voice made them both look up.

Sully stood there, his mouth gaping, his eyes wide.

Flynn looked at Kennedy, who gasped and let her go. Stood up. "Sully?"

She took a step toward him but he held up his hand. "To be clear, you are Kennedy, right? Not another twin."

She frowned, glanced at Flynn, then back to Sully. "It's me, Sul." She took another step toward him, and it seemed his entire body shuddered.

"Can I—"

She launched herself at him, her arms around his neck, and he pulled her up, buried his face in her neck. Then he set her down, cradled her face, and kissed her.

Oh, did he kiss her.

Moose raised an eyebrow, and Boo nodded, grinning.

Then Shep returned from the chopper with a litter, and they moved Axel onto it.

"This is unnecessary," he said.

"For the love—just stay there and pipe down," Moose said, shaking his head and stalking out to the chopper.

Flynn looked at Axel. "You scared him."

"Mm-Mmmhmm."

"You scared me too."

"I know. But you started it."

She sighed. Glanced at Wilson, who sat by the pit, his hand over his face. No, she hadn't. She'd just finished it.

Still, even as she looked at him, something wouldn't settle inside. She'd really thought . . .

"No more monsters," he said quietly.

She looked at him. "Let's just take a moment to breathe, okay?"

The guys picked up the litter and carried it to the chopper. London got into the cockpit. Moose was on the radio to Deke.

Kennedy held hands with Sully as some of the colony members came out.

"We're going to need to bring Donald in," said Axel. "He's hurt."

"He's fine," Kennedy said. "We have our own medical facilities, and he's already getting stitched up." She sighed. "But you should know that Dori was his daughter. He hadn't heard from her since she left, so . . ." She looked away, sighed. Then to Flynn, "Thank you for ending the questions, at least."

Flynn pulled her into an embrace. "That's what I do."

"I know," Kennedy whispered.

Flynn leaned away. "Oh, by the way . . . this is yours." She reached up and unhitched the necklace with the double hearts. Then she slid one heart charm off, held it in her grip, and made to put the necklace on her sister.

Kennedy held up a hand. "Nope."

"What?"

"That half heart doesn't belong to me anymore."

Flynn frowned.

"It belongs to him." She pointed to Axel, now being covered in a blanket and strapped into the chopper.

*Oh.* Flynn closed the chain inside her grip, then slipped it into her pocket.

"By the way, I see you bought one of my pieces." Kennedy touched Flynn's necklace. "Did I hear Axel call you Sparrow?"

"It's a long story."

"Mmm. Not even a sparrow will fall outside the Father's care." Flynn frowned.

"It's a Bible verse. Probably a good one for you to remember."

"You too."

Kennedy smiled. "Tell Mom and Dad I love them."

"You should tell them yourself."

Kennedy looked at Sully, who held her hand. His eyes shone, his gaze on her. "Maybe I will."

"Let's go, Flynn," Shep said. "We need to get Axel some antibiotics for all the goo he ingested. Deke is flying out here to take care of business."

Flynn nodded, then turned back to Kennedy. "Sorry for the trouble."

"No, you're not. But I love you for it." Kennedy squeezed her hand, then stepped back as Flynn got in, closed the door.

The rotor wash lifted Kennedy's red hair, stirred it, and she leaned back into Sully's arms, Jericho's dog barking wildly.

Flynn settled back, pulling on her headphones but hearing Barry's voice, deep and resounding through her. *"When God is in control, even death and decay can turn into good."*

*Maybe, yes.*

Boo had set Axel up with oxygen, and he lay strapped into the litter, eyes closed. Flynn watched him for a moment.

*Yes, breathing.*

Her Jack. Rescued.

She turned, her eyes wet, and looked out the window as the sun crested behind the high mountains, refusing to fall, refusing the darkness.

Then she leaned her head back, closed her eyes, and slept with her face to the light.

Axel woke up out of a pretty decent dream. He'd been diving, deep in the blue, the water cool but not frigid, so not in Alaska, thank you. Someplace warm, the sun on the water, its rays hitting deep into the reef, illuminating the rainbow fish and blue gills, and he could breathe. Deep, full breaths that satisfied his lungs, settled into his bones.

He'd drifted, letting the current take him.

And then pressure on his arm woke him, and Axel opened his eyes to a nurse—the same one as a week ago—but still, it felt like a small millennium—who'd taken care of Flynn.

He couldn't remember her name, but she seemed familiar, her eyes kind when she stripped the cuff off him. "Good morning, sunshine."

He opened his mouth, but it was caught under an oxygen mask. He reached up to move it, and something pricked his hand. An IV.

"You just keep that on until we can check your stats." She readjusted his mask. "The doctor will be in soon. In the meantime, breakfast is on the way. Oatmeal okay?"

"Never. How about a cinnamon roll from the Last Frontier?"

She smiled, patted his arm. He read her badge. Alicia. "I'll see what I can do." Then she winked, parked the stethoscope around her neck, and headed for the door. "I'll let your visitors in if you're ready."

If those visitors included Flynn, that was a big thumbs-up. He nodded.

She'd been there, deep in the darkness, when he fought to come back to himself, buried under water. Calling his name. *Phoenix.*

Maybe he did have nine lives, although clearly he'd been using them at an alarming rate.

Now, the door opened and, oh, *not* Flynn.

Moose. He carried a cup of coffee and came over to the bed. Said nothing, just nodded.

Axel nodded back.

"Want to talk about it?"

Axel looked away. About the panic of being trapped under two hundred pounds of angry killer, determined to drown him? About fighting to break free until the man finally went limp and he could detach his pack strap? About how he'd gotten caught at the bottom, had run out of air while trying to escape?

Dying, right there, below the surface, just as he broke free?

"Nope."

Moose nodded.

Axel looked at him. "Seen Flynn?"

His brother shook his head, and he tried not to let that bother him. Still, "We had a fight. I thought we were okay, but . . . I don't know. Maybe not."

Moose arched an eyebrow. "When in all this fun did you two have time to have a fight?"

"She—is . . . why didn't you stop her?"

"From what?"

"Running after Parker alone!"

Moose gave him a look. "You have met her, right? She jumped into the pit trying to save your life. I don't think I could stop her from doing anything." He took a sip of coffee. "That's what the fight was about? Her running after Parker?"

"She is . . . yes."

"She is a cop."

"Who hunts serial killers."

Moose nodded. "You were thinking you could, what . . . trap her in Alaska, get her to quit her job?"

Actually, that might be exactly what he'd been thinking, although he'd couch it differently. "I thought maybe she'd want to stay."

Moose sighed, nodded. "I get that." He looked out the window. Oh, something—"Bro?"

Another sigh. "Tillie's missing."

Tillie—oh, the waitress at the Skyport. "What? Wait—how do you know that?"

"I went to the diner . . . and she'd quit. Or left or . . . anyway, I don't know. She told her manager that she needed to take some time, but she gave no reason, and no one has seen her since."

"So, not necessarily missing, then. Simply gone from your life."

Moose's mouth tightened around the edges.

*Ah.* So they were going with missing. "You don't know where she lives?"

"How would I know that?"

Testy. Axel raised his hands in surrender.

"Sorry." Moose shook his head. "No clue. And I asked the manager. She won't give it out. I even called Dawson."

"Wow. That's desperate."

"Dawson and I are cool. And he's family, so . . ."

"Right. He dig up anything?"

Moose shook his head, and Axel hated the misery on his brother's face. He might look the same way if Flynn suddenly disappeared out of his life.

But Moose was right—he couldn't hold her hostage in Alaska.

Maybe he wouldn't have to, because a knock sounded at the door and Flynn stuck her head in. Smiled at him.

And there went the full breath, filling up inside him again. See, they'd both survived, and they'd figure this out. Because they were meant for each other; he knew it in his bones.

"Hey, Flynn," Moose said. "Did you finish up your report at the sheriff's office?"

"Yeah." She stepped inside. She wore a pair of jeans, a new Copper Mountain sweatshirt, her hair pulled back and up. And she carried car keys and a cup of coffee.

She smiled tightly at Moose, and suddenly everything felt a little . . .

"Moose, can I talk to Axel alone?"

*Calm down.* He wouldn't mind some alone time with her. But the way she caught Moose's arm as he walked by her, looked up and said, "Thank you for everything," set a boulder inside him.

He was panicking. "Moose, score me one of Mom's cinnamon rolls, will you?"

"Yep." Moose lifted his coffee. "See you 'round, Flynn."

Then he left, and she simply stood at the end of Axel's bed. Looking beautiful and perfect and . . . sad.

He moved his oxygen mask aside. "Hey," he said.

She swallowed, and even from here it looked . . .

"Have you been crying?"

She took a breath. "Uh, I . . ." Her gaze went to the window, followed by a sigh. "How are you?"

"They're pumping me with antibiotics, and I'm not at full O2 levels yet, but I'm alive. I guess you had something to do with that? I didn't know you went into the pit after me."

She raised a shoulder. And he got it. She'd gotten him into this mess.

"Flynn—"

"Did Dillon tell you anything before . . . I mean, did he say anything about the murders?"

*Oh.* "Just about Aven. Told me how he'd found her out of the river. How he'd sexually assaulted her—I shut that down. But—yeah, he was a real piece of work. How's Wilson taking it?"

"I haven't seen him. Sad to have that happen to your family, your son. I don't know what all went down in that family, but Dillon fits the profile—broken family, angry at his stepmother. Hopefully Laramie doesn't turn out like his father."

"He's got his grandfather, so . . ." He forced a smile.

Silence fell between them as she took a sip of coffee. Then she looked at him, and the boulder rolled right over his lungs. "Axel, I can't stay." She swallowed, and her eyes filled. She blinked hard, met his eyes. "And you're not leaving."

And he couldn't stop the rush of panic rolling over him, washing out in his voice. "Flynn—*c'mon.* Is this because of what I said? Because . . . I mean, I know that . . . I know you have a job—"

"I *do* have a job. And it might sound dark and creepy, but it is my job and I'm good at it. And if I don't do it, then someone else is going to have to stick their hand into the darkness and find the monster and—"he sighed. "And I have to do it alone."

She wiped her cheek, shook her head. "Watching them trying to bring you back to life might have been the worst two minutes of my life—"

"Sparrow—"

"No. Not anymore. It's Flynn. And Flynn can't wait on the helpless side of the radio, hoping you survive your next callout." She lifted her chin. "And Axel can't panic every time I go monster hunting. Can't be there to rescue me. It's not the life he wants to live."

"You should let me decide that."

"I think you already did. In the forest."

"I was . . . Flynn, that's not fair."

"I know. But let's not kid ourselves that it isn't what is in your heart. You can't help but be a hero, Axel. But that's why this can't work. Because I'll always be fighting monsters, and you'll always be trying to save me."

He looked away, his entire body burning.

"But . . . if it weren't for you, I'd still be stuck behind the falls, trapped. And very well might be dead. So . . ." She walked over to him and stood in his view.

He met her eyes, his mouth tight.

"I am sorry that I'm not Kennedy. That I can't leave my life behind. Because for a while there, I really thought . . ." She drew in a breath. "Well, let's just say that there is a part of me that belongs here with you, Axel. Just not the part that is real life."

He closed his eyes.

Then he felt her breath against his forehead. "This is for Phoenix." She kissed him. "Use that one life well."

He opened his eyes, his jaw tight, unable to speak.

Then she put the oxygen mask back on him, turned, picked up her coffee, and walked out of his life.

As abruptly as she'd appeared.

He stared at the ceiling, the air cold in his lungs. Closed his eyes. And just tried to keep breathing.

But their conversation came back to him, the one on the ham radio a week ago.

A *week* ago.

So maybe he was overreacting.

Or maybe a week was just long enough to learn to trust, to be eviscerated.

*"Maybe he was just the holiday-romance guy and not the real guy. You know, the guy who is lots of fun but deep down can't make a commitment."*

Except, he could make a commitment, right?

*"You're not leaving."*

Aw, he hadn't even thought about leaving Air One.

*Maybe she was just the holiday-romance girl.*

Maybe.

The door opened, and he looked up, the crazy thought that maybe—

"Your brother dropped this by—said he needed to head back to Anchorage." Nurse Alicia, carrying a paper bag. "I'll break regulations just this once. But only because you're a hero."

She set the bag on the bedside table and moved it up to him, then took out the cinnamon roll and put it on a paper plate. "No coffee for you, but would you like juice? I remember how you like orange juice."

He stared at her. "What?"

She gave him a motherly smile. "Axel. I was the nurse on staff when you came in fifteen years ago, after you lost your cousin, nearly drowned, broken, just like today, so much water in your lungs we had to revive you twice from dry drowning."

"I don't remember that."

She touched his arm. "Do you remember that it was my six-year-old son that you saved in the Copper River when you were ten?"

His mouth opened. "I . . . no."

"He's in med school now, down in Anchorage, but he wouldn't be if it weren't for you and your courage."

"I just . . . Listen, I didn't think, I just—"

"Did what you were made to do, clearly." She squeezed his arm. "Don't apologize for doing what God created you to do."

He sighed.

"But . . . at the same time, that's all you can do. You're not in control. As a river rat, you should know that better than anyone. All you can do is your best. The rest—all if it, actually—is in God's hands. Any other thinking is just pride."

"Wow. This is a twist on bedside manner."

"Only because I see a pattern with you. I saw the show. And I know your history. And I have my own regrets. Like nearly letting my son drown."

"An accident."

"Long ago I realized that replaying the what-ifs is just me rewriting the story so I don't have to feel embarrassed or defeated or ashamed. But with God there are no what-ifs. There is only truth. And the truth is that you're not in charge, God is, and no matter what happens, he is good."

"You sound like Moose."

"I like Moose." She winked. "You want real peace, real happiness, then it's time to have some faith. That's where you find peace. Even when your girlfriend walks away."

"You saw that?"

"I saw her crying."

"Her choice, not mine."

"Mm-Mmmhmm." She patted his arm. "I'll get that juice."

She headed out of the room.

*Her choice, not mine. Aw,* that wasn't fair. Because she was right. Rose and Jack would never have made it in the real world.

Another knock. Seriously, he'd never been so popular. And again, his heart rebelliously fell when *not* Flynn walked in the door.

*Shasta.* "Hey, Axel. I saw Moose—he said I could talk to you."

"I didn't realize Moose was in charge of my calendar."

She stilled.

"Sorry, Shas. It's fine. Come in."

She nodded. He hadn't meant to hurt her. "'Sup?"

He moved the oxygen mask away and reached for the cinnamon roll. *Yay, Mom.*

"I was hoping... I mean, I know that you don't see yourself as a hero, but... I was hoping that—"She swallowed. "Maybe you'd be willing to give me that exclusive?"

*Shoot.* But Alicia's words still hung in his head. *"Don't apologize for doing what God created you to do."*

*Fine.* He smiled at her. "Okay, yes. Sit down, Shasta, and fire away. I've got all day."

# FIFTEEN

IT WAS A BEAUTIFUL DAY TO BE MISERABLE.

Flynn sat on the bench seat in the back of the speedboat, droplets of lake water sifting into her blowing hair, the sun hot on her skin, the sky so blue, so cheerful it only turned everything inside her dark.

It didn't help that her stupid—but accurate—words to Axel kept circling her brain, even two weeks after she'd gotten on a plane for Minnesota.

*Let's just say that there is a part of me that belongs here with you, Axel. Just not the part that is real life.*

No, her real life was late-night stakeouts, crime boards, and hunting killers.

Even today, a gorgeous Sunday afternoon at Eve's parents' home on the lake, she couldn't jerk her brain away from the copycat 1039 Killer.

That and something else gnawing at her that she couldn't escape. Yes, Axel and his pained look, but . . . more.

Eve's husband, Rembrandt Stone, glanced over his shoulder and slowed the boat, then glanced at her. "Flynn! You're supposed to be watching the tubers to see if they fall out."

*Oh, right.* She turned.

Sure enough, the tube had flipped, and Eve and her daughter Ashley had flipped out, were bobbing in their life jackets in the water. "Oops."

"You sure you're okay?" He turned the boat. "Seems like you're not here."

She shrugged. "I'm everywhere today."

He slowed the boat as he came alongside his wife and daughter. "Eve says you're hunting a new killer."

"He's a copycat—grabbing girls from a bar, taking them home, assaulting them, strangling them, then dumping them in the river. So many markers from the 1039 Killer."

She knew Eve had discussed the case with him, given his past as a detective. Now he nodded as he trolled past them. "Ready for another go?"

Eve, her hair pulled back and plastered to her head, gave him a thumbs-up. "But drive us in to shore!"

He pulled the tube—more of an inflated sofa, really—close to them. Eve helped her daughter into the tube, then pulled herself in. She wrapped her arms around Ashley. "Hit it!"

Rembrandt shoved down the throttle, and the boat roared, churning up spray, pulling the tube to plane on the water.

They skidded across the top, and all Flynn could think of were the rapids and how the water had tossed her. Then the waterfall and Axel finding her and—

"Flynn, can you reel in the tube?"

*Oh.* He'd slowed the boat, bringing it in to shore, where Eve and Ashley piled off.

Flynn leaned over the back and pulled in the tube.

She refused to think about how Axel had nearly died. She'd

leave that for the dark of night, when the nightmares found her despite her attempts to let it go.

She couldn't be with a man who . . .

*What—loved her enough to save her life? To give his for hers?*

She held the tube to the boat as Rembrandt maneuvered to the long dock. Eve was there, wearing a sodden T-shirt over her swimsuit, and helped secure the boat.

Flynn pushed the tube onto the dock, then climbed out.

Eve joined her as they walked toward the yard.

The Mulligan family home, a former farmhouse, sat on a half-acre of shoreline, the path from the lake lined on both sides with legacy Hosta. It led to an expansive deck overlooking the lake.

Bets, Eve's mother, had set a long picnic table and now flung a towel around Ashley's shoulders. The seven-year-old shivered, her blue eyes big as she bit into a watermelon wedge.

Samson and Asher, Eve's brothers, played a game of catch-the-football on the lawn.

Smoke tufted from the grill, manned by Eve's father, Danny, a former police chief. He stood, grilling spatula in hand, talking with Flynn's dad, Mike. Her father stood, his hands folded across his chest, shadow from his baseball cap casting over his expression, nodding to something Danny said. Probably talking about the game.

Or her.

As if reading her mind, Eve stopped on the path. "You doing okay?"

"I guess."

"How did your parents take the news?"

"About Kennedy?" Flynn's mind went to that moment, nearly two weeks ago, when she'd given them the news.

*Kennedy is alive. And I found her.*

"She'd actually called them before I got there. Out of the blue—

they were pretty shocked. And overwhelmed with relief. I think they're planning on taking a trip to see her."

As they talked, her mother came out of the house carrying a couple cans of pop. She handed one to her husband, stayed and talked to Danny.

"You going with them?"

Flynn looked at Eve. "What?"

"Back to Alaska." Eve cocked an eyebrow.

"No. Why would I do that?"

Eve gave her a look. "Four-letter word."

"Axel?"

"*Love*. But that works too."

She'd walked into that one. "No. I knew him for a week. I don't *love* him."

"Since when does love have a time qualification? Listen, I knew I loved Rembrandt almost before we met. I'd read his first book, seen the man he was, and the feelings were already there. Meeting him in real life only ignited everything. I kissed him even before we had a real date." Eve grinned, winked. "He was the one with the brakes back then. But he knew it too, almost immediately." Her gaze cast out to her husband, now hauling the tube up the dock to the grass. A handsome man even in his early fifties, he wore a pair of black swim trunks and a T-shirt. "I couldn't wait to marry him."

"Yeah, well, you lived in the same city."

"Not always. I went to Miami for a while there. He came after me and brought me home. But he always said he would have stayed. He said home was where I was."

"Yes, well, Minneapolis and Miami have a plethora of homicides. Copper Mountain . . . not so much. And I think probably Dillon Bowie was the perpetrator of nearly all of them over the past fifteen years."

Rembrandt had walked up and now put his arm around his wife's waist, pulled her against him, her back to his chest, and kissed the top of her head. Looked up at Flynn. "So, you solved the crimes and found your sister. All done with Alaska?"

"All done."

Eve rolled her eyes.

"Did you take down the crime board in your extra room?"

*Right.* "Not yet."

He raised an eyebrow.

"I don't know why. Something... it's probably just a hard habit to break. I keep going in there and staring at it. I feel like I'm missing something."

Rembrandt nodded. Let his wife go. "I get that. Believe me, I get that. I was haunted for years over a serial killer that just kept eluding me. And then when I found him, I realized I'd been hunting the wrong person the entire time. The real killer was right next to him. And me." He looked at Eve. "The key was the first kill. But we got him."

But Eve was staring at Flynn. "Right next to him."

Flynn stared back. "That's the thing that keeps bothering me—"

"The copycat had to know the 1039 Killer. We never made the details public," Eve said.

Except Flynn had been thinking about Dillon. And the fact that—"The key is the first kill."

"Exactly," Eve said. "The first was the waitress in the river—she worked at the 1039 sometimes. But she was last seen at the Drift, a local bar with a slew of regulars and a worn-out dance floor. No cameras on the place—but I talked with one of the bouncers who said she was a regular on Tuesday nights."

"The 1039 is closed on Tuesdays." Flynn said. "Are all the victims from the Drift?"

"No."

"But all disappeared on a Tuesday?"

Eve's eyes widened. "I'll have to check, but maybe. I should have seen that pattern."

"The answers are in the details, in the mistakes they make."

"I'd ask the lead detective to look at the first victim—see if she made any enemies over at the 1039," Rembrandt said. "And the original 1039 Killer. Who did he hang out with there? Maybe he had a fan."

"Or an accomplice," said Eve.

"Besides his sister?"

"Another go-round with her might be beneficial," Rembrandt said and squeezed his wife's shoulder. "Ask the lead to check her statement, see if anything is questionable." He went up to the deck to join Ashley.

As Eve joined him, Flynn stood there, Rembrandt's words in her head. Her brain on her board in her office. On the trails of yarn, on the victims' faces, on the dates and the map and—

The first kill.

Not the first on the books, but the *real* first kill.

Aven Mulligan.

And then Axel's words at the hospital when she asked him about Dillon.

*"Told me how he'd found her out of the river. How he'd sexually assaulted her—"*

But she *hadn't* been sexually assaulted. Just captured, and hunted.

*"The answers are in the details, in the mistakes they make."*

"Flynn, want a burger?"

She looked at her mother, standing on the deck. Sweet of the Mulligans to invite them over today—probably Eve's idea.

*"Look at the first victim . . ."*

The first person kidnapped, but not killed, a woman nearly fifteen years older than Aven. According to Flynn's memory, she'd been abducted a week before Aven went missing. *Jennifer Greene.*

Flynn met her mother's gaze. "I need to get home."

Her mother seemed more vibrant today, wearing a sundress,

glasses, her honey-brown hair cut short. She came down the deck stairs. "You sure?"

"Yes. I . . . I need to check something." Flynn made to hug her mom, but her mother stopped her.

"Honey. Your dad and I are flying to Alaska in a week or so. We'd like you to come with us."

*Oh.* She'd expected that, but, "Mom, I have work—"

"Work is not life. Work is so you can live. There's a difference."

She sighed. "I know, Mom."

"Do you? Because I fear the dark life you live. It's like you and Kennedy are two sides of the same coin. She seeks the light . . ."

"And I seek the darkness? Please. Who was the one who didn't do drugs? Who finished college? I didn't run away from my life."

Flynn didn't know where those words came from, her tone turning sharp.

Her mother didn't even flinch. "No, you didn't. You embraced it—all the pain and fear and darkness—until you could master it."

Flynn opened her mouth, closed it.

"But you can't master it, can you? It's mastered you. You're so good at finding the monsters, as you call them, it has control of you."

"What has control?"

"Pride."

"Mom."

"I'm just saying that you love being the one who can solve these nightmares. But it's trapped you. You had a taste of freedom . . . Maybe you need to run to the light too. And maybe this is your last chance."

*Whatever.* "I don't live a dark life, Mom." She gave her mom a hug. "Have a great time in Alaska. Kennedy will love seeing you."

She headed up to the deck, to where Eve and Rembrandt sat at the table with Ashley. Danny set a plate of glistening burgers in the middle.

Her father came over. "You taking off?"

She frowned at him.

"You have that look. Same one I get when I'm fishing. Gotta reel in the whopper."

*Huh.*

She turned to Eve. "I think we need to take a look at the bouncer. He seemed weirdly uninterested in the case, even when I asked him to alert me to any suspicious behavior. Seems like a guy paid to protect the people inside might be interested in tracking down a killer."

Eve had put her hands over Ashley's ears. *Oops.* But she nodded. "I'll pass that along."

Flynn headed out to the driveway and got into her Subaru, turned on the radio as she drove into the city.

Oaken Fox's newest single came over the airwaves.

*"In the darkest hour, I found the strength to pray.*
*God's love embraced me, showed me a brand-new way.*
*Through the storms and struggles, I learned to stand.*
*With God's grace, I'll face life's shifting sand."*

Clearly, hanging around the Air One team had affected him too. She turned it off.

Still, Barry's words hung on in the silence. *"When God is in control, even death and decay can turn into good."*

She pulled into her underground garage and got out, headed up to her apartment. Inside, a quietness filled the loft space, just the hum of her refrigerator and air-conditioning stirring. Outside her picture window, the one that overlooked the river, people rode bicycles along the river path.

It wouldn't be long before all this turned to snow and ice.

She walked into the bedroom office, turned on the light, and stared at the wall with the web of yarn and pictures and reports, a timeline, scribbled scenarios, and a picture of her and Kennedy in the middle.

Her hand went to the two hearts, still around her neck. *"That half heart doesn't belong to me anymore."*

She dropped her hand. Took a step toward the board, her gaze on the timeline.

Jennifer's and Aven's murders occurred the same summer, weeks apart.

Then . . . nothing for five years.

She needed Axel's police statement, his exact conversation with Dillon.

And maybe Parker's also.

Opening her laptop, she googled the Copper Mountain sheriff's office. And while she was at it, she opened her Gmail.

A note from Deke, forwarded from the Copper Mountain resort, with an attachment. It had fallen off her radar after Dillon's death—Deke had had to procure a warrant for the information.

She clicked on it, read the greeting from the manager to Deke, then opened the guest list for the dates in question.

Couples, a number of family units. A college group from the lower forty-eight, and a stay by a local group called the Pathfinders, their address in Willow.

Nothing that listed the Bowie family or any of their members.

Her gut tightened as she dialed. It didn't mean that Dillon hadn't been in the area.

"Copper Mountain sheriff's office, Shasta speaking."

"Hey, Shasta, it's Flynn. I was hoping to talk to Deke. Is he around?"

"No, he's out of the office today. It's Summitfest weekend, so he's busy with crowd control."

"Summitfest?"

"End of the climbing season on the mountain. The forest service breaks camp on the higher levels and comes in. It's a blast—there's an art festival, a gear swap, a bonfire on the river shore, a concert on the last night. Even a race—it's called the Summit Scramble. Teams compete on mountain bikes and trail running and even a peak climb. It's really—"

"When will he be back?"

"I guess Monday?"

*Aw.* "Sorry, Shasta. I'm just . . ." She drew in a breath, then looked at the list from the resort. "Have you ever heard of the Pathfinders? It's a local group. The address is Willow, Alaska."

"Sure. Pathfinders is a youth group from Church on the Rock. All the kids from Copper Mountain attend—I think they're actually helping out with the Summit Scramble tomorrow."

"How?"

"They're stationed at locations to give out water and check in competitors, things like that."

"Is that the same group Laramie and Parker are in?"

"Laramie Bowie? I think so. I saw him in town earlier with his grandpa. I think Wilson is one of the volunteers, or maybe just a chaperone on trips. So sad, really. Laramie's practically an orphan, what with his mom and dad divorced."

"What?"

"Oh yeah. I heard it from Mal. He said that Wilson couldn't get ahold of Dillon's ex-wife. Apparently, she was out of the country or something. Married an Italian guy."

"When was this?"

"Oh, years ago. Dillon's been single since Laramie was a baby, I think. I remember rumors about him being cheated on, like his dad was. But you know, small-town gossip, so . . . who knows? Why?"

"Can I get Deke's cell number?"

"Um . . ."

Flynn glanced at the email. It was listed in his email tag. "Never mind."

"Okay, sure. By the way, did you see my article about Axel? The local news picked it up. He's the town hero."

"He's always been the town hero."

"For sure." Shasta sighed. "By the way, I saw your sister in town—I thought it was you. But she came in for the Summitfest with Sully."

*Sweet.* "Tell her hi from me."

She hung up, hearing her mother's words in her head.

*"I fear the dark life you live. It's like you and Kennedy are two sides of the same coin. She seeks the light . . ."*

Yeah, well.

*I am sorry that I'm not Kennedy.*

She returned to the board, and her conversation with Shasta and Moose during Parker's kidnapping replayed.

Dillon had been nineteen or twenty when his mom died. The first kill happened five years later.

Dillon was twenty-five. Newly married. His father newly divorced. Dillon hated his stepmom. Flynn's words, but it seemed to fit the profile.

But what if he also hated his ex-wife?

She looked again at the timeline.

After Jennifer and Aven, a reprieve of five years passed before the next kill. After the birth of Laramie . . . after his wife left him. Which made sense for the timeline.

It all fit—except for the first two killings, so different from the others.

Jennifer had been severely malnourished, assaulted, and strangled.

Aven had simply been shot, only a few days after she went missing.

Jennifer had been found before Aven, but time of death indicated she'd been killed *after* Aven.

What if Aven had seen Jennifer at the cabin? Maybe climbed out of the river, gone looking for help, and found Jennifer?

And what if Dillon had been there with her?

Flynn's own words to Axel came back. *Dillon fits the profile—broken family, angry at his stepmother. The real victim in all this is Laramie.*

Axel's reply was almost haunting. *"Hopefully he doesn't turn out like his father."*

What if Dillon had turned out like *his* father?

But Dillon didn't know that Aven *wasn't* sexually assaulted—because *maybe he wasn't there.*

He'd just assumed it.

*"Not like this. Not like this."* Wilson's words at the edge of the pit had razor edges through her brain.

What did that mean?

*Family bonds . . . they can be pretty strong. Cause people to do things they would never dream of. Get themselves in over their heads.*

A chaperone.

A ski trip to the resort.

Wilson Bowie, reprising his original play?

Or maybe, just like the sister of the 1039 Killer, Wilson had been trying to clean up after Dillon?

She needed a conversation with Axel about his last moments with Dillon.

Axel, who'd fought with Dillon, gotten the story out of him. Maybe even the real story—one that included Wilson's involvement, even if Axel didn't know it.

And if Wilson thought Axel might know . . .

She dialed Deke.

Voicemail. "Hey, Deke, it's Flynn. Call me back—I need Axel's statement. And . . . I know this sounds crazy, but what do you know about—"

A call came through on the other line. The sheriff's office.

She answered it. "Deke?"

"Shasta. Hey, you were asking about the Pathfinders—I was outside grabbing a hot dog and talked to Calista Roberts. She and the youth group are headed into the bush for an overnight before the big race tomorrow."

*And?*

"I saw Axel with them. And it got me thinking . . . I was on the camping trip with the Mulligans and the Bowies back when Aven was taken. We all went looking for her and . . . Dillon was with us, searching. It doesn't fit. Because he *couldn't* have taken Aven. Anyway, I just thought of that because Axel is going camping with them, and . . . whatever. It's just been sitting in my head since it all came out. It's probably nothing."

"Shasta, I want you to think hard—was Wilson with you, searching for Aven?"

Silence. "I . . . I don't remember. I'm sorry. But you could ask him when he gets back from the camping trip."

Flynn stilled. "The one Axel is on?"

"With the Pathfinders. Yes."

"Shasta, I gotta go. Thanks." She hung up.

Yeah, maybe she could call Deke again, but now she had a reason—

*C'mon, Axel, pick up, pick up.*

Her call went to voicemail.

She waited for the beep, then, "Hey, it's me. Um . . . call me before you go camping. I . . . I . . . okay, this is going to sound crazy, but I think Wilson might be our original Midnight Sun Killer."

The phone beeped, and she saved the message. Hung up.

Then she stared at the map and tried not to let the monsters find her.

If everything went as planned, he wouldn't be saving any lives today. Axel stood on the top of a mountain, one side etched with switchbacks for runners to climb, the other a plunging drop into the Copper River. The sky overhead arched blue and free of clouds, a hint of summer lingering in the air, the sun warm on his skin.

A good day to be alive. To stay alive. To mend the wounds inside.

"I see the first team of competitors." Parker Billings lowered her binoculars. She wore an orange vest with the words *Summit Scramble* on the front, just like his. She seemed to have recovered well from her ordeal, although his guess was that the memories were still hanging around, despite her smile.

She handed him the binoculars, and he trained them on a husband-wife duo hustling up the switchback. From here, they'd rappel down the cliff, landing shoreside, then take the route back to the starting line, some two miles up the shoreline.

His job, along with London's and Shep's, was to belay them off the side of the mountain as they rappelled. The Pathfinders had set up a sort of way station at the top, also, thanks to Moose's delivery of their first-aid gear as well as coolers of cold water.

The route started from the Copper Mountain River park campground, just a mile out of town but remote enough that he'd left his cell phone in his Yukon last night when he camped with the Pathfinders group. Today, he'd hiked into the location with Parker, Laramie and Wilson Bowie, along with Guy Roberts and his daughters.

He almost felt free. Healed from the trauma two weeks ago. Okay, that might be a little lie. In truth, he still woke in the middle of the night, shaking from the horror of his near-drowning.

And then he'd stare out the window at the dusky night upon the river, listening to Flynn's last words to him.

Knowing she was right.

*"You can't help but be a hero, Axel. But that's why this can't work.*

*Because I'll always be fighting monsters, and you'll always be trying to save me."*

Knowing she was right didn't make it any easier to let her go.

And that was the thought that caught him up every time. *"You're not leaving."*

No, he wasn't. But maybe . . . well, what if he did?

What if he chased after the voice on the radio, all the way to Minnesota?

What if he wasn't the vacation guy but the real deal?

"I used to run this race every year with my brother." Wilson came up beside Axel, interrupting his thoughts. "Although, back then, they didn't have the rappel. We'd run up Curry Ridge and back."

Wilson had gone back to Montana for his son's memorial service, and frankly, Axel hadn't expected him to return. He seemed recovered, at least on the outside, although pain filled his eyes despite his smile.

Terrible outcome for a man who'd spent so much time trying to care for his nephews after his brother's death, helping Mal and Hudson take over the resort operations, get the resort rolling every year when fishing season started.

"I ran it once, with Moose, right before I went into the Coast Guard. He was home on leave. We came in third place."

"I might run it next year, when I turn eighteen," said Calista, holding a bottle of water, ready to hand it to a competitor.

He walked over to the rappel stations, where London wore a harness and carabiner rig, ready to belay the rappelers. Shep wore the same, and they stood, drinking coffee from their thermoses.

Boo was stationed at the bottom, and Axel walked over to the edge and waved to her. She seemed especially happy today, what with her boyfriend, Oaken, showing up a few days ago for his appearance at tonight's bonfire and country music show.

"That's quite a fall," Wilson said as he came over to Axel. He too carried a thermos.

Sixty feet down onto a rocky beach. *Yeah, that would hurt.* "No one is dying today."

"Hopefully not," Wilson said. "But if they try, you're here to save them, right?"

Something about his voice—

Then he clamped Axel on the back. Hard—so hard that Axel jerked. His foot reached out to stop himself and found air—

Wilson grabbed his vest, yanked him back from the edge, and Axel backed up onto safe ground. "Oops."

Axel stared at him, his heart hammering against his ribs. "Sheesh, Wilson, are you trying to kill me?"

Wilson gave a snort. Then shook his head and walked away.

Okay, that was weird.

Axel walked over to Shep and London, who broke away from their conversation to greet him.

"All set on belay?"

"Just another Tuesday," London said.

He looked at her. "It's Saturday."

Shep laughed. Clearly Axel had missed out on something.

"We're good," Shep said. "Don't worry, Axel. We got this. Maybe you should go down to the bottom, help out Boo."

"I think she's got it, Shep," London said. She wore her hair back, her blonde ponytail out of the back of her cap, a pair of sunglasses. She put her hand on Axel's shoulder. "Take a breath."

He hadn't realized he'd been holding it. "I'm fine."

"You're barely two weeks out from a near-death experience. I'm not sure why you're even here," Shep said.

Because he couldn't not be?

But for some reason Alicia tiptoed back into his head. *"You're not in control. The rest—all if it, actually—is in God's hands. Any other thinking is just pride."*

*Huh.*

London took a sip of her coffee. Then, "Any word from Flynn?"

"London—"Shep started, but she silenced him with a look and then turned back to Axel.

"Nope," Axel said. "She got what she wanted here." Oh, that sounded more irked than he felt. Maybe.

Maybe not, because with the words came a rush of pain in his chest. She hadn't been here for him but for her sister. And she'd given him no promises.

He'd simply made them for both of them. *Maybe she was just the holiday-romance girl.*

"She doesn't belong in Alaska. She has a different life." And again that didn't come out right at all. But she'd been the one to say it— *"Let's just say that there is a part of me that belongs here with you, Axel. Just not the part that is real life."*

But maybe that was the problem. He didn't want real life.

He wanted the happy ending.

"Besides, we had fun, but we're not . . . we're not right for each other."

*"Axel can't panic every time I go monster hunting. Can't be there to rescue me. It's not the life he wants to live."*

Except that was the life he was *already* living.

*"Don't apologize for doing what God created you to do."*

"It's over, so I just have to live with that."

"Do you? Just because you thought of your life one way doesn't mean that God can't change course. He knows our hearts better than we do. It's probably good to listen."

He stared at her, hearing Alicia's words. *"But with God there are no what-ifs. There is only truth. And the truth is that you're not in charge, God is, and no matter what happens, he is good."*

"What do you want me to do? Get on a plane for Minnesota? Declare my love for her?" Okay, that was a little overstated.

London grinned and gave Shep a shove. "You owe me money. I

told you he was in love with her." Then she turned to Axel. "What do *you* want to do?"

*Honestly?* He sighed. Looked away. "I want to know that if I reach out to her, she'll reach back."

"Someone has to move first," London said. "Someone has to be the one with faith." She glanced at Shep, before looking away and taking a sip of her coffee.

*Huh.* But, *"You want real peace, real happiness, then it's time to have some faith. That's where you find peace."*

The first runners climbed up onto the ridge, out of breath, and London set her thermos down, picked up a harness, and walked over to them.

Shep watched her go, then looked at Axel. "The question is, Axel, will you regret it if you don't try?" Then he picked up another harness and followed her.

The question hung in Axel's head all afternoon, dogging him as he checked in competitors, affixed harnesses, oversaw the rappelling, and made sure the day spooled out without any accidents.

But that was it, wasn't it? Regrets.

He didn't want to live with regrets. With what-ifs. Didn't want to spend his life circling, wondering.

The last of the competitors reached the summit, rappelled down the cliff, the sun still doggedly hanging on to its position above the Alaska Range. He helped his team pack up their gear, then loaded it into the chopper when Moose set down on the wide ridge area. Axel decided to hike back to camp with the Pathfinders while Shep, Boo, and London flew back to Copper Mountain.

Wilson had acted as if he hadn't accidentally tried to kill Axel, and hiked down the mountain with his grandson. When they arrived back to the campground, he broke camp with the rest of the youth group.

He left with Laramie for the festival in town.

Axel dropped his gear off at his house, plugged in his dead phone, then took a shower.

Then he headed to town for the festival.

But all the while, in his mind, he was booking a ticket to Minneapolis. Because . . . faith. And maybe a little hope. And . . .

And this *wasn't* the story of Jack and Rose but of Axel and Flynn, and if he had only one life left, he didn't want to live with the what-ifs haunting him.

Not anymore.

He parked the Yukon and got out.

At the end of town, near the river, the bonfire blazed, and onstage a local band warmed up for the main act, Oaken Fox.

He'd have to swing by and say hi.

He stopped by Northstar Pizza and grabbed a takeout slice, then wandered over to the stage area and spotted Oaken standing with Boo, talking with Moose and Shep. He walked over, held out his hand. "Oaken."

"Axel. Hey, man." Oaken took his hand, then pulled him in for a back slap. Let him go. "Turns out you're the real star of the show."

Axel frowned.

"What, you don't know that your interview with Shasta went viral? It skyrocketed the views of the show. Mike's talking about another season."

Axel looked at Moose, who raised a hand. "It's just a conversation."

"And who's our victim? An actor? A football player? Maybe a politician?"

Moose raised an eyebrow. "Who pressed your buttons?"

"Sorry." Axel turned to Oaken. "Good to see you."

"I'm heading to Moose's for the weekend. You coming down?"

Axel glanced at Shep, then back. "We'll see." Then he smiled and pointed at Oaken. "Can't wait for the show."

He left them and walked over to the bonfire. Beyond the fire, the Copper River frothed and rushed in the darkness. A number of the Pathfinders were there, and he waved to Parker. She sat with Laramie, looking back at her phone as they laughed at something.

And for a moment, that night by the river with Flynn came back to him. The way she'd stepped up to him. Kissed him.

The way he'd thought—hoped—it would be forever.

He tugged out his phone. Still off, but he'd managed to charge it half-full while at home. Turning it on, the icon spun, waking it.

A voicemail popped up.

From Flynn.

He drew a breath, then walked away from the bonfire, toward the river walk, a boardwalk that overlooked the river and travelled the rocky shore. It ended in a deck that jutted out over the river.

Not far, actually, from the beach where, once upon a time, he'd nearly drowned, where he'd saved the life of a kid and maybe found his own.

He stood on the river walk and pressed the voicemail.

Drew in a breath at the sound of her voice.

*"Hey, it's me. Um . . . call me before you go camping. I . . . I . . . okay, this is going to sound crazy—"*

"Axel."

He turned, lowering the phone from his ear, and spotted Wilson walking toward him in the darkness. The man wore a jacket, his hands in his pockets.

Axel pocketed his phone, turned to him, not sure why his chest tightened. "Hey, Wilson."

Wilson held out his hand. "I wanted to apologize for nearly killing you today."

*Huh?* But yeah, okay, the fist in his chest loosened. Axel let out a laugh, mostly relief, and met his hand. "No worries. It was an accident."

Wilson smiled. Sighed.

"Something on your mind?"

Wilson shrugged. "I don't know. I just . . . you were the last one with Dillon, and I'm having a hard time with . . . everything. I was hoping you could tell me what exactly happened between you two." He offered a half smile, sad and wry.

And of course Axel got it. But, "You sure you want to hear it?"

Wilson shrugged. "Maybe we could walk a little?"

Axel nodded and then fell into slow step with him as they traveled down the boardwalk, the river roiling beneath them.

"Dillon was a good man. He just . . . he struggled. He never got over me remarrying. And his stepmom and he never got along." Wilson glanced at Axel. "I suppose he told you all this?"

Axel shook his head. "No. Not . . . really."

Wilson had stopped on the boardwalk. Turned to look at the river, the dusk shrouding it, the night starting to darken, a pale moon rising in the east.

Music rose from the band shell, Oaken greeting a cheering crowd.

"We were close. We did a lot of fishing and hunting . . ." He put his hands is his jacket. "I tried to help him."

"I'm sure you did."

"He didn't deserve to die." Wilson met his eyes. "He was . . . broken."

"He tried to kill me."

"Because you tried to kill him."

The fist in Axel's chest returned. Tightened. "Uh . . . you do know that he hunted me down—with Flynn—right? Wilson, your son was a serial killer."

"He was misunderstood." Wilson pulled his hand from his pocket and stepped back, just out of reach of Axel. "Everyone calls you a hero. You should have saved my son."

He held a gun, a .44 magnum, a bear pistol. It would stop an angry bear.

Do worse to Axel.

Axel held up a hand. "Hey—"

"Hey!"

He stiffened, and Wilson looked past Axel toward the voice. It was enough for Axel to shove him away, to turn, to warn—

Flynn.

*What—*

She sprinted down the boardwalk toward him and Wilson, her red hair aflame against the backdrop of the bonfire, her expression fierce. "Get away from him!"

Who was she—

"Wilson, I said *back away*."

*Oh.* But even as Axel turned back, she flew past him, on her way to chase down Wilson, who'd taken off running.

"Flynn! He has a gun!" But maybe she knew that.

Or didn't—he didn't know, but he wasn't going to let her find out. He took off after her, running hard. "Flynn!"

She'd come back. And he wanted to hope it was for *him*, but—

He easily ran her down, grabbed her around the waist, and pulled her up, even as Wilson disappeared into the darkness.

She elbowed him, but he hung on.

"Calm down!"

"He's the one! He's the Midnight Sun Killer!"

So many questions her words barely registered. Still. "No—Flynn. We got him. Dillon—"

She tried to unlatch his hands. "It wasn't just Dillon. Put me down. He's getting away."

And then he got it. All of it.

She *hadn't* come back for him. But it didn't change the fact that he wasn't letting her go. And yeah, if he had to simply keep rescuing her from herself, he'd do it. "Let him go."

She drew in a breath—he felt it, even as her struggle died.

"Let him go, Flynn. We'll find him again, I promise. But he's not worth you getting hurt. Or killed."

He leaned down, pulling her tight against him. "Or me. Because you know I'll run after you. Always. And this time, I'm choosing to save the person I love."

She gasped. "Let me go." Her words emerged softly, and he loosened his hold. She turned in his arms. Looked up at him.

A moment passed between them.

"I left you a voicemail," she said. "Two days ago."

He looked back at her. "I just got it."

Her eyes searched his, then she glanced down the boardwalk. Sighed.

She turned back to him, her eyes glossy, and smiled.

And maybe he was wrong. Maybe she *was* here for him. *Have a little faith—*

"Why are you here?" He met her eyes.

"Because . . ." She shrugged. "Because . . ."

"You missed me."

"Yeah."

"You're in love with me."

She rolled her eyes.

"Flynn."

"Okay, yeah."

"Because you can't live without me."

"Don't go crazy." But her eyes sparkled. "But maybe I'm . . . I'm happier with you. With the Flynn I find when you're around." She pressed her hands against his chest. "Truth is, I need someone who can rescue me . . ."

"Yeah, you do," he said.

Footsteps pounded along the boardwalk and he looked up.

Sheriff Deke, along with a couple deputies, ran up.

"He went that way," Axel said, and Deke nodded.

"You good?" Deke asked as the deputies took off.

"I am now," Axel said, tightening his hold on Flynn.

Deke nodded and followed his men.

"You're not going anywhere, Sparrow."

She put her arms around his neck, her eyes shining. "Nope."

Then she lifted herself up on her toes and kissed him. Slow and perfect and lingering, something meant for heroes and happy endings, stilling all the what-ifs in his heart.

And behind them, the Copper River sang a song of applause as the stars came out and smiled.

# SIXTEEN

MAYBE *SHE* WAS THE PHOENIX.

Flynn sat on the deck of Moose's amazing log home over-looking the Knik River, the smell of steaks grilling, some soft guitar strums from Oaken Fox, and the Air One Rescue team razzing Axel about his big appearance on *Good Morning, Alaska!*

Sure, he had fans, but she was president of the club, with first-in-line rights to his wry smile, those arms around her, the husky timbre of his voice in her ear. To the guy on the other side of the phone late at night or on her doorstep with donuts in the morning, greeting her on her way to her new job in the investigative support unit of the Anchorage Police Department. She didn't know exactly what strings Moose had pulled to land her a detective position alongside his cousin Dawson. It had included a phone call from Chief Burke, no doubt—but she didn't hate the changeup.

Mostly, she now parlayed her river-monster skills into hunting down kidnappers, robbery suspects, and vehicle hijackers.

And none of them crept up on her in her sleep.

More, she spent her evenings with Axel or hanging out at the Tenderfoot Bar and Grill.

Watching the sunsets becoming deeper, darker, more beautiful with each twilight.

"Here you go," Axel said and handed her a pop. He sat next to her on the outdoor sofa, his arm over the back, and held his can up for a toast. "Moose runs a dry house here, so it's the best we can do."

"It's fine," she said. "Those steaks smell amazing." She glanced over to where Moose stood at the grill, smoke curling out. He wore an apron and held a grilling fork, and the sight reminded her of Danny Mulligan.

"I didn't realize you guys were related to Danny and Bets."

She'd only made that connection when her parents came out a week ago to visit Kennedy. They'd met Axel and deduced the connection.

"Distant, but yeah, small world." He put an arm around her. Below, the river glistened under the rising moon. "Feels a shame that you just arrived and now you're going to be in darkness for six months."

"Not quite yet, and really, I'm not afraid of the dark."

He looked at her.

"Especially now that the real Midnight Sun Killer is in custody. Or rather, *both* of them."

Axel nodded, but pain entered his eyes. "Poor Laramie."

"Who's he with?" Flynn asked.

"Hudson Bowie for now. His mother hasn't shown up, so who knows where she is? They're petitioning the court for temporary custody."

London dropped into a chair, one leg pulled up. "That was some good sleuthing." Her comment sounded almost haunted. "How'd you figure it out?"

"Something my mentor said to me—look at the first victim. Jennifer Greene. Age 29, summer worker at the Bowie resort. She disappeared about two weeks after she arrived, about a week before Aven Mulligan went missing. Her car was found by the side of the road, the back bumper damaged, no hint of why she'd abandoned it. Forensics on it suggested paint from a Ford pickup truck, but Alaska, and especially Talkeetna, is lousy with Ford pickups, so that wasn't a good lead until I remembered Wilson Bowie's supposedly stolen blue Ford. And then something Shasta said—about Wilson being missing during the hunt for Aven. I started to wonder—so I called around to body shops in Anchorage and found one that had repaired a blue '84 Ford 150 pickup during that week. Belonged to the Bowie resort."

Silence.

"What I can put together is that somehow, Jennifer Greene and Wilson Bowie got into an accident. Maybe it was intentional, maybe not. Maybe she was wounded. There was no sign of a struggle at the scene, so maybe she went with him willingly. She probably knew him because he'd been up at the resort, fishing and helping his nephews, and probably his son, Dillon. I'm not sure if Dillon was with him for the abduction of Jennifer or if Dillon just happened upon his dad while looking for Aven a week later."

She glanced at Axel, who she'd never really outlined all this for. Took his hand. "Aven survived the river and got out. And I think she must have gone south, looking for help. My guess is that Aven found the cabin and maybe even found Jennifer tied up. I think Wilson caught her, took Aven captive, and that she broke free and Wilson chased her through the woods—hence the gunshot wound. And the MO. Maybe Dillon witnessed it, or maybe just saw it after the fact, but he did *not* know that she was *not* sexually assaulted." She looked back at Axel. *"Not."*

He swallowed, nodding.

"Jennifer was killed shortly thereafter, even though she was found first."

"Both of them in the river," said Axel.

"Yes. And that event seeded Dillon's actions, five years later after *his* wife left him. Making him a copycat MSK killer."

"How did you know Wilson would go after Axel?" Shep asked.

"Because Axel killed Dillon—"

"I didn't kill Dillon. He tried to kill *me*."

She turned to him. "I know. But Wilson couldn't hear that. You saw him at the scene. 'Not like this,' he kept saying. Maybe he'd expected Dillon to be found . . . but not killed. I don't know. I think the first MSK victims were killed out of panic. But the death at the ski resort wasn't, and that's what got me nervous."

"You mean the bride who was shot?" London said. "That was Wilson?"

"Yes." She let go of Axel's hand, drew up one knee. "He confessed to the crime during questioning, but I'd already put the scenario together. The HOA keeps a record of everyone in the vacation development, and Dillon checked in that weekend. I think he went up to the resort to visit his dad and Laramie, who were there with the Pathfinders youth group. All the resort doors are accessed by a key card, and a card issued to Dillon was used to exit the building about thirty minutes before the bridesmaids left. It was accessed again three hours later. A key card belonging to the Pathfinders exited the building after Dillon returned. I think Wilson saw Dillon come back, and Dillon confessed to what he'd done. The victim had been strangled, but Wilson feared she wasn't dead, so he went to find out—and saw her running toward the building. He shot her to protect Dillon."

"But you didn't know that before you got on a plane," said London.

"No. But I knew that when you stir up a river monster, it'll attack, and my gut said that Wilson wasn't going to let Axel get away with killing his son."

"I didn't—"

"I know," she said quietly, looking at him. "You'd never do that. But Wilson didn't know that. Or didn't care."

"But you did."

"Know, or care?"

"Apparently both."

She smiled. Nodded.

He leaned over and kissed her, and she held onto his shirt, savoring it.

"But how did Kennedy fit in?" asked London. "And who shot at you?"

"That was Dillon, both times. He hunted with Idaho, and maybe she saw them poaching. I think they both stopped by the cache cabin, and Kennedy saw Idaho's tattoo—she even sketched it in her notes, suspecting he might be a poacher. I think Dillon caught her watching them and shot at her. She ran to the Outpost, not realizing it belonged to the Bowies . . . at least, not until Sully showed up with the family, including Dillon, a year later."

"And that's when she ran to the art colony," Shep said.

"She gave her necklace to Dori, along with a letter to our family, but it never made it out," said Flynn.

"This necklace," Axel said, touching the one at his neck.

"Oh, that's so romantic," Boo said as she came over and sat down next to Oaken on the other sofa.

It sort of was, even if Axel thought it was sappy. It probably wouldn't last for long, but Flynn liked that he wore it. She wove her fingers into his.

Oaken had been lost in a song he'd been humming but had stopped during Flynn's story. Now he looked up at them. "Axel helped me with this one when I was staying here."

Then he started singing.

*"In a dusty old town, where the sun set low,*
*Lived a man named Coop with a heart of gold.*
*He'd ride the plains, a lone cowboy through,*
*With a past so dark, he couldn't undo."*

"Wow," said Axel. "I'd forgotten how sad that was."

"You have to keep listening. It's got a happy ending," Oaken said. He grinned, such a magazine cover. "Besides, you helped me write it."

"I'm not that sad—"

"Whatever. You're the one who bared his soul on national television," said Shep, coming over, holding a piece of garlic bread. "That story about the Coast Guard rescue—"

"Failed rescue."

"You rescued an entire family," Flynn said.

"Except the dad."

"Axel—" Moose started, by the grill.

Axel held up a hand. "I know. I know. I'm not invincible. I can't rescue everyone. And for the record, it doesn't haunt me." He looked at Flynn. "Anymore."

She smiled at him, then looked at Oaken. "How about the rest of that song?"

Such a nice guy—so different from the social media about him. Then again, he'd recently had some positive vibes on the internet, what with his newest single, the show, and an appearance he'd made at some teenage fan's birthday party a month ago. The video of him dipping his girlfriend, Boo, in a kiss had gone viral. Boo now sat cross-legged on the sofa, grinning at him.

He lit into the chorus.

*"But when he laid eyes on sweet Blossom,*
*A beauty that could save him, he began to understand,*
*He must rise up, though his soul's weighed down.*
*For the woman he loves, he'll wear the hero's crown."*

"Okay, that's enough," Axel said. "I really don't think you should say I helped you write that song."

"I don't know. I like it," Flynn said.

"He'll get a big head." Shep finished off his garlic bread.

"See?" Axel pointed to him. "What he said."

"Steaks are off the grill and setting up," Moose said. "Grab plates."

They got up, Oaken putting his guitar away, and Boo grabbing his hand. Shep stepped up behind London, and she had to be blind not to see the way he looked at her. But London seemed if not oblivious, then at least not biting.

Axel slipped his hand into Flynn's and pulled her away, around the back of the house, into the shadows and hues of twilight. He backed her up against the house, braced his hands on either side of her shoulders.

She put her hands on his amazing chest, caught in the sweet sizzle of his gaze on hers. "What are you doing?"

"Reminding myself of my happy ending." Then he leaned in and kissed her. Sweetly, possessively, perfectly.

And she kissed him back, just as perfectly.

"C'mon, you two! Dinner is getting cold!" Moose's voice, raised around the corner.

She pushed Axel away, and he shook his head, grinning. They sat down at Moose's long wooden outside table. Boo had lit candles, and the steaks glistened on a plate next to grilled garlic bread, a salad, and some fried potatoes.

Moose prayed. And it wasn't awkward or even imposing. Something about faith and holding on to hope.

*Thank you, God.* She tried it out and let the words sink in. Fill her. *Thank you for all the ways that light overcomes the darkness.*

The team "amened" and passed plates, and they nearly missed the ring of the doorbell. But someone sat on it, so Moose got up.

"Expecting someone?" Axel said.

He wiped his mouth, then dropped his napkin. "Nope."

*Huh.*

Then he headed into the house.

"So, Oaken, how's that movie you're working on?" Shep asked.

"I'm not in it, but I did a little video promo in a town called Ember a few weeks ago."

"Ember, Montana?" asked Shep.

"Yeah."

"I have a cousin who used to work for a smokejumper team out of Ember." Shep dug into his steak.

"There's a big forest fire raging right now, so hope he's not in danger."

"Naw, he's married and lives in DC with his wife. Directs a Red Cross SAR Team—"

"Boo! Flynn!"

She looked up at Moose's voice. He'd come out of the house, his expression turning them all silent.

"Can you guys . . . come here?"

Apparently it was a siren call for everyone, because the entire team got up and followed her into the house.

A woman sat on a bench in the kitchen. Long, dark hair pulled back, a black jacket, grimy jeans, and tennis shoes, brown eyes that widened when the crew came in. She held an ice pack to her cheek, her lip broken, her eye swollen.

Flynn stilled as Boo walked up to the woman.

"Tillie?" Boo said. "What happened?"

Flynn glanced at Moose. He stood near the end of the counter, holding on like he might need it for support. Or maybe he was about to rip it from its moorings—she couldn't be sure. He wore such a fierce, dangerous expression that for the first time she wondered exactly who he'd been before turning into a rescuer.

Then again, Axel had worn that exact same expression when he'd stopped her from running after Wilson, so maybe that was the Mulligan default when someone they loved—and she could see *that* clearly on Moose's face too—was hurt.

"I'm sorry, but I had no other choice," Tillie said quietly, looking first at Boo, then at Moose. "My daughter has been kidnapped. And I need your help to get her back."

Get the next book in the series and
continue the adventure!

ONE LAST
ALASKA AIR ONE RESCUE | BOOK THREE
PROMISE
USA TODAY BESTSELLING AUTHOR
SUSAN MAY
WARREN

She's hiding a terrible, wonderful
secret . . . but what will discovering
the truth cost him?

Moose (Arlo) Mulligan's biggest grief propelled him into the world of Search and Rescue. After years as a former Navy Rescue Chopper pilot, he returned home to start Air One Rescue—and made a name for himself. He loves his job, his life, and his routines...which include breakfast at the Skyrise, at the table of Tillie Young. She's sweet, and pretty, but Moose has no room in his life for anything more.

**And then, Tillie shows up, beaten and desperate...and needs his help.**

Tillie Young never thought her ex would track her to Alaska—but somehow he's found her, and when he kidnaps her daughter, she'll do anything to get her back. Even enlist help from her favorite grumpy rescuer at table three, Moose Mulligan.

**But Moose is no match for a former MMA boxer, and possible child trafficker, right?**

Maybe, maybe not, but he's not going to let another child go missing on his watch. Worse—when Moose finds himself accused as the kidnapper, there's no way back. Now, he must find the girl, keep Tillie safe and outwit a man fueled by revenge. It will take all of Moose's Alaskan savvy to protect them, and keep them alive...but who is going to protect him from the love he never saw coming?

**Set in the treacherous Alaskan backwoods, it's a heart-pounding tale of survival, love, and the family Moose never anticipated.**

# Note to Reader

Thank you again for reading One Last Chance. I hope you enjoyed the story! There's more to come...!

If you did enjoy One Last Chance, would you be willing to do me a favor? Head over to the product page and leave a review. It doesn't have to be long—just a few words to help other readers know what they're getting. (But no spoilers! We don't want to wreck the fun!)

I want to shout out a big thank you to the following people for helping me put together this story –

A huge thank you to my amazing editors, Anne Horch and Rel Mollet who always make my stories better with their amazing feedback. A shout out to my writing partner Rachel Hauck (of course!) and Sarah Erredge who always answer the phone and put up with my endless brainstorming questions. (and my husband, Andrew, for his technical help with all things mechanical!) The oh so talented Emilie Haney for her beautiful cover designs. Tari Faris for the way she makes the interior so beautiful, and a final thanks to Katie Donovan for their last minute proofing help. I have an amazing team—and it does take a team to make this all happen. I'm so grateful for all of you! My deepest gratitude goes out to Andrea Doering and the hard-working team at

Revell, also, for partnering with me on this story.

I'd love to hear from you—not only about this story, but about any characters or stories you'd like to read in the future. Write to me at: susan@susanmaywarren.com. And if you'd like to see what's ahead, stop by www.susanmaywarren.com.

If you like news on upcoming releases, freebies and sneak peeks, sign up for my weekly email at susanmaywarren.com, or scan the QR code below.

XO!
Susie May

# More Books by Susan May Warren

*Most recent to the beginning of the epic lineup, in reading order.*

## ALASKA AIR ONE RESCUE

One Last Shot
One Last Chance
One Last Promise
One Last Stand

## THE MINNESOTA MARSHALLS

Fraser
Jonas
Ned
Iris
Creed

## THE EPIC STORY OF RJ AND YORK

Out of the Night
I Will Find You
No Matter the Cost

## SKY KING RANCH

Sunrise
Sunburst
Sundown

## GLOBAL SEARCH AND RESCUE

The Way of the Brave
The Heart of a Hero
The Price of Valor

## THE MONTANA MARSHALLS

Knox
Tate
Ford
Wyatt
Ruby Jane

## MONTANA RESCUE

If Ever I Would Leave You (novella prequel)
Wild Montana Skies
Rescue Me
A Matter of Trust
Crossfire (novella)
Troubled Waters
Storm Front
Wait for Me

## MONTANA FIRE

Where There's Smoke (Summer of Fire)
Playing with Fire (Summer of Fire)
Burnin' For You (Summer of Fire)
Oh, The Weather Outside is Frightful (Christmas novella)
I'll be There (Montana Fire/Deep Haven crossover)
Light My Fire (Summer of the Burning Sky)
The Heat is On (Summer of the Burning Sky)
Some Like it Hot (Summer of the Burning Sky)
You Don't Have to Be a Star (Montana Fire spin-off)

## THE TRUE LIES OF REMBRANDT STONE

Cast the First Stone
No Unturned Stone
Sticks and Stone
Set in Stone
Blood from a Stone
Heart of Stone

A complete list of Susan's novels can be found at
susanmaywarren.com/novels/bibliography/.

# About the Author

With nearly 2 million books sold, critically acclaimed novelist **Susan May Warren** is the USA Today bestselling author of over 95 novels, including the Global Search and Rescue and Montana Rescue series. Winner of a RITA Award and multiple Christy and Carol Awards, as well as the HOLT Medallion and numerous Readers' Choice Awards, her compelling plots and unforgettable characters have won acclaim with readers and reviewers alike. The mother of four grown children, and married to her real-life hero for 35 years, she loves travelling and telling stories about life, adventure and faith.

For exciting updates on her new releases, previous books, and more, visit her website at www.susanmaywarren.com.